AT

A
Matthew Bishop
Novel by

BURT CLINCHANDHILL

ATACAMA
Matthew Bishop – Book 3

FIRST EDITION SOFTCOVER
ISBN: 1622536126
ISBN-13: 978-1-62253-612-2

Editor: Lane Diamond
Cover Artist: Kabir Shah
Interior Designer: Lane Diamond

EVOLVED PUBLISHING™

www.EvolvedPub.com
Evolved Publishing LLC
Butler, Wisconsin, USA

Printed in Book Antiqua font.

BOOKS BY BURT CLINCHANDHILL

MATTHEW BISHOP
Book 1: *Aldaraia*
Book 2: *Lemuria*
Book 3: *Atacama*

JAMES MITCHEL
Book 1: *Kursk*
Book 2: *47 Hours*
Book 3: *The Mogadishu Encounter*

DEDICATION

For all the men and women who gave their lives in search of the secrets that harbor our world's most northern and southern poles.

"We took risks, we knew we took them; things have come out against us, and therefore we have no cause for complaint, but bow to the will of Providence, determined still to do our best to the last ... Had we lived, I should have had a tale to tell of the hardihood, endurance, and courage of my companions which would have stirred the heart of every Englishman. These rough notes and our dead bodies must tell the tale, but surely, surely, a great rich country like ours will see that those who are dependent on us are properly provided for."

Captain Robert Falcon Scott: 6 June 1868 – 29 March 1912

NOTE FROM THE AUTHOR

One thing I always knew for sure: Matthew Bishop's adventures weren't complete when he finished his challenges in *Lemuria*. After the previous experience, where I took our friends into the heavens and into the future, I long searched for a preferably more down-to-earth adventure for Matthew, Jennifer, and Walker. Not only did I found a way to stay close to our present time, but, as in their first adventure, *Aldaraia*, they also delve into our history and, this time, beyond. I believe that their new adventure, in *Atacama*, says it all and has it all.

~~~

The research I get to do for these adventures makes the series extra special for me. In *Atacama*—in part anyway—I tried to give answers to the questions I so often ask myself—Who are we? Where are we from? What are we doing here?—albeit from my mind and fantasy, trying to use as many facts as possible, diving into the past and predicting the future, and sometimes the past. Who can say they have all that in a day's work? Researching *Atacama* was no exception to this. I read some hundred articles, more than a dozen books, and watched a few dozen documentaries, all of which gave me the ammunition to let our friends have a new adventure of their lifetime.

~~~

After our heroes' three adventures in this book, I leave myself with a dilemma. Will I line them up for a new experience, or continue in line with the conclusion in this book's interlude? Maybe when you read this, we both already know, or maybe you have an opinion. If so, feel free to contact me on social media.

~~~

For now, I hope you find as much fun in reading this book as I found in researching and writing it.

Burt Clinchandhill
~~~

PROLOGUE

Kola

Murmansk Oblast, Russia, Spring 1992

A relatively warm wind from the south gushed over the tundra, making it a nice, friendly April day of 30 degrees Fahrenheit at the North Pole. With temperatures varying between 60 degrees Fahrenheit in the summer and -30 degrees in the winter, Mitya Morozov had seen it all in the past thirty years working the drill. Little over a decade ago, they enclosed the site in a vast superstructure, with the drill itself encased in a huge three-hundred-foot tower. Unfortunately, there wasn't any heating in the building. In the winter, the workers would fire-up oil drums filled with the sparse wood they could find out there in the flatlands. Now, the men working the drill were glad winter was over, and the oil drums stayed cold. At its peak, more than thirty people worked the site. Now, only about a dozen remained, half of them working the drill, and the other half either cooking, guarding, or staffing. Morozov, leaning against an empty drum, found no happiness in anything but the weather today. He sighed at the fact he'd spent his last Kola-winter without real heating.

"Mitya," a drill-worker dressed in a bright yellow oilskin suit shouted out. "Why don't you come here and get your hands dirty for the first and last time?" His coworkers laughed.

Morozov raised his hands in front of his face. "These?" he yelled back over the sound of metal from the drill clanking as they pulled it up. "These divine instruments? No way, man, that's your job. That's why you get paid the big bucks." He gave a tiny smile as he took out a pack of cigarettes and an old, dented zippo. Before lighting the cigarette—for a long moment—he gazed at the lighter he'd bought with his first paycheck.

In 1965, Leonid Brezhnev, President of the Soviet Union, gave the order to start the deepest drill on Earth. Officially, the goal of the aimed forty-nine-thousand-foot-deep drill was to penetrate as far as possible through the Baltic Shield continental crust and perform extensive geophysical examinations. Unofficially, the reason for the drill was the fact that President Lyndon B. Johnson announced that the Lone Star Producing Company—from Washita County, Oklahoma—would start digging a thirty-thousand-foot-deep exploratory hole. Next to the arms race and the space race, the cold war rivalry now expanded to a race for the deepest drill into the Earth.

Morozov, born and raised in Murmansk, was halfway into his fifties. As a young man with scarce jobs in his hometown, he took a job guarding the new drill site some hundred miles from his home. He'd spent over half his life at the remote North Pole location, only two miles south of the Norwegian border. With only men to spend his days and nights with, he never got around to starting a family, something he regretted every now and then.

Now, almost thirty years later, his work was done. The deepest hole in the world, over forty thousand feet deep, had become a fact. They'd defeated the United States, who gave up decades ago. After forty thousand feet, the government decided they also had to give up. The greater porosity, unexpected reduction in density, and the unexpectedly high temperatures of over 365 degrees Fahrenheit at that depth made drilling any deeper impossible.

Today, they would officially terminate the drill, and at the end of the day, when they would close down the hole, Morozov would be out of work. Feeling somewhat melancholic as he smoked his Belomorkanal cardboard-tubed cigarette, he watched the drill workers retract the enormous length of drilling pipe he'd observed disappearing into the earth over the years. Many years ago, they'd offered him a job as a drilling worker. Even though it paid almost ten thousand rubles extra per month, he chose his security job over the dirty work in the mud every day. He'd never needed the money, since there were no ways to spend it at the dig. With no savings to speak of, he now regretted that. The government had arranged a small apartment for him in Murmansk, and with the small pension they provided, he could probably eat meat every day, though he wondered if it would be enough to provide his daily dose of Wodka.

Come to think of it, I never had to pay for rent or regular meals in all of my adult life. The state had always provided him with room and board.

He looked at his watch as the sun went down over the tundra and the crew freed another length of pipe from the deep. This way, he figured, it would take another three to four hours before they retracted the last pipe. Finally, the drill would see daylight again, and they would start closing the hole. Everything should be finished before midnight, and he figured he could get a good night's sleep before leaving the site in the morning.

His crewmate took off his working gloves and called out, waving at him. "Are you coming for dinner?"

Morozov waved back at the man. "Thanks, but I have some dried fish left from lunch." He took out a paper bag from his jacket and waved it in the air. "I'll pick up something later."

As the handful of workers left the building for the cantina, he realized this would probably be his last time alone in the drill building. Slowly, he walked up to the place where the remaining drill pipe disappeared into the earth beneath the thirty-foot steel construction and cranes. The hydraulics hissed, and steam vented from the valves on the side of the rig. A slight tremble vibrated from it, through the floor and into Morozov's body. He'd felt this tremble many times before when drilling, but this time the drill stood still.

He took a step forward to look inside the hole surrounding the drill pipe. The tremors seemed to generate from somewhere down there. He took a flashlight from his belt and shone it down the pit, but the drill hole itself wasn't much bigger than nine inches, and his flashlight only penetrated the first few feet.

The trembling beneath his feet increased and the drill pipe itself began to shake.

It's like something is pushing it from below, he thought.

He stretched his arm to touch the pipe, but before his hand could reach it, the tube started shaking wildly and slammed against his hand for a second. It felt warm. Under the violent shaking, the steel pipe now started to bend, accompanied by the sound of buckling steel. Morozov quickly stepped backward, keeping his eye on the construction as the sound and the trembling increased. The high-pressure valves attached to the rig gave in under the growing pressure, and high-pressure hoses—under loud hissing sounds—broke off and swung wildly through the room while venting steam. Through his steam-obstructed view, he noticed the drill pipe rising a few inches before it slammed down again with a loud bang, then a few inches more up... and then down again.

He looked around at the tables, chairs, and workbenches, all heavily shaking under the violent trembles. *Is it an earthquake?* As far as he knew, the region never had any.

The drill pipe shot some ten feet up in the air and broke the steel construction at the top, and pieces of metal started to fly around. He looked around for a place to take cover but didn't find any. Everything in the room now moved. He decided to run for the door some fifty feet away, but only a few feet underway, a gas canister rolled by and ended his endeavor. He landed on the shaking floor.

As he faced the remaining steel drill construction, which now buckled under the violence, the drill pipe fired up farther from the hole as a constant stream of pipe fragments landed left, right, in front, and behind him. He raised his hands over his head, knowing that should a piece of pipe decide to land on his head, he would be dead for sure. Each piece of drill pipe, thirty-two feet long, weighed about eight hundred pounds.

It rained pipes for a little over a minute. Then the sound of metal clinking suddenly stopped, and a chilling sound, as if a thousand voices cried out in agony, took over. Morozov removed his hands from his ears as the last pipes landed on the floor, and the sound of something rising from the drill hole grew louder and louder. Then, with a final violent rumble, a large steel object surrounded by smaller pieces of metal launched from the drill hole and high into the air. He recognized it as the drill head. It bounced off the steel roof construction and landed some ten feet in front of him, on the concrete floor, with a loud bang. In a few seconds, all the pieces had landed, and complete silence enveloped the room.

He got up from the floor and looked around at the devastation surrounding him. Furniture and tools lay strewn about, covered in a layer of grey dust and mud, pipes, and other pieces of metal. He checked out his body and smiled. He was okay.

How is this possible? I don't have a scratch.

He carefully stepped over the debris, walked over to the hole, which now lay bare in the center of the building, and gazed into the completely silent hole. Nothing. He looked around and, finding his flashlight a few feet away from him, grabbed it and pointed it at the gap. Even without the drill pipe in it, he couldn't see past a few feet down.

What the hell just happened here?

He looked around again, took a few steps back, and stopped next to the larger piece of distorted metal that had once been the drill head. Nothing stood out at first, but.... The drill head, made of three independent rotating bits, crushed everything that got in its way. One of the bits had completely broken off, and probably lay spread around the room in pieces. Morozov's attention focused on the two remaining bits, and something stuck between them—something glistening.

He bent over and carefully, briefly touched the metal to see if it was hot. It was lukewarm, so he grabbed the piece between the bits and tried to pull it out. It wouldn't budge. He wiped off some dirt to see what it was. It looked like a thin sheet of shiny, maybe golden metal. With one foot on the drill, he pulled the five-inch-long and three-inch-wide sheet of metal as hard as he could. Suddenly, the two bits rolled an inch and the sheet came loose, dropping Morozov on his back onto the floor. Upon rising, he took a closer look at the sheet and rubbed off more dirt.

Could it be gold?

"What the hell happened here?" a voice sounded as the crew ran into the building, looking at the ravage. "The entire mess hall was shaking."

"Are you okay?" another crewmember asked as he neared.

Morozov looked at the nearing man, and quickly put the sheet of metal inside his jacket. "Um, yes, I think I am."

"What did you do?" another oilskin suit asked.

"I didn't do anything," Morozov said, cleaning the dry dirt from his jacket. "One moment, I was smoking a cigarette, and the next, the whole installation started shaking and hissing, and pipes were blown all over the room. I'm lucky I wasn't hit by anything."

A crew member walked up to the drill hole, plopped down on his knees, bent over, and sniffed the spot. "We must have hit and ruptured a gas pocket somewhere on the way up," he said as he came up again.

"Well, on the bright side," one of the men said, "nobody got hurt. And we don't have to take out the drill pipe anymore. But on a less positive note, we've got an awful lot of cleaning to do."

The men laughed out loud.

Morozov took a quick look through the opening in his jacket at the shiny piece of metal, and wondered if his retirement cloud might still have a golden lining.

CHAPTER 1

The Eagle and the Turtle

Washington D.C., January 7, 1939

Franklin Delano Roosevelt turned his wheelchair, slowly rolled it up to the large window, and watched as the snowflakes peacefully found their way onto the roses in the garden. A few years back, after the White House fires, he had New York architect Eric Gugler create an entirely new office design and add extra space by creating a penthouse floor and a vast new basement with subterranean offices. At his wife's advice, Roosevelt had Gugler create a brand-new stately office in the west wing with a clear view of the rose garden.

From his new oval-shaped office, the fifty-seven-year-old President watched the snow, and his mind wandered to the springtime when the first roses would start to bloom. It wasn't often anymore that he wished he could move again like when he was younger. At thirty-nine, polio had struck him, leaving him paralyzed for life. Now, seeing the snow, he remembered himself running through it and throwing snowballs with his father when he was little.

"Mr. President," a voice sounded through the room, seconds after the door had opened. "Mr. President," the voice sounded again.

It took Roosevelt a moment to snap out of his snowball fight. As quickly as he could, he turned his wheelchair and rolled it behind the Resolute Desk. "Yes, Mary. Sorry," he addressed his secretary.

"Sir, I have acting Secretary of State, Welles, waiting for you."

"Ah, yes, send him in."

Sumner Welles, a tall, dark-haired man with a tiny mustache, had become Roosevelt's principal foreign policy adviser on Latin American diplomatic affairs when he entered the White House. Lately, at the President's request, the forty-seven-year-old wealthy and well-connected politician had shifted his attention to Europe and the upcoming Nazism.

His adviser walked in carrying a briefcase.

"Sumner, please sit down." Roosevelt pointed at the white leather chair at the other side of his desk. "How are you, and what can I do for you?"

"I'm fine, sir," Welles briefly answered, knowing Roosevelt wasn't in for other people's small talk. "You asked me to look into the 'Germany in the south waters' situation."

"And?" Roosevelt asked impatiently.

"Well, as you said, it's not good, sir. One of our men in Berlin got hold of a letter." He opened his briefcase, took a folder out of it, and handed it to the President.

Roosevelt looked at it and frowned. "What is this?" He took out a small stack of papers, scrolled through them, and waved them over the desk. "Is this German? I can't read this."

"I'm sorry, sir. Of course, I understand. The full document is being translated as we speak, and I can tell you the broad strokes of the message. But I think the logo on the first page will explain a lot."

Roosevelt looked at the logo on the front page more closely.

"German Antarctic Expedition?" Roosevelt read.

"That's correct, sir," Welles confirmed. "The document describes Hitler's orders to dispatch an expedition to the South Pole. He instructs a man called Alfred Ritscher, whom we know as a decorated World War I naval commander, to transform a cargo ship into an icebreaker. They're also making it capable of catapulting two ten-ton seaplanes, which they borrowed from Lufthansa airlines, into the air."

"But why send an expedition? To do what?"

"Well, we're not entirely sure why, but the document explicitly describes what they're planning to do."

"Which is?" Roosevelt started to get impatient.

"To establish 'Neu Schwabenland,' as it says in the logo."

"'Neu Schwabenland?"

"Schwabenland's a German region, and also happens to be the name of the ship they're sending. On paper, the mission has two purposes. First, take pictures for cartography and scientific research, and second, to claim the grounds for Nazi Germany. They're taking tens of thousands of large steel darts inscribed with swastikas, which they're planning to drop over an area of 140,000 square miles—an area conveniently located right in the middle of the mainlands of South America and Africa."

"Hmm." Roosevelt rolled his wheelchair from behind his desk and joined Welles at the front. "When you say conveniently located, you mean you think they're establishing a base?"

"That's one part of the theory," Welles answered.

"What's the other part?" Roosevelt cocked his head.

"There's also a theory about 'Lebensraum.' You heard of it?"

"Of course, it's the Nazi's idea of settler colonialism to seek out an original population and replace them with a new society of settlers. I understand they're not yet practicing it, but I heard the call is getting louder. It's the basic reason that, last year, I warned about the dangers posed by radical regimes in Italy, Japan, and Germany."

"Exactly, sir. There's a rumor that they're preparing for war, and because of it, they anticipate the need of vast amounts of fat."

"Fat?" Roosevelt lifted an eyebrow.

"Yes sir, fat. They need it as an industrial lubricant in explosives, and food. Britain even declared it a national defense commodity last month. Did you know that last year, Britain and Germany together were responsible for 83% of the world's whale harvest? In the past, the Germans got their whale fat from the Norwegians, but with the upcoming war, that line of delivery may be in danger. We think—"

"You think they're setting up their own line of whale fat production in Antarctica."

"Plenty of whales out there," Welles added.

Roosevelt gave a big sigh and stared into the air for a moment before responding. "Did I tell you that when I was five years old, my father took me to the White House, where I met President Grover Cleveland?"

Welles shook his head.

"I still see his mouth moving below his big white mustache, and I hear him saying, 'my little man, I am making a strange wish for you. I wish that you may never be President of the United States.'" Roosevelt chuckled. "You know, sometimes I wish I stayed a simple corporate lawyer."

"I think I understand," Welles replied.

"Anyway... what do we do now? Any suggestions?"

"Well, sir, do you remember Admiral Byrd? You met him back in '35 when he returned from his second expedition to the Antarctic."

"Of course I do. He's the one that put us on the Antarctic map with the Little America One and Two settlements."

"Okay, so, Byrd's been raising money for this third expedition to the South Pole, but he's having trouble getting the thing financed. He has his materials from his previous two missions to bring in, including a ship, the Bear of Oakland, but he still needs a second ship, supplies, and a crew. I suggest we provide him with it and rebrand his third mission from a private mission to a government one, a scientific mission nonetheless. With both ships, we can establish two bases of our own on the continent."

"But I don't want it to be a military expedition," Roosevelt demanded. "I can't afford to give Hitler any reason to start a skirmish with the US in the Antarctic."

"That's precisely why I suggest we make it a collaboration between the departments of State, War, and Navy, and we form a crew from civilian and government agencies, scientific institutions, and from the military ranks."

Roosevelt's mouth curved into a smile. "Sounds like a plan. But, you're also going to need the department of Interior if you want to free a ship for the expedition."

"Of course, sir."

"You think he will go for it?" Roosevelt asked.

"Who?"

"Byrd."

"I'm sure he will, sir. The man is an adventurer and an Eskimo who wants to go south today rather than tomorrow."

"And the costs?" Roosevelt inquired.

"Not sure yet, sir, but with Byrd donating a large part of the supplies and him recruiting volunteers, I think we keep the cost to a minimum."

"All right, here's what I want you to do." Roosevelt now rolled his wheelchair as close as possible to Welles. "I want you to form a committee representing the mentioned departments, and have Byrd spearhead it. I need a concrete plan I can run through congress."

"Will do, sir. I'll contact Byrd and ask each of the departments, in your name, for a delegate."

"Please do, and good luck, son." Roosevelt grabbed Welles's hand and shook it before rolling back behind his desk.

***

Three Weeks Later

The 'Old Executive Office Building' in Washington D.C., or OEOB as the vast construction was often called, housed the President's Executive Office and that of the vice president of the United States. First commissioned by President Ulysses S. Grant in 1888, the OEOB was built at the location where the White House stables were previously located. The largest office building in the United States, it contained 566 rooms, where many White House employees had their offices.

The handsome, forty-year-old Rear Admiral Richard Evelyn Byrd Jr.—descendant of planter John Rolfe and his wife Pocahontas—stood at the OEOB office window on the fifth floor and gazed out over the West Wing and the Oval office.

"How are you doing?" Byrd turned and addressed the other man in the room as he looked at his watch. In five minutes, his guests would arrive, and everything had to be ready. Especially for the occasion, Byrd had contacted a friend at 3M, the Minnesota Mining and Manufacturing Company, and asked him to lend him their successor of the epidiascope, the new prototype overhead projector. With the new overhead projector, he would beam large transparent slides onto a white screen behind him. 3M had sent their lead research scientist, Roger Appledorm, to personally assist with the presentation.

"We're good to go." Appledorm raised a thumb to the Admiral who, for the occasion, was dressed in full uniform.

Immediately after Appledorm's words, the double doors to the Victorian-designed room swung open, and the Secretaries of the Navy, War, State, and Interior entered. Each of them brought their aids and secretaries to keep a record of the meeting. Byrd watched them anxiously as they found their seats. As a career naval officer, civil servants made him nervous. His experience was that they slowed him down in his endeavors or buried him in paperwork. He usually avoided them like the plague, but this time he needed them.

He swallowed his pride and welcomed them with a broad smile. "Good afternoon and welcome, gentlemen and gentlewomen," Byrd greeted everyone. "If you will please take a seat, we can immediately start this first joint meeting of the Executive Committee of the United

States Antarctic Service. I have to say that I'm glad you all agreed to come here in person for this first meeting, and I'm sure that in the future, you'll feel confident enough to send an aid or representative." Byrd nodded at Appledorm, who flipped a switch on the massive machine.

In an instant - on the screen behind Byrd - a text, appeared in large black letters.

Joint meeting of the Executive Committee of the US Antarctic Service

The room was clearly impressed by the projection on the screen.

"Now, you've had the opportunity to read in on the subject with the documents I sent you a week ago, and we don't have much time, so I suggest we skip ahead to the questions that lay before us."

Appledorm switched slides.

1. Goal of the Mission
2. Participations of each Department/Crew
3. Planning
4. Tools
5. Funding
6. What's Next

"For your convenience, I've collected all information in the folders on the table in front of you."

Almost simultaneously, the cabinet members opened their folders, and some of them also got handed information from their secretaries.

"Are there any questions upfront?" Byrd asked.

Cordell Hull, the white-haired Secretary of State, cleared his throat. "With all due respect, Admiral Byrd, I admire your preparations for this meeting, and especially appreciate your powerful presentation on the view screen, but...." Hull took a deep breath. "I'm sure everyone attending did their homework and would appreciate the opportunity to speak their part without the need for a program. I'm sure everyone is eager to get this meeting behind us so we can attend to our daily, more important business."

"Umm... so... what..." Byrd stammered as he remembered why he hated these meetings so much.

"If I might make a suggestion?" Harry H. Woodring, Secretary of War, interrupted Byrd's stuttering while stroking his bald head.

"Please do," Byrd agreed, opening his arms.

"We've all had time to prepare and ask questions. I see you've added all the answers to our questions to the memo." He waved the folder in the air. "If you agree, we can skip the formalities and get started quickly. Does that work for everyone?"

Byrd looked around the table, and everyone nodded and mumbled. "Sure, okay, sounds like a plan, let's do that." He sighed almost imperceptibly. "All right, we'll do that. Do you mind skipping to transparent two?" Byrd asked Appledorm, who quickly changed sheets, and a series of numbers appeared on the screen. "Now, as you can see, I need one hundred and twenty-five men to man the ships, providing I have two ships to sail with, but we'll come to that soon enough." He looked around the table and stopped when facing Claude A. Swanson, Secretary of the Navy.

Swanson stroked his drooping mustache. "I can get you about half of that—a few handfuls of officers, and for the rest, A-class enlisted men."

"I've had a survey held throughout my department," the Secretary of the Interior, Harold L. Ickes, said after breathing on his glasses and cleaning them with his handkerchief. "I can easily match the other half of the personnel with volunteers. Of course, I need to pay ten dollars a month, but I don't consider that a problem."

"Great," Byrd concluded. "That's one obstacle settled then. Let's see. Planning, we can do later, and Tools, well, I will personally provide most of the tools. The only thing I need from one of you is a second ship. I'll provide the dual steam-powered and sailing ship, the Bear of Oakland. She's an old ship, but she served me fine in my previous two expeditions to the Antarctic. She will also carry a twin-engine Barkley-Grow seaplane, and I'll gladly lease her to the government for... umm, let's say one dollar a year. So...." He looked around the table again.

"That's either you, Claude, or you, Harold," the Secretary of State addressed the two men.

"We already spoke to each other on the subject," Swanson said. "And...." He paused, looking at Harold Ickes from Interior.

"I have a ship that can be ready for you in a few months," Ickes replied. "I can get you the USMS North Star, a fine 2,200-metric-ton wooden ice ship, only built six years ago for the Coast Guard, but I'm convinced she will do fine as your support ship."

"That's fantastic." Byrd grinned from ear to ear. "Thank you very much for your support."

"You're welcome," Ickes replied. "I'm absolutely fascinated by your mission and almost wish I could come with you myself."

"I can reserve a cabin for you, if you like," Byrd joked.

"*Almost* being the operative word, Byrd. Almost." Ickes smiled.

Everyone now laughed.

"All right," Byrd continued. "That brings me to the money."

"Three hundred and fifty thousand dollars?" Hull questioned out loud as the amount appeared on the screen.

"That is on top of everything and everyone you have already?" Woodring asked as the sound of the mumbling in the room grew louder.

"It is, it is, but...." Byrd paused for dramatic effect and nodded at Appledorm.

Swiftly, the 3M engineer switched the one transparent sheet for the other, and magically, a drawing appeared on the screen that quickly silenced the room again.

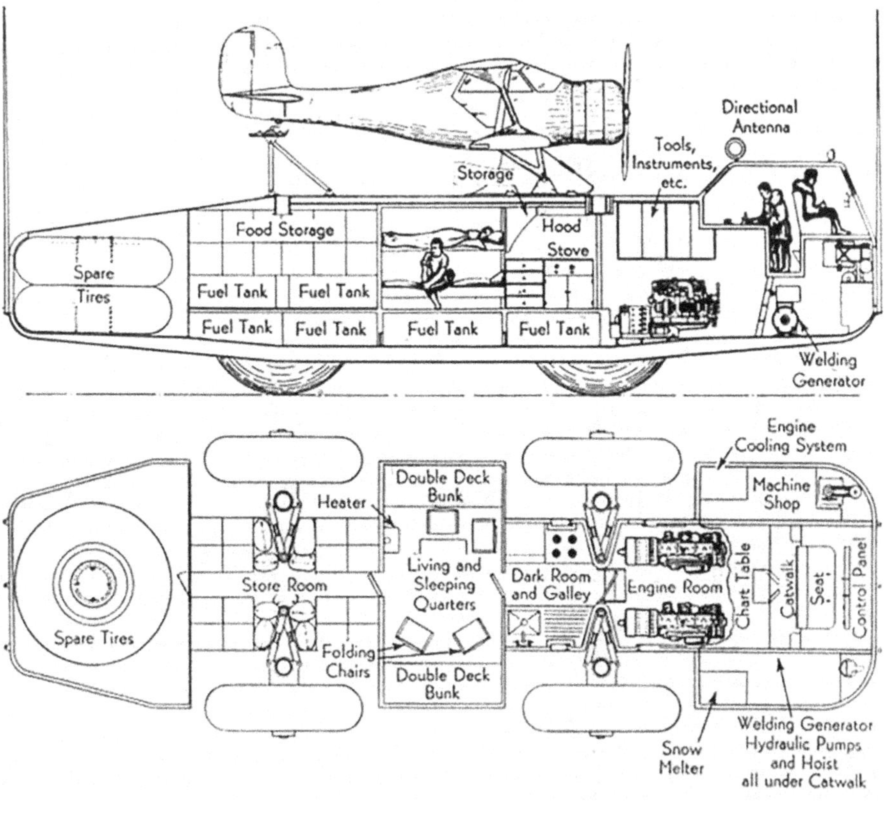

Byrd walked to the door and swung it open. A slightly heavyset man joined him, and Byrd closed the door behind him.

"Gentlemen," he continued, pointing at the screen. "Fifty-five feet nine inches long, nineteen feet eleven inches wide, seventy-five thousand pounds heavy, and a top speed of thirty miles per hour with a maximum range of 5,000 miles. And... carrying a Beechcraft Model 17 Staggerwing airplane... I give you The Antarctic Snow Cruiser, or as I like to call it, The Eagle and the Turtle." He let the image sink in for a second.

"Here to tell you all about the Cruiser is Dr. Thomas Charles Poulter, from the Armour Institute of Technology in Illinois. He's the lead designer of the vehicle, and my second in command on my previous Antarctic mission."

"Thank you," the 45-year-old Poulter said, and with a tiny nod at Byrd, he took over. "I'm afraid Admiral Byrd already gave away the Cruiser's best features, but I'll try to put things in perspective in regard to the Antarctic mission. With four sixteen-foot-tall wheels, combined with the 672-cubic-inch, three-hundred-horsepower, joined twin diesel engines, the Cruiser is designed to keep traction and keep going under the most difficult circumstances. Two thousand five hundred gallons of fuel for the Cruiser, and one thousand gallons for the airplane, and enough food and water for the five-person crew, give the Cruiser self-sufficiency for over a year under the most extreme conditions. What can I say—"

"Does it come with a stereo?" Swanson asked.

"And in blue?" Ickes added.

The room laughed again.

"Actually," Byrd took over. "All plans are ready, and the Chicago Pullman Company is standing by to start manufacturing, and will finish the Antarctic Snow Cruiser's production within three months. And," he addressed Swanson, "it's actually not a bad idea to add a stereo."

"Oh, and it's red," Poulter added. "The Cruiser will be red. We like it to stick out in the snow."

Ickes was the first to clap his hands softly. "I'm really impressed."

The others in the room soon joined him in modest applause.

"I think I speak for everyone when I say you have our blessing," Hull said, looking around.

"One more thing," Woodring said while everyone nodded. "You have my blessing too, but I need you to do one thing for me."

"You name it," Byrd responded.

"I need you to take a T3E4 Carrier and an M2A2 light tank with you for trials in the Antarctic. Of course, I'll provide the necessary personnel."

"Not a problem," Byrd agreed. "I'm sure we can find some room on one of the ships. Now, if you don't have any other questions. I'd like to finish a memo for congress, and I have a Cruiser to build."

CHAPTER 2

Cuneiform

Yale, New Haven, CT, The Present

A single book stack tower was raised in 1928 to hold over three-point-five million books in the new Yale library in New Haven. Designed by James Gamble Rogers, it was primarily funded through a gift of almost thirty million dollars from John W. Sterling, a New York attorney and 1864 Yale alumni. Sixteen levels of stacks filled with volumes rested on a for-the-time-unique, electric, self-supporting structure. They dedicated the library to the English classics. The stained-glass windows on the second floor represented scenes from King Lear, Hamlet, and Lady Macbeth, amongst others. In 1931, the Sterling Memorial Library opened its two enormous wooden doors to the European-styled Gothic cathedral, complete with cloisters, side chapels, clerestory windows, and a circulation desk altar.

Though the Sterling Memorial Library on the corner of Wall Street and Rose Walk was only just around the corner from his own office, Walker James Monroe rarely visited it.

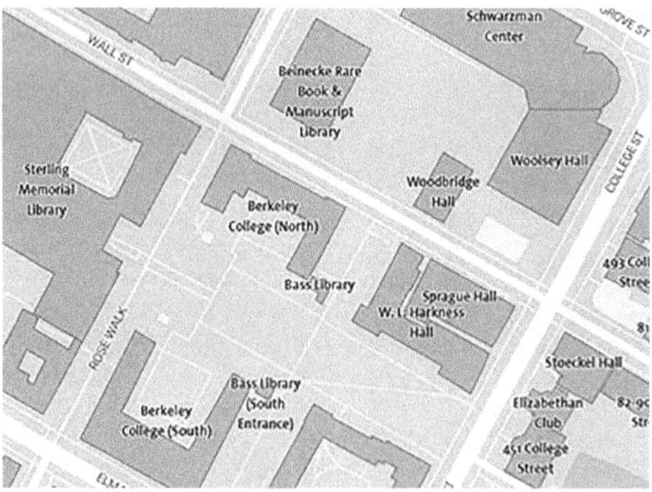

Monroe, the mid-fifties, black, bald, Brit curator of the Beinecke Rare Book & Manuscript Library, simply rarely found the time. His colleague Susan Landon, the Yale Babylonian Collection curator, had invited him to give a guest lecture during a special re-opening of the Yale Babylonian Collection. The Collection was founded in 1911 by Albert Tobias Clay, a historian and professor of Assyriology and Babylonian Literature who specialized in Babylonian business and legal documents. Yale's new permanent exhibit contained over forty-five thousand items with cylinder seals, pottery, letters, and texts, belonging to the earliest found in the world, all written in cuneiform, meaning 'wedge-shaped.' This is where Monroe came in. Landon had asked him to lecture a group of her students about the invention of writing and the oldest writing in the world.

The library's second-floor lecture hall was mostly dark, with dimmed, colored light beams shining through the glass-stained windows. All the seats in the hall were occupied, and some eighty young men and women, all first-year students in ancient literature, had watched Monroe's first part of the presentation, and so far, the curator felt he couldn't complain. Though lecturing was part of his profession, he always felt himself more of a curator and researcher. There were always one or two students who felt the need to make snotty remarks, or who accused him of being superior, which he assumed happened largely because of his British accent.

So far, so good. The audience seemed really interested this time.

"So," Monroe continued, dressed in a dark grey business suit and purple shirt. "No, writing wasn't invented in a single civilization as was long thought, and some still do. Those who do are wrong. No monogenesis. Though one of the earliest pieces of writing we found originated in Mesopotamia, ancient Sumer, it's now proven that written language individually developed in at least four civilizations." The names appeared on two large LCD screens behind him. "In Egypt around 3250 BC, China in 1200 BC, Guatemala and Mexico in 500 BC, and, here you have it, in Mesopotamia somewhere between 3400 and 3100."

"BC," a young man called out from the back of the room.

"You think?" Monroe called back in the direction of the voice, which was cause for some laughter. "But of course, you're right. BC. From there, it's believed that merchants traveling around the globe spread the writing, and in that way introduced the first written languages to the world. When you think of it, it's not that long ago."

"Five thousand years," another voice called out, from the front row this time.

"Very good," Monroe responded, smiling. "You sure you're in the right class?" Again, laughter in the room; Monroe always gained confidence when he was able to make an audience laugh. "So, what were they writing about? Anyone?"

"Bookkeeping?" someone in the front row called out.

"Okay," Monroe replied, pointing at the young woman. "A very important group I told you about were merchants who kept lists of their orders and payments. Anyone else?"

"Mail?" another voice sounded.

"Sure," Monroe agreed. "Mail. We know that merchants received messages from individuals, and for payment, they delivered them to the next village—the first postmen, so to say. Okay, and what do you think this one says?" Monroe took an engraved clay tablet from the table next to him and held it in the air. "It's written in cuneiform, together with the Egyptian hieroglyphs considered the oldest form of writing in the world. No one?" He walked into the room and, at close range, showed the tablet to the people in the front row.

While walking across the front row of students, Monroe, for a second, got distracted by two men entering the hall in the back, and he almost dropped the tablet as he bumped into a chair.

"We better not drop it." He excused himself, smiling. "I promised my wife I would bring it home tonight." He'd never actually been married to a woman, but as a British, black, married gay man, he still didn't feel comfortable sharing that notion in front of large crowds.

He looked again at the two men who had just entered. At first, he figured they were some lazy students who probably just woke up after last night's adventures. But after a closer look in the dimly lit room, he determined these weren't students. Two middle-aged, unfamiliar men had joined his lecture.

"Anyone?" He held the tablet in the air while on the screen behind him, cuneiform signs appeared.

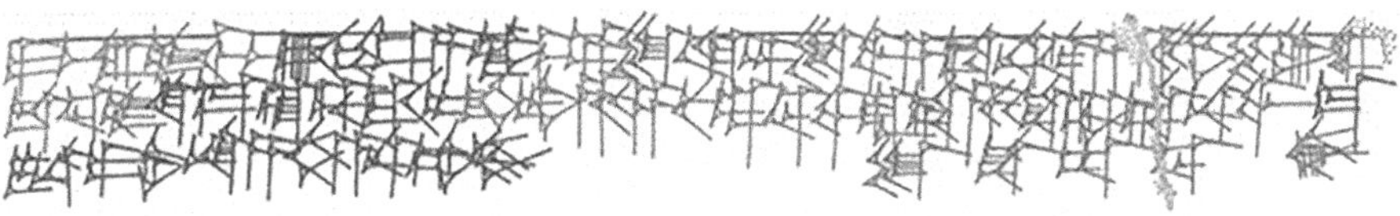

"There it is." Monroe pointed at one of the screens while he walked back behind his lectern. "That's the reason my wife wants this tablet. Still no one?" He gave a tiny smile. "I figured my wife would be a dead giveaway."

"It's a cookbook," a man's voice called out from somewhere in the middle.

"Yes," Monroe responded eagerly. "It's a cookbook. Very good. There's still hope for you yet," he joked. "In the old Mesopotamia, we literally found hundreds of these cookbooks, maybe even thousands. On this page alone, there are ten recipes for delicious dishes, complete with side dishes and herbs. I assure you we tried them all, like the one on the screen behind us. In that case—" He pointed at the screen. "—it's a recipe for an excellent stew. And trust me, some of the recipes are excellent. What's also remarkable is that out of these ten dishes, four are vegetarian. So it seems being a vegetarian isn't something specific to our time. Okay, with that, we've come to the end of the lecture. I hope you learned something about the origin of writing that you can use in your future years here at Yale. Are there any burning questions left?"

"Yes." A young woman rose from her chair. "Are there still texts that are uninterpreted out there?"

"There are," Monroe responded. "Even here in this exhibit. You have to know that once you've 'cracked' the code, that doesn't mean translating becomes easy. Often, clay tablets or papyrus writings are damaged or otherwise not easily readable. So, some parts have to be assumed. Take the script in cuneiform, for instance. There are over seven hundred symbols in that written language. Can you imagine an alphabet with seven hundred letters? It will take decades before everything is translated, and even then, new texts are discovered every day. Anyone else?"

"Do you expect any big revelations from the translations yet to come?" a young man, all the way in the back, asked.

"That's a very good question, and the truth is, I don't know. Over five thousand years have passed since the invention of writing, and I've given you only a few examples of ancient writing that we know how to translate. Many more exist out there, sometimes not even that old, which we still don't know how to translate or explain. There's the Egyptian Wadi el-Hol script, the Bulgarian Sitovo inscriptions, the... umm... Mexican Olmec writing. Oh, and the Rongorongo writings from Easter Island. That one is very interesting, because you read a line first from left to right, then turn it 180 degrees and read the next line. But what it says? No one knows, because every one of the original Easter Island Rapuni natives who could read and write were killed by the Peruvians conquering the island. So, to get back to your question... big revelations, I'm not sure, but I am certain there's a lot to learn out there. And on that note, I thank you for your attention. I wish you all the best with your studies in the coming years, and if you're interested, visit me in my workplace. It's just around the corner. Thank you again."

It took a few seconds before applause sounded through the lecture hall, followed by loud mumbling noises of students packing their things and leaving. Monroe picked up his papers and, with a sigh, put them in his briefcase.

"Glad it's over, professor?" a male voice echoed through the almost empty hall.

Monroe looked up from his briefcase at the two men who'd entered halfway through his lecture, now walking up to him.

"Who are you?" he asked while continuing his packing.

"Sorry, we didn't mean to startle you."

"You didn't." He closed his briefcase. When he looked up and more closely at the men, he noticed one was firmly overweight with a big round face, and the other was tall but skinny. In his mind, he made a reference to Stan Laurel and Oliver Hardy. The fact that the tall one wore a khaki suit complete with vest and bowtie, and the large one was dressed in a dark suit and bowtie, didn't help. A tiny grin appeared on his face.

"Anyway," the tall one said, "my name is Don Fellows, and this is William Hootkins." He gestured to the overweight man next to him as he put a briefcase on the floor. "We work for the USGS."

"The United States Geological Survey," Hootkins explained.

"I know what the USGS is," Monroe replied. "Now, what can I do for you, gentlemen? I'm in a bit of a hurry."

"Oh, sure," Fellows took over again. "Professor Monroe, we've heard a great deal about you, and understand that you're one of the country's leading experts in ancient languages."

"Actually, it's rare books and manuscripts, medieval hagiography, renaissance cartography, and in general, the history of the book. But I'm flattered." As he said it, he realized he probably sounded snotty, but he didn't care.

"Pardon our ignorance," Fellows said. "We'd like your opinion on something, but first, I need you to understand that everything we tell you and show you must be considered strictly confidential."

Monroe cocked his head. *The USGS, strictly confidential?* He'd assumed these men dug out rocks and researched them for their age. "All right, I understand."

His curiousity peaked, as he figured the USGS to be the least secretive of all government agencies. He knew they studied landscapes, natural resources, and natural hazards that jeopardized it. They did some work on geology, biology, hydrology, and geography. But as far as he knew, they were an investigative organization without any regulatory responsibility.

Hootkins nodded at Fellows, who took the briefcase from the floor, opened it, and took out what looked like a folded cloth. "Since you're in a hurry, we'll get right down to business." He slowly unfolded the cloth, revealing what looked like a thin, shiny copper or golden sheet of metal, about five inches long and three inches wide. It looked fragile.

"What's that?" Monroe asked.

Fellows reached out to hand him the metal sheet, but he somehow felt reluctant to take it.

"It's okay," Hootkins said. "You won't break it, and it's not radioactive or anything like that."

Hesitant, Monroe took the metal sheet and weighed it in his hands. It felt heavier than he expected. The edges looked carved, but as he tried to bend it between his hands, it wouldn't budge. He looked at it closely but didn't notice any markings.

"Turn it around," Hootkins said.

Slowly, Monroe turned it around and inspected the other side.

In one corner, there was something engraved that looked like symbols, written in a spiral loop. Monroe pulled his reading glasses from his jacket and put them on. The markings were hard to distinguish without a magnifying glass.

It's a very fine imprint, and there must be hundreds, maybe even thousands of characters here, he thought.

"What do you make of it?" Hootkins asked. "Do you recognize it?"

Monroe took off his glasses. "No, should I? They look like signs or characters of some kind."

"Well," Fellows said as Monroe handed him back the piece of metal. "Here." He took a piece of paper from his jacket pocket and gave it to Monroe. "This is what it looks like enlarged. Thousands of them are there, and since you are the expert on ancient writings...."

"But this isn't ancient." Monroe pointed at the metal sheet as he gave the back the paper. "And the characters used are not like anything I've ever seen." He raised his shoulders. "What is this, and where does it come from? Is it some form of secret communication? And in that case, what does the USGS want with it?"

Hootkins took a deep breath. "As we said, this has to stay between us, and though we are intrigued by the inscription, we are evenly interested in the material of the sheet itself. We hope the inscription might help shed some light on it."

"What's so special about the material?" Monroe took the sheet back and inspected it again.

"Two things, actually," Fellows answered, sticking two fingers in the air. "Do you know what carbon dating is?"

"Sure." Monroe frowned, feeling a little insulted. "That's a way to determine the age of an organic object by measuring the amount of carbon-14 present, and comparing this against an internationally used reference. But it doesn't work on metal, so...?"

"True," Hootkins said. "But the sheet came encased with some of the organic materials it was found with—mud, from a great depth into the Earth, I can say. Those materials were identified as fossilized objects, and when we tried to carbon date them, we failed because they were too old. Which means—"

"Which means," Monroe interrupted him, "they were over sixty thousand years old."

"Exactly," Hootkins confirmed.

"But that may only mean someone packed together a new thing with some really old things."

Hootkins nodded. "That's probably true, and that's why we have the piece of metal undergoing a uranium-thorium-lead test. That method works on the metal itself, and is also used to determine the age of Earth. Experts say that will definitely give better results, but unfortunately, those results won't be in for a few weeks."

Monroe shrugged. "You said there were two things that interested you about the sheet?"

"Indeed," Hootkins said. "The second thing is that the used material seems harder than anything we currently know of. We tried to determine the composition of it, but we couldn't. We tried spark analysis for bulk elemental analysis of steels, cast irons, copper, aluminum, cobalt, stainless steel, nickel, tin, and zinc alloys. We used infrared combustion to find carbon, sulfur, oxygen-hydrogen, or nitrogen, and X-ray fluorescence to search for nickel alloys, and everything else we could think of to find just about any other alloy systems. Nothing. Through ICP, Inductively Coupled Plasma, we found some tiny concentrations of copper and tin, what you might count as bronze, but the amounts were negligible."

"Hmm," Monroe replied, a little impressed by all the metals and methods spread around. "Though, for the large part, I have no idea what you were talking about, it sounds like you did your homework. I'm intrigued." He opened his briefcase and took out an old-fashioned magnifying glass. "A present from my father when I was little. I carry it around everywhere." He inspected the carvings on the sheet again. "They almost seem engraved with laser precision."

"That's what our people say," Hootkins replied.

"Where did you say you found it?"

"Well, we didn't find it ourselves, but it comes from an over forty-thousand-foot deep drill site in Russia."

"Wow, that's a deep hole. It does look like some kind of writing, but the symbols aren't like anything I've ever seen." He took his eye from the sheet again. "I must confess, at first glance, I've no idea, not about the material, not about the writing nor the way it's written. The only time I've seen writing like this before, in a spiral form, was on the Phaistos Disc."

"The Phaistos Disc?" Hootkins and Fellows asked almost simultaneously.

"Yes, wait for a second." From his suitcase, he took a round clay tablet about six inches diagonal with symbols carved into it. He handed it to Hootkins, who took it from him very cautiously.

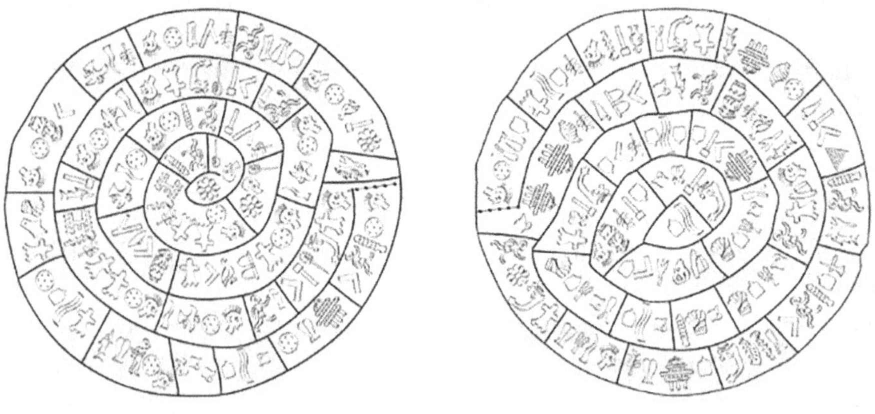

"Don't worry," Monroe said. "It's only a replica. I used it for my presentation here today. The original dates from around 2000 BC, the late or middle Minoan Bronze Age, and was found in the Minoan palace of Phaistos in Greece, on the island of Crete. There are 241 pictures of forty-five distinct hieroglyphic-like characters. But as you can see, it's nothing like your sheet of metal. This one's made of clay and much more... umm... crude."

"What does it say?" Fellows asked.

"Who knows?" Monroe answered. "No one has been able to translate it yet. The problem is it's a unique set of signs. There are no other pieces found, which makes it extremely difficult to translate."

"As with our piece," Hootkins stated.

"As with your piece," Monroe confirmed. "Fortunately, we are getting smarter by the day through looking at these translations in a more mathematical way, rather than through a lingual perspective. With a little luck, your text could be translated without ever finding a second piece written in the same language. It all depends on the structure of the characters and the setting in which they are used."

"Obviously, we've come to the right person," Hootkins said. "You seem to know everything about translating these writings."

"Well, not really," Monroe replied. "But I may know someone who did do some serious mathematical work on the subject and who might be willing and able to help you. Now, where again did you say you found this item?"

CHAPTER 3

Uakitite

Moscow, Russia

Nadya Fedorova walked up to the MGRI building at the corner of Ulitsa Miklukho-Maklaya and Ulitsa Akademika Volgina. She didn't like coming here, as she always got lost in the seven-story colossal university building, and enormous grey concrete structure built like a shoebox. She figured the architect must have been a friend or family member of the government to get such a design approved. During the day, over a thousand students attended the various colleges at the university.

In the 1930's—back in the USSR—Joseph Stalin saw the need for industrialization and ordered the education of over 435,000 engineers and technicians in five years. The Moscow Mining Academy was born, divided into seven institutes focused on Geology, Hydrogeology, International Relations, Legislation, and Resource Economics, Ecology, and Geophysics. Today, all those divisions were united in the MGRI, the Sergo Ordzhonikidze Russian State University for Geological Prospecting.

For the occasion, Nadya, in her mid-thirties, had put on a light blue denim jacket over her army green tank top, on top of a pair of dark jeans and white sneakers. Her short black hair stood in bright contrast with her pale, almost transparent skin and full pink lips. Men found her attractive, but also considered her somewhat of a threat when they saw her muscle-toned body.

As she walked into the grey-veined marble hall, voices of people roaming around echoed throughout. Somehow, it reminded her of hospitals from the nineties, like the one in which she often visited her grandma as a child. The echoes depressed her a bit. Her training at the Akademija Vnesjnej Razvedki, Russia's Academy of Foreign Intelligence, had brought her here. Ever since she graduated from the academy, she'd been given assignments in the Russian mother country, playing the liaison between her superiors and some foreign agent abroad. She hadn't signed up for this, but what was she to do? Female foreign agents were scarce. Come to think of it, she didn't know of any.

"*Dobroye utro* (good morning)," the blonde receptionist greeted Nadya.

"*S dobrym utrom,*" Nadya replied. Though security was tight, she had often visited the university and was friendly with, and recognized by, just about all the receptionists. "Can you tell me where I can find Demyan Novikov today?"

"Let me see." The receptionist worked a computer keyboard. "Where is... ah, here he is, lab B312. You take the east elevator—"

"Thank you, I think I know where to find it." She walked off into the corridor on the left.

"Miss Fedorova!" the receptions called out after her.

Nadya looked back.

"Over there." The receptionist pointed into the right corridor.

Why does everything in this building look precisely the same?

Nadya entered the elevator and punched the button reading '3'. The doors screeched closed, and after a few seconds, the elevator set itself into a bumpy upwards motion. As shrieking sounds came from between the walls, it took her almost a minute to get from the ground floor to the third, and she regretted not taking the stairs. When the doors opened again, the sign said she needed to go left. The beige linoleum floor in the long corridor matched the walls and ceiling, and every fifteen feet or so, a door, containing a ten-inch by ten-inch steel wired window, interrupted the otherwise empty walls.

Talk about a depressing environment.

'B312' read the sign on one of the last doors on the left. She stopped and peeked through the small window. The room looked sterile-white, with three rows of tables filled with a variety of lab materials. In the center row, a dark blond man dressed in a dark grey suit and a red tie sat down and looked through a microscope, while young men and women in white lab coats surrounded him.

Nadya grinned. *So that's how they distinguish the teachers from the students here.*

She opened the door and closed it behind her with a pretty loud bang.

No one looked up. The professor stayed focus on the microscope while the students looked at a large monitor next to it.

"There, you see it?" The professor looked up from the microscope and at the monitor. "There." He pointed at the screen.

Nadya had joined the group, and from behind them, she looked at the monitor. To her, the screen was filled with rough-edged spots colored from dark to light grey. "Professor Novikov," she spoke out loud. "Demyan Novikov?"

The group of white coats looked back, and then opened up a space, and Nadya came eye to eye with the professor.

"I'm professor Novikov," the man in his late forties said, putting on a set of large rimmed glasses. In his not too close-fitting suit, greasy hair, and weathered dark brown leather shoes, Novikov looked like he'd just walked out of a small accountancy office after a hard day's work. "And who are you?"

"If you don't mind, I'd like to have a word in private with you, professor."

Novikov frowned and looked around at his students. "Do you have any idea what we are looking at here?" He pointed at the monitor.

Nadya shrugged.

"This is a newly discovered mineral called Uakitite. It was recently discovered in an iron meteorite found in Buryatia, southern Russia in 2016. Do you have any idea how often new minerals are discovered?"

Nadya shook her head.

"Well, umm, it's not that rare, actually, but nonetheless, this one's quite unique. This one's probably harder than diamond, and that's unheard of. But we're still testing. It's still stuck in the meteorite, you see."

"So why don't you take it out of it?"

Novikov gave a bright smile. "That might prove difficult because, there are only a few samples in it, and they are about five micrometers in size. That means they are in size only a fraction of a grain of sand."

"That's very interesting," Nadya said, then took a deep breath and frowned.

"I'm sorry." He addressed the students while pointing at a door at the side of the room. "Please, can you give us a moment?"

Within seconds, all students had left the room.

"Please don't get up," Nadya said when Novikov moved to rise from his office chair. "The SVR has sent me," she said as soon as the door behind the last student closed.

The Sloezjba Vnesjnej Razvedki, or SVR, was extracted from the KGB in 1991. Unlike the Federal Security Service, FSB, the SVR was tasked with civilian intelligence and espionage activities outside the Russian Federation. In contrast with the GRU, its military espionage counterpart, the SVR also had intelligence-sharing agreements with foreign intelligence agencies.

"I expected as much." Novikov sighed.

"Then you know why I'm here," Nadya stated.

"As I told your colleague on the phone, there's nothing I can do. There's simply not enough material, and I don't know where the package came from. I don't know why they sent you, but there's nothing more I can do without sufficient samples— "

"Shhh!" Nadya put a finger to her mouth as she dropped into an office chair with a bounce, and slowly rolled up to Novikov, as close as she could. With her legs wide, she locked his limbs in between hers. "I guess my boss isn't entirely sure you're telling the truth, or at least has doubts whether you did your best."

Novikov frowned and shook his head.

Nadya leaned over, took his bright red tie, and pulled it, forcing him to slowly bend closer towards her. She stopped pulling when her full, pink lips were less than an inch away from his face. Then she leaned over and put her mouth next to his ear.

"You don't want my employers to doubt your loyalty, do you?" she whispered. As she leaned back again, she noticed a drop of sweat roll down from his temple. She wiped the drop away, and gave it a quick glance before she licked it off her finger. "Hmm, I think I must agree with my employers that you aren't completely honest with them."

"I am, I am," Novikov sputtered.

Nadya tightened the grip with her legs and smiled at him. "Who sent you the package?" Her voice sounded calm as she put her hands on his shoulders and pushed.

"I don't know." New drops of sweat appeared on his forehead and temples.

She bit her lip as she shook her head. "I can ask again if you want." She tilted her head, giving a wide grin.

"I'm telling you the truth. I don't know who sent it." Novikov's racing heart was now visible by the throbbing vein in his neck.

She closely inspected his face from left to right. "But I see you know how to find out."

He took shallow breaths. "And if I do?"

She raised her hands from his shoulders, tapped them a few times, and straightened his jacket. "You would make me the happiest girl in the world. I would check it out, and if it pans out, well.... That would be the end of it. *If* it pans out."

"Do you mind?" Novikov bent forward, suggesting he wanted to get up but was still stuck between Nadya's legs.

"Oh, I'm sorry. Of course. Go ahead." Nadya rolled her chair back.

Novikov got up and walked up to a locker against the wall. He opened the dial padlock, took out a small, crumpled cardboard envelope from the locker, walked back to Nadya, and handed it to her. "You see." He pointed at the label on the envelope. "There's a return address on it."

Nadya took the envelope and inspected the label. There was no name, only a postal code and street number. "Thank you." She gave a bright smile as she took her phone from her jacket, opened her maps app, and punched in the postal code's numbers: one, eight, three, zero, three, eight, and home number twenty-five, and waited. "Your Wi-Fi is very slow." She sounded strict and creased her forehead.

"I know," Novikov replied. "I've compl—"

"Shh." She interrupted him as the location appeared on the screen. "Now, that is interesting." Her face turned happy. "I must admit I'd hoped it would have been a little closer to home, but I guess beggars can't be choosers." She put the phone away, took a small plastic bag from her jacket, folded the envelope, put it in the bag and back into her coat. "Nice." She got up and, with both hands, took Novikov's hand and shook it. "Thank you, thank you so much. I will be checking in with you again if you don't mind?"

"Uh-hmm," Novikov uttered.

"Great, thank you for everything." Nadya walked to the door and left the room. "Bye now," she called out, looking over her shoulder before she turned into the hallway and disappeared from Novikov's sight.

Within minutes, she walked out of the building again, took out her phone, and punched the screen. The phone rang once, and a man's voice sounded from the other side.

"*Allo* (hello)."

"*Zdravstvuyte* (greetings, Chief)," Nadya replied.

"And?" the man's heavy voice returned.

"He doesn't know anything. He did, however, save the envelope the material came in, and it has a return address on it. No name, just an address, but I guess it's a start."

"Where is it?" the man replied impatiently.

She took a deep breath. "Just a second." Nadya took the phone from her ear, gave a big sigh, and punched some keys.

Though she'd never met the man she called Chief, when she talked to him, he rarely spoke more than a few words in a sentence. Now that she thought of it, she probably never spoke to him when he was in some kind of a good mood. She shook her head, looked at the screen, and put the phone back to her ear. "I just texted you the location."

"Wait." The line went silent, and Nadya put her phone on speaker, waiting for him to return.

"That's about 1300 miles." The throaty voice sounded loud again, and Nadya quickly put the phone back to her ear.

"I know. I can fly out from Sheremetyevo tomorrow morning and be there around noon." The line stayed silent for a long moment.

"All right," he came back. "I'll have a ticket dropped off at your address later this evening. Please hand over the envelope with the address on it to the messenger that brings the ticket. I'll have it checked out for prints. Maybe we get lucky."

"Will do."

"Oh, and Nadya...." His voice now sounded firm. "Please keep me informed of your every move, and don't do anything or talk to anyone without my approval."

"Do I ever, sir?" she asked.

The line went dead.

Touchy.

CHAPTER 4

The Buridan's Bridge

Yale, New Haven, CT

Monroe, as ever dressed in suit and tie, walked into College Street regretting not putting on an overcoat in the cold November mist. At number 451, he turned left and hopped the three steps onto the red-bricked building's arched portico. Once under the overhang, he wiped his bald head dry with his handkerchief, swung the big green door open, and walked in and down the long corridor. All the way in the back, he stopped at the door with a sign that said, 'Head of the Department of Comparative Literature and Religious Studies.' With his fist, he loudly pounded the door three times.

Two students, walking on the mezzanine, stopped and looked down to see what the commotion was about.

Monroe looked up. "It's okay. I'm just waking him up," he called out as he pounded the door again.

After a soft click, the door opened just a few inches.

Monroe gazed at the gap that arose to see if anything else would happen. It didn't, so he forcefully swung the door open, making it bounce against the wall with a loud bang.

"Please don't do that," a man's voice sounded from the inside.

Monroe went in, and in the sterile white room, behind a glossy white desk, sat Matthew Bishop, dressed in blue jeans, dark red turtleneck, and white sneakers, with his elbows on the desktop, holding his head between both hands.

"Rough night?" Monroe asked his friend and head of the department.

"Not that I'm aware," the red-curled, short-haired professor responded. "Although the headache surely suggests otherwise. How did you know I was here? I'm never in at this hour."

"I saw that electrified, ugly blue Jeep Wrangler of yours parked at the end of the street. And by the looks of your parking skills, I figured something had to be wrong."

"So, you came here to help?" Bishop frowned and squinted.

"Something like that." Monroe pulled a cord on the wall to open the shutters, and the bright sunlight beamed in.

"Why...." Bishop dragged the word out and lay his head on the desk. "That's not helping, you know?"

"Here." Monroe grabbed a thermos from an otherwise empty and spic-and-span clean table, and poured him a cup of coffee. "And here." From his pocket, he took a strip of aspirin, pushed two out, and handed them to his friend.

Bishop grabbed the pills and swiftly swallowed them with a large gulp of coffee.

"You look like shit," Monroe said while inspecting the forty-five-year-old crumpled face. "Did you get any sleep at all?" he asked the slender, steel blue-eyed, and previous 'Yale's Most Eligible Bachelor.'

Bishop took a deep breath and rose from the desk. "I went night fishing and didn't get much sleep."

"Did you catch anything?"

"Nothing."

"Well, as long as it was worth it." Monroe grinned. "Who goes night fishing on a work night?" He shook his head heavily.

Bishop stroked his trademark three-day reddish beard. "What are you doing here?" He sighed.

"Besides helping you?"

"Let me guess. You need my help?"

"Give and take, that's what friends are for," Monroe joked. "What's that?" He pointed at a row of white sheets of printed paper taped against the bookcase behind Bishop.

"What?" Bishop painstakingly slowly turned his head. "Oh, that. The papers, you mean." He now started to speak faster and more coherently. "That, my friend, are... paradoxes. I'm preparing a lecture on philosophical and mathematical paradoxes."

Monroe walked up to the papers. "Ant on a rubber rope?" he read.

"Yes, it states that an ant walking on a rubber band can reach the end even while the rope stretches faster than the ant can crawl."

Monroe frowned. "Can you explain that to me?"

Bishop grinned. "What do you know about discrete mathematics?"

"Nothing."

"Then, no, I can't explain it to you. Sorry. Maybe I can teach you sometime." Bishop smiled again. "Maybe you should start over there."

He pointed at the papers on the other side. "Those are the philosophical paradoxes. They take more of an... umm... analytical mind, I guess."

Monroe stepped up and read from one of the papers. "Argument from free will, Newcomb's paradox, Zeno's paradoxes, Buridan's bridge—"

"You'll get the last one," Bishop interrupted.

"All right, Matthew, explain it to me." He sat down opposite Bishop.

"First, it's a sophism." Bishop watched Monroe's brows grow together fast. "A fallacious argument, especially one used to deliberately to mislead."

"All right."

"Jean Buridan was a famous and influential French philosopher from the middle ages. He wrote a book called Sophismata. The book was filled with philosophical puzzles and paradoxes. For his time, it was revolutionary. I guess some of it still is. I often use it in my lectures."

As a Yale professor, Matthew Bishop's mantra had always been to send students away more confused than when they came in. That way, he always said, *'they would keep thinking of the material and learn through their own experiences, instead of just reading or listening to the material.'*

"The Buridan's bridge?" Monroe asked.

"Yes, it's a simple statement. Socrates comes to a river that he wants to cross. He walks up to a bridge a little farther down, and when he arrives, he sees the bridge is guarded by Plato. 'You shall not pass,' Plato calls out. 'You can only pass if, in the first proposition which you speak, you speak the truth. Only then will I permit you to cross. Should you choose to speak falsely, I shall throw you off the bridge, into the water.' Socrates thinks for a while and then replies, 'You will throw me into the water.' That's it," Bishop finished.

"Let me see," Monroe said. "So, if Socrates' reply was true, Plato had to let him cross. But if Plato were to let him cross, what Socrates said had to be false, and Plato must have thrown him in the water. So, there's no way Plato can keep his word?"

Bishop smiled. "You see?"

Monroe shrugged. "What if Plato takes Socrates across and, immediately after crossing, still throws him into the water. That way, they both won't be liars."

"Not sure if you get the point." Bishop shook his head. "Here." He took a small piece of paper from his desk drawer. "I'll give this to all my students after the lecture. The one that answers the question correctly gets a free meal or something like that."

Monroe took the paper and read the question carefully.

Which of the two statements is true?

The statement in the right box is true	?	The statement in the left box is false

"Hmm... and what do I get when I answer it correctly?"

"I'll take you on a fishing trip." Bishop smiled.

Monroe grunted. "All right, not sure if I want to win then. Let me get back to you on that."

"That's okay," Bishop replied. "So, did you come here to have me tell you about my paradoxes, or is there something else I can help you with?"

Monroe put away the paper, and from his jacket took a rolled-up piece of cloth and put it on the desk between them.

"A present?"

"Mwah! More of a challenge, I think."

Bishop leaned over the desk. When he picked up the wrapped cloth, he weighed it in his hand. "Heavy," he concluded as he carefully unwrapped it. "What is this?" He held the piece of shiny metal in his hands.

"Here...." Monroe handed him his magnifying glass. "Turn it around."

Bishop turned the sheet of metal into the light, and the engraving became visible. "An inscription."

"In signs I've never seen before," Monroe added.

"All right, looks unfamiliar to me too, at first glance." Bishop took his eye off the sheet again. "What am I looking at, and why is this of interest to you?"

"Remember when the Rosetta stone was discovered in 1799, or the discovery of Pharaoh Tutankhamun by Howard Carter in 1922, or the Terracotta Army—"

"I wasn't there at any of them, but I think I get your point."

"Well, this little piece here might be just as big," Monroe replied, getting more excited by the minute.

"All right, so tell me about it."

"This sheet comes from a forty-thousand-foot-deep drill in Russia, and has been dated to be at least sixty thousand years old." Monroe stayed silent for a long moment.

Bishop shook his head and grinned. "No, that's impossible. No." He shook his head even more heavily. "That's not possible for so many reasons. First, it looks like scripture, and a very fine one, for that matter. And if it is scripture, it would be more than fifty-five thousand years older than what we know to exist at present. But of course, you of all people know that."

"Big, isn't it?" Monroe stated with a smile from ear to ear.

"How deep did you say they found this?"

"Over forty thousand feet."

"Impossible," Bishop said again. "Any material we know that deep beneath the earth would have been crushed over the years by the pressure."

"You said it: any material we know." Monroe waved both hands.

Bishop tilted his head. "How did you get this?"

"The USGS brought it to me because of my knowledge of ancient writing. They asked me if I recognized it or knew of a way to translate it."

"Why is the USGS interested in an old piece of writing?" Bishop asked.

"They said they aren't, or at least, not really."

"You lost me."

"They are mainly interested in the material it's written on. It's made of nothing they've ever seen before, and they haven't yet been able to analyze what it's made of. They told me it was tougher than any other metal or alloy they'd ever seen before."

"And they just gave it to you?"

"They did. A man from the USGS named Hootkins did. I think he's the boss. He only demanded I would keep him updated about my findings."

"All right, I'm interested," Bishop said. "Let me check something out." He took a laptop from his desk drawer, precisely centered it on his desk, opened it, and started to type. "You said it was found at a depth of over forty thousand feet?"

Monroe nodded.

"Hmm," Bishop mumbled while reading the screen and typing again. "Aha, right."

"What is it?"

"Kola," Bishop replied.

"Kola?"

Bishop turned the screen towards Monroe. "Kola, in Murmansk, Russia, on the edge of the Arctic circle, the only place they ever crossed the forty-thousand-feet threshold, drilling into the earth. The Kola Superdeep Borehole, they called it."

"And you think that's where they found it?"

"You said they found it in Russia at that depth, so I don't see any other possibilities."

"Anything special about it?"

Bishop turned the screen back and started reading again. "I vaguely have some memory about the Russians setting a new record, but that's about as far as my knowledge goes. Hmm," he mumbled while reading. "Yes, you see, it says here that they set the record but were forced to stop drilling because of the higher-than-expected temperature and all sorts of other difficulties."

"Roughly eight miles deep is still immensely deep," Monroe stated.

"Not if you consider that it still is only halfway to the mantle and less than a quarter percent on the way down to the center of the Earth."

"Does it say that they found anything special?"

Bishop scanned some pages on the screen. "It says here that the biggest discovery they made was the presence of water over four miles deep. They didn't expect water because rocks that deep aren't porous. One theory says that the water came from Noah's biblical floodwater."

"Well, Genesis refers to 'all the fountains of the great deep,' so who knows."

"It says here that they also found some fossils, over four miles below, which shouldn't be there. And here's an article that mentions that they closed the hole because of a chamber of fire they stumbled upon. Supposedly, from the chamber sounded the anguished screams of the damned dead."

"Hell itself?" Monroe suggested lifting an eyebrow. "Maybe hell is literally below us after all. The Sumerians, who are by some believed to be the inventors of hell, believed that the afterlife was a dark, dreary cavern located deep below the ground, where they would go after a sinful life, and live on like shadows of their previous selves."

Bishop smiled. "Who knows? Anyway, there's no mention, on any of the Kola information pages, as far as I can see this quickly, about strange metals with inscriptions. It says here they stopped drilling in 1992 and closed the hole in 1995."

"So?" Monroe asked.

"Well, why now? Where has this piece been for over twenty-five years? Did they tell you anything? For that matter, did they just give you this to keep? Isn't this a far too important discovery to just hand over to a simple university librarian? No offense."

"None taken," Monroe replied. "All valid questions, but I have no answers, I'm afraid. You care to find out with me?"

"Well, I must admit I'm intrigued." Bishop held the sheet of metal in front of him, against the light, and inspected it. "You mind if I keep it here for now so I can have a look at it later today? I promise I will keep it safe."

"Breakfast tomorrow, my place? In the meantime, I'll see what I can dig up about that Kola hole."

"Breakfast tomorrow," Bishop confirmed as Monroe rose from his chair.

"This could be exciting!" Monroe chanted as he walked out.

***

Bishop grinned as he encased the metal sheet back into its cloth, got up, and turned to the bookcase behind him. He took out a small row of books to reveal a wall safe behind.

After putting the item in the safe and closing it again, he looked at his watch.

Damn, I'm going to be late for class. Well, at least I'm awake.

CHAPTER 5

C, G, A, T

Yale, New Haven, CT

The Beinecke Library was built in the center of the neoclassical style-built Hewitt University Quadrangle, better known as Beinecke Plaza, home of the university's administration, dining facilities, and main auditorium. The early morning sunrays beamed golden through the translucent, veined marble panels of the otherwise windowless façade of the Yale library, which was entirely dedicated to rare books and manuscripts.

The six-story-high, glass-enclosed tower of book stacks in the center of the building lit up beautifully in the morning light. Monroe, as always in a dark suit, tie, and Oxfords, walked down from the mezzanine and considered himself lucky to be the curator of the over 180,000 rare volumes. He walked up to the set table next to the glass showcase on the ground floor, which held one of the finest copies of the remaining 48 Guttenberg Bibles. He felt like a father to *all* his books—his children—but the Guttenberg Bible was his prized possession. Every other day, he cleaned the showcase and opened it to turn the book to the next page, a ritual he'd kept going ever since his commission four years ago.

The library also housed the mysterious, four-hundred-year-old Voynich manuscript, the handwritten and illustrated codex of an unknown author that many had tried—and still try—to translate. There had been a fair share of claims of deciphering the document, but after careful study, they all proved to be false. To date, the document remained an enigma that puzzled many without success. Walker Monroe and his best friend Matthew Bishop had spent many a night scrutinizing the original document for clues, but the surreptitious manuscript never revealed any of its secrets. One of their recent theories was that the writing and illustrations of—mostly unknown—plants were completely meaningless, written by who knows who to keep many puzzled for centuries.

Just as Monroe sat down at the table, his cell phone on the table started to vibrate. On the screen appeared his friend waiting at the front door of the library. He pushed a button on the screen. "What do you want?"

The man on the screen's mouth curled up. "I've heard you serve croissants and orange juice for the needy."

"Only if you need it enough." Monroe pushed another button on the screen, and the swooshing sound of the main door opening sounded through the library. Echoing footsteps sounded, followed by the sound of the doors closing again.

"Morning, Matthew," Monroe called out at his friend, as usual dressed in jeans, sweater, and sneakers, who walked up to the table carrying a laptop under his arm.

"Walker," Bishop replied.

"Better today?"

"Much better. Maybe you were right and night fishing on a weekday wasn't a brilliant idea."

Monroe smiled. He knew his friend all too well, and although it wasn't too difficult to have him admit a mistake, it also wouldn't surprise him if he were to make the same one again soon. "Orange juice?"

"Great, and coffee, please."

"Sure." Monroe poured each of them a glass and a cup, showing the red ribbon on his wrist that he always wore. "I see you brought your homework with you." He pointed at the laptop.

Bishop helped himself to a croissant and smeared a thick layer of butter on the bottom. He took his first bite and mumbled, "Hmmm, I did." He chewed down the bite. "I have something to show you after I finish this piece of delicious French pastry."

"That you can even taste it underneath all that butter...." Monroe shook his head.

"I'm glad you British are known for your excellent taste and exquisite cuisine." Bishop gave a bright smile. "Here." After finishing his croissant, he took the wrapped cloth from his pocket and handed it to Monroe. "It's all yours again."

Monroe took the cloth and unpacked the sheet of metal. "Did you find anything?"

"One second." In one big gulp, Bishop finished his orange juice, followed by a big sip from his coffee.

"And you talk about us British," Monroe remarked, smiling.

"Listen." Bishop opened his laptop. "I enlarged the engraving on the metal sheet, and there are indeed symbols on it like nothing I've ever seen before. Come sit next to me." He slapped the empty seat next to him, and Monroe quickly moved over. "Look, I've straightened a small piece of the signs so it makes a bit more sense." Bishop turned the screen to Monroe.

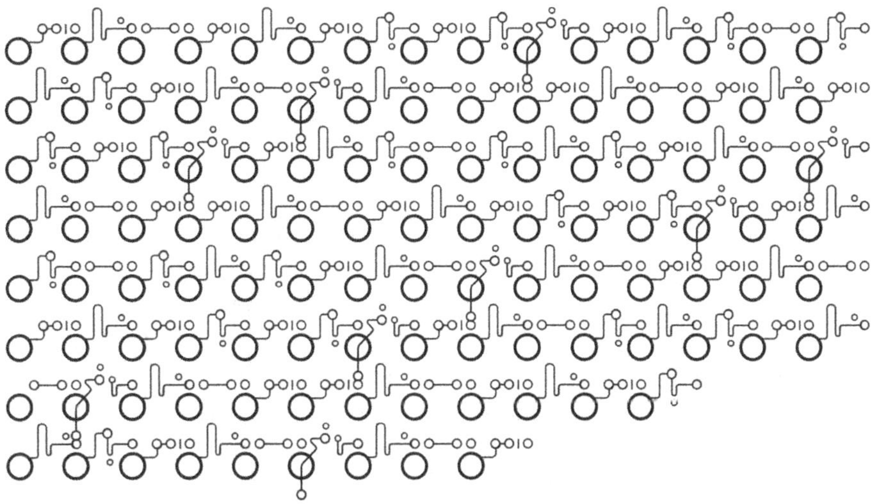

Monroe moved his face closer to the screen. "All right, a bit more sense, indeed. I've seen a lot of scripture in my time but never something like this."

"And there's lots more where this came from—thousands of times as much." Bishop swiped the laptop screen a few times, and with every swipe, a new page of similar-looking signs showed. "And all positioned in one big long string of signs, symbols, or characters, if you like."

"And you have no idea what they stand for?" Monroe asked, rubbing his chin.

"No, umm," Bishop stammered.

"Ah!" Monroe sounded eager. "There's something you're not telling me." He waved a finger in front of Bishop's face.

"Don't point." Bishop slapped Monroe's finger away. "Never point." His eyes glinted. "Of course, I took a long good look at the symbols and noticed something that looked like a pattern."

"In this?" Monroe pointed at the screen.

"Let me show you." Bishop isolated a piece of the string on the screen, enlarged it, and showed it to Monroe. "You notice anything peculiar?"

Monroe took a deep breath and slowly shook his head. He knew Bishop had the answer, and it would take him at least minutes, if not hours or days, to find a lead himself. He sighed. "Just show me."

"All right." Bishop inserted on the screen spaces between certain groups of symbols. He drew lines between the groups and finished with a circle just about in the middle. "And now?"

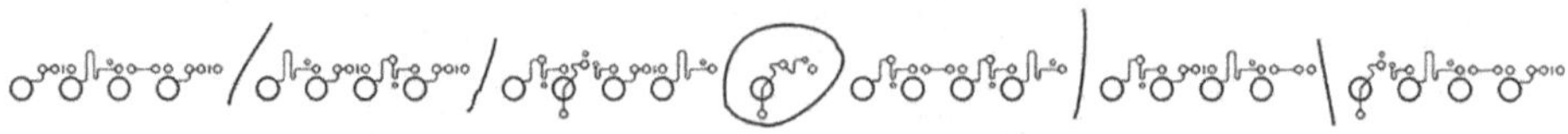

Bishop looked at Monroe, whose face no doubt displayed his wonder. Although Monroe, of the two, was the translator who'd translated hundreds of ancient documents, he needed a codec to translate large pieces of text. That's where Bishop came in.

When he was a young boy, Bishop had made his own secret languages, which he used to pass around in school. Later, after he completed his Ph.D. in mathematics at the University of California-Berkeley in 2001, he even did some *off-the-books* work as a decoder for the US military.

"You see it now?" Bishop asked.

"Tell me?" Monroe demanded, throwing his hands in the air.

Bishop pointed at the screen. "You see, I first learned that the seemingly unending stream of different symbols contains only four different symbols. Every individual character has an O-shaped form with something of a curl attached to it. Like I said, at first, I figured there were only four symbols, but...."

"But?" Monroe asked impatiently.

Bishop redrew the circle on the screen in the middle. "That one's just a little different than the others, and only occurs now and again in the complete string."

"Like a punctuation mark or something?" Monroe asked.

"That's what I thought, but if so, how about the longer and shorter strings of symbols in between the punctuations? There were still the four same symbols."

"I figure that's where the lines you drew come in?"

Bishop nodded. "Each string of symbols in between the punctuations always summed up to a number of characters divisible by four. Some parts of string consisted of three or five parts, but all of them were always and only divisible by parts of four."

"Crazy," Monroe said. "So, what are they? Words of only four characters, all consisting of the same four symbols each time in different composition?"

Bishop cocked his head. "No light burning yet?"

Monroe rubbed his chin. "Wait a second." He waved a pointing finger at the screen. "I think I've got it." A bright smile magically appeared on his face. "You think this is a DNA sequence."

Bishop rubbed his hands, opened them over the keyboard, and shrugged. "Who's to say? It seems to fit, each of the four symbols representing a nucleotide divided by a punctuation mark between strands of DNA."

"DNA is composed of four characters—C, G, A, and T—but which of the four symbols represent which character?"

"I see you watched Jurassic Park." Bishop laughed. "They're Cytosine, Guanine, Adenine, and Thymine... if indeed we're talking about DNA here."

"Look who became an expert overnight," Monroe said.

"Not really." Bishop opened another screen on his laptop. "Remember them?" He showed the homepage of the Logynous Laboratory in New Haven.

"I thought they were dismantled after the whole... umm... you know... scandal." A few years back, Bishop and a few of his colleagues exposed the laboratory and its owner for tampering and experimenting with human DNA.

"They were," Bishop replied. "Local staff bought up the place and rebooted the laboratory business. They're still the closest in the neighborhood for this kind of work. I sent them the string late last night, and I should get the results back tomorrow."

"Fast work." Monroe nodded. "Now, what if it is DNA? What will that tell us?"

"Well, I did some reading, and I figure one of three things can happen. First, if it is DNA, perhaps they can match it to a living organism, and maybe even a specific part of it. Not sure what that will tell us, but at least we'll know."

"And second?" Monroe asked impatiently.

"Then there's the second option, the possibility of it being unknown DNA. I read somewhere that only 0.2 percent of DNA of all known living and dead material on Earth has been sequenced. So, there's a fair chance they won't know what it is. I have no idea yet where to go from there. And then there's the third option, one that could possibly be combined with the first two."

Monroe tilted his head and raised an eyebrow.

"Let me explain. In 2012, a scientist named Ewan Birney sent his colleague a package with some small, empty glass vials. His colleague thought it to be a joke, but later, Birney confessed there was a speck of dust at the bottom of each vial. The dust specks were encoded with DNA. When dissolved in water and sequenced, the specks of dust contained all of Shakespeare's 154 sonnets, a PDF of Watson and Crick's paper detailing the structure of DNA, a 26-second clip of Martin Luther King's 'I Have a Dream' speech, and a jpeg picture of Birney and his colleagues at the institute they worked for. All of that information in a few specks of dust."

"So, what are you saying?" Monroe asked.

"Well, instead of coding information about living tissue in DNA, you can write just about anything else you could store in a computer, in combinations of the characters AGCT. You would get immensely long strings of characters or symbols, but it's possible. All you'd need to do is to convert the binary ones and zeros to the A's, G's, C's, and T's of DNA."

"Fascinating," Monroe replied. "So in that case, the engravings could translate to plain text or even pictures. Amazing. And could you decipher such a code?"

"Maybe, but without an algorithm, a cipher, this could prove to be extremely difficult. I suggest we first wait for the lab results."

"Sure."

"Now, you said you were going to find out everything there was to know about the Kola hole," Bishop said.

"Yes, I did. I must say I'm still a bit flabbergasted about your finding. If this is true... well, then how, or who?"

"Mind-boggling, isn't it?" Bishop stated.

"Indeed. A sixty-thousand-year-old piece of metal with strings of DNA written onto it. Or...."

"Or what?" Bishop asked.

"Well, there's one other thing I can think of."

"Which is?"

"What about the age of the metal piece? The USGS said they couldn't determine the composition of it. What if they couldn't determine it because the metal isn't from this Earth?"

Bishop laughed out loud. "You mean aliens? You're serious?" His forehead furrowed. "I'm afraid I've introduced you to one too many science fiction stories."

Monroe sighed. "You think an ancient piece of writing, of DNA, from beyond the Stone Age, makes more sense?"

"Maybe not," Bishop said. "But aliens? Let's get back to reality for now. What did you find out about the Kola hole?"

It took Monroe a few seconds to switch back. "In your quick scan, you covered pretty much all bases. The deepest hole in the world was closed in 1995, and of course, there are all kinds of conspiracy nuts who developed all kinds of crazy stories about it in the meantime, but nothing substantial. What I did find was a list of people who worked the hole at the time before its closure."

"And?" Bishop asked while pouring himself another cup of coffee.

"I figured maybe we could ask them if they know anything about a find... like maybe a piece of strange metal. Luckily, it wasn't that popular to work out there in the Russian middle of nowhere. The list of names isn't that long anymore. There are only two names on it that are still alive."

"That kind of narrows down the search. Wait, how do you know? I mean, that only two are still alive?"

"Yesterday, I talked to an old acquaintance of mine at the Russian consulate in New York. He provided me with the list and current whereabouts of the men who were on it." Monroe took a folded piece of paper from the table and handed it to Bishop.

Bishop opened it and started to read. "Damn." He took his reading glasses from his jacket and put them on. "Don't you have larger fonts on your computer?"

Monroe grinned. "You're getting old. I circled the two names of the men still alive."

Bishop started reading aloud. "Yuri Kastamarov, drill worker who resides in an assisted living home, and Mitya Morozov, security, who lives in a museum. That's curious. The first one's ninety-one years old and the second eighty-five. Hmmm...."

"What do you mean, hmmm?" Monroe asked.

"Well, I figure you're going to suggest we contact them?"

"Why not?"

"Well, it's been over thirty years, and they are at, let's say, dementia age." Bishop took a deep breath. "On the other hand, I guess there's no harm in trying. I see you already found some phone numbers to go with the addresses." He pointed at the hand-written text next to the names.

Monroe nodded. "I did, and this morning, I called them. It's eight hours later over there. Both were short conversations."

"Both dementia?"

"Both only speaking Russian."

Bishop now burst out laughing, with Monroe joining him after a few seconds.

"In my mind, I see you struggling on the phone," Bishop said. "What do you want to do now?"

"I think you know what to do next. Get the only Russian-speaking friend and colleague we both know."

"You already contacted her?" Bishop asked.

"What do you think?" Monroe responded with a wide grin.

CHAPTER 6

The Unstoppable Machine

Boston, MA, November 15, 1939

Nineteen days ago—for the first time—they had fired up the engines of the magnificent Atlantic Snow Cruiser at the Pullman Company just south of Chicago. Over the past three months, for seven days a week and twenty-four hours a day, lead designer and engineer Dr. Thomas Poulter and his men had worked tirelessly to finish the Eagle and the Turtle in time, and they succeeded.

But finishing the vehicle in time had proven to be only the first hurdle to take. Rear Admiral Byrd ran a tight ship, and had planned to depart with his two fully-loaded ships from Boston on November 15, 1939. Poulter knew Byrd well from his previous Antarctic mission, where he'd been the Admiral's second in command. Byrd, known for his ambitious planning, held himself to the same high standards he demanded from his crew.

For the past nineteen days, Poulter and his team drove, pulled, and shoved the Snow Cruiser the thousand-and-twenty-mile stretch to the Boston Navy wharf. The trip was plagued with challenges. A large truck sideswiped the Snow Cruiser in Columbia City, Indiana. In Fort Wayne, Indiana, one of the fuel pumps broke down, and many more little incidents hounded the way. Fortunately, Poulter had anticipated some setbacks on the trip to Boston, and had arranged for four large trucks with spare parts and tools to follow them along the way. He considered the trip a good way to work out the kinks. Still, nothing had prepared him for the event that happened on the Lincoln Highway near the small town of Gomer, Ohio, when the steering system broke down. The primary driver, Jay Clemency Simons, lost control of the vehicle and drove the Snow Cruiser eight feet off a bridge into a small stream.

Poulter and his men dug out the stuck vehicle while welders fixed the steering system. They tied trucks to the helpless Snow Cruiser, nose down and stuck in the mud, to pull her out of the stream and onto the road again. Poulter supervised the activities while furiously watching the days tick away on the calendar. After three days, driver Simons spoke the liberating words that the steering mechanism was fixed, and within the hour, they finally dragged Snow Cruiser out of the mud, cleaned it up, and got it back on its way.

Ultimately, on November 15, 1939, Simons drove the Snow Cruiser over the Boston city limits without a day to spare. The last mile of the roadsides were crowded with over 125,000 spectators, shouting and cheering at the passing 'unstoppable machine.' When entering the loading dock, the complete crew climbed on top of the big fire-red machine and drove a victory round across the pier, waving at the cheering crowd. First, they passed the Bear of Oakland, Byrd's old steamer that had served him well on his first two Antarctic missions. With its six-inch-thick hull, the over fifty-year-old seal hunter was the forerunner of modern ice breakers, who'd spent all her previous life in various cold-water and ice-filled environments.

"She still looks good, doesn't she?" a voice shouted from below the Snow Cruiser as Poulter waved at the crowds.

Poulter looked down at Admiral Byrd, smoking his pipe and, for the occasion, dressed up in blue coveralls and a brown leather jacket. Poulter stomped his foot two times on the cabin's roof, and the vehicle stopped.

Byrd climbed the wheel case and grabbed Poulter's outstretched arm.

He hoisted Byrd the last few feet onto the roof. "Morning, Admiral, quite a turnout." He stomped his foot again, and the vehicle slowly rolled in motion once more.

Simons opened the vehicle's side door, which swung open some ten feet above street level, and stuck his head out. "Where to, sir?" he yelled up at Poulter.

"Just circle here a bit," Poulter yelled back.

"You can say that again, Thomas," Byrd addressed Poulter. "It is quite the turnout. I knew Roosevelt ordered a large campaign, but this? I never expected so many people to show up. Most of all, I'm sure glad you're here. For a moment, I thought you wouldn't make it in time."

"For a moment, I thought so too, Admiral." Poulter shook his head and chuckled. "We had our fair share of problems getting here, but I'm quite convinced that through that ordeal, she's now fully prepared for her task on the South Pole."

"Good. So, what do you think of her?" Byrd opened his arms to the Bear.

"She does look good, sir."

"She sure is, especially when you consider that for the past few years she served as a museum and starred in the film version of Jack London's *The Sea-Wolf*. She's indestructible." Byrd sounded proud as, from the other side of the pier, the sound of barking dogs drowned out the cheering crowds.

Byrd had arranged for the hundred and twenty-five husky dogs, which he would take on the expedition, to pull small carts with crew members when they entered the harbor, as a form of attraction for the public. The crew members in their sleds on wheels paraded across the wharf like soldiers who just won a war.

"It's good for them to have their moment," Byrd said.

"I doubt if they're all sober," Poulter remarked.

"Understandable, when you think of the hardships they're yet to face on this expedition." Byrd took out a pocket watch, which Poulter knew Byrd's father had given him after he graduated from the Naval Academy in 1912.

This time *Byrd* stomped his foot twice, and the Snow Cruiser stopped precisely in front of the Bear's gangway. "I'm a fast learner." He grinned. "All right, Thomas, you better get your ass and vehicle onboard the North Star before I leave without you. I'm in a hurry to leave soon, you know. I want to sail with the tide." Byrd started to climb down from the vehicle.

"That shouldn't be a problem," Poulter assured the Admiral.

"Great." Byrd tapped his head while walking backward to the gangway. "I'll see you again in three hours."

Poulter tapped his head back and stomped the roof again.

"Yes?" Simons stuck his head out of the window. "You knocked sir?"

Poulter smiled.

"Okay, where to, boss?"

"Let's take her to her home for the coming six weeks," Poulter called out while pointing to the end of the docks.

"Aye, sir."

With a low rumble, the Atlantic Snow Cruiser's sixteen-foot-tall wheels were set in motion again. She slowly rolled straight ahead to where the United States Coast Guard Cutter, North Star, waited to take her in.

The color contrast between the all-black Bear of Oakland and the all-white North Star wasn't the only disparity between the two ships. The North Star was a modern, recently built, two hundred and twenty-five-foot-long cutter designed to sail the icy waters of Alaska and Greenland. Equipped as a support warship, the North Star also carried two single three-inch guns, six single twenty-millimeter AA guns, and two depth charge tracks. Byrd had suggested the weapons would be handy, since this time they weren't the only ones interested in their destination.

As the Snow Cruiser neared the North Star, Poulter noticed the immense wooden ramp leading onto the ship's deck. For this extraordinary cargo, they'd cleared the front of the ship, just after the nose, of any obstacles, and the fifty-five-foot-long vehicle could now find a spot there.

Simons steered the vehicle with a wide berth, lining it straight up with the ramp. He stopped with the huge front wheels just a few feet from the ramp, opened the vehicle's door, leaned out and shouted at Poulter, "What do you think, sir?"

Poulter climbed down from the roof and stepped onto the fender next to the open door, where he squatted next to Simons. "I think it's time we get this puppy on board." Poulter said. He glanced up and shouted at the people on the roof, "Okay, everybody off, and everybody out."

Everyone quickly left the vehicle.

"All right, son," he addressed Simons again. "As you can see, we need to park the Cruiser transverse on the ship. Now, I'm confident she will drive up the ramp without any problems, but the most important thing you need to take care of is to stop in time, or once on, you will overshoot the ship and land on the other side of it, into the harbor. I'll get off and guide you all the way, and I need you to follow my instructions to the letter. Do you understand, son?"

The confident Simons gave Poulter a tiny nod. "No problem, sir. I'll park her exactly where you want her."

The twenty-seven-year-old, tall and skinny, dark-curled Simons was a truck driver at the Research Foundation of the Armour Institute of Technology, the company that built the Snow Cruiser. Poulter had chosen the young man because, in his ten years of employment, and all that time on the road, he'd never had any collisions or caused any damage. For the past month, Poulter had personally trained him to drive the snow Cruiser that, with its two-stick steering, more resembled an army tank than it did a regular car.

"All right," Poulter said. "Here we go." He jumped off the fender and onto the ramp some ten feet in front of the vehicle. "Can you see me okay?"

"Yes sir," Simons yelled while sticking a thumbs-up outside the window.

"Bring her up slowly," Poulter yelled.

Softly, the Snow Cruiser's wheels started rolling and bumped onto the wooden ramp.

"Steady as she goes," Poulter called out, waving both hands.

Both front wheels now rolled onto the wooden ramp.

"That's great. Keep it going."

With a slow, steady pace, the vehicle now rolled on, and after some ten seconds, the rear wheels also rolled onto the ramp. The wood now started to buckle under the seventy-five-thousand-pound machine. Loud cracking sounds emerged from the wooden ramp.

"Everything okay?" Simons shouted out, perhaps hearing the sounds and feeling the Snow Cruiser go up and down, like dancing on calm waves.

"You're doing fine, son. Just keep it going. Whatever you do, don't stop."

Simons gave it a bit more power, and the front wheels now rolled onto the ship.

Poulter stood next to Simons' open window. "You see, it's just like cracking ice, and you know what they say about cracking ice...."

"I have no idea, sir," Simons replied. "But I suggest you tell me later."

"No problem, son." Poulter walked up with the Snow Cruiser as it continued its drive onto the ship. "Just keep it coming, keep it coming."

The rear wheels now rolled onto the ship, and with the sound of wood screeching away from under the back wheels, the vehicle drove its first inches onto the boat.

"Stop," Poulter called out after the wheels had passed little over a foot onto the ship. Simons hit the brakes and looked out again. "That's it, son. Just put the brakes on and come have a look."

Within seconds, Simons jumped out and stepped up to Poulter next to the front wheel.

"That's pretty close," Simons remarked as he looked at the front wheel just inches away from the side of the ship. He looked over the edge into the water.

"That would have been a pretty steep dive," Poulter joked. "The ship is forty-one feet wide, and the Snow Cruiser just over fifty-five feet long, so...."

"It's a good thing the nose and back stick outside of the wheels," Simons finished.

"It's a tight fit," Poulter agreed, while at the back, people were already breaking down the ramp and carrying all the wood on board. "You did good, son. We not only tested the Atlantic Snow Cruiser on the way here but also your driving skills, and both of you passed with flying colors."

"Thank you, sir."

"Now, do you have any family on the shore?"

"Only my mother, sir."

"Then I suggest you go and say your goodbyes quickly, because when the ramp is loaded, we'll leave immediately."

"Thank you, sir." Simons hustled over to the gangway next to the already dismantled ramp.

Poulter watched him walking down and over to a middle-aged woman dressed in a fur coat, and grinned. Poulter himself already said his goodbyes to his wife and two children in the hotel the day before. Seeing Simons and his mother hugging each other reminded him of his own sentimental goodbyes at the docks in the past, which he'd learned to hate so much.

A loud ship's horn, coming from the front of the vessel, disturbed his thoughts. As he walked the deck to the front, he saw the Bear of Oakland had cast off, and under the loud roar of its horn, its steampipe blew out thick black smoke as the ship removed itself slowly from the docks.

Indeed, he's in a hurry.

CHAPTER 7

The Lenin

Murmansk Oblast, Russia, The Present

It had taken Nadya Fedorova less than fifteen minutes to get from the plane, pick up her luggage, and hail a taxi in the already dark afternoon in Murmansk. This far up north, this time of the year, the sun wouldn't rise until eleven a.m. and would set again as early as two in the afternoon. Nadya had looked up the weather forecast and figured that at seventeen degrees Fahrenheit, it wouldn't even be that cold. Now that she was here, with the wind gushing around the airport, she regretted not bringing her thick Mongolian lamb fur coat. She wore only her blue denim jacket over a thin sweater. Fortunately, she figured to be out of here again later the same night.

Just as a taxi stopped in front of her, she heard the sound of the Russian anthem, 'Gosudárstvennyy gimn Rossíyskoy Federátsii,' coming from her coat pocket. She frowned at the sound. A friend of hers installed the bombastic piece of music on her phone as a ringtone, and she'd planned to change it again but hadn't come around to it; besides, she didn't know how to. She took out her phone and looked at the screen before punching the green button, and got in the taxi.

"One moment," she spoke into the phone, and then addressed the cab driver. "Portovyy Proyezd, 25." She returned to the phone. "Yes, Chief?"

"You arrived without problems?" the man's voice sounded.

"Almost a day late, but yes." A*nd I can't wait to get out of here again,* she thought as she looked at the desolate surroundings while the taxi drove off from the airport. "I'm here and just got into a cab. You have any news about the package? Did you find anything?"

"We got lucky and found two sets of fingerprints. One of them we were able to match in the Interregional AFIS database of government workers—a Mitya Morozov, eighty-five years old, born and raised in Murmansk."

"He's government?" Nadya asked.

"A former security worker on a local drill, some hundred miles northwest of the city. I have no current address other than the one belonging to the postal code you send me."

"A museum?" Nadya asked rhetorically.

"That's all I have," he said gruffly.

"Well, I'm on my way now, so I guess we'll know soon enough."

"Good luck, and you know when and where to find me."

"I know, Chief."

She hung up the phone and looked at her watch: 5 p.m. She had planned to arrive around noon, but because of heavy rainfall in Moscow, all planes were delayed, and now she wondered if Morozov would still be at his museum this late in the day.

"How far is it?" she asked the driver.

"About twenty-five minutes. Is this your first time in Murmansk?"

Nadya ignored the question, took a deep breath, and looked outside as the taxi drove onto the Tulomskoye Shosse. The rural highway ran alongside the thirty-five-mile-long Kola Bay, which ran into the Barents Sea. In the darkness of the afternoon, she barely recognized the trees in the Kola tundra that constituted the view. The absence of lights outside, and the knowledge that the next village was about three hundred miles away, gave Nadya an even more isolated feeling. She couldn't imagine why anyone would want to live here. She prayed her contact would be there so she wouldn't have to stay overnight in this God-forsaken place.

Fucking Neanderthals.

***

"I'm glad you're here," Bishop addressed Jennifer Porter, who joined him and Monroe in Bishop's office.

Jennifer, in her late thirties, was a professor of Linguistic Anthropology at Yale University. As an ex-Yale student, she had helped him and Monroe on previous research occasions. With her youthful looks, long blonde hair, and charming appearance, the ever-smiling professor was the crush of many students. Yet, due in large part to the many trips to desolated areas of the world for her studies, she'd chosen to stay single. That way, every other year or so, she could pick up her travels without feeling guilty or irresponsible. The only family she had was her mother, who was taken well care of.

"I would have come sooner, but I had a hard time finding a replacement for some courses."

"You didn't have to do that," Monroe said. "We only wanted you to help us with a telephone call. Shouldn't take more than a few minutes, half an hour tops."

"Does it ever with you?" A big smile grew on her face.

"What is it?" Bishop asked.

"I suddenly remember when I first walked into this building, and into this office, years ago. You remember?"

Bishop also smiled and nodded. "I sure do. You were still a student looking for help deciphering your father's legacy."

"I wasn't there," Monroe added, "but I do remember the aftermath."

They all chuckled now for a moment.

"I understand you want me to contact a Russian?" she said.

"Two, actually." Bishop looked at the laptop screen in front of him on his desk. "Here they are, Yuri Kastamarov and Mitya Morozov."

"What I don't understand is what you need me for. I thought you had a gizmo that did the translations on the fly for you?"

"I do. Travis," Bishop answered. "But Travis works fine when everyone is live in the room, but he's not as clear in his understanding of voices over the phone. Besides that, would you want to miss this chance of working with us again?" Bishop smiled.

Jennifer smiled back. "And you want me to ask them what, exactly?"

"Here." Monroe unrolled the cloth and handed her the sheet of metal.

Jennifer looked at it closely.

"This is the sheet I told you about on the phone. When you look at the other side...."

She turned it around.

"You see the spiral? According to Matthew here, it contains symbols or unknown characters that are grouped in parts of four."

"And there are no more than four basic characters," Bishop said.

"You suspect it to be written DNA?" Jennifer concluded.

Bishop and Monroe shook their heads as they gazed at each other. "Wow, that's much quicker than Walker picked it up," Bishop complimented.

Jennifer grinned. "He explained it to me already."

"Oh, okay," Bishop said. "Anyway, I should get the results back from the lab later today."

"All right, and what exactly do you want me to ask them?"

"Simply start with asking them whether they know anything about this piece of metal," Bishop answered. "We'll pick it up from there depending on the answer. Agreed?" He eyed Monroe.

"Sure," Monroe added.

"Okay, phone?" Jennifer commanded.

"Oh," Bishop searched his pants pockets and took out his phone.

"You didn't think I was going to pay for your call to Russia?" Jennifer smiled. "So what time is it over there?"

"Well, let's see," Monroe said. "It's just past nine a.m. here, so that means over there, it must be...." Mumbling, he counted his fingers. "Five p.m."

"All right, let's do this." Bishop put his phone in between them on his desk. "Let me see...." He started reading numbers from the laptop's screen, punched them in on the phone's screen, and put it on speaker.

After a few seconds, the phone started ringing, and Bishop turned the laptop's screen and pointed at Yuri Kastamarov's name.

A woman's voice sounded after a short moment, *"Zdravstvuyte Murmanskiy dom prestarelykh i invalidov."*

"Ah, Privet menya zovut Jennifer Porter," Jennifer replied. *"Ya ishchu informatsiyu o zhitele Yuri Kastamarov."*

As Jennifer continued her conversation, Bishop and Monroe, fascinated, looked at each other. They knew Jennifer spoke about a dozen languages, one for just about every country she'd visited in her career, but they'd never actually heard her speaking in any of them.

"Impressive," Monroe said, and Bishop nodded while pouting his lips.

"Khorosho, spasibo za vashu informatsiyu." Jennifer said after a minute, and pushed the red button on the phone.

"What happened?" Monroe asked.

Jennifer leaned back and took a deep breath. "The nurse who answered the phone told me that Mr. Kastamarov is in his nineties and hasn't spoken a word in over ten years. It seems the man is incapable of washing or feeding himself, so...."

Monroe snickered. "I guess they don't take privacy over the phone too seriously, if they give this information to the first foreigner who calls."

"Russia," Bishop replied. "Ready to try the next one?"

Jennifer nodded, and Bishop pushed the next number on the phone and put it on speaker again. In a few seconds, it rang.

"Allo," a man's crackling voice sounded.

"Allo, menya zovut Jennifer Porter," she replied again. *"Ya ishchu fr mister Morozov, Mitya Morozov?"*

"Ya ne znayu Mitya Morozov," the voice on the phone replied.

Jennifer whispered, "It's him."

"Great," Bishop said. "Ask him."

Jennifer continued the conversation, and after a minute, in a heavy accent, the voice on the phone said, "Yes, I speak and understand a bit of English, but slowly, please. My hearing is not that good, and I have trouble breathing a little. In my job at the hole, there were a lot of international scientists working at the end. They taught me a bit of English."

"That's great, Mr. Morozov. My name is Matthew Bishop, and I'm here with my colleague Walker Monroe, and you already spoke with Miss Jennifer Porter."

"Hello, Mr. Morozov," Monroe spoke.

"I understand you want to know if we found any special items at the hole?" Morozov said slowly, almost hesitantly.

"Yes," Bishop said. "To be completely honest, we've come into the possession of a gold-looking piece of metal that supposedly came from the Kola dig back in '92." For a long moment, it stayed silent at the other end of the line. "Mr. Morozov, are you there?"

A deep gurgling breath sounded through the speaker. "Yes, I'm sorry. I'm here. That is almost thirty years ago now. I didn't think anyone would care after such a long time." Again Morozov took a moment to catch his breath. "The piece of metal.... Is it about twelve by nine centimeters and two millimeters thick?"

Bishop quickly did the math. "Yes, the sheet is about that size."

"And does it have some kind of engraving in circles on the back?"

"Yes," Monroe said enthusiastically.

"So you know of it?" Jennifer asked.

Morozov's deep breathing picked up speed now. "You could say that. I guess I'm the owner of it."

"You found it and sent it to the United States Geological Service?" Monroe asked.

"I did find it. Just before the hole was closed, the hole started growling and spitting out drilling equipment. The piece of metal also was blown out of the hole, and that's when I found it."

"And you took it?" Jennifer asked.

"Yes, I thought it might be gold, and I had just been discharged from the only job I ever had. There weren't many jobs available in this region, so I thought I could sell it and maybe add something to my meager pension. I had the metal tested, but a goldsmith told me it was some kind of copper."

"But why send it to the USGS after thirty years?" Monroe asked.

"I didn't send it. I live here in a small cabin in the Lenin museum. It's a ship, you know. It was the first nuclear-powered icebreaker and the world's first nuclear surface ship made by the Soviets in 1957. In 1965, there was a nuclear accident when there was a coolant spill. Some say there still might be an increased radiation risk on board, but I've lived here for the past fifteen years and don't have any problems."

Monroe whispered, "Except for the shortness of breath and loss of hearing."

"Shhh." Bishop put a finger to his mouth.

"They let me stay here for free, and with my government pension, I'm not doing too bad."

"But you said you didn't send the item to America?" Jennifer asked.

"Oh, yes. No, I didn't. My nephew Maksim did. You see, I also had some old belongings in storage below decks that needed to be cleared out. I guess they needed the space. But anyway, my nephew from Murmansk came over and helped sort through most of it. He was the one who found the metal sheet again after all these years. He didn't know what to believe when I told him it wasn't worth anything. He took it to some gold shop in the city. They tested it and confirmed what I told him. They also told him they didn't know what it was, precisely, and if he wanted to know what it was, he should send it to some Geological university in Moscow."

"And he did?" Bishop asked.

"Well, you have to know that my nephew is rather suspicious when it comes to the Russian government, so he had some small pieces cut off at the shop and sent those to the university."

"But why send the complete metal sheet to the US?" Jennifer asked.

"Maksim asked me if he could sell it. I told him he could keep it and do with it as he pleases, so he took pictures of it and put it on Avito and tried to sell it."

Bishop quickly took his phone and searched for Avito. "Looks like some kind of Russian Craigslist," he whispered.

"But he couldn't sell it. No-one was really interested. He also placed a very detailed picture of a small piece of the engraving. That did get some people interested, but they were mostly conspiracy nutjobs who believed that a UFO caused the Tunguska incident. Anyway, no one wanted to buy it. One person told him he had a contact at the United States Geological Service and he should send it there, if he didn't trust the Russian government-run universities. So he did."

"I understand," Bishop said. "And that's it? That's all you know?"

"Yes, I'm sorry." Morozov coughed a few times.

"Well then, thank you for your time, Mr. Morozov, and I hope you get rid of that cough real soon," Bishop said.

"Not a problem," Morozov replied. "I don't get too many calls. I hope I have been of some help."

"Thank you. You've been a great help. Goodbye, Mr. Morozov."

"Are you still there?" Morozov sounded again as Bishop moved his hand to the phone.

"We're still here," Jennifer said as Bishop retracted his hand.

"There was one thing I remember, if you would like to know."

"Sure," Bishop said. "Please tell us."

"My nephew told me that after he had sent the item to America, just when he wanted to remove the advertisement, he got a call from a man from Europe, Italy or Spain, I believe it was. The man was interested in the item and wanted to pay cash. When Maksim told him he no longer had the thing, the man had insisted on knowing to whom he had sold it. He even threatened him."

"He threatened him how?" Jennifer asked him.

"I do not know. Maksim told me he hung up the phone. I remember we laughed about it later because we couldn't believe someone from southern Europe would come all the way here to make good on some kind of threat over a piece of metal."

"I understand," Bishop said.

"The nephew," Monroe whispered.

"What?" Bishop whispered back.

"Mr. Morozov," Monroe said, "do you think it's possible we can speak to your nephew?"

"I think so," Morozov replied. "I have his phone number here somewhere..." Morozov's voice silenced suddenly, followed by the sound of a screeching door.

"Kto ty, kak ty syuda popal," ounded softly in the background, and Bishop and Monroe immediately eyed Jennifer, who moved in closer to the phone.

"I believe there's someone at the door," she said, "and he asks who he is and how he got in."

The sound of Morozov rising from the chair and moving through the room followed. In the distance, a woman's voice replied.

"Okay, he is a she—Sadia, Inaya, Nadia, Dahlia, or something like that." Jennifer concentrated on the conversation that continued, now clearly farther away from the phone. Morozov raised his voice, while the woman stayed remarkably calm.

"What's going on?" Monroe asked when the voices grew louder again.

"Shhh," Jennifer replied when a loud thud followed. "I believe she pushed him back into the chair."

"What are they talking about?" Bishop asked.

"She says she works for the MGRI and was sent to get the original sample from which he sent the shards to her organization. He tells him he doesn't have it." Jennifer continued listening attentively. "He says he threw it away when he didn't hear anything back, but I'm not sure she believes him."

"Chto eto? Vy s kem-nibud' razgovarivayete po telefonu? S kem?" The woman now raised her voice.

"I think she sees the phone, and she asks who he's on the phone with." Jennifer said.

A loud crackling sound through the phone's speaker followed.

"Allo." The woman's voice sounded crisp and clear from the phone.

In a reflex, all three leaned back in their chairs.

"Hello," Bishop answered after a second.

A click followed.

"She's gone," Monroe concluded, reading from the screen on the phone. "Try again," he said, and Bishop pushed the redial button on his phone.

"Nomer, na kotoryy vy pytayetes' dozvonit'sya, v nastoyashcheye vremya nedostupen...." An automated voice message sounded, and Jennifer hung up the phone.

"It says the number is currently unavailable." She took a deep breath. "What do we do now?"

"That didn't sound too good," Monroe said.

"We need to do something," Jennifer replied.

Monroe shook his head. "There's nothing we can do."

"There is one thing we can do," Bishop concluded. "And that's the same thing we were going to do if this woman hadn't interfered. We're going to find the nephew."

CHAPTER 8

Ata

Yale, New Haven, CT

Jennifer, with Monroe standing next to her, watched as Bishop rolled the mouse, punched the keys, and swiped the screen of his laptop.

"It says here that the surname Morozov is derived from the Russian word moroz, meaning frost," Bishop read from the screen.

"I can only imagine," Monroe said.

"Nothing on Maksim Morozov?" Jennifer asked, stroking her eyebrows. The young professor got her impatience from her father. When she was little, her father used to urge her to finish dinner quickly, and when she didn't finish quickly enough, she risked not getting dessert. Often, when she had dinner these days, dessert reminded her of those moments.

"Give me a minute," Bishop answered. "I'm getting there. Wait, here... I think I found something. I have an Inna Morozov that appears to be working as an organizer of holiday decorations, whatever that might be, and one without a first name that repairs household appliances—all according to the automatic translation."

"Here," Jennifer commanded as she stretched her arm out over the table. "Let me see."

Bishop turned the laptop towards her and shoved it to her.

"Let me see." She worked the screen for a short moment. "I believe you're correct. One man and one woman go by the name of Morozov here."

"And that in a city of over 300,000," Bishop said. "That means we could be lucky." He took his phone from the table and unlocked it. "Give me the man's number."

"That's zero, zero, seven, eight, one, five, two, six, five, five, zero, and two."

"Got it." Bishop punched the last digit and put the phone on speaker in front of them on the table. It rang within seconds.

After a short moment, a man's voice sounded. "*Remont bytovoy tekhniki, Morozov govorit.*"

"*Da,*" Jennifer replied. "*Eto Jennifer Porter zvonit iz ssha.* Do you speak English?"

"Hello," the man replied. "I do speak English."

"Great," Jennifer said. "Listen, you don't know me, but I'm here with my colleagues from Yale University, and we just spoke to your uncle Mitya. We don't have much time, and to be blunt, we think he might be in big trouble."

"What are you talking about?"

"I don't think we should waste any time on the details, but we spoke to him about the piece of engraved metal that you sent to the USGS. We understand you also sent some smaller pieces of it to a Russian university. We believe that someone is now after your uncle to obtain the entire piece."

"But he doesn't have it!"

"We know," Jennifer continued. "But we accidentally overheard a conversation when we called your uncle, and we believe he might be in danger."

"I will call him immediately," Maksim said.

"We already tried to call him back, but the phone seems to be disconnected."

"Then I'll go there now. Thank you for calling, but I need to hang up now and get over there."

"Maksim," Monroe inserted. "One quick question, if you don't mind."

"Please keep it quick," Maksim sounded, breathing more heavily. "I'm already on my way down to find a taxi."

"A simple request," Monroe continued. "We understand that you had some people reacting when you advertised with the metal piece."

"Yes."

"We believe that one of those names might have something to do with the trouble your uncle is in. If it's possible, could you send us everything you have on the people who contacted you? I understand there was a southern European man, whom we are very interested in."

"I'll see what I have saved on my phone and send it to you later. To this phone number?"

"That would be great."

They heard Maksim now calling out loud over the sounds of heavy traffic.

"I need to go now," he said.

"All right, good luck," Jennifer said. "Please let us know how everything goes."

It was too late; Maksim had already disconnected the phone.

"Let's hope he gets there in time," Monroe said.

Bishop grunted. "But in time for what?" He looked at this watch. "Talk about time... I need to go or I'll be late for my appointment at the lab. It's only a five-minute walk, but still. Listen, I'll be back here in... let's say... two hours. You have time to meet me here again?"

"No problem," Monroe said.

Jennifer nodded. "I cleared my schedule for today, so.... You mind if I tag along?"

"My pleasure." Bishop rose from his chair and put his jacket on. "See you here later," he addressed Monroe.

"Sure, leave me all alone. No problem," Monroe mocked and smiled. "I have an idea of my own where this is going, so I want to check something out anyway."

Bishop and Jennifer frowned.

"All right, let's go," Bishop said, and the three walked out of the office and onto the Rose Walk.

Monroe split off at the end, and the three waved their hands and talked at once: "Catch you later." "Later." "Good luck."

After a short walk on Wall, Bishop and Jennifer turned onto College Street.

A minute later, Bishop pointed left as they passed the Grove Street Cemetery. "Did you know Walter Camp is buried here?" The graveyard, surrounded by Yale University, was the first private, nonprofit cemetery in the world, built in 1796. It was also the first one to have paved, named streets and avenues. Many notables from the region were buried there.

Jennifer cocked her head. "Who's Walter Camp?"

"What?" Bishop called out. "Shame on you! Camp was the inventor of modern football. He was a writer, railroad expert, inventor, and became the first modern American football coach. He was a Yale alumnus and coached the Yale football team at the end of the nineteenth century, and won the national championship three times."

"Because they were the only team?" Jennifer mocked.

"Very funny."

"We should cross here," Jennifer said.

"Ah yes, I forgot for a moment. You've been there before."

"It feels like a lifetime ago."

A few years back, Jennifer underwent a medical procedure that cured her of a potentially fatal illness, but also, without her consent, changed her DNA, temporarily enhancing some of her senses.

"And everything that happened to you back then," Bishop said. "I mean, nothing ever came back?"

"Nope," Jennifer said as they crossed the street. "It just vanished after a few months. I stayed under medical supervision for a while, but I'm fine."

"Better," Bishop said.

They walked into a large, industrial-looking, office building, and up to a desk in the center of the otherwise empty, clean white hall. On the front of the reception desk, a sign read 'Logynous Laboratory New Haven.'

"Hi, I'm Matthew Bishop, and I have an appointment with Elise Aldridge."

The young woman behind the desk started typing on her computer. "Yes, I see it. Please take the elevator behind me to the third floor, and I'll ask Dr. Aldridge to welcome you there."

"Great, thank you," Bishop said.

After a few loud, echoing steps, they entered the elevator and went up.

"Nervous?" Bishop asked.

"Not so much nervous as reminiscent. The last time I was here, I was heading for a rough time."

"Last time, I wasn't here with you." Bishop tried to console her.

"I know." She smiled as the doors opened again.

A woman, in her early forties and dressed in a white lab coat, welcomed them to the floor with an outstretched hand. "Dr. Aldridge, but please call me Elise."

"Elise, I'm Matthew," Bishop said, shaking her hand. "And this is my colleague professor—"

"Jennifer Porter, nice to meet you." She also shook the doctor's hand.

"Please follow me." Elise started walking down a long hallway. "Interesting piece you sent me," she said as they passed a long row of doors on either side.

"We figured as much," Bishop said.

Elise's long blonde hair waved all the way down to the slender woman's lower back.

"And what do you do at Yale?" Elise asked Jennifer.

"I'm a linguistic and cultural anthropologist."

Elise chuckled. "Then I'm sure you're going to like this."

Jennifer eyed Bishop as they walked into a windowless conference room at the hallway's end. A round table, surrounded by five chairs, stood in the center of the small room.

Elise sat down in front of a laptop on the table. "Please take a seat at that side. That way, you have a good view of the screen." She pointed at a sizeable sixty-inch flatscreen on the wall. "Coffee?"

"Yes, please," both guests said almost simultaneously as they sat down.

"Let me first say that I'm extremely curious as to where you found the sequence."

"Why?" Jennifer scrunched up her brows.

"That's okay," Elise replied. "Maybe later. Let me put the screen on and explain." She worked the laptop and the screen switched on. "All right, now, as you suggested, we replaced each of the four symbols from your sequence with one of our bases—A, C, G, and T. That way, we got four different strings that could possibly match an existing DNA string, or part of it. As these things always go, we didn't get any hits on the first three attempts, but when we ran the fourth, something happened."

With a click of the mouse, a short list of chemical abbreviations and their full names appeared on the screen.

KMT2D : Histon-lysine N-methyltransferase 2D

PCNT : Pericentrin

COL1A1 : Collagen Type I Alpha 1

COL2A1 : Collagen type II Alpha 1

FLNB : Filamin B

ATR : Serine/threonine-protein kinase ATR

TRIP11 : Thyroid Hormone Receptor Interactor 11

At the sound of a vibrating phone, Jennifer looked at Bishop. "Is that you?"

Bishop searched his pockets. "I believe it is." He took his phone out and read the screen.

"You need to take that?" Elise asked.

"No, it's a message." He turned to Jennifer. "From our Russian nephew." He put the phone away and turned back to Elise. "Please continue."

"All right," Elise continued. "It's good for you to realize that we can only be about ninety percent certain of the outcome, because we found only parts of a string that we could match. There simply wasn't enough material, but what we did find matched almost a hundred percent with KMT2D, better known as Histon-lysine N-methyltransferase 2D, and PCNT, Pericentrin." With a laser pointer, she pointed at the two top rows in red.

"And that is in human DNA?" Jennifer asked.

"Not all of it. There are some pieces of code that we have no match for. But for the large part, it most likely is. In theory, it could be a closely related primate, but there's only less than 0.1 percent chance of that."

"Meaning?" Bishop asked impatiently.

"Please, indulge me for just one more moment." Elise folded her hands as if starting to pray. "We did not only find recognizable parts of those strings, but we also found some anomalies in it."

"What kind of anomalies?" Jennifer shifted in her seat.

"Well, our references suggest that the DNA described in the code, or rather the person the DNA belongs to, was most certainly be inflicted with diseases like rib anomalies, cranial malformations, premature joint fusion, and osteochondroma, or skeletal dysplasia."

"Wow," Bishop reacted. "No idea what you just said, but it sounds bad."

"It is bad."

"Male or female?" Jennifer asked.

Elise raised her shoulders. "No way to tell with this information."

"So, what now?" Bishop asked.

"You're still impatient," Elise said. "You see these other genes in grey on the screen?"

Both Bishop and Jennifer nodded.

"We ran the deformities through just about every national and international database we could find. We figured that, if we were lucky, we'd find a place where the combination of these two specific genes, with each of their particular abnormalities, had been registered before."

"And did you get lucky?" Bishop asked.

She smiled back.

"You did?" Jennifer leaned even farther over the table.

"We did. And that's where the other genes on the screen come in. You see, the complete list on the screen is a list with abnormalities found in one specific specimen on Earth. So, all the evidence at hand suggests that the code you gave me must also belong to this subject."

Elise took a quick, deep breath, then clicked the mouse again, and the image on the screen changed.

"Jennifer, Matthew, meet Ata."

CHAPTER 9

Start Packing

Yale, New Haven, CT

In the small conference room, the TV screen's image changed to a picture of a tiny skeleton with a conical-shaped head. The bones lay next to a ruler to show its six-inch shape. Elise kept silent for a long moment to let the image sink in.

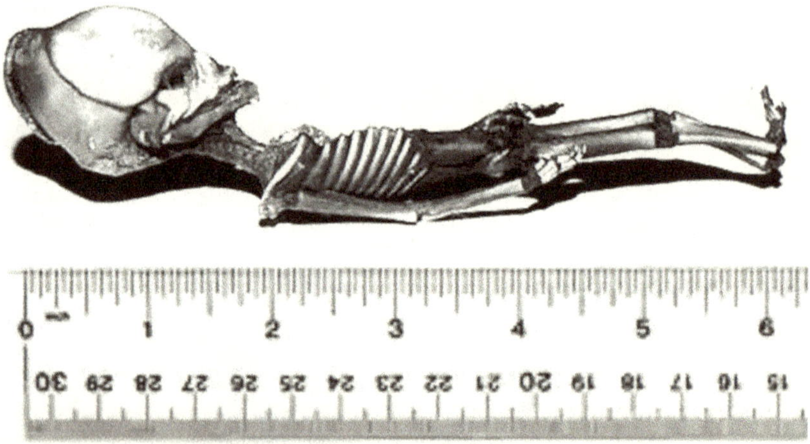

"That is, umm...." Jennifer stammered. "What is that?"

Elise grinned. "That is the Atacama skeleton, or as some like to call her, Ata, the mummy."

"Her?" Bishop asked.

"It's a she," Elise answered. "In 2003, the tiny skeleton was found in the desert region of Atacama in Chili. Until 2018, when Stanford University researchers studied the skeleton's DNA, there was wide speculation about the origin of the mummified skeleton. You can imagine the theories that developed about the origin of Ata."

"Alien, probably," Bishop said.

"Amongst others," Elise replied.

"Grist to the mill for the conspiracy nuts," Jennifer added.

"Indeed," Elise confirmed. "Anyway, the Stanford researchers determined that Ata was a young female fetus with genetic abnormalities that explained the skeleton's perceived abnormal characteristics, like the cone-shaped head and ten instead of twelve ribs. They believe that Ata must have died shortly after birth, or that she was even prematurely stillborn."

Bishop shook his head. "But the skeleton looks so full-grown. I cannot believe that's how a newborn's skeleton looks."

"I understand, and that's still one of the mysteries," Elise confirmed. "Estimates of the age of the skeleton structure are consistent with a human child of at least six to eight years old. You have to know that the Stanford research is not undisputed. I read that the University of Otago reviewed the results back in '19. They call into question the efficacy of the skeletal and genomic analysis Stanford did."

"The University of Otago?" Jennifer asked.

"New Zealand," Bishop answered. "One of the top one percent of universities in the world."

Jennifer cocked her head.

Elise nodded. "The Otago-led research team didn't find any evidence of skeletal anomalies, as reported by the Stanford researchers. They claim that the abnormalities reported are normal in a fetus."

"But if there weren't any anomalies, what were they?" Jennifer asked.

"Unfortunately, I'm not the expert in this field," Elise replied. "As a matter of fact, I had never heard about the Atacama mummy before today, but I sure would like to get my hands on that mummy to see for myself."

"Of course, you would." Bishop eyed Jennifer and gave a tiny smile.

"Absolutely." Elise nodded heavily.

"Is there anything else?" Bishop asked.

"Not now," she answered. "Not without more materials to study."

"Well, doctor, in that case, thank you for your time. We'll dig a little further, and if it's okay with you, we'll get back to you if anything new happens."

"You're still not going to tell me how you got this sample?" Elise asked.

Bishop rose from his chair and moved for the door, and Jennifer followed him. "Maybe next time, doctor," he replied. "I think we first need to find out some extra information for ourselves."

"All right." Elise gave a tiny smile. "Good luck with that. I'll send all the information I have to your email address in a moment. I hope to hear from you again, professors." She walked to them and shook their hands. "You know your way out?"

"Thank you." Jennifer nodded as they left the room.

In the hallway, Jennifer frowned as she eyed Bishop.

"What?" Bishop asked as they entered the elevator.

"Nothing much. I just wondered why you weren't your charming self."

Bishop gave a deep sigh. "I guess you're right. Somewhere during her talk, I got a vibe that there's more to this than just a simple finding. I'm not sure how to describe it, but I guess my vibe made me cautious."

"Because of our previous experiences?"

They left the elevator again and went for the exit.

"Probably. Let's see what Walker thinks of it. After all, it's his finding. I think I just want to be cautious, and maybe for now, just keep it between the three of us, without the risk of others interfering, if you know what I mean."

"I think so."

They crossed the street again and walked parallel to the Grove Street Cemetery.

"Any other famous dead people I should know that are buried here?" Jennifer asked.

"Well, let's see... ever heard of Charles Goodyear?"

They continued quietly for a few minutes, until they turned back onto College Street and walked back into the only red brick building on the street.

There, on the staircase, sat Monroe, laptop on his knees and a stack of papers next to him. "Since when did you change your lock?" he asked.

"Ah, sorry," Bishop said. "I have a new key in my office that I forgot to give you."

"That took you some sweet time," Monroe complained as he picked up his stuff and followed them back into the office.

"Uh-huh, but was it worth your wait?" Bishop raised a finger, circling it in the air.

"You tell me." Monroe fumbled with his laptop and papers, finally dropping everything on Bishop's desk. "Was it worth my wait?"

Everyone sat down at the desk again.

"Do you mind?" Bishop stacked Monroe's papers and put them on the corner of his otherwise clear desk. Then he opened his laptop and, for a moment, worked the keys and mouse. Then he turned it to Monroe with a picture of Ata on the screen.

Monroe pulled the laptop towards him and inspected the image for a second. "Ata, the mummy?"

"You know of this?" Jennifer asked.

"Sure," Monroe replied. "Ata, the mummy, found in the Atacama Desert in Chile. An intriguing story that anyone with some interest in ancient history and conspiracy theories knows. But what does Ata have to do with your DNA sequence?" For a moment, the room stayed silent, and Monroe finally said,. "No! You're telling me that.... Ata's DNA.... Are you sure?"

"Ninety percent sure, according to the doctor at the lab," Bishop confirmed.

Monroe turned to Jennifer for confirmation.

She tilted her head and nodded almost imperceptibly.

"You're yanking my chain." Monroe shook his head.

Bishop took the laptop back, worked it for a second, and then turned it back to Monroe. On the screen was Dr. Aldridge's email with her findings.

For a minute, Monroe worked himself through the attached document.

"Basically," Jennifer explained, "the DNA written in code on your metal sheet contains human DNA anomalies that in part are also found in your mummy."

"So, now she's my mummy?" Monroe smiled as he stopped reading. "But what does this mean? Ata was believed by many to be an alien skeleton, until research confirmed that it was just a deformed baby left in the desert some fifty years ago. How does DNA in a fifty-year-old mummy turn up in a fifty-thousand-year-old piece of engraved metal?"

"What exactly do you know about this Ata?" Bishop asked.

"That's a good question. It's been a while."

"And the man's age starts counting," Jennifer remarked, smiling.

"Thank you for that," Monroe replied while Bishop joined the laughter. "Anyway, the story starts. I believe it was in 2003 when the skeleton was found near a ghost town in, umm... La Noria, it was, an abandoned nitrate-mining town in the Atacama Desert in Chile—really in the middle of nowhere. I remember now because I looked it up at the time, but couldn't even find it on any of the maps back then. Ata was wrapped in a white cloth tied with a violet ribbon. I don't think it's known who found the mummy, but it quickly was sold to a Spanish businessman and collector of rare oddities named Castillo, Catalino, or something or like that. Years later, in 2012, an American doctor named Steven Greer, who happens to be the founder of the so-called Disclosure Project, got permission from the Spanish owner to scan the skeleton with CT scans and X-rays."

"What's the Disclosure Project?" Jennifer asked.

Monroe tapped some keys on the laptop and turned it to Jennifer, who read aloud, "The Disclosure Project is working hard to fully disclose the facts about UFOs, extraterrestrial intelligence, and classified advanced energy and propulsion systems."

"Doctor Greer is the founder of the project," Monroe added.

"Wow," Bishop said. "That's a mouthful. I can imagine what his conclusions were."

"Maybe," Monroe replied. "But the radiologist who analyzed Ata's images couldn't account for the mature formed bones on a human fetus-sized mummy. Greer also supplied samples of Ata's bone marrow to immunologist Gary Nolan from Stanford University. Nolan concluded that the genetic material was from a human being."

"Without a doubt not alien?" Bishop asked.

"Nope," Monroe answered. "Although he also couldn't explain Ata's appearance. From there, Nolan, together with people from other universities, analyzed Ata's genome. I believe they found mutations in a handful of genes that could all be involved in human growth."

"And a mystery was solved," Jennifer added. "The doctor at the lab told us a leading New Zealand university did a review on those results and disputed them."

"Otago, the University of Otago," Monroe said. "I heard of that but don't know the specifics of their research."

"Alien or no alien," Bishop concluded. "That still doesn't explain the DNA writing on the sheet of metal thousands of years before Ata was born."

"Coincidence?" Jennifer suggested.

"Do you have any idea, one in how many billion a chance it is to find two exactly the same DNA aberrations that far apart in time?" Monroe answered.

"No," Jennifer said.

"Well... umm... neither do I," Monroe stammered. "But the odds must be astronomical."

"I agree," Bishop said.

"What do we do now?" Jennifer asked.

"Wait a moment." Bishop took his phone from his pants.

"The nephew's message?" Jennifer sounded enthusiastic.

"Indeed," Bishop replied, and mumbled as he worked the screen. After a short moment, a wide smile appeared on his face.

"What?" Monroe spread his arms wide over the table.

"What did you say the name of your mummy owner was?" Bishop asked.

"Catalina, Castillio, something like that. Why?"

"Does the name Rafael Gervasio Castellano ring a bell?"

Monroe cocked his head and frowned. "That could very well have been it," he replied after a short moment. "But how?"

"Remember our phone call with Morozov's nephew, Maksim?"

"Sure," Monroe answered. "This was the message he promised to send, with information about the people who reacted to his ad when he tried to sell the metal sheet. It's a short list of names, which he concludes with the name of the person who even threatened him on the phone."

"I remember," Jennifer said, "the southern European man."

"From Spain," Bishop said.

"Wait a minute!" Monroe called out. "So the man who owns the Atacama mummy is the same person who tried to get the sheet with DNA from the Russian?"

Bishop raised his shoulders. "It would seem so."

"But that can only mean one thing," Monroe said.

"Castellano knows about the DNA on the sheet," Jennifer concluded. Both men nodded. "But what does that all mean?"

"More riddles," Bishop said.

"Indeed," Monroe said. "What do you want to do now?"

"It's your project," Bishop replied. "But the doctor who analyzed the DNA from the sheet told us she would love to get her hands on that mummy to research it herself."

"You want to call that Castellano?" Monroe asked.

"To be honest, I think we spent more than enough time on the phone," Bishop answered. "Besides that, I believe that if we want to convince Castellano to give us the mummy, we'll stand a much better chance if we were to ask him in person."

"You want to go to Spain?" Jennifer asked.

"Barcelona," Bishop addressed both. "And only if you join me."

"I kind of hoped and figured it would come to something like this," Monroe confessed.

"What do you mean?" Bishop asked.

"Remember I said I had to run an errand when you went to the lab?"

"Sure."

"Well, I visited my good friend and our colleague, Susan Landon. She just reopened the new Babylonian Collection, and I explained to her we were working on a lead that could possibly provide her with interesting new items for her collections."

"Let me guess," Bishop said. "You convinced her to spend a portion of her yearly research budget to finance your little project."

"Our project," Monroe said.

"You lied to her?" Jennifer said.

"Not necessarily," Monroe said. "There actually is a possibility we might stumble onto something interesting for her collection."

"Sure." Jennifer shook her head and smiled.

"You both can find the time to accompany me to Spain?" Monroe asked.

"Give me a day," Bishop said, sighing.

"Why not," Jennifer agreed, still shaking her head.

"Great, okay," Monroe concluded. "I'll make the arrangements while you both start packing."

CHAPTER 10

Little America Three

The Ross Ice Shelf, Antarctica, January 12, 1940

For the past nine weeks, the Bear of Oakland and the North Star had sailed the North and South Atlantic Ocean and the Antarctic Ocean to find their destination, the cold and desolate plains of the South Pole. For the most part, both ships had sailed together within viewing distance of each other, but one week ago, they had split up to reach their destination and start their separate missions.

Both were to set up field bases from which they could map the geography of the coastlines, construct meteorological outposts that made weather reports twice a day, measure the height of the ice shelves above the sea, and analyze magnetic readings. Geologists on board both ships would also examine volcanic rocks, and biologists would gather and study biological samples. As a 'secondary objective'—as Roosevelt had called it—the military on board were to secure the mission's safety and do reconnaissance on the Germans' activities at New Schwabenland.

At 1.4 degrees Fahrenheit, ice-cold Gale winds gushed at over forty knots across the vast and icy plains of the Antarctic Ross Ice Shelf.

Some five hours ago, the North Star had moored at the shelf. Charles Poulter himself—under loud applause by all crew members on the deck of the ship—had been the first one to jump from the ship. He drove a large wooden pole into the ice that served both as bollard and as a symbol of their arrival and the start of the mission.

Now, a significant number of crewmembers were creating a large ramp from the timber they'd unloaded the past hours. The men were all fully dressed in matching, custom-made, thick winter clothes, which Admiral Byrd had commissioned from the Alaskan-Indian Arts and Crafts Section of the Office of Indian Affairs for ten-thousand dollars.

For that money, native craftsmen had made mittens, caps, parkas, trousers, mukluks, robes, trousers, and sleeping bags. Poulter watched the men work the timber barehanded as he blew warm air into his folded hands.

"No mittens?" Simons asked as he walked up to the expedition leader.

"Maybe later," Poulter answered. "I always like to get my body used to the cold before it gets even colder. Then it's time to dress up."

"It gets even colder?"

Poulter smiled. "It probably will. Excited?"

Simons rubbed his arms in his parka. "I guess I am, sir. I'm curious about how she will behave on the ice and in the snow."

"Me too. We'll know in a few hours."

"Any word from the Bear?"

"Yes, the latest was the day before yesterday, shortly after they reached the Weddell Sea. Admiral Byrd had successfully landed the ship and was starting to set up camp."

"And the war in Europe?"

"I heard Roosevelt declared the US neutral in the conflict, as did many other countries in the war, like Belgium, Portugal, Spain, Sweden, and Switzerland. They all try to maintain their independence, and offer economic concessions to the Germans to make up for their military weakness."

"So why did the USA also declare themselves neutral?" Simons asked.

"President Roosevelt publically opposed the aggression by Japan, Italy, and Germany. He even gave a speech to quarantine the warlike countries, and was condemned for it by the Nazi government in Germany. Congress, however, opposed intervention. Those democratic isolationists only think about themselves and don't want to get entangled with strange countries and wars overseas."

"I heard there were also Germans on the South Pole, sir. Do you think there's a chance we run into them?"

Poulter took a piece of paper from his parka pocket and unfolded it over the railing.

"You see, we are here at the Ross Ice Shelf." He pointed at the lower part on the paper.

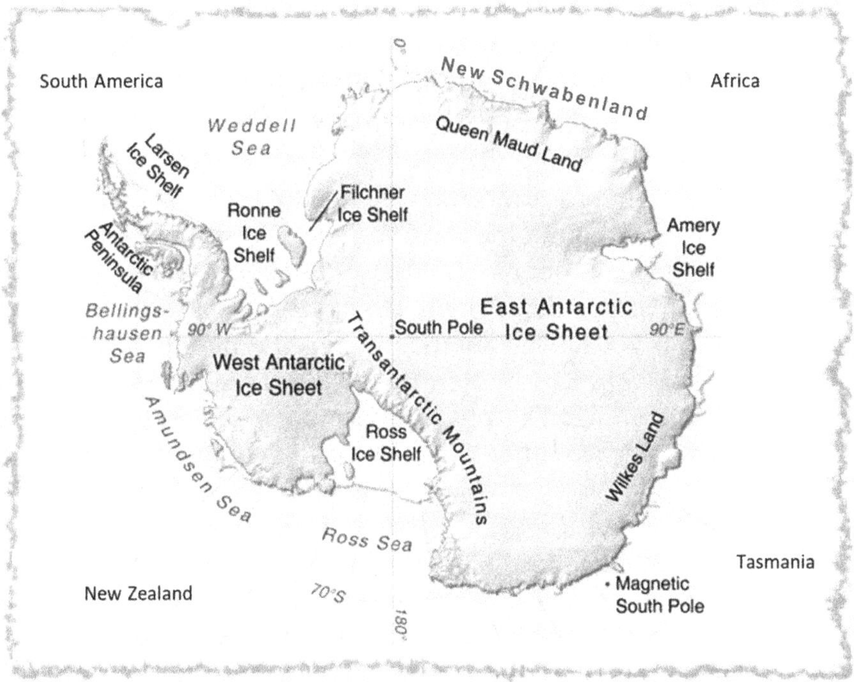

"And here are the Germans." He moved his finger to the top of the paper. "You see, New Schwabenland."

Simons nodded.

"If anyone should worry, it's Admiral Byrd. He landed somewhere here, at the Weddell Sea. That's where he'll create a temporary settlement and drop most of the soldiers, the tank, and the T3E4 Carrier—right next to the Germans' front door. Later, he's supposed to join us here after we've made the first preparations for a permanent settlement. That's why we carried most of the scientists, and of course, you, who will drive us over the ice in our Turtle." Poulter smiled.

Simons smiled back. "How long do you think they'll need?" He pointed at the men working the ramp.

"Not long. I think that in a few hours, you'll be able to drive down the Cruiser and take her for a spin on the ice."

"Sounds good," Simons said. "You think this weather will clear, sir?"

"Unfortunately, we don't have a weather forecast this far out, but from my previous experience, I know the weather here can change in an instant, so let's hope so."

"It sure as hell would make my work a lot easier," Simons said, shaking his shoulders. "Now, if you don't mind, I'd like to get below decks, have a cup of tea, warm up, and prepare for the drive down."

"You do that, son. Get something to eat too. You're too skinny for this climate."

"Will do, sir." Simons turned and walked away.

For almost three hours, the men worked the ramp, trying to beat the heavy weather conditions. The extreme circumstances and poor visibility had already claimed their first victim. One of the soldiers working the ramp got his leg jammed between a plank and the ice. A beam broke loose from its ropes on top of the ramp, and rolled down. He never saw it coming. The physician on board concluded a broken ankle, and the soldier would be condemned to operate the radio for the next six weeks.

The North Star and the Bear of Oakland were two of the first ships retrofitted with 'bridge to bridge' radio. That way, the ships could be in constant contact with each other. Up until then, communication had been restricted to morse code. Even the Snow Cruiser was outfitted with this innovation.

Just as they finished the ramp, the wind decreased, and even the clouds opened. Rays of sunlight now lit up the ice like a large field of diamonds.

***

Simons came back on deck, putting on his mittens. "Wow," he said to Poulter, who didn't seem to have moved for the past hours. "That's an entirely different sight."

"Much friendlier?" Poulter asked.

"Something like that."

"You better watch out, son. The icefields can be treacherous. There are caverns below, and thin layers of snow can hide large cracks that you can fall through at any moment."

"I'll be careful. Everything ready?"

"She's all yours." Poulter pointed at the Cruiser.

Simons climbed the ladder welded to the side of the control cabin. Once on top, he opened the door and disappeared inside. Seconds later, a loud rumble broke the Antarctic silence and thick streaks of smoke rose into the air from the Cruiser's large exhaust pipes. Simons pushed a button on the huge but otherwise almost empty dashboard, and a loud horn sounded. While the engines were heating up, he climbed out onto the Cruiser's fender and squatted to watch the deck quickly fill up with curious crew members who came to watch the Turtle drive off onto the ice.

After a minute, Simons rose again, and the crowd started cheering. He took off his wooly cap and waved it into the air, and the crowd went wild. They all too took of their hats and ecstatically waved them in response. Simons looked around and gave a tiny smile. If only his father could have seen him now. He had only some vague memories of his father left. When he was a young boy, at the age of five, his father, who was a butcher, was killed during a freak car accident. When unloading his meat truck, he'd forgotten to put on the parking brake, and when the car rolled back, he got stuck between the car and loading dock and died within minutes. The only clear memory he had was when he rode on his father's back every night as he was carried in to bed in the evening.

This is for you, Dad.

After Poulter, accompanied by two other crew members who wanted to enjoy the view, climbed on top of the Cruiser, Simons went in again and closed the door behind him. After one more honk, he pushed the gas pedal and the engines rumbled even more. With a screech from the enormous wheels coming into motion on the wooden deck, the seventy-five-thousand-pound machine slowly came into motion. He put the pedal further down, and the front wheels folded themselves over the ship's edge and onto the ramp. He slowly drove on, and in seconds the back wheels also left the boat.

The ship rose up five inches in the water, and the watching crew all appeared to hold their breath as the ramp's loudly creaking wood protested under the weight. About two-thirds down, the Cruiser's front suddenly tilted down as the left front wheel plunged through the wooden structure and onto the ice.

The three men on top of the Cruiser were struggling to stay on top, hopefully grabbing onto whatever stuck out of the roof as the Cruiser banked to one side and threatened to keel over. Simons heard a loud thump above his head and hoped no one had been seriously injured. He had no time to think about what happened, having slipped from his seat and now pulling himself back into his chair. He grabbed onto the two steering sticks, found the pedals again with his feet, and instinctively pushed the throttle fully down. With both engines' extreme effort, the Cruiser's left front side climbed back on top of the ramp's remaining part. The vehicle straightened itself again and, only a few seconds later, it drove off the ramp and onto the ice.

With full force, Simons hit the brakes and, after regaining his breath, opened the cabin door and climbed out and onto the roof.

After two full seconds of silence, everyone realized what happened, cheered, and again threw their caps into the air.

Poulter stood next to him. "That was a close one. Nice driving, son." Poulter shook Simons' hand. "Now wave at the crowd," he ordered, and both men waved at the crew on the ship. "On this kind of mission, we need to celebrate our successes because, in my experience, there will be at least just as many failures."

"You're wounded, sir," Simons said, pointing at Poulter's head where a small streak of bloop ran down from under his cap.

Poulter wiped it off with a handkerchief and looked at it. "It's nothing." He put it away again. "Now, if you don't mind...."

It took Simons and the other men on the Cruiser a second to realize that Poulter wanted them to get off of the top.

Poulter waved his arms up and down, silencing the crew as he took the deck of the vehicle all to himself.

"Men," he yelled, raising both hands in the air. "Today, not only will you all be making history, you'll be an active part of it. Your names will be called out when in the future they speak about the first settlements on the Antarctic continent, the same way they talk about the pilgrims that settled in America. As you can see, the sun came out to lift some of the heavy burdens that, without a doubt, we will endure in the coming months. But our burden will be alternated with the richness of new discoveries, and you will experience and see things that no human before has seen."

Poulter made a fist and stretched his arm, as far as he could, into the sky. The crew shouted out his name and waved their caps to him like he was the Messiah himself.

Simons looked up to the charismatic man on the Cruiser, shook his head, and smiled. *Incredible.*

Poulter again waved his arms at his audience, urging them to be silent again. "You all have your assignments and know who your team leader is. Our first goal will be to set up base camp, to swap our bunks on the boat for a stable sleeping place on land—or rather, on the ice. All right, men, I'll stop wasting your time now and wish you good health and Godspeed when creating Little America Three." He again waved at the cheering crowd, then climbed off of the Cruiser.

"What do you think?" Poulter asked Simons.

"I think they love you," Simons answered.

"They do now, but wait until the first person loses a finger or a toe due to frostbite."

"It's clear you've done this before, but if you don't mind me asking.... What do you expect of me? I don't have a task yet, and I take it we don't take the Cruiser farther out before base camp is ready."

"All right. As a priority, I've given the order to install the crane and unload the Eagle."

"The Eagle, sir?"

"The Eagle, yes. Have you met Dougal McConnel?" Poulter asked.

"The pilot? Sure."

"His Beechcraft 17 Staggerwing biplane is nicknamed the Eagle. I want you to find him, and together you'll coordinate a series of reconnaissance flights and set out a research path for the Cruiser. When you return, and camp is ready, you'll load the Eagle onto the Turtle, and we'll assemble a crew for the Cruiser's first adventures."

"What are we to look for on the flights?" Simons asked.

"I don't know, son. You'll be the first to set eyes upon the land and ice you'll fly over, so you'll tell me."

Simons gave a bright smile and chuckled. "Will do, sir. I'll give you a journey you will not soon forget."

CHAPTER 11

The Reporter

Murmansk Oblast, Russia

"I'm about to walk in," Nadya said into her cell phone. "It's only a hunch, but from our short conversation, I have the feeling he was covering for someone, and that something or someone is going to show up here.... Yes sir.... Thank you, sir.... I will call you again if something comes up, and please let me know if you find out whose phone number that was the old man was speaking to.... Will do." She punched the screen and put the phone away.

At the corner of Perovskoy and Mapxca, the Gorodskaya Bol'nitsa Hospital reminded her of the Soviet regime buildings often portraited in movies as the only building style in Russia. Unfortunately, here the prejudice proved right. The entire city was layered with these simple, functional high-rise buildings filled with square windows, and most of them painted in beige. This hospital building, though an exception being painted light blue, checked all the other boxes. '*Boxes with windows,*' Nadya called the buildings.

She straightened her clothes, took a few deep breaths, and walked fast-paced into the hospital. Fortunately, it had been a typical rush hour that brought many drunk drivers to the hospital's emergency rooms. In the crowded lobby, nobody gave the woman much notice as she walked in and wiggled herself to the front of the line at the reception.

"*Travmpunkt* (Emergency Room)?" Nadya sputtered.

The young woman behind the desk pointed right to a set of closed double doors. "Press the doorbell at the side, and someone will come for you."

Nadya walked over and arrived just as the doors opened for a doctor to come through from the other side. She quickly slipped through into a long hallway containing windows on the right side, with chairs below them, and treatment rooms on the left. All the entrances to the rooms were closed off with a white curtain. As she looked further into the corridor, she noticed another reception in the middle. She walked up to it just as a nurse took a seat behind a computer on the other side.

"Excuse me," Nadya said, and the nurse looked up from her computer. "I'm looking for a Mr. Morozov?"

"And who are you? Are you family?" the nurse asked.

"No, I'm Olya Kovalchuk, a reporter for the High North News." Nadya took a business card from her coat pocket and flashed it in front of the nurse's face. Reporters were a common sight in the ER, and accidents, in large part, filled the local news section in the papers.

"Mr. Morozov is still being treated, but if you please take a seat near ER number twelve, there will be a doctor coming out soon, and you can ask him your questions."

Nadya nodded. "Thank you."

As the nurse focused on her screen again, Nadya looked over the reception area. At the end of the desk sat a notebook and pen. She moved swiftly along the desk and snatched them, then moved to the end of the corridor, stopped at number twelve, and sat down. She took out her phone, opened a web browser, and searched for any news from the events at the Lenin Museum on any of the local papers or blogs. She didn't find any.

"That's good," she mumbled.

For almost half an hour, she waited, and just as she started to dose off, the doors to the corridor opened and a young man barged in, fully waking her up again.

"I'm looking for Mitya Morozov?" the man asked the first man he passed in the corridor.

The second man shrugged his shoulders.

"Mitya Morozov?" he asked the next person, a woman, even louder.

The woman pointed at the reception desk.

In a few big steps, he arrived at the desk and, out of breath, asked, "Morozov, Mitya Morozov?"

"Are you family?" the nurse behind the desk asked.

"I'm his nephew, Maksim Morozov."

"He's in number twelve at the end," the nurse pointed out. "But you—"

Maksim didn't hear her as he rushed to the end of the hallway.

"They will not allow you in yet," Nadya addressed Maksim as he neared the room.

"What?" Maksim stared at her.

"I couldn't help overhearing. I also came to see your uncle, but the doctors are still with him."

Maksim walked up to the curtain and peeked through it.

"*Vy ne vozrazhayete?* (Do you mind?)" One of two men in white coats, leaning over a bed, yelled at him. "We'll be out of here in ten minutes."

Maksim closed the curtain again.

"I understand he's still unconscious," Nadya said.

"Who are you?"

"I'm sorry. My name is Olya Kovalchuk, a reporter for the High North News." She held up the notebook and pen.

"A reporter? Do you know how he is? When I came to his house, the police were there, and they said he was assaulted, but they couldn't tell me how bad he was."

"I understand you're family. Do you mind if I ask you a few questions?"

"What questions? What do you mean?"

"Well, you said you saw the police when you visited your uncle's house. Did they tell you what happened? Do you mind me asking?" She sat down next to him.

Maksim took a deep breath. "Umm, no, I guess I don't mind. They only told me he was assaulted and brought here to the hospital."

"They didn't tell you why or by whom?"

"I asked, but I think they didn't know yet."

"All right, thank you." Nadya put the pen and paper down on the chair next to her. "Then I guess we'll just have to wait. I'm sure your uncle is going to be fine." She put a hand on his shoulder.

"Thank you." Mitya ran his hands through his hair. "How did you get here?"

"Police scanner in the car." She pointed out of the window. "And I was in the neighborhood." Mitya gave a tiny smile. "Did you visit your uncle often?" she asked.

"Once a week... on Fridays." His voice broke.

"I'm sorry." For a moment, they both kept silent. "Then why today?" Nadya came back after a short while.

"What?" Maksim shook his head.

"I mean, it's Tuesday. Why visit him today?"

***

"Oh, that. Well, umm...." Maksim hesitated to tell her, a reporter. He hated it when he read all kinds of sad, personal stories in the newspapers. Just keep it to yourselves, he used to think. On the other hand.... *What if I were to tell a reporter my story? What if I were to make this story public? Maybe they would leave us alone when they knew we didn't have anything related to the item anymore.* He gave a deep sigh. "You want to know what happened?"

"Sure." Nadya nodded as she retook the pen and paper.

"Well, my uncle used to work at the Kola drill not far from here. One day, just before they closed the site, over twenty-five years ago now, he found a shiny piece of metal with something engraved on it."

Nadya's brows drew together. "What kind of engraving?"

"I don't know. It looked like a circle with small dots in it. But anyway, my uncle kept it all those years, and I only learned of it some short time ago. First, I tried to sell it as gold, but some goldsmith told me it wasn't gold, so I had it tested at the Geological University in Moscow. I sent them some small pieces, but when I didn't hear back, I tried to sell it for my uncle on Avito. At first, no one was interested, and then, all of a sudden, people from all over the world seemed to want it."

"What do you mean all over the world?" Nadya asked.

"Well, first, it attracted only conspiracy wackos. One contact said I shouldn't have trusted the Russian government with it and suggested I send it to a contact of his in America, at the USGS, The United States Geological Services."

"And you did?"

"Sure, why not? By that time, I felt I wouldn't get any money for it, but I was curious enough to want to know what it was."

"Do you remember who at the USGS you sent it to?"

Maksim closed his eyes and looked up. "Umm, what was it.... Hutch, Hoover, Hotchkiss.... No, Hootkins." He opened his eyes and looked down again. "Yes, a William Hootkins, I remember now."

"You're sure?" Nadya wrote the name down.

"I'm sure."

"Thank you. And you said there was interest from all over the world?"

"Yes, after I shipped the item, a man from the south of Europe responded and was very interested in obtaining the item. When I told him I didn't have it anymore, he became very angry with me."

"Oh, did you tell him what you did with it?"

"No, I didn't. When he became unreasonable, I hung up the phone. And then there was today."

Nadya tilted her head.

"Today, I got a call from some American lady college professor who told me my uncle was in danger, and that it was all about the piece of metal."

"What did she tell you about the item?"

"Not much, just that she knew I'd sent it to the USGS and that because of that, my uncle was in danger. And now this." He opened both hands in the direction of the curtain.

Nadya put a hand on his shoulder and paused for a short moment. "He's gonna be okay," she picked up again. "I'm sure of it. Do you also remember the name of the college professor and what college she was from?"

Maksim sniffled. "Of course, I have an excellent memory. Her name was Jennifer Porter, from Yale University."

Nadya wrote down the name. "Thank you." She rose from the chair. "Thank you. Oh, and one more thing. Do you by any chance happen to remember the name of the southern European who was interested in your item?"

Maksim smiled.

"What is it?" Nadya asked.

"I know now. You see, you're the second one today who asked for the name. The first time I had to dig deep, but now I found it back on my phone. It was a Spaniard, Rafael Castellano, from Barcelona."

"That's great." Nadya also wrote down this name. "Thank you. I think I have enough for now."

"When will the article be printed?" Maksim asked.

"Well, that's up to my publisher, but I'd guess tomorrow." Nadya smiled. "Thank you again, and all the best with your uncle."

Maksim nodded.

***

Nadya walked away and tore off the top piece of paper from the notebook. When she passed the reception, she put the book back on the desk. "Thank you."

"You're welcome," the nurse replied without even looking up from her computer.

A few minutes later, Nadya walked out of the hospital, took out her cell phone, and dialed a number.

"Yes," a man's heavy voice sounded through the phone.

"Chief," Nadya replied. "I think my little hospital visit was successful. I met Morozov's nephew, and now I have a few names for you to check out. I'll send you everything in an email after I hang up."

"That's fine," the Chief's emotionless voice replied.

"Have you been able to find out who the phone number belonged to that I sent you?"

"I did. It was the last number Mr. Morozov spoke to, you said?"

"Yes."

"The number belongs to an American University professor named Matthew Bishop. He works at—"

"Let me guess," Nadya interrupted him. "Yale University."

"Yes, don't tell me you called the number?"

"I didn't, sir. It's a long story, but one of the names I'll send you is from an American college professor, a woman this time, who also happens to work at Yale. Don't you think that's too big of a coincidence?'

"Agreed," the Chief said.

"Sir, did you know the metal has some kind of engraving on it?"

For a moment, the other end of the line stayed silent. Then the Chief came back. "No, I didn't. What kind of engraving?"

"I don't know. Some dots in a circle, the nephew told me. But anyway, what did you find out about this man, this Yale professor?"

"You have all the details in your inbox, but in short, he teaches mathematics and is known for his code-breaking skills. You think he has the item?"

"Hmm... I'm not sure about that," Nadya said. "Either he has it, or someone at the USGS does. I have a name for you to run. I'll send it to you."

The Chief stayed silent for a long moment before saying, "That's okay."

"You think you can arrange a ticket to the United States for me? I'd love to take a look at this university."

"I'm sure you would," the Chief replied. "But even if I'd agree to let you go abroad, I don't think it would do us any good. Professor Bishop is out of the country for guest lectures in Spain."

"Spain?" Nadya's raised her voice.

"Yes, Barcelona. What is it? You know something?"

"Just another hunch, sir. That ticket, do you think you can change that to Barcelona, Spain? I have a feeling you won't regret it."

CHAPTER 12

The Alchemist's House

Barcelona, Spain

The hotel Gargallo Rialto, at 40 Carrer de Ferran, was one of the smaller hotels in Barcelona. Monroe had chosen the hotel not only because of its proximity to the Ramblas, the Port, and the Boquería Market—all places he wanted to visit while there—but mainly because it was close to Castellano's house in the center of the city. On the ten-hour flight here, they had argued about which places to visit in the third most popular city in Europe, after Paris and Amsterdam. After a two-hour argument, Gaudi's Basílica de la Sagrada Família, the National Museum of Art of Catalonia, and the Casa Batlló, another Gaudi building and one of his masterpieces, made the cut.

The small hotel lobby offered only two corner sofas opposing the reception. Jennifer sat down on one of them. The bar behind the entrance looked a lot cozier to her, but at breakfast, the three friends had agreed to meet in the lobby after freshening up. She took a leaflet on the works of Antoni Gaudí from her backpack, and started reading as a woman sat down next to her.

"Did you know that he never made detailed plans of his works?" the woman said with an accent.

"Excuse me?" Jennifer asked, turning to the woman.

"Gaudí," the woman replied with a closed smile. "He never made any detailed drawings or plans of his designs. Instead, he made three-dimensional scale models."

"I didn't know that. Are you a Gaudí scholar?"

"No, not at all. Just an aficionado, visiting the city to admire his works," the woman replied.

"Your accent... it's Russian?" Jennifer asked.

"Ukrainian, actually." She gave a bright smile. "You're on holiday?"

Jennifer looked up and thought for a short moment before answering. "Umm, no, I'm a college professor giving guest lectures at the University of Barcelona, with some colleagues."

"Oh, that sounds interesting."

On the far end of the narrow lobby, a loud ping sounded from the elevator. As the doors opened with a swoosh, Jennifer turned to see Bishop and Monroe coming out.

***

In the blink of an eye, Nadya clipped a tiny, black, button-like gizmo at the inside of Jennifer's open backpack.

When the unsuspecting professor turned back, Nadya had already risen from the sofa. "Nice to meet you," she said. "I need to go now. Have a great time in Barcelona."

"You too."

Nadya quickly turned and walked out the door.

***

"Who's that, Jennifer?" Monroe asked as he neared the couch.

She tilted her head. "Not sure. She didn't introduce herself." Jennifer walked to the reception desk. "Excuse me," she addressed the man behind the desk.

"Yes ma'am."

"That woman that I was just talking to... did you see her?"

"Sure, ma'am," the man said.

"Do you know if she's staying in the hotel?"

"I don't think so, ma'am. I've never seen her before. I thought she was with you."

"All right, thank you." Jennifer turned back to Bishop and Monroe.

"What is it?" Bishop asked.

"Probably nothing," she replied. "Shall we go? We have a long day ahead of us."

Both men agreed and walked the three steps down from the hotel stairway and onto the street.

"This could be a perfect holiday," Bishop said as he donned a pair of Chopard sunglasses.

At seventy-five degrees Fahrenheit, it was an abnormally warm day for the time of year.

"This way," Monroe said. "It's only a few minutes, according to Google." He pointed right as he picked up the pace.

Soon they snaked their way through the narrow ancient streets, feasting their eyes on the hundreds of differently styled, ancient, and modern facades.

Monroe asked, "Did you know that Gustave Eiffel offered his design for his tower to Barcelona for the World Exposition in 1888? They rejected the offer because they were afraid that the monstrosity would be a blemish on the city's skyline."

"You're a regular tour guide," Jennifer reacted, smiling.

They turned a corner into an even narrower street, no more than ten feet wide, and Bishop pointed at a street sign. "Is this it?"

"Carrer de l'Arc de Sant Ramon del Call," Monroe read. "This must be it."

The three looked into the empty street, where on both the left and right the beige stones in the building's facades were only interrupted by closed blinds, full of graffiti.

"Let me guess, number eight," Bishop said.

"How do you—"

Bishop placed his hand on Monroe's bald head and turned it backward.

"Ah, I see."

At the corner of the street were two tall, green-painted wooden doors. Each door had a large wrought iron lion's head on it, with a large ring through its nose serving as an opener.

"Indeed, that must be it," Jennifer agreed.

For a second, Monroe searched for a doorbell, but when he found a large brass nob left of the door, he grabbed it and pulled it. Inside, behind the closed doors, loud chimes sounded.

"Rustic," Bishop said.

After a minute, just as Monroe appeared ready to ring again, a small hatch in the door opened. "Ola," the man behind the hatch said.

"Ola," Monroe replied. "I'm Walker Monroe, and these are my colleagues. I called to arrange a visit."

The hatch immediately closed again, and the sound of deadbolts moving behind the door sounded, followed by the screeching opening of the left door. Jennifer peeked inside, but the hallway sat empty.

"Come, quickly." An arm waved them inside from behind the door.

"After you," Bishop said.

Jennifer cautiously walked in, followed by the others. Once inside, with a loud bang, the heavy door closed behind them.

***

Just before they went in, a silent electric scooter turned the corner at the other end of the street and stopped at the side of the road. Once they were inside, Nadya stepped off, removed her helmet, and searched her pockets for her cellphone and headphones. She put the earbuds in, worked the phone, and leaned back against the scooter.

***

"Excuse me for the secrecy," said a blond man in his early seventies, dressed in khakis and a blue striped shirt under a dark blue sweater. "It's the paparazzi, and the tourists."

"You are Rafael Gervasio Castellano?" Jennifer asked.

"Indeed, I am, young lady. And you are?"

"Sorry," Monroe said. "I'm Walker Monroe, we spoke on the phone, and these are my colleagues, Matthew Bishop and Jennifer Porter."

Castellano shook all their hands. "Please, follow me." He walked to the end of the hallway and onto a wrought iron spiral staircase.

"Paparazzi and tourists?" Jennifer asked.

"Yes, but fortunately, it's a Monday. On Mondays, both of them are not as active, you see."

"They come here for your collection?" Jennifer asked.

"If only," Castellano answered. "The paparazzi are waiting for me to come out so they can take my picture. Since the tabloids got wind of my collection, they pay handsomely for pictures of me, preferably on a bad hair day." The staircase spiraled up another two stories. "And tourists come to see 'The Alchemist's House.'"

'What's that?" Monroe asked.

"You're in it," Castellano said. "It's this building. You're now in the heart of El Call, the Jewish Quarter. Didn't you see Satan's Coffee Corner at the end of the street?" Castellano didn't wait for the answer while he slowly ascended the stairs. "A famous Jewish alchemist lived here in the fourteenth century. The legend goes that his beautiful daughter was in love with a Christian. When they wanted to marry, the young woman asked her father for permission, but he declined. The daughter told her lover about the rejection, who in turn decided to poison his former girlfriend."

"Different times," Monroe said.

"They sure were," Castellano replied. "The lover visited her father, the alchemist, who sold him a poisoned rose that could kill with a single sniff. Later that night, the lover climbed up the façade to the daughter's window, begged her to take him back, and gave her the rose. She smelled the rose and was stricken immediately."

"Effective," Bishop said.

"Indeed it was," Castellano conformed. "The next morning, the alchemist found his daughter with the rose next to her. He recognized the flower as the one he had poisoned. That same day, he fled the house, put a curse on it, and never came back. Ever since then, the whole street has been cursed. At night, the daughter's ghost is often seen roaming the pavement. Sometimes you can hear her crying, and the water in the pond on the patio turns black."

Castellano fell silent as they stood still in a small corridor in front of a large wood-carved door.

After a long moment, Jennifer asked, "And your collection?"

"How good of you to ask." With a dramatic swing, Castellano opened the large door.

Dimmed, flickering electric candlelight automatically came on, giving the room an eerie golden glow. The entire floor had been converted into one big room. All the windows were boarded up, and in the center of the room sat an old wood carved oval table with chairs, surrounded by paintings, magazines, weird-looking metal items, stone-carved objects, and strangely formed skeletons in glass showcases.

Castellano walked in and spread his arms. "My collection."

"Wow," Jennifer said.

"Wow, indeed," Monroe added.

"This is a museum," Bishop said as the group spread out in the room.

"But not open to the public," Castellano replied, raising a finger. "I made it available to the public a few years ago, and I'm still paying for that mistake."

"The tabloids and paparazzi?" Bishop concluded.

"El diablo de Barcelona, they called me."

"I can imagine," Monroe whispered in Jennifer's ear.

"Please sit." Castellano pointed at the table in the center. "Tea?" He presented an antique silver teapot.

"Yes, please. Thank you. Please," they all agreed.

Castellano filled up the antique red and silver stoneware tea cups that sat on the table. After filling the cups, he walked away from the table and disappeared behind a large cupboard. Seconds later, he reappeared carrying a small blue velvet cushion on both hands. "Gentlemen and woman, this is Ata." He put the cushion down on the table in front of his guests.

The three responded in rapid fashion.

"Wow, so tiny."

"Smaller than I thought."

"Incredible."

The tiny Ata appeared as a full-grown human body on the cushion, slightly out of proportion and with a big cone-shaped head. Though the bone structure seemed to be complete, the tiny bones appeared weather-beaten and leather-like, given the dark brown and beige color.

"May I?" Bishop asked, stretching out at the pillow.

"Of course, you can pick her up." Castellano handed out white velvet gloves he took from an antique-looking box on the table.

Bishop pulled the cushion towards him, put on the gloves, and carefully picked the little woman up. He held her in his palm, and the skeleton was smaller than the total length of his hand. He weighed it by moving his hand up and down. "It weighs almost nothing."

'What can you tell us about it?" Monroe asked.

"I'm afraid nothing much other than I told you on the phone, which you already knew. On the one hand, I have a report saying she's a young newborn baby with a stack of deformities. And on the other hand, there's a university that disputes, at least in part, the findings."

"But what do *you* think?" Jennifer asked, quickly putting on gloves as Bishop handed her the mummy.

Castellano gave a deep sigh. "For a long time, I was convinced she was not of this world—alien of some kind—but I'm not so sure anymore."

"Why is that?" Monroe asked.

"Look around you," Castellano demanded. "All my life, I've been collecting so-called proof of alien existence. And time after time, I came up with new evidence." He waved his arms around the room. "Experts have scrutinized every piece of evidence in this room, and for almost every item, I have a report saying they can't explain it completely, but...." He paused for a moment. "But, there's probably a perfectly plausible, earthly explanation for it. There's never irrefutable proof, you see. So, it doesn't matter what I find or how many experts say they don't know. I'll always be the nutjob collector in the Alchemist's house."

Jennifer gave Monroe the mummy.

"Can I see the metal tablet?" Castellano asked.

Monroe put the mummy down on the cushion, and from his jacket pocket, he took a small case he had specially made to transport the tablet in. He handed it to Castellano, who opened the case.

"It's beautiful." The collector took it out and stroked the surface, then removed a small folding magnifying glass from his pocket, opened it, and put it on the engraving. "You still don't know what kind of metal it is?"

Monroe shook his head.

"And these etchings?"

Monroe eyed Bishop, who nodded. "We believe they are part of multiple DNA strings."

"Incredible. It looks the same. DNA, really? So, you know what kind of DNA?"

"What do you mean, it looks the same?" Monroe asked.

"Uh, yes, sorry, later," Castellano uttered, waving a hand. "The DNA, you know what it is? Is it human or something else?"

"We don't know yet," Bishop answered quickly, attracting the looks of Jennifer and Monroe. "From the owner, we learned that you were interested in the sheet. Can you tell us why?"

Castellano ignored the question as he put the magnifying glass down again, placed the sheet back into the case, and handed it back to Monroe.

"That's it?" Monroe asked. "That's why we came to Barcelona?" He turned to Bishop.

"Hey, there's still the Sagrada Família to visit." Bishop gave a tiny smile.

"Wait a moment," Jennifer said, addressing Castellano. "What about the Russian ad? Why did you contact Maksim Morozov when he tried to sell this item?" She pointed at the box.

"Ah yes, of course," Castellano answered. "Well, that was not directly related to Ata. It's really a bit of a long story."

"We've got all day," Bishop interjected.

Castellano sighed again. "All right, then. More tea?" He put his hand on the teapot. "Ah, I see you haven't touched your tea yet."

All three picked up their cups.

"All right, where to start.... Did you ever hear of Alyoshenka?" When all three shook their heads, Castellano chuckled. "Of course you didn't.

Alyoshenka, or as some like to call her, 'the Kyshtym Dwarf,' was kind of Ata's sister. Her older sister, that is. This story dates back to 1969, Russia. In the small town of Kyshtym, some eleven-hundred miles east of Moscow in the Ural Mountains, an old woman named Tamara Vasilyevna Prosvirina went on her daily walk. When she left the village and walked into the woods, she found something wrapped in a blanket lying against a well."

"Another mummy," Monroe stated.

"Not a mummy this time." Castellano raised his voice. "According to the story, when Tamara opened the blanket, she found a tiny, ten-inch tall, humanlike creature, and it was alive. The creature looked fully grown and had an abnormal, long, conical-shaped head with unusually big eyes. Tamara took the creature with her, and when she talked to the blanket on her way home, neighbors noticed it and asked her about it. She told them it was her baby, Alyoshenka. You have to know that Tamara was known to have mental issues, so at first, no one took notice. Later that day, Tamara's daughter-in-law came by, and Tamara asked her if she wanted to see her daughter. Knowing the old woman was nuts, she indulged her. Tamara took her to the bedroom, where Alyoshenka lay on the bed.

"The creature looked dead, but when Tamara tried to feed her cottage cheese, it moved and nibbled some of the cheese. The daughter-in-law warned the town doctor, but when he showed up and wanted to take the creature with him to examine it, Tamara didn't let him take her. She said that without her, Alyoshenka would die. The doctor left empty-handed, and from there, Tamara took care of the creature. She would take daily walks with it in a stroller, but no-one was allowed to see it. She would always cover it. Days later, the daughter-in-law insisted on taking a look at the alleged baby again, and when she forced herself into the bedroom, she found Alyoshenka dead on the bed. The body was already decomposing. They took Tamara away into an asylum, and from there, the reports become more fantastic."

"From *there*, the story gets fantastic?" Bishop asked.

Castellano continued unrelentingly. "The story goes that first the creature's skin became darker and leathery, and some say the skeleton completely vanished, leaving an empty shell. There are lots of pictures, and there's even film of it." Castellano nodded heavily. "They are all on my website. I'll send you a link."

"So the body vanished?" Bishop asked.

"The story goes that a local police officer named Vladimir Bendlin confiscated Alyoshenka's body, but his boss showed no interest in the case. Bendlin, who I guess these days, we would probably call the Fox Mulder of Russia, kept the body in his fridge at home. He had the body examined by a local pathologist who said that she wasn't human, while a local gynecologist said that it was simply a child with terrible deformations."

"Like Ata," Monroe suggested.

"Maybe," Castellano said. "Anyway, Bendlin finally handed Alyoshenka's body over to a group of Russian ufologists. They took it, and from there, nothing was heard about her ever again."

"That's a good story." Jennifer looked at her watch. "But what has that got to do with the metal sheet?"

"I was coming to that." Castellano waved a hand slowly over the table. "Almost twenty years ago, just a few years after this story played and after I got my hands on Ata, I decided to go and visit the town of Kyshtym and see for myself. When I got there, I learned that the crazy, now old woman, Tamara, had been released from the asylum and lived in solitary just outside the small town. So, I went to visit her. I met her when she was outside, tending her garden. She seemed barely approachable, and when I asked her about Alyoshenka, she threw down her tools and fled inside. As she left the door open, I followed her inside. She lived in a one-room cottage with barely any windows, and that's when I saw it."

"Saw what?" Jennifer asked impatiently.

Castellano pointed at the box with the metal sheet. "On all the walls, Tamara had scribbled spiraled drawings of characters. Exactly like the one your Russian friend Morozov had an enlarged photograph of, which he placed with his ad."

Bishop, Monroe, and Jennifer all leaned over the table.

"How can you be sure those were the same drawings?" Bishop asked.

"Of course, I cannot be a hundred percent sure, and that's why I tried to buy the item. You can see now how disappointed I was when I learned that it was already sold. But from what I saw, it looked very much the same."

"Do you have any pictures of the drawings on the crazy woman's walls?" Monroe asked.

"I'm sorry. I didn't have a camera with me that day. Nowadays, we all carry our cameras with us everywhere on our phones, but back then...."

The four of them fell silent for a moment, and their breathing into the silence gave the place an extra creepy atmosphere until Bishop broke the silence. "Do you still have the old woman's address?"

"I do, but I don't think it'll do you any good. She died shortly after I visited her—ran over by a truck in the middle of the night."

The three of them frowned and deflated.

"That's how I felt, but the story goes she liked to dance in the middle of the road at night. She had schizophrenia, you know. On the other hand, the story also goes that many of the people who had anything to do with Alyoshenka died or mysteriously vanished shortly after the incident."

"Hmm," Bishop mumbled. "But I'm still interested in the address, if you don't mind?"

"Sure, let me see." Castellano left the table and opened a drawer in a desk with a large crystal skull on top.

"What do you think of all this?" Jennifer whispered.

"I can't say I'm sure what to think of all this yet," Bishop replied. "But I would still like to know more about it."

"You have an idea?" Monroe asked Bishop.

"Ah, here it is," Castellano called out, waving a small piece of paper into the air.

Bishop grinned. "I do, but I'm not sure you're going to like it."

CHAPTER 13

Category Six

Barcelona, Spain

"Thank you for the tea and warm welcome," Jennifer said as the three left the haunted house and stepped back into the street.

"You're welcome," Castellano said as a small group of young tourists entered the street, making loud noises. He spoke fast. "Have a safe trip, and do keep me informed if you find anything new." With a bang, he closed the door.

"I guess he doesn't come out often," Bishop said.

"I guess not," Monroe agreed. "What was that all about, you having a plan and me not going to like it?"

"What I meant was that I was intrigued by his story about the crazy woman, and the only way to see if there is any merit to this story is to find out for ourselves and go to Russia."

"Okay, but what's not to like?" Monroe replied, smiling.

"Well, we both know how you were always complaining about your only trip to Russia when you got invited for a guest lecture." He nodded at Jennifer, who grinned. "You got stuck in heavy snowfall on the road from the airport, somewhere in the middle of nowhere, and stayed in a small worn-down motel for three days—too cold to get outside and with only Russian food to eat."

"And with a driver that didn't speak a word of English," Jennifer added. "And when you finally got freed from the snow, the university was closed for some kind of a winter holiday. So after a week, you came back to New Haven, empty-handed, so to say."

Both Bishop and Jennifer now burst out laughing.

"Yeah, sure, you laugh," Monroe said. "Let's see how you would do after three days in a stinky hotel room, sharing a bed with a smelly Russian who was clearly in love with his vodka."

They laughed even louder.

After a second, Monroe joined the laughter. "But anyhow, I was also quite intrigued by the crazy woman story. And besides that, my previous adventure in Russia took place in one of the colder areas in mid-winter."

"And where do you think we're going now, and what season do you think it is over there?" Jennifer asked.

Bishop took the piece of paper Castellano gave him from his jacket pocket.

"And?" Monroe raised his hands.

Bishop mumbled, reading from the paper. "Umm... a lot of Russian names but.... What's this?" He showed the piece of paper to Jennifer.

"It looks like a small village near Kyshtym," she translated. "In the Chelyabinsk Oblast, Kaolinovy, last gray house on the main street."

"That's it?" Monroe asked.

Jennifer nodded. "That's it. No other address or number, just the woman's name."

"Can I see?" Monroe asked.

Bishop handed him the paper.

Monroe had already taken out his phone and was working the screen. "I can confirm the existence of the village, but that's just about it—no hotel listings, no schools, shops, nothing. Hell, Google Maps doesn't even know the place."

"So?" Bishop pointed to the end of the street, and they started walking. "Still sure you want to go there?"

"Of course," Monroe replied, still concentrated on his phone. "If we want, I have already found three tickets from Barcelona to Chelyabinsk, with a layover in Zurich. From there, it's one and a half hours to Kyshtym by car."

"Ad some extra time to Kolanivy, or something like that," Bishop concluded.

"Kaolinovy," Jennifer corrected.

Monroe counted on his fingers. "It's about a thirty-hour trip in total."

"I can't wait," Jennifer mocked.

"So?" Monroe raised a finger over the screen, ready to push the reservation button. "What do you say?"

"I'm in. Sure I'm in," Bishop said.

"What do you think?" Jennifer's mouth curled into a smile.

Monroe pushed the button on the screen and looked at his watch. "We have about four hours to see the sights before we have to be back in the hotel, gather our things, and leave for the airport."

"The Basílica de la Sagrada Família first?" Bishop asked as he pointed the way and started walking.

***

After they turned the corner, Nadya raised herself from leaning against her scooter, where she'd been watching them, and sat down on the saddle again. She took her phone out and dialed a number. After a few seconds, there was a single tone, then nothing. "Umm... hello?"

After a long moment, a voice sounded. "Nadya, is that you?"

"Ah, yes, it's me, Chief. I guess there was something wrong with the connection. I'm still in Barcelona."

"Is everything okay?" his dull voice asked.

"It is, sir. The three just left from a visit to the collector. I've listened in to the meeting after I planted a bug inside one of their backpacks. I'll send you the complete conversation after this call."

"Okay, and I assume you have an excerpt of the conversation for me now?"

"I do, sir. They have the item on them, but there seems to be more to it than just the material itself. They said the etchings are part of written DNA strings."

"Hmm, so it might still be true." His voice sounded soft.

"Excuse me, sir?"

"Uh, nothing, nothing. So that's it?"

"No sir. They were particularly interested in some mummy in the man's collection. A tiny one, I understand, named Ata. Does that mean anything to you?"

"It doesn't," the Chief answered.

"Well, the collector told them about a similar mummy back in Russia, where he also found similar writing like on the item." Nadya waited for a second, but when there was no response, she continued. "I suggest you listen to the complete story in the recording I'll send you. Anyway, they will be on their way to Russia to a village near the city of Kyshtym. I couldn't hear the name of the village over the sound of loud scooters in the street, but if you want, I think I can beat them to Kyshtym, wait for them at the airport, and pick up their trail over there."

"They still have no idea they're being followed?"

"I'm absolutely sure of it," Nadya confirmed.

"All right, go ahead and come back to Russia, to Kyshtym. You'll be closer to home, anyway. But remember one thing: I absolutely want to hear from you if there's any chance of you being discovered. Are we clear on that?"

"Completely clear, sir."

"All right, then. Get yourself on that plane, and please send me the recording immediately after we hang up."

"Will do, sir. Thank you." Nadya put the phone away, and grimaced when she realized the Chief had never wished her good luck. Who was that man whom she'd never met face to face? She shook her head as she worked her phone and sent him the file. Then she put on her helmet and started the scooter.

***

Kyshtym, Chelyabinsk Oblast, Russia, The Present

Thirty hours had passed since the three walked down the most dangerous spiral staircase in the world. The staircase in the Sagrada Família church was notorious for lack of an inside railing. The only handrail, placed on the outside of the spiral, gave you a false sense of security. One small misstep on one of the five hundred and four steps and....

"Do you know you still look pale from descending the church tower?" Bishop asked Monroe while they were on their way south.

"Ha-ha," Monroe replied. "Truth be told, I never expected it to be that frightening."

"I think we were all a little bit frightened," Jennifer added. "Still, I'm having second thoughts, wondering if I wouldn't have rather stayed in the warmth of Barcelona instead of this." She pointed outside.

Thirty minutes ago, they had landed at Chelyabinsk airport in the south of Russia, where only a handful of passengers got off the airplane. After exiting the plane, the eighteen degrees Fahrenheit air and gushing, icy cold wind had prompted Monroe to bring up memories about his previous trip to Russia—bad memories.

In less than fifteen minutes, they had retrieved their luggage, and another five minutes later, they were in a taxi—a twenty-year-old Lada Riva—driving even farther south in the direction of Kazakhstan, on their way to the village of Kaolinovy.

"At what time do we arrive in Kaolinovy?" Jennifer asked the driver.

"*Okolo poludnya,*" the man answered in a cheerful tone.

"We should arrive around noon," Jennifer translated.

"Thanks," Bishop said as he pulled down the zipper of his parka. "I'm glad we were able to buy these warm clothes in Spain."

"I don't think I will have much use for my bikini out here," Jennifer replied, grinning while playing with her hair.

"From eighty to eighteen degrees...." Bishop smiled back.

Monroe chuckled while reading on his tablet. "Do you remember Kyshtym?" He raised an eyebrow.

"Sure," Bishop said. "We just passed it, the largest city near the airport."

"That one," Monroe confirmed. "Did you know that the biggest nuclear facility in the Russian Federation, the Mayak Production Association, is in Kyshtym?"

"How would I know?" Bishop asked, while Jennifer shrugged.

Monroe pointed at the tablet. "It says here that the third biggest nuclear disaster, after Chernobyl in the Ukraine and Fukushima in Japan, happened over here decades ago. Huh, did you know that nuclear disasters have a similar categorization as hurricanes? It's called the International Nuclear Event Scale. It runs from zero, being what they call a deviation like a small leakage without consequences, to a seven, a major incident like Chernobyl."

"And what category was your disaster out here?" Jennifer asked.

"A six. It's officially called a serious accident. The cooling system in one of the tanks, containing eighty tons of liquid radioactive waste, failed. When the temperature started to rise, a chemical explosion thrusted a hundred-and-sixty-ton concrete lid into the air, spilling the dried waste. At least two villages were exposed to radiation. A total of ten thousand people were evacuated after a week. Even more people were evacuated from the area in the following two years."

"Never heard of it." Bishop shook his head.

"Neither did I," Jennifer said. "When was this?"

"September 1957," Monroe answered. "Over twenty-thousand square miles, with two hundred and seventy thousand people living on it, were contaminated."

"Wow," Jennifer said. "And now? I mean, how contaminated is this area now?"

"According to this, the current level of radiation is less than 0.1 millisievert per year. Harmless, they say."

"Sure it is," Jennifer nodded, squinting. "I suggest we get in and out as fast as we can."

"Agreed," Monroe said.

"You know what this means, don't you?" Bishop said.

"What do you mean?" Monroe replied.

"Regarding Alyoshenka." Bishop paused for a short moment. "The creature was probably just a heavily deformed baby, most likely from a mother suffering from radiation sickness herself."

Monroe sighed. "Possibly, but how do you explain the spiral text on the walls of the crazy woman?"

"I can't. Yet," Bishop answered. "But I guess we'll know soon enough now."

"*Tvoi druz'ya?*" the taxi driver asked, looking in his mirror.

Bishop and Monroe looked at Jennifer.

"He wants to know if the car behind us is a friend of ours."

"How so?" Bishop asked, looking back while Jennifer talked to the driver.

"*Otlichno,*" Jennifer thanked the driver, then addressed Bishop and Monroe. "He says he drives this route about once a week, and this is probably the first time in his life that there's been a car behind him for about the entire route."

Now they all looked back.

"An interested party?" Monroe suggested.

"But who? How?" Bishop asked.

"Slow down, please," Bishop said, and Jennifer translated. The driver slowly decelerated.

The car behind them rapidly got closer and then slowed down.

"I believe there's someone in the front and back," Monroe said.

"I can't see it with the sun coming from behind," Bishop added.

The car behind them slowed further, maintaining some distance between them.

"What's he doing?" Jennifer asked.

Suddenly, the car changed lanes, accelerated, and speedily overtook them and passed. On the side of the car, they read 'TAKSI,' and they tried to gaze inside.

"An empty taxi?" Jennifer asked.

"I could have sworn I saw someone in the back," Monroe said.

"Very strange," the driver replied in a heavy accent. "Must be someone in the back. There are no empty cabs driving here."

"Someone hiding in the backseat?" Jennifer asked.

"Possibly," Bishop answered as the car quickly moved out of sight.

"But who knows we're here?" Monroe asked. "We told no one. Not even our Spanish collector knows."

"I can't be sure," Jennifer said, "but do you remember the woman in the hotel lobby in Barcelona?"

"Sure," Bishop said.

"I can't really explain it, but I got a strange vibe from her."

"A vibe? Like a few years back?"

Jennifer shrugged.

"What did she say?" Bishop asked.

"Nothing much. We talked about Gaudi. She told me she was on holiday from Ukraine, and I told her I was giving a guest lecture at a university over there. That's it."

Bishop nodded. "Even if there's something to it, how would she know we are here? I suggest for now we do not overthink it. It could easily be nothing." He took a deep breath, exhaled slowly, and looked left and right at the same wintergreen forest landscape they'd seen for over an hour now. "How far is it?"

Jennifer asked the driver, and said, "Not far, about fifteen minutes."

CHAPTER 14

The Crazy Woman

Kaolinovy, Chelyabinsk Oblast, Russia

As the taxi drove from the dense forest into the bright sun and onto a narrow mountain path, the driver started talking to Jennifer.

"What's he saying?" Monroe asked after a minute.

"He explains that the Ural Mountains run from north to south in Russia. He says the mountains, for a large part, form the frontier between Europe and Asia. The region is known for its wide variety of mixed forests, mountains, steppes, and forest-steppes. Still, there's also a lot of pollution from factories and mineral mines in the region. During the second world war, almost all the Russian tanks and military vehicles were produced there."

"Ask him what he knows about nuclear activity in the region," Bishop said.

Jennifer talked to the driver for a moment. "He only knows about the Mayak Production Association some hundred miles north of here. Apparently, they made nuclear bombs during the cold war. He lived over there with his parents when he was a young boy. The rumors go that over forty thousand prisoners of war and gulag prisoners built and worked at the factory after the second world war. He thinks the plant is closed now, but he never goes there anymore."

"Then how do you explain this?" Monroe asked, pointing at his tablet.

Jennifer read the screen out loud. "In September 2017, a large cloud of radiation was detected over Europe, reaching as far as the Caribbean." She sighed. "It originated in this area, the Chelyabinsk region of the Ural Mountains. Russia even confirmed that they detected a cloud of nuclear radiation at the time but never acknowledged any responsibility for a radiation leak. It also says that the total radioactivity was between thirty and a hundred times the level of radiation emitted from the Fukushima, Japan disaster in 2011. Russian officials claim it was a natural occurrence."

"Sure it was," Bishop says. "I become more and more convinced that Alyoshenka might not have been as alien as some thought it was."

"Eto staryy kar'yer," the driver said as he drove down from the mountain.

Jennifer translated: "He says that's the old quarry. The road runs along a small lake that over fifty years ago served as a clay quarry. The white clay mixed with the liquid gave the water its current opaque bright blue color. It's beautiful," Jennifer added while listening to the driver. "The village should be right around the corner now."

As the taxi turned the corner, they passed an old, weary street sign that, at one time, must have said Kaolinovy. Now the 'lin' and the 'y' were no longer readable on the weather-beaten sign. The driver stopped the car next to it in the middle of the road.

"This must be it." Monroe pointed at the sign.

"He wants to know where to go now," Jennifer translated.

"Please let him drive to the end slowly," Bishop said.

The taxi passed the few dozen old, detached, and mostly wooden houses on both left and right, and a handful of cars parked at the curbs.

"There's the other taxi." Jennifer pointed at a green car parked in front of what looked like the only store on the street.

"It's empty now, except for the driver, who seems to be asleep," Monroe said.

***

From inside the store, Nadya gazed onto the street and then quickly ducked away. A few minutes earlier, she'd jumped out of the taxi and ordered the driver to wait for her. She then hustled into the store and strategically took a position with a clear view of both sides of the street.

***

Bishop shook his head as an uneasy feeling mounted.

"Empty like everything else," Jennifer pointed out. "It seems there's no one out here."

"I think there's a distinct possibility that everyone left town when they shut down the quarry," Bishop replied. "I understand there are hundreds of similar ghost towns all over Russia. They all left as soon as the work vaporized. Only a handful of mostly elderly people with nowhere to go stayed behind."

Within seconds, the taxi neared the end of the quarter-mile-long street, where the road ran into the woods again. On the left, a big lumber-like shed defined the end, and on the right, a small red cottage ended the road.

"So much for a gray house," Monroe said.

"Hmm...." Bishop stroked his chin. "Let's get out and ask. Can you ask the driver to wait here?" he asked Jennifer.

Jennifer addressed the driver in Russian, who nodded in agreement.

"Will he wait?" Monroe asked as they got out of the car.

"We didn't pay him yet. He'll wait," Jennifer said smiling.

"Let's check out the red one." Bishop pointed to the other side of the street.

"I wonder how this looks at night," Monroe said as he crossed the muddy road.

"Sad," Jennifer answered behind him, with Bishop close behind her.

Bishop stopped in the middle of the road and inspected the house—one floor and a gable roof. The surface area couldn't be much more than 175 square feet. The only windows seemed to be the two flanking the door in the center of the façade. The front of the tiny house bordered the curb, and as he walked up, Bishop inspected the doorframe. On one side, some minor damage appeared in the plaster.

This could very well have been painted gray before.

"I don't see anything," Jennifer called out as she peered through the left window, both hands clamped between the glass and her head.

"Nothing here," Monroe replied, doing the same at the other window.

"This has to be the place," Bishop said, and banged three times on the door. "No bell," he said after seeing he'd startled the others.

Monroe shook his head. "Subtle. Whoever dead inside must have risen after that knocking."

When after a minute nothing happened, Bishop walked up to the window and tapped it. Again, nothing happened.

"*Zdravstvuyte,*" a man's voice sounded behind them. When they turned around startled, a man hanging out a window in a house behind them waved a hand.

"*Dobryy den'* (Good day)," Jennifer replied as she walked up to the man.

"I'm glad she's with us," Monroe said.

Bishop nodded. "Indeed."

Jennifer stopped below the window, looked up, and conversed with the man for a minute.

She then turned back to Bishop and Monroe. "I asked him if he knew where the owner lives, and he said we should ask at the grocery and hardware store." She pointed to the middle of the road.

"All right, what are you waiting for?" Monroe took the first steps in the direction of the store.

"He's in a hurry," Jennifer said.

"Who wouldn't be?" Bishop waved his arms in both directions of the street.

***

"Is there a back?" Nadya asked the store manager behind the counter. She waved a fifty-thousand-ruble note—a month's salary—in front of his face while nodding outside, where Bishop and his friends neared the store.

The store manager grabbed the banknote from her hand, handed her a key, and pointed to a door at the other end of the store.

She bolted to the back of the store, opened the door, and went through just as her marks opened the front door.

***

"*Dobryy den'*," the store owner greeted the three. "You're English?"

"American," Jennifer replied.

"I speak English," the man said. "I worked in London as a cabbie for over five years."

"Great," Jennifer said. "Maybe you can help us."

"We're looking for the owner of the red house at the end of the street," Bishop said.

"And who are you?" the man asked.

"Excuse me," Bishop replied. "My name is Matthew Bishop, professor at an American University, and these are my two colleagues, Jennifer Porter and Walker Monroe."

Both gave a tiny nod.

"American professors!" the man said. "We don't get many of those, and most certainly not three in one go."

Bishop laughed. "Can you help us?"

"You're looking at him."

"Excuse me," Bishop said.

"The owner of the red house." The man proudly threw his chest forward. "You're looking at him," he repeated. "I'm Alexei Prosvirina."

"Pleased to meet you, Mr. Prosvirina," Bishop said.

"Alexei, please."

"All right, Alexei." Bishop nodded. "You live in the red house at the end of the street?"

"I didn't say that. That's no place to live in. I live here above my shop. I inherited the place years ago from my sister."

"Tamara Vasilyevna Prosvirina?" Monroe asked.

The shopkeeper frowned. "You knew my sister?"

"We didn't," Monroe answered. "We heard of her for the first time a few days ago."

The man nodded knowingly ."Then you're here for the legend."

"What do you mean?" Jennifer asked.

The man smiled. "Years ago, we got a lot of visitors asking about the baby alien my sister found and raised for a short while. These days, we don't get many visitors about anything around here. So, why are you here?"

"You don't believe it was an alien?" Monroe asked.

"I'm not sure what to believe. I worked in London at the time and came back to take care of my sister after she had her accident."

"You mean the accident with the truck?" Jennifer asked.

Alexei nodded.

"I understood she died from the accident."

"She didn't, although you might say she did, in the long run. After her accident, she was disabled, confined to bed, barely able to speak. She was hardly approachable. The only thing she called out now and then was that 'they were here!'"

"Who? Aliens?" Bishop asked.

"You tell me. I took care of her for eleven months till she died."

"How did she die?" Jennifer asked.

"Who's to say? My sister wasn't a sane woman, you know. She was institutionalized several times, and every time she got back, I believe she was a little worse. Now...." He leaned over the counter with his knuckles on it. "I still don't know why you are here."

"Sure," Bishop said. "It's a long story, but if it's possible, we would like to take a look inside her old house."

"Why?" Alexei cocked his head.

"We're not sure," Monroe took over. "We spoke to someone who visited her there years ago, and spoke about your sister drawing spirals all over the walls of her house. We think we might have found similar drawings somewhere else, so we wondered if they're the same. Are they still there, the drawings?"

"I know the drawings you speak of, but if they were there once, I figure they are not still there."

Monroe frowned. "What do you mean?"

"When I inherited it, I had the place renovated, hoping I could sell it or rent it out. Neither happened, of course. I had the outside painted red, and on the inside, I had the wood painted and put new wallpaper on the walls. I never saw any drawings, but I never visited the place before it was renovated. So the drawings could be there, I guess, right behind the wallpaper."

"Can we see it?" Bishop asked.

"Sure you can, but like I said, everything will be carefully worked away behind the wallpaper now."

"Nevertheless," Bishop said.

"Sure, no problem." Alexei took a key ring from the drawer below his register and stepped away from the counter. "Follow me."

Within seconds they left the store and crossed the street.

"You can just leave the store and don't have to lock up?" Jennifer asked.

Alexei laughed. "There are about a hundred fifty people living in Kaolinovy. Most of them belong to one big family. If something was to happen here, everyone would know. Besides that, by leaving the store open, a customer can always get inside, do some shopping and wait for me. When the door is open, they know I won't be long."

They all looked behind them when an engine broke the silence of the empty street. The green taxi drove away from the grocery and back out of town.

"Do you know who that was?" Jennifer asked.

"I've no idea," Alexei answered.

"So much for knowing everyone," Monroe grunted.

"Here we are," Alexei said, opening the door to the red house. "Please go in." He waved the three inside.

***

At the end of the street, the green taxi drove off the road and parked in the tree line. Nadya tapped the driver on the shoulder, gesturing him to shut down the engine while dialing a number on her cellphone with her other hand.

"Chief?" she said into the phone after a second.

"Nadya, how's the south?"

"Cold, sir. I followed the Americans to a hole called Kaolinovy, near Kyshtym, an old mining town."

"And?"

"Well, to be honest, I'm not sure. I planted a bug on the woman's backpack, but they left the taxi and left their luggage behind, so I'm without ears."

"It probably wouldn't matter anyway," the Chief replied. "The battery will be about empty. Where are they now? Do you still have them in sight?"

"They visited a grocery, and the storekeeper took them inside a house across the street. That's where I lost sight. I could try to get a look inside, but it's a tiny house with only a couple windows, and there's a chance I might be spotted. What do you want me to do?"

The line went silent for a moment, and Nadya heard the Chief take a deep breath. "Here's what I want you to do. Stay with them as long as you can, without being seen. If they travel elsewhere, try to find out where they are going, but again...."

"All right, sir, will do. But it's kind of difficult since there are no other cars, or people for that matter, anywhere in sight, so everything I do will likely raise suspicion."

"Just see what you can do. Avoid any risks, and as soon as you think it isn't safe any longer, you head back to Moscow. In that case, we'll find a way to pick them up from there."

"Will do, sir. Thank you."

"Take care."

***

The wooden floor and walls in the tiny house were completely empty. The only thing breaking the surface was a small kitchen sink at the end of the room.

"Just enough space for a fold-out bed and a small table, I guess," Monroe said.

"For many, that's more than enough in Russia," Alexei remarked. "It's just there are simply not enough people left in Kaolinovy, and no teenagers are looking for a home."

Bishop rubbed a hand over the new, white, pristine-looking—if a bit dusty—wallpaper and looked at his hand.

Alexei smiled. "You can imagine I don't dust here very often."

Bishop chuckled. "That's no problem." With his hand, he wiped the wallpaper looking for an edge. When he found one, he looked back to see if Alexei was looking. When the coast was clear, he gave a fake cough and pulled at a corner of the paper. It easily came loose.

"What are you doing?" Jennifer whispered in his ear, but Bishop didn't answer.

"It's removable wallpaper," Alexei said, watching Bishop from a reflection in the window.

"Sorry," Bishop replied, "but it's essential for us to know what's behind this paper."

"I'm sure it is," Alexei replied.

"How much?" Monroe asked.

"You're willing to pay to remove the wallpaper?" Alexei asked.

"Why not?" Monroe shrugged as Jennifer gave him a frowning look. "Nobody lives here, and Alexei can redo the wallpaper anytime, should he want to."

"A hundred thousand rubles," Alexi said.

"How much do you have on you?" Monroe asked Bishop and Jennifer while opening his wallet.

"Thirty," Jennifer said.

"Twenty," Bishop added.

"One, two, three," Monroe counted. "That's eighty in total." He took the money from Bishop and Jennifer, stacked everything together, and waved it in front of Alexei.

"But the taxi...." Jennifer uttered.

"We'll get some more on the way back," Monroe replied. "Well, can we have an hour alone in this house?" he asked Alexei.

Alexei grabbed the money, took another bill from his pocket, and put everything together and back in his pants pocket. "Miss, gentlemen," he said as he stepped to the door and opened it. "It's been a pleasure doing business with you. Just close the door behind you when you leave, will you?"

"No problem," Bishop said. "Thank you."

Alexei left the house, and Bishop closed the door behind him.

"Well," Jennifer said, "I think this is a men's job. You start pulling, and I'll be outside informing the cab driver we'll be a little while longer. You know where to find me."

"That shouldn't be too difficult." Monroe smiled.

A second later, Jennifer left the house, leaving Bishop and Monroe behind. Bishop turned to the wall and again found the piece of paper he'd started peeling off. He slowly pulled it a bit farther down, and a beige-painted stone wall materialized. He wondered if that always had been the color of the paint, or if dust and dirt had accumulated over the years. He looked at his fingers and had to contain himself from getting nauseous.

"Your mysophobia acting up?" Monroe asked.

"Please feel free to find a strip of your own," Bishop replied.

"Sure, no problem." Monroe stepped into another corner and started peeling.

"Here we go," Bishop called out as a drawing on the wall emerged. For a second, he stopped as Monroe joined him.

"Wow," they both said instantaneously.

Bishop pulled the paper farther down, and tiny scribblings in a huge four-foot-wide spiral materialized.

Monroe put his head closer to the writing. "I can barely see the individual signs. How can the crazy woman have written this? There must be thousands of characters here."

"Hundreds of thousands," Bishop said.

"Amazing. At first glance, they appear to be the same kind of symbols like on the metal."

Bishop nodded. "Let's pull everything down and see." As he pulled the strip of paper all the way down, the complete spiral revealed itself.

"Wow again," Monroe said as he walked back into his corner and started pulling again.

For the next fifteen minutes, a heap of paper grew steadily as they stripped the walls naked, and spiral after spiral emerged on the bare stone walls.

When Jennifer entered the house again, she stopped in the doorway with wide eyes. "One, two, three, four, five, six, seven...."

"Amazing, isn't it?" Monroe said.

"Unfortunately," Bishop said, "not every piece of writing is as clear as we could hope for, but there's a lot of material to work with here."

"Where to start?" Jennifer asked.

"Pictures," Bishop replied. "I think it's smart if we all make as many detailed pictures as we can."

"Agreed. Let's do that," Monroe replied as they all took out their cellphones and started taking pictures.

"Got it?" Bishop asked after a few minutes, and they all checked the images on their phones.

"Amazing." Monroe enlarged one small group of symbols to full screen. "They look exactly the same."

"I think so too," Jennifer agreed.

"I think they are," Bishop said. "If we have everything, I suggest we get back to the cab and get out of here as soon as possible."

"Back to the airport," Monroe agreed.

A minute later, they were back in the cab and driving out of the village.

"There's that green taxi again." Jennifer pointed at the tree line at the end of the street as they passed it.

"Indeed it is," Monroe said. "Let's see what happens."

They looked back to see if the taxi would pick up after them, but instead, the green car turned out of the tree line and turned into the village again.

"It's not following us," Monroe said.

"I still don't trust it." Jennifer shook her head.

"Let's just keep an eye out for anything unusual," Bishop suggested.

"What do we do now?" Monroe asked.

"I think we first need to get all the images into the computer and see if we can straighten out the symbols and get them readable. Then we should send them to the lab to see if Dr. Aldridge can make anything of it."

"Sounds like a plan," Monroe said.

"And we have twenty hours on a plane to carry out that plan," Bishop added.

"Umm...." Jennifer looked at her watch. "And a five-hour wait at the airport, I'm afraid."

"That'll give me more than enough time to update Hootkins at the USGS," Monroe said.

"No news from those guys at the USGS?" Bishop asked. "I thought they were still researching fragments of the metal?"

Monroe nodded. "They are, using some kind of different techniques that could take up to two weeks before they'd have any results."

"Well, I guess this is something we obviously can't hurry," Jennifer said.

CHAPTER 15

Deformities?

Yale, New Haven, CT, Two Days Later

The city's Graduate Hotel had only been an eight-minute drive with the taxi that brought Nadya there from Tweed-New Haven Airport. The small but luxurious hotel was conveniently located just across the street from Yale's School of Art, and the closest place to stay near Bishop's, Monroe's, and Jennifer's office. Only once before she had left Russia on a work assignment, and that had ended in a disaster and a co-worker's death through no fault of her own. It had taken her almost three years to regain her Chief's trust, and she was determined not to break that trust now.

Across the street from her hotel, Nadya walked onto the University grounds on her way to check out the offices as her cell phone rang.

Nadya stopped and picked it up. "Chief, what did you find?"

"Not that much, I'm afraid. We assume that the spirals you photographed relate somehow to the etchings on the metal sheet, but since we haven't seen that one, we can't be sure."

"And the symbols?"

"In your transcript from their visit to Barcelona, we understood that the etchings on the sheet somehow identify strings of DNA, but our decoders haven't been able to identify anything like that on these spirals."

"Basically, we know nothing," Nadya stated as she started walking again.

"That's all I have for you at this time. Where are you now?"

"I just walked onto the street with the mathematician's office. They came back over a day ago now, so I figure the best chance to find him would be at his office."

"What are your plans?"

"Not sure yet, but he doesn't know my face. I figure I can always pretend to be an exchange student should it come to a confrontation."

"All right, but be careful. You never know."

"Will do." She pushed the button on the screen and put the phone away as she turned onto College Street. "Three hundred," she read out loud from the face of the building on her left. She took a piece of paper from her pants pocket and mumbled, "Four-fifty-one." She had to be close.

***

Monroe didn't like spending much time in his basement office. He spent most of his time here on the ground floor library, behind the small desk sandwiched between the showcase with his copy of the Guttenberg Bible and the glass tower filled with his books—his babies, as he liked to call them. He loved to see students enter the library for the first time and look in awe at the six floors of old books and manuscripts in their glass tower.

This time, he'd chosen the more private environment of his chamber office to meet with Bishop and discuss the results of their trip to Russia.

The basement offices straight beneath Beinecke Library's great stack of books were called the chambers, a name well-deserved because most of the rooms in the basement were completely deprived of sunlight. It looked as if they'd built the crude concrete offices to create as the greatest possible contrast with the magnificent, meticulously handcrafted books and manuscripts stored in the library.

Like Monroe's workplace, some of the offices had one small strip of glass in the wall where sunlight could penetrate the otherwise dark, gray room. To make the office a bit more habitable, Monroe had one wall filled with old books from his private collection that he'd gathered over the years. On another wall, surrounding a large LED flatscreen, hung framed single pages of old official documents, like an 1867 U.S. Revenue Tax Document and an old South Shoreline Bill of Lading from 1876, New Haven Co. Erie Railway.

He was exceptionally proud of his Widow's Mite, a framed, half-inch, round coin that stood on one corner of his desk. They'd used the coin as currency two-thousand years ago in the Holy Land, at the time of Jesus, and it was even mentioned in the Bible. In Mark 12:41-44, 'Jesus observed a poor widow giving two small bronze leptons, known as 'mites,' to the treasury.' Etched on one side of the coin was King Alexander Jannaeus's name, and on the other, an 8-rayed star was depicted. Though not exceptionally rare, most of the recovered coins had been heavily battered through the years, but Monroe's specimen remained exceptionally well preserved. More important, he especially liked the idea that Jesus himself could have held his coin.

"Where's Jennifer?" Bishop asked as he picked up the framed coin from the desk. Then he sat down opposite Monroe.

"She called a moment ago to say she would join a bit later. Did I ever tell you about that coin?"

"Only a hundred times." Bishop laughed as he put the coin back.

Monroe laughed back. "Probably the age. I suggest we get started. Jennifer will catch up when she gets here. What did you find out?"

"Well, after we came back, I first straightened out all the text and noticed that there were substantially more unique symbols used than we previously found on the piece of metal."

"More than four?"

"Substantially more. Thirty-two, to be exact."

"That's a lot more than the four letters used in DNA," Monroe remarked. "So it's not DNA?"

"Well, the first four DNA symbols and the one decimal we found earlier are also in the drawings. Actually, more than half of the hundreds of thousands of symbols that are drawn in the spirals are still those same five signs."

"Thirty-two, you said?" Monroe gazed up for a second, squinting.

"Yes, thirty-two signs, of which we've identified five as being the same ones we found on the metal sheet. Like our mummy's DNA, so to say."

"Remarkable," Monroe replied.

"What do you mean?" Bishop asked.

"That's exactly the same number as the European cave signs and the original English alphabet."

"What are you talking about?"

"Let's see." Monroe pulled the laptop towards him to the center of his desk and worked the keyboard. He then turned the screen to Bishop. "Here."

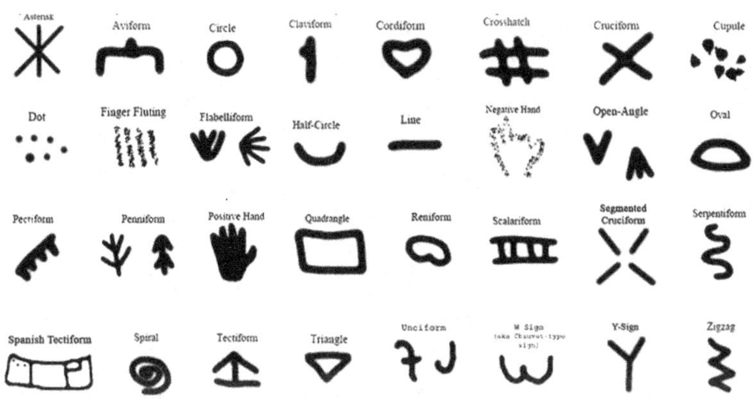

"What am I looking at?" Bishop asked.

"On ancient cave walls all over Europe, those same thirty-two signs appear over and over again. And only those same signs, drawn over a timespan of thirty-thousand years."

"Early writing?" Bishop asked.

"It doesn't look that way if we look at the groupings of the symbols. The earliest writing we know of is some 3,500 years old, so there's a tremendous gap."

"And nobody knows what these signs are about?" Bishop asked.

"Well, we have an idea of what some of them depict, but what they mean, or why and how they are there.... As you can see, some actually look like something we know today, but others...."

"But they don't look anything like we found on the metal sheet or in the home in Russia," Bishop remarked.

"I didn't say they did. It's just a remarkable coincidence there are exactly thirty-two signs in both cases."

"A remarkable coincidence," Bishop concluded.

"Probably," Monroe agreed. "Strange enough, the English language originally also had thirty-two characters." He retook the laptop, typed something, and turned it back to Bishop. "Look."

Eth (ð), Wynn (ƿ), Thorn (þ), Ash (æ), Ethel (œ), Yogh (ȝ)

"These are the lost letters," Monroe explained. "Do you know that you can still find these characters on every modern word processor?"

Bishop shrugged.

"As the language evolved, we lost six characters we simply didn't need anymore. And the way we're still evolving language, we're about to lose a lot more in the coming years."

"Are you saying you still think the signs in the symbols simply stand for a letter in our alphabet?" Bishop asked, frowning.

Monroe thought for a long moment. "No, I don't think that. I think it's just a coincidence, but a weird one. Still... I can't help wondering if the signs somehow are an evolved version of our alphabet or, for lack of a better word, a 'prevolved' version of it."

"I still think it's a remarkable coincidence," Bishop repeated.

"Probably." Monroe took a deep breath and nodded. "Now, what did Elise have to say about the symbols?"

Bishop looked at this watch. "We can call her now and find out together." Bishop took out his phone, put it on speaker, and set it in the middle of the desk.

After two rings, a voice said, "Doctor Aldridge."

"Doctor, Matthew Bishop here together with Walker Monroe, my colleague. In your email, you said I could call you around this time for your results on the symbols."

"Yes, Matthew, hi, and hi to Mr. Monroe. A pleasure to meet you."

"The pleasure's all mine, and please call me Walker."

"Walker it is. I'm Elise.... The writing, yes. Well, of course, I didn't have much time to look at it, but with the previous knowledge of the mummy's DNA, so to say, I'm ninety-nine percent sure that more than half of the new strings are also human DNA."

"More than half of it?" Bishop repeated.

"Yes, well, as you know, there were thirty-two signs, so I first filtered out the other twenty-eight of which I have no idea what they are."

"I understand," Bishop replied. "When you say it's human, you mean the same as the mummy's? I mean, with the same deformities?"

"Again, for the most part, I do believe so, yes. Although I must say that I'm becoming less sure that they are indeed deformities."

"How's that?" Bishop asked.

"Well, the cells described in the DNA code don't have all the traits of abnormalities. It's hard to explain, but, umm...."

"Maybe you shouldn't *explain*, but just tell us what it means," Monroe said, tilting his head to Bishop.

"All right," Elise responded. "It looks like the cells in this DNA could be exactly as they were meant to be."

"So no accidental abnormalities?" Bishop asked.

"I don't think so, but it's still a possibility," Elise answered. "I'm planning to look into it further, but that's going to take a while."

"Let me see if I get this straight," Bishop said. "If the DNA is deliberately so, then there are no deformities on the mummy's body? Everything is exactly as it should be... umm... on purpose?"

"Like in evolution?" Monroe added.

"I've no idea," Elise responded. "I can only tell you what I scientifically see in the DNA. But there's still much more research to be done."

"But if I understand correctly, and your conclusions also prove to be correct, we're talking about a new kind of human?"

"Different would be a better term. I cannot determine if Ata's a newer or older version of regular humans. So, *different* would be better, for now."

"Cool," Monroe replied. "And you have no idea how or why? I mean. Is this through some kind of natural process or what?"

"I really can't say yet, and I'm not sure if I will be able to ever tell for sure, with the limited data at hand."

"Elise," Bishop asked, "could it still be that the changes are created from exposure to radiation?"

Elise took a deep breath. "Well, I doubt it, but I can't be sure. If so, it wouldn't be a first-generation change. I mean, the changes I see suggest they were traded through at least two generations of humans."

The door to Monroe's Beinecke chamber swung open, and Jennifer walked in. "Did I miss anything?" she asked.

"Shh!" Monroe put a finger to his lips, and she sat down quietly.

"Anything else, Elise?" Bishop asked.

"Not for now."

"All right," Bishop replied, "Thank you for your intriguing work so far. Please keep us informed on anything else you find."

"Will do. It is indeed intriguing work. I'll send my findings to your email address and talk to you later." With a click through the phone's speaker, the call ended.

"That *is* interesting," Monroe said.

"What did she find?" Jennifer asked.

Monroe cleared his throat. "She thinks Ata might not be a deformed child, but rather a different kind of human species."

"You heard her," Bishop took over. "It could still be from exposure to radiation through generations of humans. If someone was exposed in '57 at the age of twenty, and gave birth herself twenty years later...."

"That's '77," Monroe counted.

"...And who had another child twenty years later," Bishop continued.

"That's '97," Monroe concluded. "Still fits."

"So it could be that Ata, after all, still was the product of radiation exposure," Jennifer concluded.

"Sure," Monroe said. "But we forget one thing. Unlike the Kyshtym Dwarf, Ata was found in the Atacama Desert thousands of miles from the nearest radiation source. I know that doesn't prove everything, but still...."

"I agree," Bishop said. "That would be quite a travel, especially for a tiny mummy." He grinned.

"What do we do now?" Jennifer asked.

"Let's have a look at the other twenty-eight signs," Bishop replied. "Let's see if we can make any sense of them."

"Twenty-eight signs?" Jennifer asked.

"We're going to be here a while," Monroe said. "Coffee, anyone?"

CHAPTER 16

The Rosetta Stone

Yale, New Haven, CT

"So, what are your thoughts?" Monroe took a sip from his coffee while working his laptop to switch on the flatscreen hanging on the wall. "You already send me the file?" he asked Bishop.

Bishop nodded. "You should have it."

"Ah, here it is." Pages full of signs immediately appeared on the big screen. "Why do you think whoever's behind the signs wrote out the DNA? I mean, why not store it in actual DNA, as those two scientists did with Shakespeare's sonnets? Look at all the signs or characters needed to show a tiny bit of DNA."

"I'm not sure," Bishop said. "I know that, at this moment, DNA as a storage medium has enormous potential because of its high storage density, but its practical use is far from ideal. Reading and writing times are extremely slow, and you have to harvest the DNA and 'grow' it, so to say, to make it readable. Not to speak of the extreme costs. Besides all that, the potential reader would first need to figure out the fact that he was looking at DNA. I mean, with written signs, you automatically would know what to do: try to translate or decode. What would you do if you found a dust particle on another planet? How would you know to search in it for DNA?"

"You're talking aliens now." Jennifer grinned.

Bishop shook his head. "I'm just saying that making it visible to the naked eye... writing seems like the most sensible thing to do if you wanted to convey a message. By the way, while you were getting coffee, I had some prints made." Bishop gave both of them a stack of stapled papers. "On these papers are all the signs that Elise could not relate to as possible strings of DNA."

"And the same on the screen?" Monroe asked.

"Yes, may I?" Bishop asked, pointing at the laptop.

Monroe turned the laptop to Bishop, who worked the keyboard and mouse for the next few minutes.

"I've logged into my account, and ran some decoding algorithms on parts of signs, but nothing so far. As you can see, it's still working one of the more complex algorithms right now."

On the top half of the screen, a bright yellow cursor ran across the signs, while on the lower part, words—sometimes looking like English—appeared.

"When one of the algorithms finds a string of three consecutive English words, it will flag it as a possible match," Bishop continued. "To be honest, this could take days, weeks, or maybe even months. Even then, we might not be sure of the outcome."

"We're not even sure if the signs are some kind of alphabetic, polysynthetic, or logographic language?" Jennifer asked.

"To name a few," Monroe said. "There are far more forms of writing and combinations possible when you look at it from a historical perspective. Ancient languages like cuneiform or hieroglyphs are structured completely different from modern languages. For example, Inuktitut, a Canadian Inuit language, is a polysynthetic language. Words are composed of many morphemes that have independent meaning but may or may not stand alone. Did you know about half the world uses a primarily logographic or mixed writing system? You know, a picture for every word?."

"Like Chinese, Mandarin, Wu, Yue, and Min," Bishop stated.

"Exactly," Monroe concurred. "But also Japanese, Ancient Egyptian, Mayan, and partial Arabic and Hebrew use symbols for consonants and leave the reader to fill in the vowels."

"Can your algorithm also translate the signs if they're in any other form than alphabetic?" Jennifer asked.

"In part," Bishop replied. "But there are more algorithms available where this one came from. It's always a question of time. Unfortunately, we don't know how much time we are talking about. When I get back to my office, I'll dedicate some computer power to it, and continuously work on decoding the signs. Still, the question remains: was someone trying to hide something behind some kind of code, or is someone trying to tell us something?"

"What we need is a Rosetta stone," Monroe said. "You remember?"

A few years ago, the three of them had visited the British Museum and took a brief look at the Granodiorite Stele—Rosetta Stone. The stone dated back to 196 BC, when King Ptolemy V Epiphanes—during the Ptolemaic Dynasty—in Memphis sent out a decree in both Egyptian

Hieroglyphic, Demotic script, and ancient Greek. Because the stone held the same decree in three languages, the Rosetta Stone became key to deciphering the Egyptian writings.

"That would come in handy now," Bishop replied.

"I'm afraid there's never a Rosetta stone when you need one," Monroe joked.

Jennifer rose from her chair, tore the papers loose from the staple, and placed them in rows in front of her on the desk. Then she took a step back and stared at them with her left eye closed, while squinting through the other.

"What are you doing?" Monroe asked.

Jennifer didn't answer. She took another step back, looked left, then slowly turned right, and squinted again, keeping her eyes focused on the papers.

"What is she doing?" Monroe asked Bishop, who shrugged.

For minutes she gazed over the papers. "A pen!" she suddenly ordered, reaching with her hand open while keeping her eyes focused on the papers.

Without her looking at it, Bishop put a pen in her hand.

While focused and holding her breath, she bent over and started putting vertical dashes between groups of signs. She drew on the papers for a minute, then raised herself again and exhaled loudly.

"What was that all about?" Monroe asked while Jennifer sat down.

A tiny grin appeared on her face. "Would it help if we could differentiate between letters and numbers?"

Both men now cocked their heads and frowned.

"Not every language has numbers," Monroe stated with a frozen frown. "In a more historical sense, numerically fixated people like us are the uncommon ones. For the large part, in humans' two-hundred-thousand-year lifespan, we didn't even use numbers. Even today, we have over seven thousand languages in use, and some of them don't have any numbers in them. Like the Munduruku and Pirahã in Amazonia, some of them have only two exact numbers in their alphabet."

"Walker!" Bishop spoke. "You're babbling, lecturing again."

"She asked," Monroe defended himself.

Jennifer shook her head. "I asked if it would help if we could separate the numbers from the letters."

"Sure it would," Bishop said. "But how? What did you see?"

"I think I did more than just separate them. I think I found the Rosetta Stone for the numbers in the text itself."

"What? How? Where?" Monroe asked, looking at the scribbles she put on the paper.

"Patterns." Jennifer pointed at the sections of signs between her dashes. "Can you put one on the screen for me?"

"Which one?" Monroe asked.

"Doesn't matter." She grinned. "I believe they're all the same."

"Fascinating," Bishop uttered.

"Patterns," Jennifer said. "Patterns in the Christmas tree."

"What?" Bishop uttered.

"How?" Monroe added.

"Did you ever hang the Christmas lights in the tree with your parents?" Jennifer eyed the two sightly confused men. "How would you check if the lights were evenly distributed?"

"Just put them on, I guess," Monroe said.

Bishop cocked his head, frowned for a second, and said, "Like looking at snake trails in books. That's what you were doing right now." Jennifer gave a bright smile while Bishop heavily nodded. "What pattern did you see?"

"Will someone please tell me what you two are talking about?" Monroe demanded.

"Sure," Jennifer replied. "My dad taught me that when we'd put the lights in the Christmas tree, I should put the lights on in a dark room, take some distance, and look at it through my squinted eyelids. If the lights were equally distributed, the tree would evenly light up, in a constant pattern, so to say. If not, there would be gaps in the pattern where the tree would have dark spots."

"The same works for books," Bishop added. "When you look at a page in a book while squinting, the characters will disappear, and patterns will emerge. Snake trails are white curving lines that appear on the page and are made up of spaces that run in a pattern from top to bottom."

Monroe rose from behind his desk, took a step back, and squinted while looking at the desk. After a few seconds, he gave a deep sigh. "I see what you mean. The pattern begins and ends where you put your dashes." He opened his eyes again.

"Can you put one on the screen for me?" Jennifer repeated.

"Ah, yes, sorry." Monroe sat down and worked his laptop, and on the screen appeared a large string of signs.

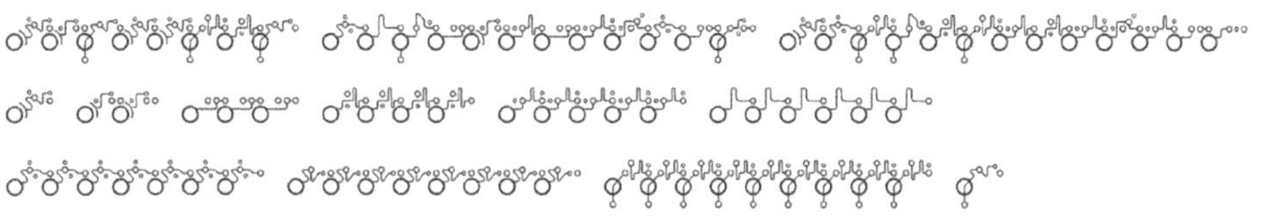

"Seventy-nine characters, eighty-nine including spaces," Monroe read from the bottom of the screen.

"Excellent," Jennifer said. "Now, take a good look."

"You said the Rosetta Stone was in the fragment?" Bishop asked.

Jennifer nodded. "Uh-huh."

Monroe shifted on his seat and raised two hands in the air. "Can we please stop the riddles and get on with it?"

"All right." Jennifer walked up to the screen. "The fragment is nicely lined up. Now, this part—" She pointed at the top row. "—we need to decode, but these next two, I believe, are the Rosetta Stone for the top row."

"I believe you're right," Bishop said.

"It's unbelievable, but I think I see it too," Monroe added. "They are numbers, and the number one is pictured with one sign, the number two with two signs and the number three...."

Jennifer ran a finger along the series of numbers until she came to the last, single sign.

"Zero?" Bishop asked.

Jennifer shrugged. "Maybe."

Monroe meticulously looked at the signs again. "But why such a simple one-on-one translation matrix?"

Bishop gave a tiny grin. "I guess the answer to that question will reveal whether someone is trying to tell us something or trying to hide it from us. If you wanted to hide something from someone, this would be a much too easy way to do it."

"So someone wants to tell us something," Monroe concluded. "In that case, what do the numbers say?"

Jennifer grinned. "Do I have to do all the work here?"

"Ah, sorry, let me see." Monroe worked his laptop again while Bishop rose from his chair and squinted at the papers on the desk to see if he could find any other patterns.

"Anything?" Jennifer asked after a minute.

Bishop shook his head. "Nothing. The rest of it seems random."

Jennifer nodded. "Much in the same way that it would look if I were to spread random book pages on the table, I think."

"Here we go," Monroe called out as a row of numbers with some question marks in between them appeared below a row of signs on the screen.

76?32?35?7?? 179?49?45?5?? 12011940

"I'm afraid not all the signs could be related to a number." He pointed at the question marks. "Now, what are we looking at?"

For a minute, the three were completely silent, gazing at the screen.

A deep female sigh broke the silence. "Did you ask Google?" Jennifer asked.

Monroe frowned.

"Why not?" Bishop asked.

Monroe raised his shoulders before copying the sequence and pasting it into the Google search bar. Immediately after he pressed enter, links appeared to pages about numbers, a geological survey water supply paper, an energy band period limits, and a bibliography of the physical equilibria.

"That can't be it," Bishop said.

"What if you replace the question marks with points," Jennifer suggested.

Again Monroe filled in the search bar and pressed enter.

'Your search - 76.32.35.7.. 179.49.45.5.. 12011940 - did not match any documents.'

"What if we look at the grouping of the numbers?" Bishop suggested. "We have three groups."

"The first two look a little like computer IP numbers," Monroe hinted.

"And IP addresses lead to locations, don't they?" Jennifer asked.

"Nice one," Bishop said.

Monroe worked his keyboard. "The first one leads to a location in the Cheney Reservoir in Kansas." He continued typing. "The second one leads to a place called Cuenca in Ecuador. Do these two seem like suitable locations to any of you?"

They all shrugged, frowned, and again the room fell completely silent for a while.

Bishop, after a long moment, broke the silence and pointed at Monroe's laptop. "May I?"

"Sure." Monroe shoved the computer to his friend, who started typing. "You have an idea?"

Bishop stayed focused on the screen.

For three minutes, the only sound in the room was that of the laptop's clicking keys, and Jennifer and Monroe watched his hands on the keyboard.

"There!" Bishop yelled, startling the other two. "How do I get this to the screen?"

Monroe reached for the laptop, and in a second, the image appeared on the screen.

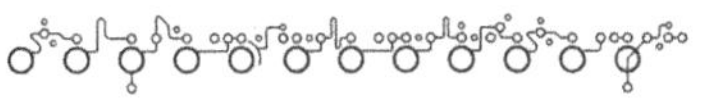
76°32'35.7"S

179°49'45.5"W

12011940

"What are we looking at?" Jennifer asked.

"I figured, what if the first two are indeed indicating a location, but not as an IP address but as regular coordinates."

"Good idea," Jennifer said. "But do these coordinates lead to a sensible location?"

Bishop shrugged. "Can you find out?" he asked Monroe.

"Sure, the simplest way is to feed them to Google again." He copied the numbers to the search bar and hit enter. Immediately on the screen, a large blue rectangle appeared with a red teardrop sign in the center.

"Where's that?" Jennifer asked.

"Looks like the middle of an ocean," Monroe answered.

"Can you zoom out?" Bishop asked.

Monroe clicked the image and slowly started to widen the area. It took a while before, at the bottom of the screen, a jagged white coastline appeared. In gray text on the white expanse, a word appeared.

"Antarctica?" Bishop spoke.

"The South Pole," Monroe confirmed. "The exact location is in the Southern Ocean, a few miles of the ice coast."

"That makes *a lot* more sense than the other two locations," Jennifer said, nodding.

"It does?" Monroe asked.

"It doesn't," Jennifer explained.

"Sarcasm," Monroe muttered. "Now, what about that other number, 12011940? What could that be? Wait," he stopped for a second. "Could that be a date?"

"December first, nineteen-forty," Jennifer read, and Monroe immediately started searching, and as the results appeared on the screen, he read out loud: "'Greek troops captured Pogradec,' 'The last of the three worst nights of the Southampton Blitz occurred,' 'Manuel Ávila Camacho became 45th President of Mexico,' 'Allied convoy HX 90 was sighted by German submarine U-101,' and 'Richard Pryor was born in Peoria, Illinois.' Any thoughts?"

"Nothing related to Cuenca, Ecuador, the Cheney reservoir in Kansas, or Antarctica, I think," Bishop answered.

"The Germans were in Antarctica at the time, I believe," Jennifer added.

"But I doubt the allied convoy met a German submarine over there," Bishop replied.

"So, no date?" Jennifer asked.

"Wait a second," Monroe came back. "You Americans put the day behind the month. So the date would read December 1. We Europeans, including Russians, would write 1 December. Which would make the date..."

"The twelfth of January," Jennifer and Bishop spoke in choir.

"Already ahead of you." Monroe worked the laptop and started reading again. "'The Danish tanker Danmark was torpedoed and sunk by the German submarine U-23 off the Orkney Islands,' 'The horror science fiction film The Invisible Man Returns was released.'"

"A classic," Bishop interrupted.

Monroe continued speedily while shaking his head. "'NBC initiated its first network television programming,' and...." He slowed down his reading. "'Admiral Byrd landed with two ships and a total of hundred and twenty-five men at the Weddell Sea and the Ross Ice Shelf on the South Pole for his third Antarctic Service Expedition.'" He skillfully worked the laptop again, and as the image of the Antarctic reappeared, he zoomed in on the coordinates they found.

"Ross Sea," Bishop read from the screen where the red teardrop was placed.

"But the text spoke of a Ross Ice Shelf," Jennifer said. "This location is in the middle of the ocean."

Monroe zoomed out again. Where the white ice of the Antarctic on the bottom of the screen appeared, it read 'Ross Ice Shelf.'

"Figures," Bishop said. "The location is now placed in the ocean because of the ice that melted or broke off over the years."

"All good and well, but," Monroe stammered. "What has an Antarctic expedition to do with a drill on the North Pole, mummies with strange DNA, weird signs in sheets of metal, and in writing from a crazy old woman?"

Bishop looked at his watch. "All valid questions, but they have to wait for later today. I have an appointment in my office. Can we meet over there in... let's say... two hours?"

"No problem." Jennifer smiled. "I can use the time to do some actual work myself."

"I have some time to spare, and will keep looking for connections," Monroe said. "I'll meet you later in your office."

"Great," Bishop said. "See you then and there. I wonder where this is going."

CHAPTER 17

The Shadow

The Ross Ice Shelf, Antarctica, January 19, 1940

From a distance, a group of thousands of Adélie penguins watched Little America Three, and got startled for a second as Simons fired up the Antarctic Snow Cruiser's engines. Every day for the past week, Simons had run the two, ten-liter diesel engines for five minutes, to make sure everything ran smoothly and nothing would freeze up, doing permanent damage.

The camp consisted of rows of tents neatly placed upon the ice, each tent reinforced with two dozen guy ropes attached to two-feet-long guy-outs driven deep into the ice. That way, the frequently gushing winds would not blow them away. In the past week, the weather had been in their favor. Fair winds and bright sunny skies had kept the temperature at an average of forty-three degrees Fahrenheit.

"How are you holding up?" Poulter asked Simons as he sat down at the Cruiser's chart table. "Join me." He patted on the bench.

Simons tilted his head and pouted his mouth as he climbed down from the driving chair and sat down on the bench. "Well, I gotta admit that living in daylight twenty-four-seven kind of gets to you, but otherwise...."

"Most people get used to it after two weeks max, or they never will," Poulter replied.

"I feel lucky I can sleep in the Cruiser. I heard the tents are not very light-tight, and most people sleep with blindfolds on."

"That's true," Poulter said. "And we have three months of daylight left before it gets dark for half a year. What do you think?" He spread out a map of the Antarctic on the Cruiser's table.

"I think we're ready to go, sir," Simons replied. "We've been here for a week now, and we've only driven ten feet forward and back every day now. The Cruiser's proven she can withstand the cold, and McConnel and I think we've plotted some great routes over the ice to research."

Poulter pointed at the map. "All right, then, show me."

Simons took out a pen, wrote the numbers one, two, and three on the map, and drew a line between the two and the three.

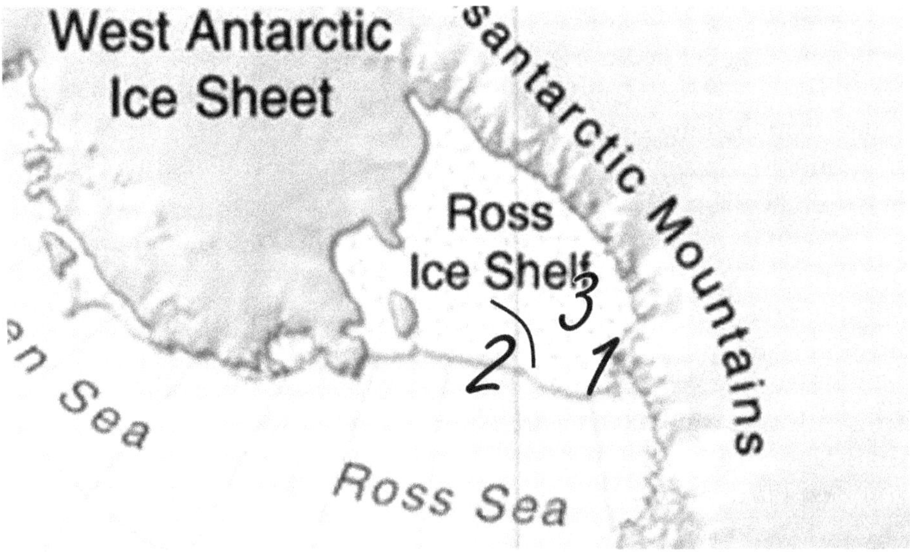

He pointed at the one. "Here we are, sir. And around three, we checked out the smoke plumes we saw earlier this week, you remember?"

Poulter nodded.

"We believe it was from Mount Erebus, sir, the volcano Sir James Clark Ross discovered on his Antarctic expedition in 1841. The active volcano spits out smoke all the time. Usually, the sea wind takes it land-inwards, so we can't see it from Little America."

"I see you did your homework, son. And you think it's worth checking it out?"

"Well, sir, I spoke to some of the geologists. They would love to get samples from the volcano and the nearby mountain."

"Mount Terror," Poulter said. "Named after Clark Ross's ship, the HMS Terror."

"From the air, it doesn't seem that terrifying, sir. I think we can take one of the geologists with us and get there without much trouble."

"All right, and what's that number two?" Poulter asked, pointing at the map again.

"Good question, sir. We made several passes, but it seems like there's a dark shadow below the ice, as if something is frozen into it."

"Could that be parts of Franklin's lost expedition?"

"I'm sorry, sir?"

"Captain Sir John Franklin departed from England in 1845 on the HMS Erebus and HMS Terror. There's little known about what happened, but none of the hundred and twenty-nine men were heard from ever again. I wonder if what you see below the ice could be the remnants of that expedition?"

"Maybe, sir, but from the sky, that shadow appears to be more of a square than the long shape of a ship."

Poulter took a deep breath. "Doesn't matter now. Good work. How long will the drive take to Mount Erebus?"

"About a full day, sir, and another to the shadow, and another back to camp."

"Sounds like a plan. Oh, and what's that line between the two and three?" Poulter pointed at the map.

"That's a steep ridge, sir. I'm not sure we can pass that with the Cruiser. If not, we'll have to drive around it and add another day to the trip."

"Sounds doable."

Simons nodded.

"All right, then," Poulter continued enthusiastically. "How long will it take for you to load up the Cruiser for a five-day trip?"

"We're going, sir?" Simons gave a tiny smile.

"I think those two are excellent locations to check out."

"I can have her ready and fully stocked by tomorrow morning. If we leave early, we'll be at Mount Erebus by the end of the day."

"Please make it so, son."

"Who will come?" Simons asked.

"You and me, of course. We'll also take the plane, so we need a pilot. You ask Dougal McConnel, and please pick one of the geologists. Your choice."

"Thank you, sir, for the trust." Simons smiled from ear to ear.

"No problem. We leave after breakfast at eight." Simons nodded while Poulter climbed out of the vehicle.

"I'll have her ready, sir," Simons shouted after him.

***

Though Simons went to bed early that night, he slept very little. During that night, his mind wandered off into dreams where he and his colleagues took the Atlantic Snow Cruiser and ran it off a cliff, fell through the ice with it, or drove off the shelf and sunk to the bottom of the Antarctic Ocean. After each dream, he had woken up bathed in sweat. The last time had been around 5:00 AM, when he decided to get up. He woke the small group of soldiers he'd recruited the day before, to help him get the Cruiser ready.

Now, at 6:30, the soldiers were finalizing the slope they created from snow and ice, and they piled up against the rear of the Cruiser. The slope would serve as a ramp to load the Eagle—the Beechcraft 17 Staggerwing biplane—onto the Cruiser.

"How's your Turtle holding up?" A tiny black-haired man, dressed in khakis and a brown leather jacket with a fur collar, walked up to Simons as he checked the tire pressure.

"Morning, Dougal," Simons replied. "She's doing okay, I think."

McConnel lit up a cigarette and offered one to Simons.

"No, thanks, I quit just over a year ago now."

"What do you mean by okay?" McConnel asked.

"Last night, I took her out for a final test spin, but she had little to no traction. The air must have been extremely damped, freezing up the ice and making it extremely slippery."

"What did you do?"

Simons slapped the back tire of the Cruiser. "I had the soldiers slap under two extra tires at the back. She now has two tires on each side. Together with the extra weight of your plane on top, she should have all the traction she needs to get us underway."

"I just hope we won't fall through the ice," McConnel replied.

Simons laughed out loud. "I heard the ice is over a thousand feet thick and at some places even over two-thousand, so...."

McConnel laughed back now. "Great. Now, when do you think we can go?" He pointed at the snow ramp at the back of the Cruiser.

"Sergeant!" Simons shouted at one of the men working on the ramp.

"In a minute, sir," the sergeant shouted back, raising a thumb.

"All right," McConnel said, walking off. "I'll get the Eagle."

As the sergeant and his men stepped away from the slope a minute later, a roar emerged in the otherwise quiet early morning. Seconds later, McConnel's biplane materialized from behind a row of tents and drove up to the Cruiser, leaving a trail of snow, blowing up behind the plane.

"That should get everybody up and awake," Simons heard a dark voice behind him say.

"Burt, good morning," Simons replied.

Burt Kippler, a tall, slightly heavyset man with a prominent reddish beard, was the geologist Simons had selected for the mission. Simons had to choose out of five specialists, and, knowing nothing about geology, he'd chosen Burt because he was a nice guy... and the only one he'd been able to beat during a card game days before.

"Are you ready?" Simons asked.

Burt raised a small duffel bag and dangled it in front of Simons. "Kind of anxious to get underway."

"That's everything you're taking with you?"

"This is my personal stuff. All professional gear is already loaded."

"All right. Great."

"Morning," a loud voice sounded, and Poulter, fully dressed for the occasion in warm khakis, joined them. "Everything okay?"

"I think so, sir," Simons shouted over the sound of the nearing Eagle's engines. "I'll be right back." Simons swiftly climbed onto the Cruisers roof and, standing on top of it, waved both arms at McConnel, who drove his plane onto the ramp.

"Keep it coming, straight ahead," Simons shouted.

Not that McConnel could hear him, but his symmetrical waving arms led him to believe he could keep McConnel on a straight path. Slowly but surely, the eagle drove up the forty-foot ramp and onto the Cruiser.

"Keep her coming." Simons walked backward to the front of the Cruiser as the plane drove off the ramp and onto the back of the truck. He then shouted while crossing his arms.

McConnel immediately hit the brakes, and the aircraft stopped. Seconds later, the engine stopped, and McConnel got out under loud applause from a group of expedition members gathered around the Cruiser. "All right, let's tie her up," he shouted while throwing a stack of rope in Simons' direction.

A few minutes later, Simons and McConnel climbed off the Cruiser and joined Poulter and Kippler.

McConnel smiled. "You realize that the four of us have to shovel a new ramp when we need to take her off?"

They all laughed.

"Everyone ready to get on our way?" Poulter asked.

"Ready."

"Everything's loaded, sir."

"Good to go."

"All right, then," Poulter almost yelled. "Everyone throw in your gear, and let's make some miles."

They all loaded their gear and entered the Cruiser except for Poulter and Kippler, who had decided to ride on the roof and enjoy the sun until they lost sight of Little America Three.

Simons waved at the audience from the side window, pushed down on the throttle, and the Cruiser's engines roared above the ice shelf. He released the clutch and the massive vehicle slowly rolled into motion. Simons sounded the horn, casting a ten-second long blast over the ice, and he spectators cheered and applauded as the Cruiser drove off. Simons planked the throttle, but the vehicle picked up little speed. He opened the window and shouted at Poulter.

"Can you see what's happening out there?"

Poulter leaned over the vehicle's side, and Simons waited for a response.

"There seems to be little traction," Poulter shouted back.

Simons picked a lower gear and cautiously lowered his foot again. Then he started to mumble as he read from one of the few meters on the huge dashboard. "Five, six, seven, eight, nine, ten." Then he stopped when the meter did.

"What's going on?" McConnel asked, lying flat on his belly on the roof and leaning into the driver-side window.

Simons pushed some levers before answering. "It seems we lose traction when the engine hits over two thousand RPM."

"What does that mean?" McConnel asked.

Simons shook his head. "What it means is that we won't be able to drive speeds over ten miles an hour."

"Even though I designed her to drive over thirty," Poulter replied, listening in from the roof.

"How can this happen, Captain?" McConnel asked.

"The ice," Poulter said. "Because of the humid air, the snow on the ice freezes up at night, creating an ice-skating rink the size of France."

"And we're sliding our way to our destination while our wheels turn twice as fast as we're moving forward," Simons added.

"What now?" Kippler asked.

"Let's see if I can make an estimate on fuel consumption with current speed and efficiency." Poulter took a piece of paper and pencil from his fur jacket, licked the tip of the pencil, and mumbled as he started writing. "Two times... by four... makes thirty-two...." He raised his head towards the sky.

"And?" Simons asked.

"We use a lot more diesel than we anticipated, but we should be able to make it with over a third of the diesel left when we return."

"*If* we return," Kippler added.

"Not so somber, Burt." McConnel patted him hard on the shoulder.

"How are we on food?" Poulter asked.

"We've stocked enough for about a week," Simons answered. "Ten days if we ration."

"That won't be necessary," Poulter said. "Even at the current speed, we'll be back in five days, and I trust the weather conditions will change." He pointed at a few light clouds in the sky. "When it starts snowing again, we'll pick up traction again and double or triple our speed. You're up to it?"

"Yeah," Simons said, sounding the horn again.

"I say we do it," McConnel added.

"Hmm," Burt uttered.

"Then let's do this," Poulter shouted.

The seventy-five-thousand-pound Cruiser slowly drove out of sight of Little America Three on its way to Mount Erebus.

CHAPTER 18

The Descendant

Yale, New Haven, CT, The Present

Monroe leveled a loud bang on Bishop's office door.

"Yes?" Bishop's voice sounded almost agitated.

Monroe drew a face at Jennifer before they stepped in.

"Wow," Jennifer uttered.

"What the hell happened here?" Monroe said, stroking his face with both hands. The usually sterile-looking office now lay covered with papers all over the floor, and the furniture was turned over. The bookcase behind the desk sat almost empty, with the books now scattered around on the floor. The only things left standing were a one-foot-square showcase on a chrome metal pole, and the desk. Strangely enough, the bureau was empty and sparkling with only a laptop in the center and a chair behind it.

"I cleaned that one already," Bishop said upon spotting Monroe looking at the desk.

"The place was broken into?" Jennifer suggested.

Bishop nodded.

"Any idea what they came for? Did they take anything?" Monroe asked.

Bishop shrugged. "They took my laptop. This is my spare." He pointed at the one on the desk. "For the rest, there's only grading papers and books in here. Nothing of interest, I would think."

"And the laptop?" Jennifer asked. "Anything of value on that? Maybe about our latest... umm... endeavors?"

"It's my regular work laptop, password-protected. And besides that, all my data is stored in the cloud. I've already changed my password and revoked access to it from this laptop, so no risk there. I came here to set up the decoding algorithm, which runs on the server, so that's no problem either. I finished that, by the way."

"Finished what?" Jennifer asked.

"Setting up the algorithm on the server. It's running now, but as I said, it could be days, weeks, months, or maybe forever."

"Hmm." Jennifer cleared her throat. "It could be simple vandalism or theft."

"You really believe that?" Monroe asked when Bishop hesitantly nodded.

"Truth be told," Bishop said. "I'm getting the feeling this case has drawn more attention than we're aware off. And looking at this mess, I'm getting the feeling they aren't the cooperating types, if you know what I mean."

"Hey," Jennifer said, "at least they left this one straight up." She pointed at the glass showcase with the leather-bound book.

"You remember that one?" Bishop asked.

"Sure, the Voynich Manuscript. You told me about it when we first met. It's the book written in a language no one has been able to translate, with illustrations of plants and animals that have also never been identified. You told me a close friend of yours—" She eyed Monroe. "—gave you the copy while the original was in his library." She grinned. "Did you ever run it through your algorithm?"

"I did, for years—through all kinds of algorithms, but nothing ever came up. I'm more and more convinced it's just a fake book, a hoax made to confuse and keep those who would find it busy for years."

"In that case, it worked," Monroe added.

"Do you mind?" Jennifer asked, pointing at a chair buried underneath the papers.

"Sure," Bishop said.

Both Jennifer and Monroe dug up a chair, and they sat down.

"Did you call Campus Security?" Monroe asked.

"They'll be here later today. I'm to leave everything as it is. I doubt they'll find anything, though. That's okay. I'm just not looking forward to cleaning up this mess."

"We'll help you when Security is finished here," Jennifer offered while looking at Monroe. When the Brit stayed silent, she gave him an elbow.

"Sure, we will," Monroe abruptly agreed. "What do we do now? You wanna know what I found out?"

Bishop shook his head a few times rapidly, then nodded. "Yes, sure, tell me."

"Tell *us*," Jennifer added.

***

Some thirty feet from Bishop's window, on a bench on College Street's sidewalk, Nadya pretended to be reading Tolstoy's *War and Peace* while listening to Bishop's conversation. Some time ago, she'd placed a small microphone on the bottom of the Voynich Manuscript's showcase after searching his office. And now she could listen without standing out, just another young woman reading a book in the daily campus street scene.

***

"The Ross Ice shelf." Monroe took a small tablet computer from his jacket. "First reported by the British polar explorer James Clark Ross."

"A Brit, of course." Bishop smiled.

"Of course," Monroe confirmed. "Anyway, about five hundred miles wide and up to two hundred feet high, the ice shelf is what it sounds like. A huge chunk of landlocked ice, fed by glaciers and ice streams that run from the land into the sea. The glaciers feed the shelf where a huge ice barrier rises to three hundred feet high above the shelf itself. Although the barrier seems stationary, it grows, but also melts and refreezes again, as part of the ice shelf, slowly moving the shelf north."

"Wait a minute!" Jennifer said. "I thought you said before that the ice shelf had shrunk over the years, and that's why the coordinates of the 1940 mission were now in the ocean."

"Well, it seems the ice shelf itself melts faster than it can grow."

"Figures," Bishop added.

"It says here that the net effect is about minus forty-seven to eighty-seven inches a year, and the shelf ranges in different spots from a thousand to almost three thousand feet thick."

"Sounds like a place you don't want to be," Jennifer said. "What about the 1940 expedition with the admiral? What's his name?"

"Byrd," Monroe answered. "Rear Admiral Richard Evelyn Byrd Jr., to be precise." He read from the screen. "Byrd, together with his non-military counterpart, a Doctor James Poulter, was sent by Roosevelt on a both scientific as well as military expedition. In 1939, Hitler presented a four-year plan to have Germany completely self-sufficient in both military and economic aspects by 1944. One of the ways to achieve this was to gain control over the whale hunt."

"Whales?" Jennifer asked.

"Apparently, in the late 1930s, Germany and Britain purchased about thirty-eight percent of all the world's whale harvest. They used the fat to wage war those days. At first, they used it as fuel, but with the invention of kerosene, they started using it to create the margarine that Hitler needed to keep his troops fit. In liquefied form, the blubber served as a potent machine lubricant for tanks, and it was used in manufacturing nitroglycerine explosives too. Britain by then, in 1938, had declared it a national defense product. At that time, most of the whales were bought from Norway, who hunted the whales along the unclaimed Antarctic coastline. By sending troops to claim the Antarctic, the Germans planned to gain exclusive access to those waters, in order to disrupt the Norwegian flow of whales to other countries, keeping all the resources to themselves. That's why, in '38, Göring approved the plan to create a settlement called 'New Schwabenland.' The claim served two purposes: that of the exclusive whale hunt; and to test his war-machine engines at low temperatures. I guess they were anticipating a Russian invasion even back then."

"And did they succeed?" Jennifer asked.

"In a way," Monroe continued. "Just before the Germans arrived in the Antarctic, the Norwegians had claimed the territory for themselves. However, that didn't stop the Germans from staking a new claim on the same stretch of land and ice. They flew Nazi seaplanes over ten-thousand miles of unexplored Antarctic land, where they dropped thousands of four-and-a-half-foot darts, inscribed with swastikas, bordering their 'New Schwabenland.'"

"When was this?" Bishop asked.

"Umm...." Monroe worked his laptop. "January 14, 1939."

"Hmm...." Bishop shrugged. "We always assumed World War II started on September 1, 1939, but in a way, you could say that it started almost nine months before that, when Germany annexed a piece of land that belonged to the Norwegians."

"Except for the fact that the Norwegians didn't fight for it, I guess you're right."

"Wow," Jennifer replied. "But besides watching the Germans, what was Byrd doing out there? And how does it relate to our findings?"

"Good question," Monroe said. "Unfortunately, I don't have a clear answer. Apparently, they also had geologists and biologists on board who researched the land and the animals. I found a list of animals they researched—many new species, by the way. They also brought back lots of rock samples, but no mention of anything weird or really out of the ordinary."

"Aren't there some kind of archives anywhere we can look at? Storage, perhaps?"

"The Smithsonian has a few things on the U.S. Antarctic Service Expedition, as it was called in those days, but that's all on botany. I skipped through that collection, but I don't think there's anything there. They also have one of Byrd's scrapbooks, but that doesn't go beyond his 1930 expedition. You have to know that, because of the start of World War II, the mission was called back early. I think much of the knowledge they brought back got lost in the hectic circumstances of that time."

"So, it's a dead end?" Bishop asked.

"Maybe not," Monroe answered. "As you would suspect, anyone who actually attended the Little America Three expedition is long gone, but—"

"I knew there'd be a 'but'." Bishop smiled.

"But...." Monroe grinned back. "I found on the internet a decade-old appeal in a local newspaper, in which a man claims that there were things kept secret about that Antarctic expedition. He urges anyone who knows anything to come forward with any kind of information they'd have. I can't find if anyone came forward."

"That's it?" Jennifer asked.

"That's about it, except for the fact that the man mentioned in the article claims to be the son of one of the original expedition members."

"And he's still alive?" Bishop asked.

Monroe nodded while smiling.

"Uh-oh," Jennifer said. "I see another trip coming."

"I guess we're in luck this time," Monroe replied. "He lives in a gated community in Wallingford. It's a twenty-minute drive if we take the I-91. If we leave now, we can be there and back before dinner."

Jennifer eyed Bishop, who tilted his head. "All right," she said. "What are we waiting for?"

"Don't you have to wait for Campus Security?" Monroe asked.

"They have a spare key to my office, so they can get in. I'll call them from the road to tell them I had to go. Your car?" Bishop asked Monroe.

He nodded. "I'm parked on High behind the library."

"What about your algorithm?" Jennifer asked Bishop as they got up to leave.

"It'll continue running when we're on route. If necessary, it'll run forever."

***

Nadya's three targets walked out of the building, and as they turned off College Street onto Wall, she jumped off the bench to follow them, waving *War and Peace* in her hand. After another minute, she watched them get into Monroe's Vauxhall Astra. "*Piz-dets* (Damn it)," she called out as she looked around to see if there were any cabs around.

Nothing.

She slapped the book on her leg.

***

"I still don't know how you can call this a car," Bishop complained, with his knees raised in front of his chest in order to fit Jennifer in the back behind him.

Monroe smiled. "This is one of the last UK-produced cars, and one of the few right-hand-drive versions you can buy over here. It's the least I can do for the home country, since I pay my taxes over here. Need I remind you that your Jeep doesn't have any seats in the back at all!"

"He's got you there," Jennifer said.

They laughed as he drove off, and twenty minutes later, they drove off the I-95 and onto the North Farms Road, where a large road sign said:

Welcome to the Estates at Wallingford – Wallingford, CT.

"This must be it." Jennifer pointed at the sign. "Did we miss the gate?"

"Yeah, I guess we missed it."

"Better," Jennifer said. "I always found there's something spooky about those communities. What's the number?"

"826," Monroe answered.

"Left here," Bishop said immediately, and Monroe instantly hit the brakes.

They looked left, where a three-foot-high, medieval-looking wall circumvented a vast lawn, with a paved road running neatly in the center of it.

"Wow," Jennifer muttered.

"Again, no gate," Bishop remarked.

"I guess that means we're welcome," Monroe said as he turned left and steered the car onto the driveway.

Thirty seconds later, the driveway took a slight turn left, and a large Tudor-styled mansion emerged with steeply pitched gable roofs, elaborate masonry chimneys with chimney pots, and decorative half-timbering.

"Wow, again," Jennifer said as Monroe stopped the car at the central, embellished doorway.

Bishop immediately got out of the car. "It is impressive." He stretched his body while Jennifer and Monroe also got out of the vehicle.

"I wonder if we're welcome," Jennifer said.

"I guess there's only one way to find out." Bishop walked up to the door and rang the bell.

A few seconds later, a middle-aged man opened the door.

"Good afternoon," Bishop said. "Are you Mr. Cooper?"

The man grinned. "No, I only work here. Can I help you?

"Well, we're looking for Mr. J. Cooper," Bishop said. "Does he live here, and is he available?"

"Are you journalists?" the man asked.

"Oh, no. Sorry, we're professors from Yale University, and we're researching an old Antarctic expedition Mr. Cooper's father was on. We'd like to ask him some questions about it."

"One moment please." The man turned and walked into the house, leaving the door open.

Jennifer put one foot over the threshold and inspected the hallway on the inside. "You know what this place reminds me of?"

Both men shook their heads.

"Did you ever see 'the Sopranos'? Their New Jersey home? It looks exactly like that." She must have spoken a little too loud.

"You know, I get that a lot," a deep man's voice sounded from the hallway.

"Oh, I'm sorry," Jennifer replied. "I didn't mean to imply—"

"No apologies necessary," the big man said as he approached. He had gray hair, mainly at the sides of his head, a big gray brush mustache. "I'm Jay Cooper, and yes, the Junior stayed even though I'm eighty-two."

The three of them now stared at the amazingly fit eighty-two man.

"You're from Yale and want to know about my father?"

"Yes, excuse us," Bishop said and introduced them. "We're doing some research on the Little America Three expedition, and we understand your father was a part of it. To be completely honest, you're the last living descendant of the expedition members we could find."

"How did you find me?"

Monroe gave a tiny smile. "I found you through an old local newspaper article, where you searched for information about the expedition yourself."

"Wow. But there must be more descendants out there," Cooper said. "Anyway, please come in." He waved them inside. "Let's sit down in the back yard. The weather is great, don't you think?"

They followed him through the house into the garden, where they sat down at a small table in front of a large swimming pool.

"Beautiful," Jennifer said.

"Thank you. Can I pour you some iced tea?" He raised a carafe and took a glass from a stack.

"Sure."

"Please."

"Yes, please."

"Now, what do you want to know?" Cooper asked as he poured them their drinks.

"Well, basically," Monroe said, "we want to know what you know about that specific mission to the Antarctic. What did your father tell you?"

The man chuckled. "My father didn't tell me anything. I never even met my father."

They all frowned.

"You see, my mother was already pregnant with me when my father took off, and he never returned from that mission."

"What happened?' Jennifer asked.

"To be honest, I thought you came here to talk to me about just that."

"What do you mean?" Bishop asked, sipping his tea.

The old man frowned. "As I said, my father never returned from that mission. From the moment I was old enough, I tried to find out what happened over there. My mother didn't know any specifics about my father's demise. I must have spoken to dozens of other expedition members and government officials over the years, but nothing concrete ever came of it."

"I take it your father died in Antarctica?" Monroe asked.

"That's the official version," Cooper said.

"But you don't believe that?" Bishop asked.

"Oh, I'm pretty convinced by now my father did die down there, but it's the circumstances—the how—that never became clear. You have to know that my father was the only one that didn't return from that expedition, and if someone had given me a reasonable explanation for it, I probably would have accepted it."

"But they didn't," Bishop concluded.

Cooper shook his head. "Most of them had conflicting stories, and that made me so suspicious of it. Some say he fell through the ice. Others say he got attacked by something. And again, others claimed he was killed by the military that was present because he discovered some dark secret."

"What did your father do on the expedition?" Monroe asked. "We know your father was on it, because of your appeal in the newspaper form years ago, but I've thoroughly searched through the lists with names of participants, and as far as I know, there was no Cooper."

"Hmm." Cooper chuckled. "When my father didn't return, my mother had me re-registered under her name. Simons... Jay Clemency Simons was my father's name. He was the driver of the Antarctic Snow Cruiser. Maybe you heard of it?"

"A little," Monroe answered.

"Well, it was a seventy-five-thousand-pound, huge expedition vehicle with a real plane on its back. The Cruiser was supposed to drive over the Antarctic Ross Shelf and over the land."

"Supposed?" Jennifer asked.

"Yes, well, most of the people I interviewed over the years reported that the Cruiser had been a failure and didn't perform that well. Others stated that the Cruiser went missing on its first exploration, and there were also reports of it breaking through the ice and sinking to the bottom of the ocean."

"The vehicle didn't return from the mission?" Bishop asked.

"Just like my father," Cooper answered. "There are reports, however, that the Cruiser was left behind and was spotted again on later expeditions."

"Is there anything specific that makes you suspicious about his demise?" Jennifer asked. "Other than the conflicting reports?"

"Back in the day, I spoke to another member of the expedition, a geologist.... What's his name? I can't remember.... Well, anyway, I once spoke to him on the phone, back in the nineties. He told me that there was much more to the story than the public was led to believe, but he wouldn't give me details over the phone. When days later I met him in person, he told me a story of how he, a pilot, along with the expedition leader and my father, got into an accident near Mount Erebus, and the Cruiser sank, taking my father with him."

"That doesn't sound like a story that needed to be kept from the public," Monroe remarked.

Cooper nodded. "Exactly what I told him, but he insisted that was everything there was to it."

"You think someone got to him?"

Cooper nodded again. "I always suspected so."

"What do you think happened?" Jennifer asked.

"Good question." He shrugged. "I must have spoken with over a hundred people on the subject, people who were directly involved in the expedition, and people with all kinds of theories on the area. Some claimed there are mysterious structures, arguing amongst themselves whether or not they were built by the Nazi Germans. Others spoke of mysterious holes and hollow Earth theories. Of course, nothing panned out, but I'm convinced there's more going on in the Antarctic than we know about. Did you know that over thirteen thousand feet beneath the ice, under a dome of oxygen, they recently found a freshwater lake? It's true—millions of years preserved and full of all sorts of life. Anyway, I'm afraid that, now that there are little to no survivors of the Little America expeditions, we might never know the truth." He gave a deep sigh. "Now, why are you here? Why the sudden interest of three Yale professors after eighty years?"

"Umm...." Bishop stammered for a second. "We think you might be right that there was possibly more to that expedition than we know at this moment. It's a bit hard to explain, but we found documents pointing to something that happened down there during that mission."

"What happened?" Cooper asked.

"Good question," Monroe said. "That's what we came here for. We were hoping you could give us some clue as to what occurred there."

Cooper shook his head. "I'm sorry. I've told you just about everything I know."

"So another dead end," Jennifer said.

"That man," Bishop asked. "That geologist you spoke of. I take it that man is dead too, but does he possibly have any living relatives you think we could talk to?"

"I'm afraid not. Years later, when I tried to contact him again, I learned, through his only son, that he was dead. And I'm afraid the son himself also died a few years later." For a moment, Cooper silenced.

"I'm somewhat reluctant to say, but there might be someone who could give you some extra information on everything that happened on that mission."

"But you're hesitant to tell us who that is?" Bishop asked.

Cooper released a big sigh and paused for a long moment. "It's another Cooper, my son, J.J. Cooper. But there's a distinct possibility he won't talk to you, especially if he knows you talked to me."

"What do you mean?" Monroe asked.

"Well, I guess that's in large part my fault. We don't talk to each other that often anymore. When he was growing up, I became a sort of obsessed with the mystery about his grandfather. On the one hand, it clearly rubbed off on him, given his interest in the North and South Poles. On the other hand, I guess that fact dominated his upbringing, leaving very little room for developing social skills, so to say. He's not the most trustworthy kind, but he is a real man of science. He studied Marine Biology at the Boston University, and wrote his dissertation on the Little America expeditions and their influence on the native marine life in the area."

Bishop said, "Would he talk to us if we didn't tell him we visited you first? No offense."

"None taken. I'm not sure. I know the subject is no longer a favorite of his, and after our falling out, he had a hard time on a more personal level. I think it might have cost him his relationship."

"Maybe if we gave him a surprise visit?" Bishop suggested.

"Or maybe if you visited him," Monroe added, pointing at Jennifer.

"Umm... well...." Cooper stammered, hesitating.

"What is it?" Bishop asked.

"Well," Cooper picked up. "A surprise visit might do the trick, but—"

"Great," Monroe interrupted the man. "Let's do that."

"Let the man finish first," Bishop said, shaking his head.

"Cooper smiled. "Thanks. As I said, a surprise visit might do it, but I'm afraid you would have to travel to the Victoria University of Wellington, where he works at the Centre for Antarctic Studies."

"Wellington?" Jennifer asked.

"Yes, Wellington... the capital of New Zealand, to be precise."

"Figures." Bishop sighed.

CHAPTER 19

Eukarya

Yale, New Haven, CT, The Present

Monroe turned his Vauxhall onto the I-95 back home. Quickly now, miles of green bushes along the road went by.

"It always feels kind of crazy driving a right-hand-drive car," Bishop said behind the wheel, looking at his watch.

"I told you we'd be back before supper," Monroe said, sitting next to him and taking a tablet from his backpack.

"I was just wondering if we would be back before Campus Security would be gone again from the office. I wanted to see if they could install a new alarm system."

"I thought you had one?" Monroe replied.

"I did, but it stopped working some time ago, and I hadn't given it much thought... until now."

"So, what do we think?' Jennifer asked from the back.

"About?" Monroe answered.

She huffed. "Our visit to the eighty-two-year-old Cooper Junior, of course."

Bishop took a deep breath. "I think he was a nice, kind man. Though he sounded reasonable, I'm not so sure if there's anything to his story about the people involved with the expedition collectively hiding something."

"It wouldn't be the first time," Monroe said.

"What are you typing?" Jennifer asked Monroe.

Monroe demonstratively raised a finger high above the tablet and landed it back on the screen. "And gone," he said. "I was writing a small summary about our visit, and just now sent it to Hootkins, my friend at the USGS."

"You have friends at the USGS now?" Jennifer mocked.

"Well, sort of. He was kind enough to loan me the metal sheet under the condition I would keep him informed. And who knows where the USGS comes in handy again."

"Aha," Jennifer replied.

"I don't know." Bishop shook his head. "I mean, here we have a man who never knew his father, and who's desperate to add something to his family history, to find some truth in the different stories he was told as a kid about his daddy."

"That's not all that strange, is it?" Jennifer asked.

"It isn't," Bishop confirmed. "But it doesn't necessarily make him the clearest mind we ever came across, is what I'm saying. I mean... the man is talking about Nazis building mysterious structures on the South Pole, the hollow earth theory, and mysterious life way down below the Antarctic ice."

Monroe raised his tablet. "And yet...." He paused for a moment. "Did you know there are thousands of people that, in some way, embrace the hollow Earth theory?"

With one hand on the wheel and the other rubbing his face, Bishop exhaled a long, stretched-out breath. "And probably even more people hang on to the theory, or fact, as they claim, that the Earth is flat."

"And enclosed by one big fence of ice called the Antarctic, preventing us from falling off," Monroe added. "But seriously...." He took another look at the screen. "Did you know that in the early twentieth century, a spiritualist writer and close friend of Queen Victoria, named Helene Walburga Ehrengarde, mentioned the hollow Earth hypothesis in her book *Colloquies with an Unseen Friend*? She claimed that beneath a desert, cities exist where the people of Atlantis lived. She also claimed that the entrance to the subterranean empire would be uncovered in the twenty-first century."

"That's about a desert!" Jennifer frowned.

"Not to encourage him too much," Bishop said. "But... Antarctica is also a desert. In fact, it's officially the largest desert on Earth. A desert is a region that is very dry because it gets little to no water. Another way of defining a desert is that it's a region that evaporates more water than it receives back through the rain, mist, snow, or whatever. That's why deserts are in nature an inhospitable environment for humans."

"There, you see? Thank you." Monroe raised two arms, smiling.

"You're being a smartass," Jennifer said to Bishop.

Bishop shook his head. "I shouldn't have encouraged him. Sorry."

Monroe enthusiastically picked up again. "What about the Piri Reis map, made by the Ottoman admiral Piri Reis in 1513? It was considered the standard for over a hundred years. Some say that map depicts Antarctica without the ice. Now how do you explain that?"

"Aliens?" Jennifer asked, giving a tiny smile.

Bishop laughed out loud. "Do you also believe Hitler didn't commit suicide but left for Antarctica on a sub to flee to hollow Earth through a hole in New Schwabenland?"

Monroe grinned back. "Of course I don't. But, Matthew...." His voice sounded strict now. "You yourself are a big fan of Plato, aren't you?"

Bishop nodded reluctantly.

"Well, then you must know that Plato himself talked about an island that around 6900 BC sank into the ocean in twenty-four hours, and he named it Atlantis."

Bishop sighed. "I know. I also know that some suggested he was talking about Antarctica, but there's also sufficient evidence to suggest he was speaking metaphorically."

"Sure," Monroe confirmed. "For every theory, there's another one disproving it. Even for every piece of evidence in science, there's someone who, years later, will challenge it. You do know Antarctica wasn't always covered in ice? I read that as recent as twelve thousand years ago, it was still fertile land and, around that time, shifted two thousand miles."

"I heard about that. Five minutes to go." Bishop said as he turned off the highway and onto Trumbull Street in New Haven. "To stay a bit more on the scientific side.... Is there anything on there about that freshwater lake Cooper Junior was talking about?"

After working his tablet for a moment, Monroe mumbled to himself a few seconds before answering. "It took the Russians twenty years to dig a hole about two-point-five miles below their Vostok Station on the Antarctic."

"That's about the same amount of time it took to dig the Kola hole in the North Pole," Bishop remarked. "The Russians are digging everywhere. What are they looking for?" He smiled.

"No idea." Monroe smiled back. "But anyway, it says here that at that depth, they found an almost five-thousand-square-mile freshwater lake with an average depth of one mile."

"Wow," Jennifer said. "That's a gigantic splash of fresh water. Anything about the life forms that Cooper was talking about?"

Monroe mumbled again. "Umm... they found strange magnetic readings that some believe to come from possibly ancient metals, buried beneath the surface."

"Like our metal?" Jennifer asked.

"Stick to the science," Bishop uttered.

"Sorry, the life forms... let's see...." Monroe ran his finger up and down over the screen of his tablet. "It says here that they found lakes beneath the ice before, but that they were all sterile. Lake Vostok, however, contains a unique ecosystem. They estimate the completely isolated lake to be over twenty million years old, and found more than thirty-five-hundred different kinds of living bacteria in it."

"They only found bacteria?" Jennifer asked. "No fish or anything else?"

"They only dug a hole, and brought up water samples," Monroe replied. "I figure they didn't go down there or go fishing. Anyway, a professor named Scott Rogers, from Bowling Green State University in Ohio, performed DNA and RNA sequencing on the water samples in July 2013. They deducted the metabolic pathways exemplified in the ice and lake. He and his team found over thirty-five hundred unique gene sequences. About 94% were from bacteria and 6% from Eukarya." Monroe mumbled. *"What's a Eukarya?"*

Jennifer grinned. "It's a biological domain. I learned of them when I was having my health problems a few years back. There are three domains to the tree of life: Archaea, Bacteria, and Eukarya. Organisms in the last domain have cells whose nuclei are enclosed within a nuclear envelope."

"Sure," Monroe pouted. "Any examples at hand?"

"Umm, sure. Eukaryotes, as they call members of the domain, are the plant life we know, and, I think, all animals and algae."

"And humans?" Bishop asked as he parked the car on Wall Street between the Beinecke Library and his office.

Jennifer nodded. "Absolutely."

The three got out of the car, and Bishop took the first steps in the direction of his office, and Monroe in the opposite direction towards his library.

"Gentlemen!" Jennifer called out.

"Sorry," Bishop said. "My office? Campus Security, you know?" He pointed towards College Street.

"Sure, no problem." Monroe strode up to Bishop, and they started walking.

"I was thinking," Bishop said. "Does it say whether they identified the DNA they sequenced?"

"Let's see." While walking, Monroe worked his tablet. "It says here that Rogers was able to classify and match over sixteen hundred of the sequences. They matched them to organisms previously found in deep sea sediments, marine environments, lake sediments, animals, and plants."

***

As they walked up to the office building, Jennifer's gaze was drawn for second to a woman sitting on a bench a bit farther down the street. The woman seemed to duck away behind a book.

"Watch out," Bishop called out, grabbing Jennifer at the shoulder when she came dangerously close to a fire hydrant in front of her.

"Ah, sorry," she said, shaking her head.

They walked into the building, where they were greeted by a small group of students who were debating something on the stairs.

"You're late, professor," one of the female students called out.

Bishop stopped, frowned, and looked at his watch. "Shit."

"You forgot, professor?" one of the young men asked. "We were going to debate Newcomb's problem."

"No, of course not. Sure, can you please give me fifteen more minutes to wrap up something?"

"No problem, professor," another young woman said.

Bishop took a deep breath as he took a pink sticky note from his door. "Damn."

"What does it say?" Jennifer said.

"I missed them, but they left a cell phone number. I'll call them back later." They walked into his office, where Bishop fell into the chair behind his desk.

"Walker," Jennifer said, "does the text say anything about what kind of Eukaryotes?"

Monroe worked his tablet for a few seconds, and said, "It doesn't, but it does suggest they're related to the fact that, about sixty-six million years ago, Antarctica was still connected to Australia and had a subtropical climate."

Jennifer, in silence, looked up to the ceiling.

"Are you okay?" Bishop asked after a minute.

"Yes, I am." She snapped out of her trance after a second. "You know, I was thinking.... If Rogers matched sixteen hundred out of the thirty-five hundred unique gene sequences, that's still less than half. I think we should try to get our hands on those gene sequences and have your lab specialist, what's her name, try to match them with the genes found in Ata and those we saw in Russia."

"Elise Aldridge," Bishop replied.

"That one." Jennifer grinned.

"That's actually a great idea," Bishop said.

"You sound surprised," Monroe replied.

"No, I'm sorry," Bishop addressed Jennifer. "My mind was wandering around to too many things. I'll contact Elise later today and see if she can get her hands on the DNA and do the matching."

"Not a problem," Jennifer said. "I kind of know how your brain works, so...."

Bishop gave a tight smile.

"Now, what do we do with the knowledge from Cooper Junior?" Monroe asked.

"What do you want to do?" Bishop asked. "It's still your project. Do you want to wait for the results of the DNA or—"

"Is it, though, still my project?"

"Sorry, I'm not having the best of moments," Bishop said. "What I meant to say was that you are still the one who started this all. And although I'm curious as hell, I still feel you should be the one to call the shots on this one. I wouldn't want you to get the feeling I was taking over."

"I understand," Monroe replied, "and I thank you for that. In that case, I wonder what the influence of the DNA results would be on a possible next step."

"You mean the step of going to New Zealand to visit Cooper Junior?" Bishop asked.

"Well, I'm all for it," Jennifer said. "I always wanted to visit the land of the Māori people. And besides that, wouldn't it be great to give Cooper Junior some closure at eighty-two?"

"And you, Matthew?" Monroe asked.

Bishop smiled.

***

Nadya had her earplugs back in and had listened in on the conversation from the bench outside the office. As Jennifer and Monroe left the office again, she quickly got up, walked out of sight, got her phone out, and dialed a number.

"There you are again," the voice of the Chief sounded as she walked in the direction of her hotel. "How are you doing?"

"I'm okay, thank you, but I'm sorry to say that I lost contact with them for the large part of the day."

"But you're back in contact now?"

"I am. Or I was. They split up now, but I was just in time to pick up that they are probably planning a trip to New Zealand. Something to do with Eukaryotes found in Antarctica, but I don't have the details on that."

"That's okay for now. Let me see what I can find out about that. In the meantime, you find out for sure if they're going to New Zealand, and if so, get yourself a ticket out there."

Nadya gave a big smile. "Will do, sir, and thank you for your trust."

"It's okay. Now, let's see where this all leads."

CHAPTER 20

The ARC

Wellington, New Zealand, Two Days Later

The taxi took a little over fifteen minutes to get from the International Airport to Kelburn Parade in Wellington's center, through the crowded streets of New Zealand's capital.

"I always figured New Zealand was one of the lesser populated countries in the world," Monroe remarked, pointing at the rows and rows of buildings, neatly packed next to each other as close as possible.

"Number hundred-sixty-six of just under two-hundred countries," the cab driver replied. "We have less than five million people, most of them living packed together in a few handfuls of cities. We've got the most and best nature in the world. If you like, I can show you around."

"Thank you," Bishop said.

"The Cotton Building," Jennifer called out, pointing to a street sign with a large arrow pointing at the other side of the street.

"Yes, Victoria University of Wellington," the cab driver replied, and swiftly turned the car, drove into a narrow back alley, and stopped at a five-story-tall concrete office building.

"Wow, this is it?" Monroe asked.

"There, that green and gold sign." Bishop pointed at the sign identifying the building.

"This is the location you asked for," the cab driver responded.

"Umm, yes, sorry," Monroe replied.

"You expected something else?" Jennifer asked as she and Monroe got out.

"Well," Monroe turned around in the narrow back alleyway. "Maybe I expected a bit more space." He looked straight up into the bright sun, and then down again while pointing at the gray, concrete buildings that surrounded them at close distance.

Bishop paid the driver and also stepped out. "Breathe," he said, smiling at Monroe while the cab's trunk popped open behind them.

"Let's get our luggage and see if anyone's expecting us."

With their luggage, they rolled onto the long and winding ramp towards the Cotton Building's entrance.

"All this snaking reminds me of my times in Disneyland with my parents," Jennifer remarked. "An endless row of people waiting for a thirty-second rollercoaster ride."

"I know what you mean," Bishop said. At the top, he pushed the bell next to the red double doors.

"Are you sure they're expecting us?" Jennifer asked Monroe.

"I sure hope they do," Monroe replied, smiling.

"And if not," Bishop replied, "I understand there's plenty of nature to enjoy. It is spring over here, so we're in the right season."

"Weird," Monroe said.

"What is?" Bishop asked.

"The fact that back home, winter is starting, and out here, summer is around the corner."

"Sound like a perfect time to visit Hobbiton," Bishop replied.

One of the doors swung open, and a smiling young woman said, "Hi. This is not Hobbiton."

"Thanks for clearing up that misunderstanding." Bishop smiled back. "We're actually looking for a Dr. J. Cooper."

"Ah, Jay-Jay," she replied. "Please come in." She waved them in. "Just wait here, and I'll get him for you."

She walked down the long, narrow corridor and disappeared through a milk glass door at the end. Two minutes later, the door opened again, and a tall, dark, muscular man, dressed in blue jeans and a white T-shirt, came through and neared them with big steps.

"Welcome." The man stretched out his hand. 'HAKA 2019' was printed in large black letters on his shirt. A large tattoo on the man's right arm seemed to run from the top of his shoulder all the way down to his wrist.

Bishop shook his hand. "Hi, I'm Matthew Bishop. You're Dr. Cooper?"

"Ah no, I'm sorry. Dr. Cooper was on the phone, so I came to pick you up. I'm Hemi, Tipene Hemi, Jay-Jay's co-worker on most of his projects. If you'll allow me, I will take you to him. You can leave your luggage there. We'll have it sent to your hotel later." Hemi pointed behind a small counter to the left.

"Great," Bishop said, and when they started to walk, the others introduced themselves.

"I'm glad you're expecting us," Monroe said.

"I can imagine," Hemi said. "It's been a long trip, I figure. How was it?"

"Long indeed," Monroe answered. "But we're glad to be here now."

"You're Māori?" Jennifer asked.

Hemi laughed.

"I'm sorry, did I say something wrong?"

"No, no," Hemi spoke rapidly. "It's just that when people ask that, they usually don't have an idea of what they're really asking. But yes, I am Māori. Do you know what Māori means in our native language?"

"I have no idea," Jennifer replied.

Hemi lowered his voice as he looked back at her. "It means 'normal,' 'ordinary' or 'natural.'"

"Oh, I'm sorry. I didn't mean to—"

"I'm just messing with you." Hemi gave a big smile and, when at the end of the corridor, opened the door. "After you." He bowed slightly to Jennifer and pointed inside.

They walked into the large open space, and a man in his mid-forties, dressed in black jeans and a thick wool knitted vest, stood just outside a large square made of tables. On the phone, he looked at them and waved them forward. When they neared him, he pointed them to some chairs scattered around the tables. Then he raised a finger and mouthed, *one moment,* before he continued his conversation.

Before sitting down, they inspected the large hall filled with what looked like electronic research equipment, snow climbing gear, oxygen tanks, and racks with thick winter clothing, all scattered around the floor, racks, and tables.

"This is your storage room?" Bishop asked Hemi.

Before he could answer, the man on the phone raised his voice and smacked the phone handset onto the base. "I'm sorry," the tall and slender, almost white-haired, pale-skin man said. "Funding conversations. I'm sure you recognize the problem. We're finalizing packing our stuff to get to our Antarctic base in two days, and still lack a large piece of funding, so...."

"I think we all recognize that problem," Bishop replied, and introduced himself and his colleagues.

"I'm J.J. Cooper. Please call me Jay-Jay. You've already met my co-worker, Dr. Tipene Hemi. But please, sit down."

"Please call me Tipene," the big man said as he sat down. "There's a pot of coffee and cups on the table. Please help yourselves."

"What does the J.J. stand for? "Jennifer asked Cooper.

"J.a.y. J.a.y." Cooper smiled. "My father figured it was a nice twist doubling his name and giving it to me."

"It does have a nice ring to it," Jennifer agreed.

"Thank you, and welcome to ARC, the Antarctic Research Centre, probably the world leader in Antarctic studies."

Hemi chuckled. "He always likes to say that."

Cooper gave him an eye and continued. "From this location, we work together with the School of Geography, Environment, and Earth Sciences."

"And what exactly do you do?" Jennifer asked.

"That's a good question, one we often asked ourselves," Hemi replied, looking at Cooper.

"Please, continue." Cooper tilted his head. "Now I'm curious too."

Hemi smiled and continued. "Basically, here at the ARC we research the Antarctic climate history, the ice sheet processes, and their impact on the Earth system and specifically New Zealand."

"And...." Cooper took over when Hemi fell silent. "When we're not trying to find the funding, we do both undergraduate and postgraduate teaching, and research supervision in Antarctic affairs, glaciology, sedimentology, and paleoclimatology."

"That's a lot of work for two men," Monroe said, smiling.

"We are a small group of about a dozen people," Cooper replied. "Nice and cozy, as I like it."

"You also do work on location?" Bishop asked.

"You mean in Antarctica?" Cooper asked, and Bishop nodded. "Sure, I, or rather Tipene and I, try to spend at least four months of every year on location, working from New Zealand's Scott Base Research Facility. But now, I'm curious. Tell me, why are you here, nine-thousand miles from home?"

Bishop and Jennifer looked at Monroe.

"Okay, that's me, I guess," Monroe replied.

"We're just along for the ride," Bishop said, pointing at Jennifer and himself.

"Thank you," Monroe said, giving half a smile. "Anyway, in our email conversation, I told you that, on behalf of my library, I am researching ancient writings or signs that somehow seem to have a link to Antarctica, more specifically to the Little America Three mission back in '39. Since you seem to be the expert on both subjects, we thought we'd pay you a visit."

"And the reason you couldn't tell me this over the phone?"

Monroe took a deep breath, and Jennifer took over. "Let me. To be honest, we spoke to your father first."

Cooper shook his head, grinned, and raised an open hand to Hemi.

Hemi shook his head, searched his pocket, and came back with a ten-dollar bill that he put in Coopers' hand.

"I figured as much, as I told Tipene when I got your request," Cooper said. "He didn't think so, so we made a small bet. However, I have to say that I never expected that three professors from a well-respected university like Yale would fall for the fairytales of that nutcase, let alone that those three professors would travel halfway around the world for it."

"Well," Bishop replied. "We spoke to your father because of his link to his father, your grandfather, who was on the original Little America Three mission. I cannot and will not attest to the sanity of your father or the relation between you two, but for our research, it seems to me he did send us to the expert we're looking for."

Cooper chuckled. "Flattery will get you everywhere. Did my father tell you his fantastic story about the Antarctic Cruiser and how it reported a cavern of gold at the end of a dark tunnel before it went down?" He didn't wait for an answer. "Did he also tell you that shortly after he met my mom, years before I was born, he was crazy enough to join the U.S. Navy as a reporter? All of that, only to serve on the icebreaker Edisto, which did oceanographic research in the Ross Sea? His only goal being to see if there was anything left of the mission and to find a trace of his father?"

"And the gold?" Monroe asked.

"I don't think he cared about the gold, but he was obsessed with finding out what happened to my grandfather. The mystery in general, I guess."

"The question, I think, is: did he find anything?" Bishop asked.

"Yes and no." Cooper rose from his chair, walked up to the table behind them, and picked up a large stack of papers, which he brought back to the table. He smiled as he sat down again and slapped the stack down. "Every now and then, this pile comes in handy."

"Research," Jennifer suggested.

Cooper grinned as his fingers leafed through the papers. "All the prints I made of the research I did for my doctoral thesis. On February 24, 1963, the Edisto, a U.S. Navy Wind-class icebreaker, sailed the Bay of Whales some three hundred miles west of the original Little America

Three location, when they noticed something strange on a huge, miles-wide iceberg they passed. Some forty feet below a hundred-fifty-foot-tall floating blue and white iceberg, a dark streak of what looked like metal, wood, and cloth stuck out. When they took a closer look, they identified the materials as Little America Three's remains exposed in the ice face. Ah, here it is." He opened a folder and shoved it over the table to Bishop. "You see that?"

Bishop first tried it without his reading glasses. "Hmm," he mumbled as he zoomed in and out of the paper. Then he took his glasses from his jacket pocket, put them on, and tried again. "Ah, well, it still looks like it could be anything, buried in the ice and snow." He took out his phone and made a picture of the photo before he handed the folder to Jennifer.

"Did they take a closer look?" Bishop asked.

"They did, but only after my father convinced them to do so. Together with a pilot and two sailors, my father took Edisto's helicopter and flew it to the iceberg. When it was impossible to get to the remains from the top, my father persuaded the sailors to rappel from the side to see if they could get in. That's where things went horribly wrong. Just as the sailors almost reached the remains, a chunk of ice from the top broke off, and the two sailors plummeted to their death, more than a hundred feet below in the freezing ocean."

"Wow," Jennifer said. "That's horrible."

"It was." Cooper nodded. "And that's why it was kept out of the news back then."

"I understand," Monroe said. "And I'm sorry for how you feel about the part your father played in their deaths. But what does it imply?"

"What do you mean?" Cooper asked.

"Well, our research leads to the Little America Three mission. Are you saying that everything that remained was lost in time?"

"Maybe." Hemi took over when Cooper waved his hand at him. "Where Jay-Jay is the expert on the past, I'm the one that's working more in the present. The 1963 sighting of the floating ice shelf held a large part of the site, if not all, that washed into the sea. But that doesn't mean it's lost for all time."

Cooper jumped back in. "The chunk of ice that the Edisto encountered seemed to have broken off somewhere in the middle of base camp. So, half of it could still be there on its original location."

"And that was the only time someone laid eyes on the remnants?" Jennifer asked.

"It was the last time, but not the only time," Cooper answered. "You heard about the Antarctic Snow Cruiser?"

"Your father told us about it," Monroe answered. "The seventy-five-thousand-pound vehicle that proved to be a complete failure."

Cooper shook his head. "Not sure if he was right when he told you it was a failure, but that's the one. Just after World War II, in 1946, the US Navy started another Antarctic campaign called Operation Highjump. When members of that expedition reached Antarctica, they came across the Cruiser again. It was still sitting near the basecamp, where it was left behind. They reported that the tires were flat, but that the vehicle was otherwise in pristine condition."

"They didn't explore anything back then?" Bishop asked.

"There wasn't much to be seen. Anyway, years later, in 1958, another expedition accidentally stumbled upon a series of bamboo poles sticking out of the snow and ice. When they started digging with a bulldozer, they also found the left-behind Cruiser. It was still completely intact with papers, cigarette stubs, plates, and soda cans right there on the table where they were left behind decades before."

"And again, they didn't look any further?" Monroe asked this time.

Cooper shook his head. "The Cruiser was all they found. The camp was probably hidden below a thick layer of ice that broke in two later on. But I'm still interested in why you're here. The writing or symbols you talked about in your email... can I see them?"

"Sure." Monroe took a small tablet computer from his backpack, worked it for a moment, and handed it to Cooper. It showed a picture of the metal sheet with the spiral writing.

"Where did you say you found this writing?" Hemi asked, watching as Cooper enlarged the writing on the screen.

"We didn't tell you yet," Bishop answered. "But it came from a deep dig near the North Pole in Russia, and—"

"The Kola dig?" Hemi interrupted.

"You know it?" Monroe asked.

"I know *of* it," Hemi replied. "There are not that many deep digs out there, and Kola was the deepest. But sorry for the interruption. Please go on."

Bishop continued. "We found the same kind of writing a second time in a small mining village in Russia."

"All right," Cooper replied, giving Monroe the tablet back. "That's interesting, but how do you think this writing relates to Antarctica?"

Monroe picked up again. "Well, unfortunately, we can't translate most of the writing yet. Matthew here has some algorithms working on that as we speak, but... well, who knows. Anyway, Jennifer found a recurring sequence of signs in the strings that we could decode to a set of numbers. These numbers turned out to be a set of coordinates and a date. These coordinates lead us to a spot on the Ross Ice Shelf, and the date was January 12, 1940."

Cooper gave a tiny smile and a chuckle. "The date Byrd and his men arrived at Antarctica."

"As I understand, it was exactly the date Dr. Poulter moored the North Star at the Ross Ice Shelf," Bishop said.

Cooper nodded. "You did your homework, but I'm still a little fuzzy on why you came here. What were you expecting to find? Am I missing something?"

"Three facts," Bishop said. "First, the metal sheet found at Kola is at least sixty thousand years old."

"But could even be much older," Monroe added.

Bishop nodded. "And secondly, Walker here told you that we translated the numbers from the signs. Well, we also translated some other parts of the sequences." He paused for a moment to take a deep breath. "It was written out deoxyribonucleic acid."

"DNA?" Cooper frowned. "You found DNA in a sixty-thousand-year-old specimen?"

"Well, not the actual DNA," Jennifer corrected. "But rather the written-out code."

"But, how," Hemi muttered. "We only found out about DNA somewhere in the fifties."

Cooper straightened himself in his chair. "You said you had three facts?"

Bishop nodded. "Yes, we were able to match parts of the DNA code with a unique set of DNA found in something else." He took another deep breath. "A small mummy of what looks like a deformed infant that was found in the Atacama Desert in Chile."

Cooper shook his head, and started a grin that quickly changed into a loud laugh.

Hemi joined him while Bishop, Monroe, and Jennifer sat there with straight faces.

"This has to be a joke," Hemi came back after a few seconds.

"You're serious." Cooper eyed the straight faces, and frowned. "If you're not pulling my leg, and I'm starting to think you aren't, what's your conclusion about all this?"

Bishop shrugged. "I assure you we're deadly serious, and just as confused as you are. The simple reason we're here is because the trail leads to these coordinates, and we don't have any other leads. So yes, we're here for your area of expertise on the South Pole and knowledge about the Little America expeditions."

"You *are* serious." Cooper gazed at their faces.

For a long moment, the large room fell silent but for the echoes of their breathing.

Bishop broke the silence. "So you don't have any knowledge about something out of the ordinary that happed or found on the Little America Three expedition?"

Cooper shook his head. "No. If anything, the expedition was cut short because of World War II. I guess the most exciting thing that happened on the mission was the death of my grandfather."

"They never recovered his body?" Jennifer asked.

Cooper again shook his head. "Do you have the coordinates you were talking about?"

Monroe worked his tablet for a moment and handed it to him.

"All right." Cooper took a rugged-looking laptop from the table next to him and, after a few seconds, put in the coordinates. "Aha."

"Aha?" Monroe asked.

Cooper turned the laptop to him. "Exactly what I expected. The coordinates lead straight to the center of Byrd's third expedition."

"At the edge of the water?" Bishop looked at the screen.

Cooper explained. "I think it was there where the piece of the iceberg broke off, tearing the base camp in half."

"And nobody checked it out after the break?" Jennifer asked.

"Why should they?" Hemi asked rhetorically. "It wasn't a special place, to begin with."

"Could it be that now it is?" Monroe asked.

"What do you mean?" Cooper asked.

"Well, I mean...." Monroe now leaned his body over the table. "Don't you find it interesting that your grandfather disappeared under... umm... let's say suspicious circumstances? And now, over eighty years later, we come across sixty-thousand-year old writings that not only translate to mummy DNA, but also give us the exact coordinates and date of the Little America Three expedition?"

"I find it more than fascinating," Cooper replied. "But what would you have me do? Get out there and have a look?"

Monroe, Bishop, and Jennifer stayed silent again while gazing at Cooper and Hemi.

"But... now... no... you can't...." Cooper stammered and eyed his colleague, who tilted his head and shrugged. "Oh, no, you really think we should go there."

"It's not as if we won't be in the neighborhood in a few days," Hemi replied.

"Can we come?" Jennifer asked in a rush.

"What?" Cooper asked.

Bishop grinned. "We *are* scientists. Or don't you have any room left?"

Cooper grinned, and Hemi answered. "There's room enough. Hell, the part where we are going is almost overcrowded with three airstrips and a complete set of roads between all base camps. Did you know there are more than twenty airfields in Antarctica? There's almost a flight coming and going every day of the week this time of year. Your own United States and their McMurdo Station alone houses over twelve hundred people during the summer. I'm sure they would love to take you in for a while."

"To be honest," Bishop said, "if we're going, I think we would rather go with you. And I think I speak for all of us." He looked around at his colleagues' nodding heads.

"Now, be careful what you wish for," Cooper replied. "We research the climate, and don't regularly go on treasure hunts. You have to know that Scott Base is rather spartanly equipped in comparison with McMurdo. During the summer, there's never more than a hundred people out there, and the three of you would probably have to share a room, in bunk beds."

"And you'll be stuck over there for at least a week," Hemi added.

"The question is," Bishop said. "If we were to go with you, can you take us to the place where Little America Three used to be?"

Cooper sighed. "I guess we could get out there and have a look, if the weather cooperates."

"So, we're going?" Jennifer said enthusiastically.

Cooper shook his head. "Not without the proper preparations, you aren't."

CHAPTER 21

The Road South

Wellington Airport, New Zealand, Two Days Later

At Air Movements Rongotai—the Royal New Zealand Air Force part of the Wellington civilian airport—a gigantic C-130H Hercules fired up its turboprops. As it geared up, its four propellers started to rotate slowly. The gray Royal New Zealand Air Force plane was getting ready to begin its twenty-eight-hundred-mile flight to the Ross Ice Shelf in Antarctica. At the plane's back, the let-down rear cargo door served as a ramp to load a vast amount of boxes with supplies like food, drinks, repair materials, tools, and four snow scooters.

"Are those for us?" Monroe asked Cooper, pointing at the scooters.

Cooper didn't answer. For the past two days, more often than he'd initially planned, he and Hemi had been busy preparing their visitors for their stay at the cold and treacherous South Pole. Together, they'd been buying warm polar clothing. Where Cooper and Hemi were dressed in army green, Bishop and Monroe bought dark blue polar clothing, and Jennifer chose red. They were made aware of the most basic security measures, and learned how to stay warm using layers of clothing creating warm air pockets. They also learned how to stay hydrated, cover their extremities, and always, always, always—Cooper had urged them—keep dry at all times.

"It's time," Hemi shouted from the back of the plane as he walked up the ramp.

Cooper nodded at the three, and together they walked to the back of the plane and up the ramp. Inside, they sat down on folding seats attached to the side of the aircraft, and strapped in. Both sides of the aircraft were fitted with rows of seats, all empty except for the five of them. Through three little windows on either side of the plane, a little daylight came in, and the orange-looking cabin lights gave the inside of the aircraft an eerie look. In the center, the vast leftover space was filled entirely with carefully tied-up cargo.

A man dressed in a flight suit walked up to them from the cockpit. "You all safe and sound here?" He checked their seatbelts.

"We're good," Cooper answered after giving his guests a quick look.

"No inflight entertainment?" Bishop's question got lost in the increasing roar of the engines.

The co-pilot hit a large red button at the end of the bulkhead, and almost immediately, the ramp started to rise, and the plane rolled into motion.

"Have a good one," the co-pilot said. He passed them and walked into the cockpit, and closed the door behind him.

A minute later, the plane turned onto the runway that ran all the way from the Evans Bay in the north to the Cook Strait in the south. The turboprops geared further up, running the plane down the six-thousand-foot runway. The sound of the propellers cried through the cabin.

As the plane raised from the runway and the sound of the wheels resonating through the cabin dissipated, Hemi raised his head.

"Tipene," Bishop addressed the Maori sitting next to him. "You don't like flying?"

Hemi shook his head. "I get seasick too. Otherwise, I would gladly exchange the flying for a boat trip. I tried everything to get rid of the anxiety, but nothing helped. You know, someone once said, 'Expose yourself to your deepest fear. After that, fear has no power, and the fear of freedom shrinks and vanishes. You are free.' He was lying."

"Jim Morrison." Jennifer said, sitting on the other side next to Hemi.

"What?" Hemi asked.

"It was Jim Morrison who said that."

"Figures." Hemi gave a tight smile.

***

Back at the airport, a woman watched the plane take off from behind a mesh iron fence. Her phone rang, and she took it out of her pants pocket, looked at the number on the screen, and sighed. She gazed at the skies for a second before answering.

"Chief, Nadya here."

"I see you're back at the airport," the man said.

"You're following me now?"

"Just your phone's GPS signal. What happened?"

"They left again."

"We anticipated that. To Antarctica?"

"Yes, and I have no way of following them there," Nadya replied. "And even if I had a way to get there, that woman would probably recognize me in a heartbeat."

"I know, but that's no problem. Since they left from New Zealand, they're without a doubt on their way to Scott Base. So we know where they will be. Within, umm... in about seven hours, a C-17 from the United States Antarctic Program will land at the same airport you're at right now. On board are an American scientist and two of our colleagues, who will travel as guest scientists to Antarctica's U.S. McMurdo Base. The plane will leave again after re-supplying, one hour after landing."

"With what orders, and what about me?" Nadya asked.

"One of the Russian guests will have the orders on what to do once you get there."

Nadya stayed silent for a short moment, letting the message sink in. "I'm going with them?"

"Sure, what did you think? You wanted this mission, in part to redeem yourself, didn't you?"

"Yes."

"Well, if that's still the case, I suggest you spend the time until departure wisely. Prepare yourself and get some warm clothes."

"Okay." She sighed.

"Is there a problem, Miss Fedorova?"

"Of course not, sir," she rapidly replied.

"All right, then, I will send you the specifics on the flight and your contact in a secure email."

A soft click revealed the Chief had cut the connection, and Nadya looked at her phone's screen to ensure he was gone. "*Seven hours,*" she mumbled.

***

Some five hours later, the Royal New Zealand Air Force C-130 flew over the Ross Ice Shelf's edge.

"Wow," Monroe said as he looked out of the small window. "How tall is that thing?"

"The shelf itself?" Cooper asked, not waiting for the answer. "It rises between fifty and a hundred sixty feet above sea level."

"And it's safe to walk all across the shelf?" Jennifer asked.

"You won't fall through if that's what you're afraid of," Hemi replied. "The ice is between a thousand and almost three thousand feet thick. In the winter, the thickness of the ice can grow over twenty inches in a night."

"If the shelf rises so tall above sea level, how did the early explorers manage to get onto land by boat?" Bishop asked while looking out a window.

"Good question," Cooper answered. "Perhaps you can see it. At some places, there are stretches of ice that are almost like a beach. But make no mistake: even at those edges, the thickness of the ice is over tens of feet thick."

"You need to strap in now," Hemi said, pointing at a red light flashing in the front of the plane. "We're almost there, and the landing has started, as you probably feel."

"Great," Bishop said. "I'd love to stretch my legs again."

"In a few moments, we'll be walking on the South Pole," Monroe said. "Isn't it exciting?"

"It's more than exciting," Jennifer replied when the plane took a sharp right turn.

"Is it far from the airfield to the base?" Monroe asked.

Cooper and Hemi both laughed.

Monroe shrugged. "What is it?"

"Oh, nothing much," Cooper said. "It's just that you called it an airfield. We're landing at the Ice Runway, as it's called. And, well, I guess it's exactly that. However, it's the main runway for the Antarctic Program, a strip of flat ice that's been kept free from snow, to the extent that's possible. There are no buildings or terminals, you see."

"Let me explain," Hemi said. "The airstrip is located on the ice between the Antarctic mainland and Ross Island, where we are going. You probably won't notice, but we'll be on an iced-in island the entire time."

"How do we get from the runway to the station?" Monroe asked.

Hemi laughed. "By car, what did you think? It's about a half an hour drive."

"Has there ever been an accident with an airplane?" Monroe asked. "I mean, I figure the weather can be bad with lots of wind, and a landing strip on ice... isn't that slippery?"

They all grinned for a second now.

"You should be fine," Hemi said.

"Although," Cooper added. "On October 31st, 1960, a Lockheed EC-121 from the Oceanographic Development Eighth Squadron crashed while attempting to land on the Ice Runway. The pilot and co-pilot were the only ones badly injured. The other crew members had only some minor injuries."

"And what happened then?" Bishop asked. "I mean with the wreckage. I suppose they don't have much recovery materials out here."

"The crashed aircraft was left in place and never recovered. When the ice thawed in spring, it was simply allowed to sink, and another runway was created on top of it when the water froze again."

Monroe swallowed. "Not helping," he mumbled.

After the plane leveled again, it lined up with the landing strip, and when it almost hit the ice, a big stream of blown-up snow and ice emerged behind each propellor. A soft thud gave away that the plane had landed on the ice, and it rapidly decreased its speed. The aircraft came to a full stop in less than a minute, and immediately the red light in the front turned green.

"Gentlemen and woman, welcome to Antarctica," Cooper said loudly.

At the sound of hydraulics pumping, the rear door of the plane opened. The bright sun rays nearly blinded the passengers, who got up from their chairs and got ready to leave the aircraft.

Hemi raised his sunglasses in the air, checking them before he put them on. "The temperature outside is a fine nine-point-one degrees Fahrenheit, with a lot of sunlight, so it won't feel too cold out there. However, I advise you to put on your sunglasses, or you'll be snow-blind within a few hours. And believe me, that will pretty much ruin your stay here."

"Wow," Bishop said as the back door slowly transformed into a ramp, and the icefield emerged—ice as far as their eyes could see.

With the ramp now fully down, they walked outside, Cooper first.

Monroe stepped carefully onto the ice and stomped his feet.

"There's a plane behind you on the ice," Jennifer said.

"Smartass," Monroe replied.

"What now?" Bishop asked as he looked around but the endless ice and snow.

"Give it a minute," Hemi said. "Trust me. They know we're here and will join us in a minute. Relax, take a deep breath of the cleanest air you ever breathed, and take in the scenery."

Bishop did precisely that. He closed his eyes, raised his chin, took a deep breath, then slowly exhaled and opened his eyes again. It reminded him of the only time his father, a traveling salesman for Boeing when Bishop was a child, had taken him on a business trip to Alaska. He encountered his first major snowstorm there. Somehow, he expected the Antarctic to be something like that, only worse. But this was like nothing he expected. He even opened the zipper of his jacket, feeling warm.

"I know what you're thinking," Cooper said. "If this is the Antarctic, bring it on. But trust me: it's a great day out here, and it won't be like this the entire time. You'll see."

When the plane's last propellor came to a complete stop, an overwhelming silence came over the place. They all kept silent, enjoying the moment.

Jennifer broke the silence. "Isn't this absolutely fantastic?" She took a picture with her cellphone of the plane in front of the immense white vastness.

"That'll be our ride." Hemi raised a finger in the air.

"Where?" Monroe asked, and Hemi pointed north.

"I don't see anything," Bishop said.

"Hemi has ears like no one else," Cooper said.

Thirty seconds later, a trail of dark dots materialized on the horizon.

"There they are," Monroe said, smiling as if he was getting rescued from being snowed in for a week.

The dots rapidly came closer and transformed into a small caravan of vehicles. In the front drove two dark blue Toyota Hilux AT44 trucks. With their raised suspension, three-hundred-liter diesel on board, all-wheel-drive system, and increased wheelbase, they were specially converted for the extreme conditions on the continent.

"Not bad," Monroe said. "That'll get us to our destination fast."

"There's a twenty-five-mile-per-hour speed limit in Antarctica," Hemi replied. "We're trying to prevent the ice from melting even faster than it does already, you see."

Monroe nodded. The AT44's, as they were called, were closely followed by a series of PistenBullys dragging empty trailers behind them. As opposed to the AT44's, the PistenBullys ran on tracks like a tank, which gave them greater traction on the more slippery and snowy Antarctic fields. In less than a minute, the caravan of vehicles stopped next to the plane.

From the first AT44, a man casually dressed in a thin winter coat and wearing dark sunglasses jumped out. "Cooper, Hemi," he shouted as he walked up to them. "It's so good to see you again."

"Mike, how are you?" Hemi called, shaking the man's stretched-out hand. "Mike, this is Jennifer Porter, Walker Monroe, and Matthew Bishop." He pointed them out one by one. "Our guests I warned you about in my email." He grinned.

"Nice to meet you," Mike said. "Are you ready to get to the most beautiful base in the entire Antarctic?"

"Sure."

"Of course."

"Show us the way."

"Hi, Mike." Cooper casually waved a hand from the back.

"Hi, Jay-Jay. So, let's hit the road then."

They all followed Mike the few steps to the first AT44.

"Get in, get in," Mike said.

"And our luggage?" Jennifer asked.

"I see you have your most personal belongings on you." He pointed at the backpacks they were all carrying. "The rest of your stuff will be brought in a little later, together with everything else. It's not like it's going anywhere here." He stretched out an arm over the vast plains of white and blue ice. "Please." He walked around the car and opened all four doors, and everyone took a seat on one of the three rows of chairs. "Please strap in, and we're on our way."

Seconds later, the car turned, while at the back of the plane, men were walking up and down the ramp, unloading the cargo and packing everything onto the PistenBully's trailers. A few seconds later, the car drove onto the icefield, where only the tracks from the vehicles that had just arrived gave away a route going somewhere.

"How do you know where you're going?" Bishop asked from the front seat.

Mike tapped on a compass glued onto the dashboard, straight in the middle, behind the steering wheel. "And of course, you can follow the tracks or, in this weather and this time of day, simply follow the sun."

"And in bad weather?" Monroe asked.

"Around here, well... umm... I would strongly urge you not to get out in bad weather." Mike, Cooper, and Hemi laughed loudly. "But I guess that if you were caught in bad weather, with little to no sight, there's always the GPS."

"And if that doesn't work anymore," Cooper added. "Just drive in a straight line to the coast, where the rocks turn into the flat frozen, make a choice, left or right, and keep driving along the coastline. You're bound to run into a base."

"Better stay inside," Hemi urged them.

A little over half an hour later, the snow and ice way steadily turned into a real muddy road, the snow spots gradually subsiding.

"This looks like a real road now," Jennifer said.

"It is," Mike answered as he drove off the icy rocks, where the road went up to what looked like a small mountain ridge. "If you look to your left, you'll see those black spots in the snow that look like buildings in the distance."

They all mumbled.

"That's McMurdo Station. Over twelve hundred of your countrymen live over there."

"That's as much as a small village," Bishop remarked.

"It is," Hemi added. "They have literally everything over there a small town has."

"And more," Cooper said. "They even had their own nuclear power plant back in the '60s and '70s."

"They don't anymore?" Monroe asked.

"Nope," Cooper answered. "Hairline cracks in the reactor, and water leaks, made an end to that. They switched back to conventional diesel generators, like we use."

"And Scott Base?" Jennifer answered. "I mean, how big is it really, and does it also have all the conveniences of a small town?"

"Well," Mike said as he drove the AT44 down from the ridge. "Just give me a minute." He stretched his words before he hit the brakes.

"What is it?" Jennifer asked.

"Look right," Mike answered.

About ten feet away from the car stood a large road sign:

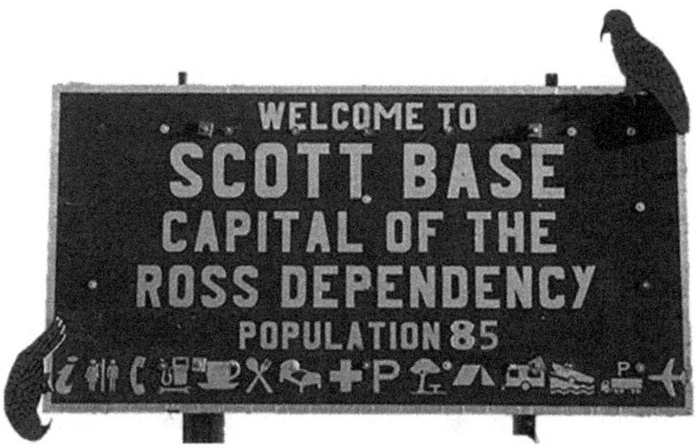

A large row of icons was drawn below the text, like a telephone, coffee cup, tent, a large P, gas pump, and a man and woman toilet sign.

"I guess we've got it all," Mike said when he drove off again. Seconds later, he turned left from the ridge, where the ice and snow had vanished entirely and an open shelf of rock, like on a mountaintop, appeared. "Now, lady and gentlemen, if you look right in front of us...." He pointed a few hundred feet ahead. "Scott Base."

CHAPTER 22

Beyond Mount Erebus

The Ross Ice Shelf, Antarctica, January 20, 1940

The wind breezed softly around the Antarctic Snow Cruiser as the sun began to rise at 3.30 a.m.

"Good morning," Poulter said to Simons as he climbed from the living quarters into the driver's control cabin.

Simons was lying in his sleeping bag with his legs stretched out on the dashboard. "Morning," he replied. "You couldn't sleep either?"

"I guess it takes some time getting used to," Poulter replied, stretching out. "Anything worth seeing out there?"

"The sun's just coming up now. Half an hour ago, when there were only stars above, you could beautifully see the silhouettes of the ice ridges appear. And that mountain over there. You see it?"

The day before, Poulter and his crew had arrived an hour before midnight, when darkness had just set in. "I see it now. Wow, could that be?"

Simons sat up straight, took off his sleeping bag, and picked up a map from a compartment in the door and pointed to it. "According to this, that, out there, is Mount Erebus. And if you look closely, you can see smoke coming from the top."

Poulter squinted, and with his face as close to the glass as he could get, he looked up. "You're right. There is smoke out there. Wow. We're in the right place."

"You ever doubt it?" a voice sounded from behind, as Burt Kippler also came up into the cabin.

"Did we wake you?" Poulter asked.

"Maybe, Captain. I'm a light sleeper, so.... But no problem. What are we looking at?"

"A geologist's dream, I guess," Poulter answered, pointing outside.

Kippler bent his heavyset body over Simons' shoulder to look outside, following Poulter's finger. "So we did get there. Congratulations." He patted Simons on the back.

"Our brazen pilot still asleep?" Poulter asked.

"And snoring contently, Captain." Kippler grinned. "I'd like to take a look outside."

Simons looked at Poulter, who nodded and said, "Sure. Go right ahead."

Simons grabbed the door handle next to him. "You remember where the ladder is?"

"I already used it a few hours ago." He smiled. "When you gotta go, you gotta go."

The men smiled back while Kippler put on his fur coat and his Cossack hat. "You better dress up warm, Burt," Simons said. "There's a bit of a nasty wind out there."

"I think I can handle it." Kippler put both hands below his waist and shook his belly. "What is our schedule?"

"Well, don't make it too long," Poulter ordered. "I'd like to leave around noon so we can get to our next destination before the sun sets. On our first run, I prefer not to take any risks and would rather get home a day early. If everything works out as planned and we don't run into too many problems, we can prepare for another trip in a few days or so."

"That's no problem. I'll just be out for fifteen minutes, max. I'm not planning on climbing the volcano yet." Kippler smiled brightly. "Though I wouldn't mind getting up there for a bit the second time around."

"I'll make sure you'll get your chance to take a second look," Poulter replied.

"Mind if I come with you?" a voice came from the back of the Cruiser. McConnel stuck his head through the door opening. "I need to take a whiz and a dump anyway."

"Always good to know." Poulter shook his head. "And a good morning to you too."

"Sorry, good morning. You all sleep well? I did. A bit short, but otherwise...." McConnel spoke fast and loud as he closed his jacket.

"Please get out there," Poulter said. "You're hurting my head."

As Kippler opened the door, the cold wind blew inside. "Get out, get out, get out," Simons yelled as the two men slowly climbed out. He quickly closed the door behind them. "Pfff!" He blew a raspberry and shrugged. "Them rather than me. What do you think so far?"

Poulter took a deep breath. "Except for our speed limitations, I think we're doing okay. At this pace, we'll be back in four days total.

What do you say we leave those two to do their thing, and we have breakfast?"

"Sounds like an excellent idea. I brought some orange juice and powdered milk to go with the biscuits."

Poulter laughed.

"What is it?" Simons asked.

"Oh, you just reminded me of the previous Little America expedition. Admiral Byrd brought three Guernsey cows with him for fresh milk, and promotion, of course. They were named Klondike Gay Nira, Deerfoot Guernsey Maid, and Foremost Southern Girl. We ended up working a dairy farm in Antarctica for a year. We even had a calf born on the way here. The ladies became quite the celebrity when we returned in thirty-five." Poulter chuckled. "Well, anyway, let's eat."

Half an hour later, Poulter and Simons finished breakfast, and another thirty minutes later, they'd performed all the pre-drive checks as Poulter looked out the door-window and watched McConnel and Kippler walking up. He opened the door for them just as Simons let the Cruisers engines roar over the icy plains.

"You took your sweet time," Poulter said. "Fifteen minutes, you said." He looked at his watch. "That was almost one hour ago."

"Sorry, but it's absolutely amazing out there," Kippler replied. "You were right. It's a geologist's wet dream."

"I don't recall using those exact words," Poulter said. "But anyway, I'd like to hear everything about it in a minute. If you will, please get into the back first, so we can get on our way again."

"Again, sorry, Captain." Kippler stumbled in carrying a box with rocks, and staggered to the back closely followed by McConnel.

"And stop calling me Captain, you two."

"All right, Captain. Oh, sorry," McConnel said.

"Are you ready?" Poulter asked Simons, who took place behind the wheel.

Simons pushed the gas pedal, released the clutch pedal, and just as the Cruiser's clutch grabbed on and the Cruiser started to rock, he put his foot down on the clutch again. Immediately, the Cruiser stopped shaking.

He nodded. "Ready, sir."

"All right, then, let's go." Poulter pointed forward.

Seconds later, Simons set the Cruiser slowly into motion and drove away from Mount Erebus.

"What did you find?" Poulter asked Kippler.

"It's really a massive geographical wonder, this island. Did you know that the ice shelf surrounding the island is roughly the size of France? It is in fact...."

***

For over four hours, the Cruiser moved north, and for most of the journey Burt Kippler had kept on talking about how he enjoyed the exceptional views, marveling at just about every rock that stuck out of the snow and ice.

"That doesn't look too good," Simons interrupted Kippler during one of his adorations.

"What's that?" Poulter asked.

"Over there." Simons pointed at the sky in the distance, where dark clouds were forming a thick layer above the dark blue waters.

"That's over the ocean," Poulter said. "That could still go in any direction. How far away are we from your 'shadow'?" He bit his lower lip for a second.

"I'm not sure, but according to my trip meter, we shouldn't be out more than a few miles. Can you see if Dougal is awake? He was with me up there. Maybe he recognizes something in the area."

"That man can sleep where he stands. McConnel," Poulter shouted into the back of the Cruiser.

Simons suddenly and abruptly stopped the Cruiser. Everyone fell forward, and McConnel cried out from the back as he rolled out of the top bunk bed and onto the floor.

"What is it?" Poulter asked, bracing himself.

Simons raised himself and looked down in front of the Cruiser. "It seems like a steep end down. I doubt we can make it with the Cruiser."

"Damn, what's going on? What is it? Are we there yet?" McConnel stuck his sleepy head around the corner of the door.

"That's what we wanted to ask you," Poulter answered. "For now, it seems we hit a dead end."

"Come up here," Simons said. "You were there with me. Do you recognize anything?"

McConnel stumbled up front and sat down next to Simons. "There's some bad weather up ahead."

"We know," Poulter snapped. "But do you recognize anything?"

"All right, take it easy. Here on our west side. That's the ice ridge we saw from the sky that prevents us from taking a shortcut back home."

Left of them, a row of massive shards of ice, which stretched out as far as they could see, seemed to be forced up from below the ice and rose over forty feet into the air.

"Those shards of ice are called sails," Kippler said. "They're part of a pressure ridge."

"A what?" Simons asked.

"A pressure ridge. It develops through underwater currents that grow new layers of ice at the bottom of the existing ice, and which are then pushed up by the currents. These sails can have keels up to a hundred and fifty feet below the ice."

"You see anything else?" Poulter asked Simons and McConnel.

For a moment, they all kept silent and looked out.

A minute later, Simons broke the silence. "I think we should have a look outside," he suggested.

"All right, then," Poulter said. "Let's have a look outside. This time we're all going. Get dressed, get your gear, and get out there. It'll be good to stretch our legs for a moment."

Simons opened the door for a second to check the weather. A freezing wind carrying swept-up snow blew inside, and he quickly closed the door again. "It looks like summer's over. We'd better dress up extra warm."

Ten minutes later, all four men dressed in thick pants, fur jackets, and hats walked up to the Cruiser's nose.

"Can you see the end?" Simons shouted at Poulter, trying to rise above the sound of the snowy wind.

"I'm not sure," Poulter replied, while looking over the edge of the cliff.

"I think it's the ocean," Kippler called out.

"What?" McConnel said.

"The ocean... I think we're standing on the beach."

"There's water down there?" Simons said.

"I didn't say that. There's probably a few hundred feet of ice before you'd find any water."

"Can we get down there?" Simons asked.

"I see no technical reason why not," Kippler replied.

Poulter took a few steps down and inspected the terrain. The blue-lit ice sails that sparkled into the air slowly turned gray. He looked up to the skies and saw the sun disappear behind a vast set of dark clouds. "I'm not sure it's a good idea to get down there now."

They all looked up.

"Maybe not," McConnel said, "but I've seen many depressions from the sky, so to say, and I believe that once this one hits us, it won't go away for a long time."

"Meaning?" Poulter asked.

"Meaning we could be stuck in the Cruiser for more than a day, Captain," McConnel answered, making Poulter draw his brows together.

"Meaning we'd run out of supplies and need to cut our trip short and head home," Kippler added.

"Shit," Poulter said. "How long?" he asked McConnel.

"Hard to say. Thirty minutes to an hour, I'd guess."

Poulter sighed. "You all wanna give it a go?"

They all nodded and mumbled in agreement.

"All right, then." Poulter nodded slowly. "Let's see how far we can get, but at the slightest sign of danger, we head back. Deal?"

Again they agreed.

"Okay, follow me."

Step by step, they followed Poulter carefully, planting their feet firmly in the ice and snow.

"This place looks like a maze," Simons said as they worked their way down between the sails of ice and snowy elevations that, at some places, rose to over twenty feet. "There's never more than a few feet of visibility."

"As long as we're going down, we're going in the right direction," Poulter replied. "You're doing okay back there?"

Simons turned to Kippler, who was closely followed by McConnel. "Seems like we're doing okay, si—" A loud thud followed, and before he could finish his sentence, Simons fell flat on his back and immediately began to slide down. "Shiiiiit," he yelled as he turned himself over and picked up speed. It felt like minutes as he tried to grab on to protrusions sticking out of the ice at the sides. In less than a minute, he felt his body rise again, and then, as if he'd been jettisoned from a slide, he felt weightless for just two seconds before he dropped face down in a deep layer of snow.

"Pfff!" Simons raised his head out of the snow and blew out small pieces of snow and ice from his mouth. He turned swiftly, sat up straight, and looked around. Behind him, the pink-blue pressure ridge appeared as a giant snow wall with sails of ice sticking out, while in front of him, there was nothing but a vast field of flat ice and snow.

"Jay, are you okay?"

"Simons, where are you?"

The voices called out to him from within the ridge.

He rose to his feet and, with his gloves, brushed off the snow from his clothes. "Yes, I'm fine. Get down here. It's beautiful."

"Is it safe?" Poulter shouted down.

"Totally safe," Simons shouted back up. "I can recommend the ice slide."

***

"Yeehah," McConnel said as he dropped himself into the place where Simons fell and started to slide down. "Yeah...." His voice quickly dissipated.

"I think I'll walk," Kippler said.

"My sentiments exactly," Poulter replied as the two started their walk down.

Two minutes later, Poulter and Kippler exited from between the ice sails in front of Simons and McConnel.

"You took your sweet time," McConnel said.

Poulter grinned, then looked up. "I think we'd better hurry. I really don't like the look of that." Above the men, dark clouds moved in quickly, adding up to one giant wall of darkness that seemed to close in fast. "Now, what are we looking for? A shadow?"

"One below the ice," Simons said. "A hundred-square-foot one."

"It shouldn't be far from the pressure ridge," McConnel added.

For over five minutes, they walked around, whipping off layers of snow and searching through the ice for dark edges. Suddenly, a loud whistle sounded. As they turned, they saw Kippler, who had walked back and climbed back up the ridge, where he had a good view over the ice.

"Over here!" He wildly gestured his arms.

The men quickly climbed up the ridge and joined him.

"You see, over there." Kippler drew a square in the air with his hands.

"Wow," Poulter said. "You're right. It looks like a perfect square."

Some fifty feet onto the icefield, a large, dark shadow appeared below the ice.

"Could this be man-made?" Poulter asked.

"Hmm," Kippler grunted. "I've seen lots of natural formations in my days, but never one with such straight lines, and in a perfect square. I've no idea what that could be."

The wind cranked up.

McConnel shrugged. "It's getting cold up here."

"It is," Poulter confirmed. "Whatever we want to do, we need to do it fast. Any idea how deep below the ice that thing is?"

"It's hard to say without a drill," Kippler said. "I'd say somewhere between two and ten feet down."

"This is getting crazy," McConnel said as the gushing of the wind now sounded like giants whistling from behind the ice sails. He adjusted his collar as pieces of snow and ice were swiped from the ground and blew into his face. "This wind is starting to hurt!"

"He's right," Poulter said. "Besides the weather, we don't have the proper tools. We need to get back to the Cruiser and wait for the wind to settle down, and when it does, get back here with the right gear."

"Agreed," Simons said.

"Let's go," Kippler added, adjusting his clothes.

Poulter turned to the ridge and looked up. "We can't get up any farther this way. We first need to get down, and get up again where we came down. Follow me."

They all followed Poulter as he climbed down again and walked some twenty feet left to where he and Kippler had gotten out from between the ice sails.

"Here we go," Poulter shouted, and started climbing the ridge.

Less than ten feet up, a loud roaring sound they all felt in their bodies emerged from everywhere between the sails. Poulter stopped for a second and looked back to see if everyone was still there.

"Keep going," Simons shouted. "Go, go, go."

Poulter looked back up again, and just as he took the next step, a large piece of ice tumbled down towards him. A few feet in front of him, the lump of ice bounced off the floor just as he turned and squatted. His effort to avoid the fast-falling piece was pointless.

***

The chunk of ice hit the back of Poulter's head, striking him down and knocking over Simons, who at his turn fell, rolled over, and took Kippler and McConnel with him on his way down.

Seconds later, the four were back on the icefield.

"Dr. Poulter." Simons shook the man's shoulders. "Thomas, wake up." He checked his breathing. "He's unconscious but alive."

"So what do we do now?" Kippler shouted in the storm.

"We need to carry him and find shelter," Simons shouted back.

"Where?" McConnel shouted out.

The men checked their surroundings. On one side, they knew, was the flat icefield, but since the visibility had become less than ten feet, they couldn't see it. On the other side, their way to the Cruiser was obstructed by the immense pressure ridge.

"We need to follow the riff and seek shelter somehow," Simons called out.

"Which direction?" McConnel asked.

Simons looked at Kippler, who shook his head. "The only thing I can think of is that way." Kippler pointed right. "That's where the ridge is highest, so there might be a chance there are openings on the lower side."

"Then right we'll go," Simons agreed. "Help me," he said to McConnel, and together they hung the unconscious Poulter between their shoulders and slowly walked off.

For minutes that felt like hours, they walked against the searing wind, Kippler leading the way and inspecting every foot of the riff for an opening to a cave or other place to hide.

Suddenly, he stopped, looked up, and raised an arm. "Wait here," he yelled, and climbed a few feet up the riff. For a few seconds, he disappeared behind an ice sail, then reappeared. "Can you get him up here?"

"We better put our backs into it," Simons yelled at McConnel, who nodded back.

With small steps, the two, each with one of Poulter's arms over their shoulders, dragged him up the riff. As they reached the ice sail, Kippler waited for them and assisted them forward into what looked like the entrance to a cave.

"Wait a second," Kippler said as he reached into his fur coat and came back with a flashlight. He pushed the button but nothing happened. He pushed the button again and again, but still, nothing. "Shit!" He smacked the back of the flashlight against the wall, and the light came on. "Yes!" He shone the light into the cave. "Let's get in as far as we can."

The three worked together to carry Poulter into the cave, and seconds later, what little daylight was left disappeared from the front.

Kippler pointed his flashlight farther down the cave. "Come on."

The searing wind subsided, and the crystalline-formed ice walls seemed to warm them up rather than cooling them down.

"Let's put him down here," Simons said, and together with McConnel, carefully put Poulter against the wall.

As they put him down, Poulter grunted.

"He's regaining consciousness," Simons said.

"Where... where... are we," Poulter stammered.

"We're safe, sir, in some kind of a large tunnel system," Simons said. "We dragged you inside."

Poulter cautiously shook his head.

"How are you doing, sir?" Simons asked.

"I think I'm ok." He felt the back of his head and looked at his hand. "No blood. Well that's something, at least. What happened?"

"You got knocked on the back of your head by a falling rock, Captain," McConnel took over. "Then the storm came in, and we dragged you here."

"You couldn't get back to the Cruiser?"

McConnel grinned. "Not while carrying you."

Poulter grunted as he tried to get up.

"Carefully." Kippler helped him up.

"I'm okay," Poulter said. "Seriously."

Kippler let go of him.

"You see?" he said as he took a few slow steps. "Where is this tunnel?"

"Somewhere inside the pressure ridge," Simons answered. "I think we're straight below where we parked the Cruiser."

"And the storm?" Poulter asked.

Kippler raised a finger. "You hear it? We just got here, so...."

"Any thoughts on where this tunnel leads?" Poulter asked.

"I was just planning on having a look inside," Kippler answered. "It looks like there's a corner some fifty feet up ahead." He pointed inside with his flashlight.

"You wanna go check it out?" Poulter asked. "I'll stay here behind."

"I'll keep you company," McConnel added.

"I'll join you?" Simons said.

"Great," Kippler said. "Let's go, then."

"Thanks for staying with me," Poulter said.

"No problem, sir, I could use the rest myself."

Seconds later, Simons and Kippler came to the end of the corridor and moved left. After taking that first corner, they quickly came to another turn.

"What do you think of these tunnels?" Simons asked.

"Not sure, to be honest, but do you feel we're slowly going down?"

Simons nodded.

"And the rough edges and crystal form seem to indicate the tunnels were formed through a landslide or some other kind of geological phenomena. The structured shape, on the other hand, and the organized way these tunnels snake through the ice would almost suggest...." Kippler rubbed his chin.

"Are you suggesting these tunnels are man-made?"

Kippler tilted his head. "Impossible. If these tunnels were human-made, the walls would be much smoother, and there would be signs of where they were carved out. Unless...."

Now Simons tilted his head as they proceeded.

"...Unless the ice would have had time to grow on, so to say. The tunnels would have been wider and higher before, and through time and weather influence, the tunnels would grow close again."

"How much time are we talking about?"

"I don't know anyone alive who could tell you this," Kippler replied. "I would think much longer than the average man on Earth lives."

"This ice shelf was discovered in 1841 by Sir James Clark Ross. That's a hundred years ago. Are we talking that old?"

Kippler sighed and cautiously shook his head as they turned another corner.

"What's that?" Simons asked.

"It's a cave, at the end of the tunnel. It looks like a dead-end from here."

Once inside, they inspected the square-looking cave with its blue, somewhat smooth icy walls.

"Damn," Simons said.

"What did you expect? A treasure room? Or maybe the lost crew of the HMS Erebus and HMS Terror?" Kippler asked, grinning.

"I have no idea." Simons walked up to the end. For a second, he stopped and stared at the wall, then touched it. With his gloved hand, he softly stroked the large ice crystals on the wall.

"Beautiful, aren't they?" Kippler asked as he shone the light on Simons' hand, where the crystals beneath it reflected blue diamond-like light.

"They are." Simons took a deep breath. "It's a pity, but this seems like the end of the line. I think we'd better head back. How far down do you think we went?"

"Well...." Kippler raised his head and counted, mumbling. "Maybe five hundred feet into the tunnels, and some fifteen feet down into the ice."

Both men turned to walk back, and Kippler shone his flashlight along the walls and in the direction of the tunnel again.

"What's that?" Simons asked.

"What?"

"Over here." Simons walked up to the wall and pointed at the ice.

Kippler aimed the flashlight against the wall. "Indeed, what is that?"

Inches below the ice, a dark, rectangular form stopped the light from penetrating deeper.

"Looks like something's frozen inside the wall," Simons said. "How big do you think it is?"

"I'm not sure how deep that is, but it's maybe one foot high and two feet wide? Wait." Kippler searched his jacket and took out a big jackknife. "It can't be too deep in there. Let's see if we can dig it out. Here, you take the flashlight."

Kippler started slamming his knife into the ice, and in seconds big chunks of ice flew around the cave. "It's a pity I didn't bring any bourbon," he joked.

A minute later, the shape was completely cut out, and Kippler tried to take it out. "It looks like a metal plate." He forced his knife between the ice and the metal, but the plate wouldn't budge. He carved out more ice from the edges, wrapped his fingers around the edges, but still the plate wouldn't come loose. He sighed. "There must be some kind of anchoring behind it."

"Shit." Simons wiped away the icy remainders from the plate and took a closer look. "What's that? Are those engravings?"

"Not possible," Kippler said. "Give me the flashlight."

Simons gave him back the flashlight, and Kippler pushed him away from the plate. "My God, you're right. It looks like drawings of some kind."

"Are those circles?" Simons asked. "Are you sure we can't get it out?"

"Be my guest." Kippler stepped aside. "Give it a try."

Simons pried his fingers between the plate and the ice. He put one foot up against the wall and pulled as hard as he could. "Help me," he cried out, moaning. Kippler joined him with a hand on top and one below the plate. "One, two, three," Simons counted, and both men gave it all they had, but still....

"It's no use," Kippler said.

"Damn, what do we do now?" Simons thought for a moment. "If only we brought a camera."

"We have some in the base camp," Kippler replied.

"That's not very helpful, Burt."

"Sorry," Kippler said. "But maybe...." He searched his jacket again. "Here." He showed a piece of folded paper and a lead pencil.

"What's that? Do you want to copy the thing? You can barely even see what's on it."

"I've something better." Kippler unfolded the paper and put it up against the metal plate. Then he took the lead pencil and carefully started rubbing it over the sheet. On the paper, the shape engraved on the metal slowly materialized on the paper.

"Amazing," Simons said.

"I always carry it around in case I want to make rubbings of fossils that I come across and can't take with me."

"Brilliant."

Kippler finished and handed him the piece of paper. "You see. Just as good as a photo. Perhaps even better. More details, you see."

"I don't know many, but you're definitely the best geologist I know," Simons said.

Kippler gave a bright smile.

"Now, I suggest we get back to the others and see what the storm does. But I feel we must absolutely come back here."

"I agree," Kippler said. "Let's leave a marker outside and get back here as soon as we can."

CHAPTER 23

Chelsea Cucumber Green

The Ross Ice Shelf, Dependent Territory of New Zealand, Antarctica, The Present

Heavy rain battered the airstrip at Air Movements Rongotai. Nadya watched a dark grey C-17 taxi onto the runway. On the side of the airplane, she read 'United States Antarctic Program.'

Thank God! I'm freezing out here.

She raised her umbrella and walked onto the tarmac where the plane stopped, and the loading dock at the back slowly opened.

As soon as the hatch hit the asphalt, a stream of American soldiers carrying duffle bags came out of the dark cabin and ran to the terminal, trying to stay as dry as possible. The rest of the plane seemed empty at first, until the lights came on. From a bench, on the left side, three men rose and walked her way. Two of them wore light grey coveralls with name tags below the letters 'USAP,' which read M. Yakovlev and Y. Pavlov. Without speaking, they stopped next to her.

"You must be Miss Fedorova," the third man called out as he left the plane. The heavyset man wore a dark suit and white shirt with red bowtie under a long khaki raincoat. He spoke Russian. Listening to his accent, Nadya suspected he'd worked abroad for a long time, yet she couldn't quite put her finger on it.

"Nadya," she replied.

"Great, and I am Andre Melnyk. Do you mind?" He pointed at the terminal.

"Of course not," Nadya answered. "Let's get out of the rain." She shared her umbrella with Melnyk.

"By the way," the round-headed man said. "These two gentlemen are Miroslav Yakovlev and Yuri Pavlov."

"Madam," they both replied, nodding.

"Both men are military trained. Miroslav is a versatile pilot who can fly just about anything, and Yuri here's an expert on the polar caps."

"And you are?" she asked as they went into the terminal.

Melnyk laughed. "Indeed, who am I? I'm an anthropologist and geologist by profession, and avid archaeology enthusiast."

"And your orders are?"

"Let's sit over there." Melnyk pointed at a small table in front of a McDonald's. "Let's see if we can grab something to eat before the plane leaves again in thirty minutes." They all walked up to the table and sat down. "Do you mind getting me a quarter pounder and a Big Mac?" he asked Pavlov, who got up again, nodded, and gestured Yakovlev to join him. "Anything for you?" Melnyk asked Nadya.

"No thanks."

"All right." He waved at the two men, who walked away. "What are my orders? From now on, my orders are the same as yours. We're to find out what the Americans are up to, and intercept any knowledge or goods they gather in any way we can."

"At what cost?" Nadya tilted her head.

Melnyk shrugged. "The only thing that's important is that you know that our employer thinks that, if everything pans out, they might be onto something big out there—earth-shattering big."

"Like?"

He shrugged again. "Big enough to give us an unlimited mandate to get our hands on whatever they find."

"How are we supposed to do that? And what about the risk of being discovered?"

"From now on, that's of secondary importance." He turned to see if his burgers were coming. "As for your first question... we are guests at McMurdo Base. It's only a few miles from Scott Base, where they are staying. The Americans at McMurdo think we're there to research rocks that provide clues for reconstruction on how and when the supercontinent Gondwana broke apart."

"And what if we are discovered? How are we supposed to get out of there?" Nadya asked.

"That's why I brought our own pilot. If we cannot find a plane or helicopter—" He slapped his jacket pocket. "—I have a satellite phone with a direct connection to Vostok Station, and they will immediately come and pick us up."

Nadya nodded. "Impressive. And that's how you're going?" She pointed to his suit and bowtie.

"Ha! I have proper clothes on the plane. I will change on the way there."

Pavlov set a plate with wrapped burgers on the table in front of him.

"Ah, great, American food... let's first eat."

***

"Actually, it's called Chelsea Cucumber Green," Cooper said.

"I'm sorry?" Bishop said.

They sat at a long table in the spacious, almost white dining room, where a self-service cabinet gave an excellent view to the open kitchen behind it.

Cooper smiled. "Chelsea Cucumber Green... it's a pistachio mint fresh green. I overheard you talking about the exterior color of our buildings here at Scott Base. Do you mind? Are you working?" He raised the tablet with his breakfast on it.

The main green buildings on the base were all built on pillars ten feet off the ground, rising above the snow, and placed at least twenty feet apart to prevent the risk of spreading fire. All buildings were, however, linked to each other by tunnels made of galvanized iron.

"Of course not," Monroe said, smiling as he closed his laptop. "I was just updating our contact at the USGS about our findings so far. I can continue later. Sit. I insist. You're our only rescue out of here, so.... You were saying?"

"Chelsea Cucumber Green. The original buildings were yellow and orange, or red and yellow, but when the base needed to be re-painted in '65, they decided to paint it green like the New Zealand landscape. On the other hand...." Cooper considered his words for a moment. "There's also a version of the story about the then superintendent, Bob Thomson, who came back from a trip to Ireland, where he liked the white cottages surrounded by green, so he reversed that image for Scott Base. Anyway, how did you sleep?"

"Great," Jennifer said. "Sleeping in a bunkbed reminded me of when as a little girl. I often stayed the night at my niece's place, who always let me sleep on the top of her bunkbed. I remember climbing up the ladder and finding it quite a challenge." She grinned. "Not so much now, of course, but still... good memories."

"I slept like a baby," Monroe added. "I expected it to be much colder, but it's actually a comfortable temperature everywhere."

"In here it always is," Cooper replied. "Summer and winter."

"Breakfast is great." Monroe pointed at his scrambled eggs, croissant, orange juice, and coffee.

"I'd say we've come a long way since Robert Falcon Scott on his Terra Nova expedition in 1910. They cooked with penguin blubber, ate salted almonds, turtle soup, roast beef, and stewed penguin breast in red currant jelly, or seal meat."

"Brr." Monroe shook his head.

"Where's Tipene?" Bishop asked. "Is he still asleep?"

Cooper smiled and looked at his watch. "Seven-thirty... I figure he's finishing up our transportation as we speak. Tipene's always the first one to wake up, somewhere between four and five, and doesn't eat until lunch."

"Finishing up transportation?" Bishop asked.

"You'll see." He gave a tiny smile. "It's a sunny day out there with little to no wind, so I figured you wanted to get out there as soon as possible."

"Where are we going?" Jennifer asked.

"Your coordinates." Cooper answered. "I figured that's where you wanted to start your search."

"Where else?" Bishop replied.

"You mean the place where Little America Three supposedly broke in two?" Jennifer asked.

Cooper nodded. "It's not that far, and I think it's a good way for you to get acquainted with the Antarctic. And again, it's a beautiful day out there."

"How far is it?" Monroe asked.

"I think we can reach it in less than an hour. It's familiar terrain, so we won't have too many problems."

"Not too many problems?" Bishop asked.

Cooper shook his head and pouted his lips. "Normally, when we scout new terrain or terrain we haven't been to for a while, the biggest risk is the cracks in the ice. These cracks can form overnight and be covered by a thin layer of snow. You have to be vigilant while crossing such terrain. The main cause of death in the Antarctic is falling into those crevasses. The cracks can be hundreds of feet deep, and sometimes they swallow entire vehicles. We have a PistenBully outfitted with a crevasse probe held on the end of a long arm in front of it. The sensor triggers an alarm in the cabin when a crevasse is detected. But as you probably can imagine, you can only travel *real* slow, because you need the time to be able to hit the brakes. But we won't need that today."

"Umm... overnight, you said?" Monroe looked nervous.

"Don't worry. We know these parts of the woods, so to say, like the back of our hand. You'll be completely safe. Now, if you're finished?" He pointed at the empty plates, and they all nodded. "Great. If you put your trays in the cart and get ready, I'll meet you in thirty minutes in the general assembly hall. Just follow the signs through the tunnels, and I'll meet you there."

Cooper got up and, in a minute, disappeared through the swinging doors.

"What do you think?" Bishop asked.

"I can't wait." Jennifer sounded enthusiastic.

"I'm still wondering how we'll get there," Monroe said. "With what kind of transportation."

"All right, then, let's get ready." Bishop rose from his chair. "Thirty minutes in front of your door?" he asked Jennifer.

"I'll be ready."

***

Thirty minutes later, Bishop and Monroe turned a corner in the hallway and stopped in front of number 114, Jennifer's cabin. Bishop tapped on the door two times.

A second later, Jennifer opened the door and stepped out. "You two look great." She pointed at their possum fur collars and Cossack hats.

"You look good too," Monroe said, pinching her thick red coat.

"Shall we?" Bishop asked.

The three took off in the direction of the signs that said 'Maintenance and Assembly.' From the main building, the first tunnel snaked its way to the Research building. From there, they walked through the Recreation building to finally end in the Maintenance and Assembly hall. When Bishop opened the double swinging doors, a cold wind entered the corridor from the hall.

"Brrr," Monroe said. "I thought it was warm everywhere."

"Sorry," Cooper's voice sounded from behind a large stack of wooden crates just before he emerged.

Mesh metal containers were mounted on all the walls, filled with climbing gear, pickaxes, spiked shoes, and other cold weather gear. In the center of the hangar-like hall, all sorts of vehicles were parked.

Cooper pointed. "They just closed the main hangar door after rolling out a helicopter. It'll be warm again soon."

"Wait until you get out," Hemi called out from the back while working on a snowmobile.

"Good morning," they all greeted him back.

"Ready to take a ride?" Cooper asked.

"How?" Monroe asked quickly.

"We have one old gasoline slurping machine." Cooper pointed at the machine Hemi was working on. "And...." He pointed behind them at a row of snowmobiles. "These four babies are ours to try."'

"Wow," Monroe said, looking at four brand new, sleek, shining black and bright red snowmobiles.

"I don't trust anything that doesn't smell like gasoline," Hemi said.

"That's why you don't get one." Cooper smiled.

"These are electric?" Bishop asked.

"They are."

"But how?" Bishop asked. As a great fan of electric vehicles replacing gasoline ones, he himself drove an electric converted Jeep Wrangler. "I always thought current electric engines couldn't perform in these cold weather conditions. Or rather, the battery packages would give out at extreme colds."

Cooper nodded. "True, but now there's a Canadian firm that claims to have overcome all problems associated with cold. The university negotiated with them to give us four of these on loan." He waved his arm at the vehicles. "The TS3 Taiga Electric Snowmobile, from zero to sixty in less than three seconds, without transmission—hundred and eight horsepower, two hundred and fifty newton meter of instant torque. It guarantees a range of sixty-two miles at even twenty-two Fahrenheit, and all of that at full speed. Direct drive, like I said, meaning no transmission, integrated GPS, and DC quick charge in twenty minutes."

"You sound like a commercial," Jennifer joked.

Monroe nodded toward Bishop and said, "Jennifer, can you please help Matthew? He's starting to drool."

"Don't you love the idea?" Cooper asked.

"Just let them talk," Bishop answered. "They don't know how to appreciate real beauty."

"All right, any of you ever driven a snowmobile?"

They all shook their heads.

"Bikes?"

Now they all nodded.

"Same thing." Cooper walked up to one of the machines and started pointing at parts. "On/off, steering—hat will make these two skis at the front go left and right—gas... just turn it with your hands like a motorcycle. That will start rotating the track here beneath your seat. And these are the foot brakes, the mirror, and GPS. All your GPS's have the coordinates you gave us programmed into it. That's all you need to know. Tipene will drive in front all the time, and I'll be at the back making sure we don't lose any of you. You'll all be wearing a helmet equipped with a Cardo Packtalk, so we're connected to each other all the time. You don't have to push any buttons. Just say, 'Hey Cardo,' then say what you want, and the rest of us will hear you."

"I will tow a toboggan." Hemi pointed at what looked like a covered sled attached to his snowmobile. "The toboggan is stocked with search equipment, food, drink, and other supplies."

"What do you think?" Cooper said. "Are you up to it?"

"I say we get underway," Bishop replied.

"Agreed," Jennifer added.

"It's an adventure." Monroe smiled.

"Good. Please try on a helmet and a pair of snow goggles for size." Cooper pointed at a large rack with helmets. "Then take your seats when you're ready. Oh, and please keep in mind: you won't hear an engine running, but be assured that when you turn the throttle, it will run. Just turn it a tiny little bit at first. One thing more: when the doors open, drive out straight without trying to steer. You can only steer in the snow and a little bit on ice, but not on concrete. Clear?"

"Clear."

"Yes."

"Okay."

Within a minute, they all sat down on a snowmobile. When Cooper opened the door, Hemi cautiously drove out, dragging his toboggan behind him. Bishop, then Jennifer, then Monroe, followed him.

"Are you all there?" Cooper sounded in their helmets. Then he pushed a button on a remote, and the door behind them slowly shut again. "And don't forget to say, 'Hey Cardo,' when you reply."

"Hey Cardo," Bishop said, "Matthew here, I hear you loud and clear."

"Walker here," Monroe sounded next.

"This is cool," Jennifer sounded as they drove from the asphalt and wood onto the snow.

Hemi sounded next. "I'll pick up some speed now, but please call out if anything is going on back there. And of course, we'll be watching you. Please enjoy the ride and the sights."

Hemi opened his throttle, and snow sprayed wide from below the steering skies at the front.

For the next thirty minutes, they crossed the icy planes of the Ross Ice Shelf, which reflected blue and golden in the early morning sun.

Hemi throttled down for the first time, and the others neatly parked next to him in a row. "Over there, you see? The ocean." He pointed north, where a white ice-shelf ended in a streak of dark blue that could have been either sky or water.

"That's where we're going?" Bishop asked.

Cooper pointed at the GPS. "If you didn't already switch on your GPS, do so now, and you'll see that in about three miles, we'll reach our destination, your coordinates. Ready to see what's out there?"

They all agreed, and Hemi nodded to Cooper, who took the lead as he geared up again.

When they neared the coastline, they could smell the salt in the air, and the snowy underground became icier.

"Do you feel that?" Cooper sounded over the radio. "The grounds are getting slipperier. It's frozen from the cold Antarctic winds called katabatics. These winds are formed by cold, dense air flowing out from the polar plateau, and at the steep vertical drops along the coast, they create cold air that rushes back over the mainland."

In another ten minutes, he stopped his snowmobile, got off, and took off his helmet.

"This is it?" Monroe asked.

"This is it," Cooper said as he tapped his GPS. "Where would we be without this little American military invention?"

Everyone got off their machines, looked around, and inspected the area. Except for the north, where the ocean started below a thirty foot cliff, there was nothing else in sight but a blueish white, flat surface of snow and ice.

"Whatever you do," Cooper said, "keep your snow goggles on at all times. Fifteen minutes of sun reflecting on the snow, and we can carry you home snowblind."

"Great view," Monroe said. "But what do we do now?"

"We start digging," Hemi said, and they all went silent for a moment. "I have shovels and pickaxes in the toboggan."

Bishop, Monroe, and Jennifer eyed each other, frowning.

"Hey, you wanted to come here and search," Cooper added when Hemi couldn't keep a straight face, and they both burst out laughing.

"You should have seen your faces," Hemi said, trying to regain a straight face.

Bishop shook his head. "Good one."

"You really got me going," Jennifer said. "I was already starting to regret ever coming here."

"And almost ready to get a shovel," Monroe added.

"But seriously," Bishop said. "What now? Do you have a metal detector in that thing?" He pointed at the toboggan.

"We've got something better," Hemi said. "We brought GPR."

"GP what?" Monroe said.

"Ground Penetrating Radar," Cooper replied.

Hemi opened up the toboggan and pointed at a black box with a white cover. He took out the one-by-one-foot wide and six-inch-thick box, and with a thud, placed it in the snow.

"Looks heavy," Jennifer remarked.

Hemi huffed. "It is."

"And expensive," Cooper added.

Hemi took out what looked like a long leather belt, which he connected to the box. He then dragged the apparatus to the back of Cooper's snowmobile and attached it.

"Just one more thing," he mumbled as he took another, much smaller box from the toboggan. He took a small digital screen from the box and attached it to the snowmobile's steering. "That's it. This one's all set up. Who'll do the honors?"

"What do you mean?" Bishop asked.

"One of you will have to drive," Cooper answered, smiling. "We have two of these sets and a pattern for both programmed into the GPS. I need two volunteers who will ride the patterns."

"I'll do it," Jennifer said. "I like driving these things. What do I do?"

Cooper pushed a few buttons on the GPS. "Simple. You follow these lines on the GPS screen and this other screen. Don't drive too fast. As long as the green light is lit, you're doing okay. Should it turn red, you slow down. Here on the left, you see what's beneath the snow." On the screen, a grey square showed some straight, horizontal, darker lines. "Should one of these lines start to show peaks, like a mountain, you'll also hear loud beeping, and you should stop and call it in through Cardo. We'll set up a speaker so we can hear you all the time. All clear?"

"Clear." She immediately got on the snowmobile again.

"If you need anything or get hungry," Cooper said, "you simply drive back here. We brought a nice lunch. When you think you found something, the first thing you do is mark it with one of these little flags." He pointed at a small bag next to the saddle. "Okay then."

"Wait a minute," Hemi said, and tossed her a bottle of water. "You need to finish this first. In fact, we all do." He handed Bishop a tray of bottles. "We must stay hydrated at all times."

"You carry water in a cool box?" Monroe laughed.

"Actually, it's a heating box," Hemi replied. "To prevent the water from freezing. It has a battery that'll keep our water liquid for up to twelve hours."

"It's the world upside down," Monroe replied.

"Literally," Bishop added.

Jennifer gulped down the full bottle, put her helmet back on, and turned the throttle up. Slowly, she drove away to the starting point on her screen.

"I'll set up the second GPR," Hemi said, and walked away.

"Who'll take it?" Cooper asked, and Bishop and Monroe looked at each other. "You can switch after some time," Cooper added.

Monroe raised his shoulders. "I'll take it. As long as I'm here, I'd better earn my keep."

"All right," Cooper said. "That also means that as soon as any of you find something, it's up to us to see if we can dig it out."

"Now I'm happy I volunteered." Monroe gave a wide smile.

A minute later, Hemi called out from the second setup. "Ready?"

"You have to find something first." Bishop smiled back at Monroe. "Now go."

A minute later, Monroe drove in the opposite direction of Jennifer and started following the pattern on his screen.

"Sandwiches, anyone?" Hemi said, walking up to Bishop and Cooper carrying three small folding camp chairs and another heating box.

CHAPTER 24

The Turtle

Monroe paced the ice and snow, rubbing his hands and looking at his watch.

"A little over an hour," Hemi said.

"Sorry?" Monroe replied.

"We've been searching for a little over an hour now," Cooper said.

"And still, completely nothing," Monroe said while Bishop, some thirty feet behind them, completed another round on his snowmobile.

"Don't worry, if there's anything out here, we'll—"

A loud horn sounded from behind them. They all turned to see Jennifer standing next to her vehicle some three hundred feet in the distance, making broad gestures with her arms above her head.

"Heeeey," she called out.

"She's got something," Monroe said. "Why is she not using her comms?"

"No idea," Cooper said. "She probably forgot in her excitement. All right, let's grab the gear and get over there." He planted a flag on their present location, and as quickly as they could, they threw everything in the toboggan and drove off towards Jennifer, who was still jumping and waving her arms.

As they drove off, Bishop, who'd watched the spectacle from a distance, also came racing by on his way to her.

They pulled up near her and hopped off their snowmobiles.

"You found something?" Bishop asked.

"I think I did," she replied.

"Let's see," Hemi said as he worked the GPR's screen and everyone gathered around. "Hmm, look here. Keep your eyes locked on the horizontal lines." He pushed a 'play' button on the side of the screen. The horizontal lines trembled a bit over the screen, then suddenly spiked all over.

"Wow," Bishop said. "Can you see what it is?"

"No," Cooper replied. "But the height of the peaks suggests it's relatively high in volume, more than three meters."

"And how deep beneath the snow?" Bishop asked.

"It varies a bit," Hemi answered. "But at average, about... umm... no more than four or five feet." He disconnected the GPR from the snowmobile.

"What do we do now?" Jennifer asked.

"First," Hemi said, "we see if we can find the edges, which means we simply drag this thing around and see where the wavy lines end and begin, and we mark it with flags. Who's with me?"

"Sure," Jennifer said, and picked up a bunch of flags.

"Follow me." Hemi reset the GPR and the straight lines reappeared. "Now, you came from that direction, so let's head back there first."

Within thirty feet, the lines started to wave on the screen.

"Check," Hemi yelled, and stopped for a second while Jennifer planted a flag behind the GPR. "Here we go." He started walking and dragging the machine. "Check... check... check...." It sounded every other minute, and each time Jennifer planted a flag in the ice. "Check. That must be about it."

After Jennifer planted the eighth and final flag, everyone took a few steps back and virtually drew lines between the flags.

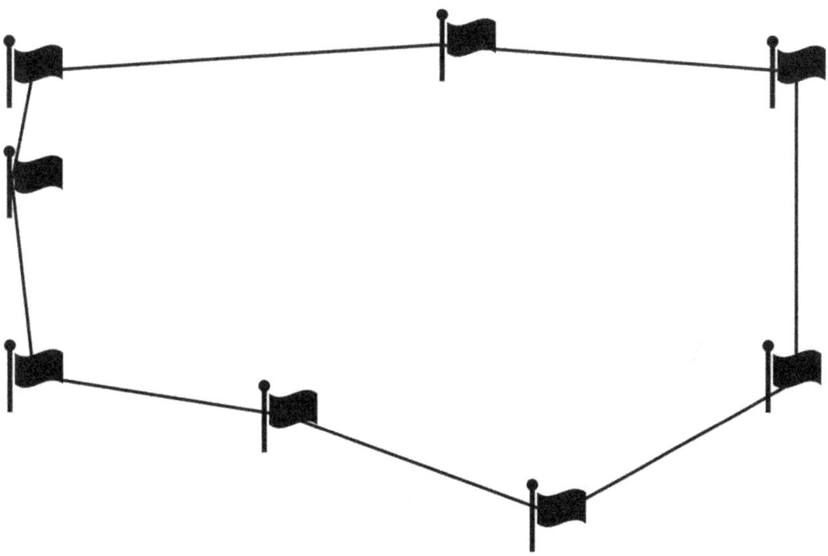

"Cool," Monroe said. "What do you think?"

"How big was the Antarctic snow Cruiser?" Hemi asked Cooper.

"About seventeen by six meters. Umm, some fifty-five by nineteen feet."

"That's some fast conversion," Jennifer said.

Cooper smiled. "People forget that we've only used the metric system for thirty years now. I grew up using the same antiquated system that you Americans still use."

Bishop chuckled. "What do you think?"

"Might be a fit," Hemi said.

"Can you determine the material of whatever's down there?" Bishop asked.

"There's no way to determine what it is. The GPR can only detect a disturbance in the soil's consistency, or this case, snow."

"What do you think?" he asked Cooper.

Cooper shrugged. "I think it's a tight fit, but who knows. There's only one way to find out."

"That's the part I was afraid of." Monroe grinned.

"We dig!" Hemi opened the toboggan and took out some gear, which he put in the snow.

"What's that?" Monroe asked when Hemi took out a large chrome pipe attached to what looked like a gas canister.

"That's what they call a Bare Blaster Propane Torch."

"Now we're talking," Monroe replied.

"We can try it," Cooper replied. "But we have to be careful not to melt the snow only to have it freeze up into ice immediately."

"I figure that wouldn't make our work any easier," Jennifer said. "And those?" She pointed at a row of large white plastic bags.

"That's 96 percent pure calcium chloride pellets."

"Like road salt?" Bishop asked.

Cooper shook his head. "Not really, except for the fact that you use it for the same purpose. Generic salt doesn't work very well at these temperatures. Calcium chloride works at extremely low temperatures and at multiple times the speed of salt. You know those hand warmers where you click a small piece of metal inside, and the liquid inside crystallizes, and they get warm?"

Bishop nodded. "Sure."

"Same chemical. It gets warm by itself and melts the snow."

"So what's the process? What do we do?" Monroe asked.

At almost the same moment, Hemi appeared in front of him and handed him a large shovel and a pickaxe.

"Here," Hemi said. "Pick a nice spot in the center of the rectangle and start digging, and make sure to throw everything you dig out of the area. Otherwise, your colleagues have to dig it up a second time. The next one starts to dig some ten feet behind or in front of him, and so on. Once you find something, there are small scoops in the toboggan."

"When you find something," Cooper added, "call out, and we'll check it out. From there, we can see if we can use the blowtorches or the calcium chloride."

"Clear?" Hemi said.

Mumbling, they all nodded. "All right, get yourselves some gear and let's go."

Monroe was the first to put a shovel into the icy snow in the center of the marked area. "Ouch," he said when the ground appeared more challenging than he'd anticipated.

Hemi said, "You'd better first clear some ice with your pickaxes, and then use the shovels."

Soon, all five of them were chopping, digging, and shoveling ice and snow.

"Not to complain," Monroe said, opening the top of his jacket. "But I expected it to get very cold out here. Not so much now."

"It's the sun reflecting on the snow," Cooper explained. "Like in winter sports. You ever ski?"

"I'm a black man from Liverpool originally. So, that's a no." Monroe smiled, and everyone joined him laughing.

For the next forty minutes, they dug snow, drank water and ate sandwiches.

Hemi started singing a song about working on the chain gang. "That's the sound of the men... working on the chain... ga-a-ang. That's the sound of the men. working on the chain... gang. All day long, they work so hard, till the sun... is goin' down...."

Clunk. Bishop's shovel hit something hard, something that sounded metallic. Immediately, the singing stopped and everyone ceased shoveling, and everyone standing in their pits turned toward Bishop.

"What is it?" Jennifer asked.

Bishop fell to his knees and with his gloved hands, removed more snow to get a good look at what was underneath his feet. Then he came up again waving a shard of something dark red in his hand.

"What's that?" Monroe asked.

"I think it's old red paint," Bishop replied. "What color did you say that Snow Cruiser was?"

Everyone climbed out of their pits and raced up to Bishop. Below

Bishop's feet, a dark red square had appeared. It looked like a heavily scratched and dented piece of metal.

"That has to be her." Cooper jumped down next to Bishop, kneeled, and tried to free more snow from the sides. "This has to be the roof. We need to know where the front or back is and where we are. There should be a hatch in the front, on top of the steering cabin."

"Try to dig a narrow path in both directions," Hemi suggested. "That should give us some indication."

"Good idea," Cooper said. "You start digging that way." He pointed at Hemi, then turned to Bishop. "And will you start that way?"

"No problem," Bishop said.

"Jennifer, Walker," Cooper said. "Can you both please continue the digs in line with this?" He widened both arms in the extension of the line between Hemi and Bishop.

Everyone agreed and started digging. Minutes later, a small red line started to take shape in the otherwise pristine white surroundings.

"I've got something," Monroe called out.

"All right, everyone," Cooper said. "Please continue. I'll take a look." He walked up to Monroe. "Okay, let's see if we can widen this a little."

Monroe worked one part of the hole while Cooper dug out the other end.

"It goes down here," Cooper said.

"That must be the end."

"Or the beginning," Cooper said. "Help me dig it out further."

"Here." Monroe handed him a small scoop he'd taken from the toboggan.

Both men scooped compressed snow from the bottom of the pit and swept the icy snow over the edge into the air.

"Stop. We can stop," Cooper said.

"What?" Monroe asked as Cooper climbed out of the hole.

"This is the wrong end," Cooper called out. "We need to focus on Jennifer's end."

Monroe joined him next to the hole. "How do you know?" he asked as both men got their gear and walked up to the other side.

"This side goes straight down, but the front of the Cruiser was slanted, so it should go down at an angle."

"You sure?" Monroe asked.

"Positive. We need to dig a few more holes near Jennifer, and I'm convinced we'll find the front over there."

"Okay."

Cooper explained his theory to the rest of them, and said to Monroe, "Pick a side." He waved an arm to the left and right of Jennifer.

Monroe walked left, and just as he raised his pickaxe to make his first swing, Jennifer called out.

"Got something!" The dark red color appeared beneath her feet.

"All right, everyone," Cooper said. "Pick a direction, and let's see where this thing goes."

Seconds later, everyone was either standing or sitting down on their knees, freeing everything surrounding Jennifer from the snow.

"I've got the end," Bishop called out.

Cooper immediately joined him, and together, within a minute, they'd dug down about a foot, where the metal went down into the ice.

"You see. Slanted." Cooper sounded proud. "And I think I feel a window down here. The hatch must be to the left or right of this."

"I've got a metal edge here," Hemi called out at Cooper's left.

"Let's dig it out," Cooper said, and crawled up to Hemi on his knees.

Two minutes later, all five of them surrounded a hole in the snow, looking at a three-by-three-foot square, dark red, metal plate, a few feet down in the ice.

"Wow," Monroe said.

"This is exciting," Jennifer added.

Bishop said, "What do we do now? How do we open this? There's no grip or anything."

Cooper left for the toboggan, and returned a minute later carrying a crowbar.

"Step aside," he said, and jumped in the hole again. He put the crowbar in between the hatch and the frame and pushed it down. He grunted as he gave it more power, but nothing happened.

"Here, let me." Hemi jumped down and took the crowbar from Cooper. He leaned down on it with all his power, and as it slid away, the crowbar slipped from under the edge and Hemi fell on his knees with a loud clunk on the metal plate. "Damn, this isn't going to work." He climbed out of the hole again.

Cooper had returned to the toboggan again, and was already on his way back carrying a large white plastic bag in one hand and a propane torch in the other. After he kneeled next to the hole, Cooper took a jackknife from his jacket and cut the white bag open.

"Why not heat everything?" Monroe asked. "Wouldn't that be quicker?"

"It probably would," Cooper responded. "But I don't know what the ceiling of the cabin is lined with, and I don't want to risk a fire."

"You think there's a chance of fire?" Bishop asked. "I doubt there's any oxygen in there."

Cooper shrugged. "Probably not, but I don't want to take any chances now that we've gotten this far." He poured the bag of white pellets on the hatch, and used his shovel to evenly distribute the pellets along the edges of the hatch. "Now we wait."

"How long?" Monroe asked.

"Probably no more than a minute or five," Cooper replied.

"I can't wait to get a look at what's inside," Bishop said.

"Temper your enthusiasm, professor," Hemi said. "There's always the possibility the Cruiser is filled up with snow or moisture got in, and everything is rotten in there. Or maybe chemicals they carried affected the inside."

"We'll know soon enough now," Cooper said. "Let's stay optimistic. Everyone's got a flashlight from the toboggan?"

"Shit," Monroe said, and immediately left for the sled.

"Bring one for me," Jennifer called out after him.

"And me," Bishop added.

When Monroe returned with the flashlights, he also brought a tray with bottles of water, which he distributed. "You need to stay hydrated."

For another few minutes, they paced the surroundings, drank their water, and Monroe threw snowballs at Jennifer until Cooper, with a loud thump, jumped onto the metal roof again.

"Now, let's try this again." Cooper waved his crowbar in the air, wedged it between the metal parts, and pushed down hard as he could. For a few seconds, nothing happened, but then a screech sounded from the hatch, and the crowbar moved an inch farther down.

"It's happening," Monroe said.

Cooper leaned down harder on his crowbar, and with a sharp and shrill sound, the hatch sprung open some four inches, and he fell on his knees.

"Yesssss," Hemi cried out.

Cooper got on his feet again, raised the crowbar, and gave it to Hemi. Then, with two hands, he grabbed onto the edge of the hatch and pulled with all his might. Still, the hatch wouldn't open any further.

Bishop jumped down into the hole and put his hands next to Cooper's. "Here, let me help."

Both men now gave it all they had, and with the sound of screeching metal, it slowly opened. They pulled it all the way up and over, revealing the dark square hole that led into the vehicle. Both Cooper and Bishop took out their flashlights and lit up the interior.

"What do you see?" Monroe asked, the sight from above obstructed by the two men leaning over the entrance.

"It's the steering cabin," Bishop said. "It looks empty but intact. It's incredible."

"Let me see." Monroe tried to join the two in the narrow hole.

"Wait!" Cooper held up a hand. "Let me first check it out and see if everything's safe."

"Looks safe enough," Bishop said. "And it survived seventy years."

"All the more reason to see if there are any rotten places, like in the ceiling. We wouldn't want the whole place to come down on top of us. Here, help me down." Cooper sat down with his legs through the hole and stretched both arms to Bishop. "Let me see if I can reach the dash with my feet."

Bishop grabbed Cooper's hands and, with the flashlight between his teeth, shone the beam on Cooper's waving legs.

"A bit more to the front," Cooper said. "Almost there. Yes, a little lower."

Everyone seemed to have stopped breathing.

"Yes," Cooper called out as one foot rested on the dash, and he quickly added his other. "All right, now lower me."

Bishop carefully lowered Cooper, who retracted his arms and grabbed onto the hatch. Then he dropped himself from the dashboard onto the floor.

Bishop shone his flashlight at Cooper as he sat down on the bench behind the steering sticks and the windows.

"I'm ready to drive off," he said, as he realized that he sat at the exact same spot his grandfather would have sat seventy years ago, when he was the first to drive across the Antarctician ice and snow.

What an experience that must have been in that time. For a moment, he fell silent.

"Are you okay?" Bishop asked.

Cooper sighed. "I am, it's just that... umm... well, it somehow feels that this place is filled with other people's memories. Family, if you know what I mean." He shook his head. "I probably sound crazy."

"Not at all," Bishop said. "It would have surprised me if you reacted otherwise."

"Thanks." Cooper chuckled. "All right, let me see what's back here."

"Here." Bishop handed him a flashlight.

Cooper took it and climbed into the back. For a few minutes, the only sound came from below, where Cooper tapped the metal walls to see if the structure was still sturdy enough to hold the ice outside.

"It is amazing," Cooper said as he climbed back into the steering cabin. "Hemi, you need to get down here."

"Yes, will you help them down from there?" Hemi called back. "I'll help them first at my end, and when everyone's inside, I'll swap with you. That way, there's someone up here at all times."

Cooper nodded. "All right, Tipene."

"Ladies first," Monroe said as he pointed Jennifer to the hatch.

Supple, guided by the men, Jennifer lowered herself and moved away into the Cruiser.

"Next," Cooper called out.

Within two minutes, they were all down, and Cooper was on his way up again.

"You don't want to stay down longer?" Hemi said.

"Sure I do," Cooper replied. "In time."

"Okay." Hemi lowered himself into the hatch being helped by Bishop below.

***

"All right," Bishop said. "Let's see what's back there." He climbed over the driver's bench and lowered himself into the engine compartment. The two huge, dark blue diesels looked dusty, but there was nothing to give away their age. He tapped the gray-painted metal surrounding them. Everything looked just as sturdy as it probably was in the mid-previous-century.

"How is this possible?" he said to Hemi, who joined him from behind.

Hemi said, "The extreme temperatures, low salt content, and dry environment are perfect for preservation."

"Makes you wonder what will be hidden beneath all the ice here in Antarctica." Bishop moved into the next room. On the left sat wooden cupboards with a sink on top, and on the right sat a stove, atop which rested two pans with closed lids on them. He opened one of them and peeked inside.

"Well, at least they did the dishes before they left." He smiled and opened a drawer, which banged loudly as a tray with cutlery appeared. "It's all perfectly usable. Unbelievable." He opened all the drawers and cupboards, but found only some pans and empty metal boxes.

He passed an open corridor into the next room, where Jennifer and Monroe were sitting down on folding chairs. In the center of the room was a small table with some papers, plates, cigarette stubs, and empty soda cans. Along the walls were two bunk beds.

"Welcome to my office," Jennifer remarked.

"What do you think?" Monroe said, smiling.

"Amazing, isn't it? Did you find anything yet?" Bishop pointed at the drawers beneath the table and along the walls.

"Not yet," Monroe said. "We checked out the back first, but there's nothing there but some empty fuel tanks and supply racks."

"Also empty," Jenifer said as she opened one of the drawers, and a single pencil rolled up to the front. She raised it in the air. "Souvenir."

"Let's see what we've got here." Monroe opened a small door beneath the table and took out a stack of papers.

"Be careful with that," Hemi said. "It might break."

"I will." Monroe carefully took the papers from the stack one by one.

"What are they?" Bishop asked.

"Maps, manuals, and inventory lists, as far as I can see."

"And what's that?" Jennifer pointed at a dark piece of folded paper.

Monroe took the paper and tried to unfold it, but the paper cracked and tore from the edges.

"Warm it up first," Bishop suggested.

"How?" Monroe asked.

"Give it to me," Jennifer said. Monroe handed her the paper, and she started to blow warm air along the edges.

"What kind of a librarian are you anyway?" Bishop joked.

"I promise you this wasn't in the librarian course." Monroe smiled.

A minute later, Jennifer carefully unfolded the paper and put it in front of her at the table. "Here you go."

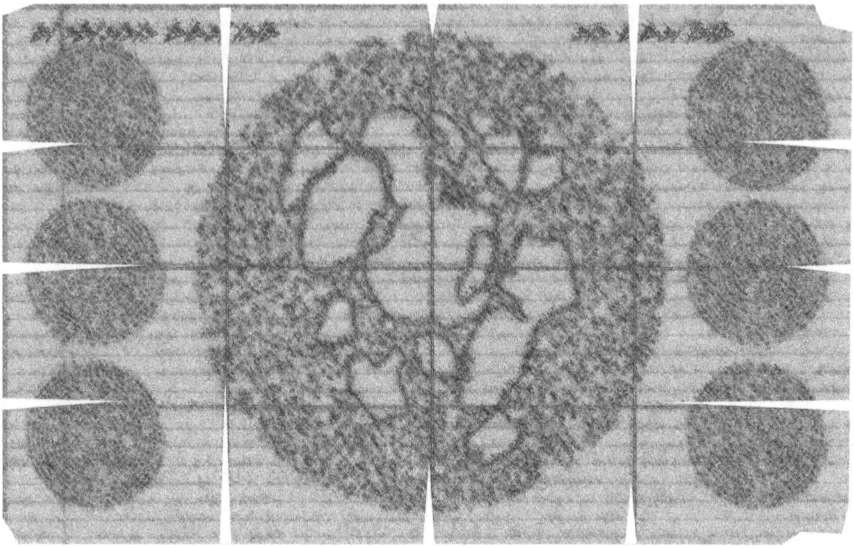

"What's that?" Hemi asked.

Monroe turned his head in line with the paper. "I have no idea what it says, but I'm pretty sure it's a rubbing."

"A what?' Jennifer asked.

"A rubbing, like when you put a piece of paper on something imprinted, and you take a lead pencil and rub it over to get a print of whatever's underneath."

Bishop turned the paper towards him. "But what does it say?" He stared at the paper for several seconds.

"What do we do now?" Monroe asked Hemi.

Hemi looked left and right, and picked up a small, metal meshed crate from the floor. "Here, I suggest we collect everything you want to take with you and put it in here."

"Do we need to go out?" Jennifer asked.

"Not yet," Hemi replied. "Jay-Jay also wanted to take another look, so I'll switch with him in a moment. Besides that, we now know where the Cruiser is, so we can always take a second look. I just hope there's something here that can help you."

"I hope so too," Monroe said. "What do you think, Matthew? ...Matthew?" Monroe asked again when Bishop didn't respond.

"Umm... what?" Bishop snapped out of his trance, staring at the rubbing.

"What do you think? Is there anything here that can help us?"

"I'm not sure." He pointed at the rubbing. "I'm not sure yet."

CHAPTER 25

Air New Zealand's Flight 901

Scott Base, Antarctica, Evening

The Scott Base lounge looked like any lounge at any middle-class hotel. It had comfortable brown and white leather seats surrounding glass-topped wooden tables with reading materials on top. On one side, a large bookcase occupied the wall, while on the other side, a large open fireplace sat between two windows that overlooked the Ross Ice Shelf within the distance, and the mountainous coastline of White Island on the mainland, at the other end of the frozen sea.

Bishop and Jennifer took seats at one of the tables, where Bishop stacked the papers he'd taken from the Cruiser.

Monroe fiddled with a telescope in front of one of the windows.

"That won't do you much good," Cooper said as he walked into the lounge, followed by Hemi.

"What do you mean?" Monroe asked.

"Wrong time of year. In a few months, when the nights turn dark again, you have a great view of the Aurora Australis from here."

"Aurora Australis?" Jennifer asked.

"The southern lights," Cooper answered. "Like the Aurora Borealis near the North Pole. Small particles emitted by the sun attracted by Earth's magnetic field, lines that light up as they enter our atmosphere. You must have seen pictures of those green and orange lines lighting up on the horizon. A magnificent sight."

"I was looking at the seals," Monroe said, still behind the telescope.

"There are a lot of them this year," Hemi said.

"They look big," Monroe replied.

"They are," Hemi confirmed. "Weddell seals can be twelve feet long and weigh over thirteen hundred pounds. You don't want to mess with them. They're the apex predators in the Antarctic. They've been seen killing emperor penguins up to a hundred pounds and forty inches, and just for the sport of it."

"I always figured seals were those nice little furry creatures you see on TV," Jennifer said.

"Just stay out of their way, and you'll be okay." Hemi grinned.

They all sat down as Cooper tapped the stack of papers on the table. "Did you find anything yet?"

Bishop shrugged. "We just got here too."

"Ah," Cooper said. "Do you mind?" He took the top piece of paper from the pile.

"Of course not," Bishop said.

"Whose property are these, anyway?" Monroe asked, walking up to the table.

Cooper grinned. "Good question. The Antarctic soil belongs to no one, but the Cruiser was originally American, and from my perspective, it's fine if these papers wind up in an American college library."

Monroe smiled. "I will take good care of them, but before that time comes, let's see what we have here."

"Looks like a list of fuel consumption." Cooper waved his paper around.

Bishop pulled the stack towards him and leafed through it.

"What are you looking for?" Hemi asked. "Anything specific?"

"Just filtering out anything specific," Bishop answered. "I think we can start by eliminating all kinds of lists and pre-printed documents."

"There can always be additional writing on those," Jennifer said.

"True, but we need a place to start." Bishop sifted through the pile. "Here... and here... these are the two that stand out to me."

"A map and a...." Hemi scrunched up his nose. "What did you call it before?"

"Rubbing," Monroe said.

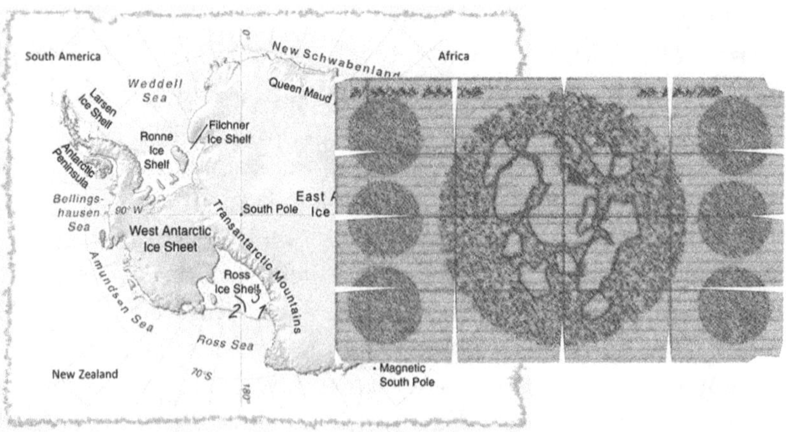

"Yes," Bishop said. "You recognize the map of Antarctica?" He eyed Cooper and Hemi.

"Sure," Cooper answered. "It's a bit outdated, of course, but I've seen the exact same copy of it when writing my dissertation on the Little America expeditions. It was a standard but rather crude map from that time period. They made it with the little-to-no information they had on the continent back then. There were no satellites, and only a few handfuls of expeditions ever made it to the continent, and very little data about those missions was shared between countries."

"They did know where the Germans were located," Monroe stated, pointing at the top of the map, which read 'New Schwabenland.'

"I guess they did have spies at that time." Cooper laughed.

"And what are those numbers?" Jennifer pointed at the one, two, and three that were handwritten on the south of the continent.

Hemi turned the maps towards him. "Not sure." He cocked his head. "They're not far from where we are now."

"Locations the Cruiser visited?" Bishop suggested, rubbing his chin.

Cooper nodded. "Could be. I think number two could be Mount Erebus, an active volcano not far north from here on the island." He pointed to the back of them. "When you look out the window of the café on the other side of the building, you can often see plumes of smoke rising from the mountain."

"Anything of interest out there?" Bishop asked.

Cooper shrugged. "I'm not sure, but I don't think so. It's one of the three volcanos on the island, the others being the smaller Mount Bird and Mount Terra Nova."

"There's one thing that happened out there," Hemi added. "In 1979, Air New Zealand's Flight 901, which was doing Antarctic sightseeing with passengers, flew into Mount Erebus, killing all 257 people on board. The wreckage is still out there."

"Could that be something?" Bishop asked. "Could that perhaps be the place they made the rubbing?"

"I don't immediately see how," Cooper answered. "But you never know."

"And the other numbers? One and three?" Jennifer asked. "What about them?"

Now Hemi turned the map towards him. "One looks somewhere around the location where we were yesterday."

"Little America Three?" Bishop asked.

"Sounds logical," Cooper said. "It could very well have been their point of origin on a trip they were planning, number two being Mount Erebus."

"Which leaves number three," Jennifer concluded.

Monroe took out his cellphone and took a picture of the map. "Let me see." He worked his phone for a moment before he raised it into the air in front of the others. "Does this help?"

The map was now projected as a transparent overlay over a satellite image of the area on the screen. Spreading two fingers on the screen, Monroe zoomed in on the part with the three numbers.

"Number three seems to be on the edge of, or even in, the ocean," Jennifer noticed.

"That could very well be," Cooper said. "Seventy years ago, the ice shelf was a lot bigger. It's well known that with the rising of ocean temperatures, the ice sheet is melting about six times faster than forty years ago. According to NASA, in Antarctica, 252 gigatons of ice are melting each year, roughly the equivalent of three-point-five Olympic swimming pools every second."

"That's an amazing amount," Jennifer said.

"Whatever they were going for, it could very well have been lost," Monroe concluded.

"On this map, however rough, it looks like it was on the edge of the ice shelf now," Hemi said. "But that doesn't mean whatever it is was lost to the sea."

"It could have broken off and still be on a rogue ice shelf," Cooper added.

Hemi nodded. "Anyway, there's no way of telling from this map. There's far too little detail."

"And the location?" Bishop asked.

"Too little detail," Cooper replied. "It could be anywhere within the range of tens of miles of coastline."

"And what about this line?" Jennifer asked, tapping on the paper map. "This also seems to be drawn by hand."

Cooper picked the map up and closely inspected the line drawn between the numbers two and three. Then he tilted his head and mumbled, "Could it be?"

"What is it?" Hemi asked.

"Well, do you mind?" Cooper stretched out his arm towards Monroe's phone.

"Sure." Monroe handed it to him.

Cooper worked the phone for a moment, and then raised it into the air, running the screen in front of everyone's face. "You see?"

"What's that?" Jennifer asked. "Ice sculptures?"

"It's the Ross Sea ice ridges," Hemi answered. "Floes of ice. They're separate plates of ice that collide with each other and, from below the ice, are thrust upwards into the air. They form what we call Ice Sails, massive sculptures up to forty feet tall."

"But these are at the edge of the ice shelf bordering the water," Bishop said.

Cooper handed Monroe back his phone, and said, "Indeed. Only emphasizing the fact that in the past, another ice shelf pushed against the one we see now. But that still doesn't help with determining its location. About 40% of the overall mass of sea ice in Antarctica is a build-up of those pressure ridges."

They all went quiet for a moment before Jennifer broke the silence. "The question remains: what did they find over there?"

Monroe took a deep breath. "Whatever it was they were searching for, they probably didn't find it."

"How so?" Cooper asked.

"Because if they did find anything, we probably would have found traces of it in the Cruiser."

"Didn't we?" Bishop tapped a finger on the rubbing on the table.

"What do you mean?" Jennifer asked. "You think that was made at location number two?"

"Why not?" Bishop said.

Hemi picked up the rubbing from the table and took a closer look at the top of the drawing. "May I?" He pointed at Monroe's phone.

"Am I the only one who has a cell phone in here?" Monroe complained before handing it over.

"You are the only one who has one on him." Bishop smiled as Hemi took some pictures of the rubbing.

"Umm...." Jennifer sounded reluctant as she took her cell phone from her jeans.

"Here." Hemi handed Monroe back his phone. "Can you enlarge the two images I took and raise their contrast?"

Monroe swiped the screen a few times and showed it to Hemi.

"Hmm...." Hemi shook his head.

"What are you looking for?" Bishop asked.

Hemi pointed at two places at the top of the rubbing. "You see over here and here. It looks like there was something added on both the left and right side after the rubbing was made."

"Something was written in lead pencil?" Bishop suggested.

"That's what I thought, but...." Hemi turned the phone in Monroe's hand towards Bishop. "You tell me?"

"It looks like writing indeed, but what it says, I have no idea."

Hemi now passed around the phone, and everyone took turns analyzing the screen and zooming in and out. They all ended up shaking their heads.

"And the other picture?" Hemi asked.

Monroe got back the phone, did his thing, and reached out to give it to Hemi again. "Hey," Monroe said, taking back his arm, looking at the screen while enlarging the image between two fingers.

"What is it?" Bishop asked.

"Here." Monroe showed the screen to everyone.

"Numbers?" Jennifer asked.

"I believe so," Monroe replied. "Anyone have a pen and paper?"

Bishop searched his pockets for a second and said, "Yes. Go. I'll take notes."

"Well, let's see," Monroe mumbled with one hand holding the phone and the other working the screen, focusing on the screen as he deciphered and called out numbers and letters for a minute or so.

"That's it," he finally said. "What have you got?"

Bishop put the paper down on the table.

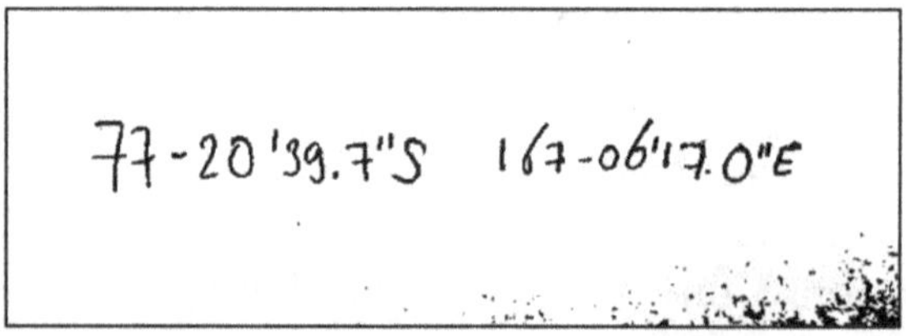
77-20'39.7"S 167-06'17.0"E

"Is that what I think it is?" Jennifer said.

"Quick," Cooper demanded, waving his hand to get Monroe's phone. "Seventy-seven, fifty-one south are the base coordinates."

"Our base coordinates?" Monroe asked. "Scott Base?"

"Yup," Hemi confirmed.

"Here." Cooper raised the phone and let it go around. On the screen, a satellite image of Ross Island was shown with the shape of an upside-down red teardrop projected along the coast in the north. "Wow. I think we've found a new location."

"Wow indeed," Jennifer said.

"Is it far?" Bishop asked. "Can we go there?"

"It's not that far," Cooper replied. "But if we were to go there, I'd suggest we do so tomorrow and leave early, so we have a full day to work with."

Bishop smiled from ear to ear. "Sounds like a plan."

"And what do we do in the meantime?" Monroe asked.

"There's a pool table in the café behind us," Hemi replied. "Could that be a good place to start?"

"Sounds like another good plan," Monroe agreed.

CHAPTER 26

The Tunnel

Antarctica, Morning

"I miss the sunrise," Monroe said as he walked into the Maintenance and Assembly hall, where the snowmobiles were already waiting under the rolled-up hangar door. The sun was shining bright, and not a single cloud floated in the sky.

"You're late," Bishop replied.

"That's how I know I miss the sunrise." As long as Monroe could remember, he had set his alarm clock half an hour before sunrise. In fifteen minutes after waking up, he would dress, grab a cup of tea, put on his walking shoes, and walk off into the sunrise—every day.

"Your early morning walks?" Bishop asked, and Monroe nodded.

"I totally feel you," Jennifer agreed. "I miss the darkness of the evening."

"You'll get used to it," Cooper said.

"Trust me," Hemi added, "it's much better than the other half of the year in total darkness."

Jennifer huffed. "I can't imagine how I would possibly cope with constant darkness."

"Same here," Monroe said. "I once knew an English professor who moved to Tromsø, a Norwegian town located over two-hundred miles north of the Arctic Circle. He told me that during what they call the Polar Night, from November to January, the sun wouldn't rise at all."

"Terrible." Jennifer shuddered.

Two loud pings sounded from Bishop's jacket pocket. He took out his cell phone and read the screen: *You have one new voice message*. "Do you mind?"

"Of course not," Cooper said. "If you have a connection out here, you should use it. It could be gone before you know it."

Bishop dialed a number and listened.

"Don't you have a satellite phone?" Jennifer asked.

"I have one," Hemi said. "When we go out, one of us always carries a sat phone."

Bishop took the phone from his ear and said, "You should listen to this." He put his phone on speaker.

"Hi, Matthew, this is Elise... umm... Aldridge, in case you know more Elises. You asked me to look at the gene sequences from the eukaryote they found in the Russian Antarctic drill, and compare them with those from your mummy. Well, it took me some time before I could get my hands on the samples from Lake Vostok, but as soon as I got them, I ran some tests, and, well...." The line went silent for a moment. "There are definitely similarities. Of course, you only gave me a fragment, so it isn't much, and I have to find out if there's a chance the results are in any way tainted. But for now, I did find trace similarities between the genes from Lake Vostok, the ones you gave me in the files, and the ones found in Ata, the mummy. It looks like a three-way match. Anyway, I will send you the results through email, and call me back when you can. Elise."

As the line went silent again, Bishop pushed the red button on his phone.

"What do you think?" Monroe asked.

"Not sure," Bishop replied.

"It's all connected," Jennifer said. "It has to be."

Bishop nodded. "It sure seems like that. The question is how, and why?"

"Maybe we'll find the answers out there." Monroe pointed to the snow outside.

"Who knows, who knows," Bishop said softly.

"And on that note," Cooper said, "any saddle pain from yesterday?"

"Nope, nothing," Bishop and Jennifer stated in unison.

"And?" Bishop eyed Monroe.

Monroe spoke reluctantly. "All right, just a little, but I've taken my precautions for today." He slapped his behind.

"I don't want to know," Bishop said, laughing.

"Agreed," Cooper added. "That being said, I feel the new electric snowmobiles worked like a charm. Don't you think?"

"I don't know how a regular snowmobile performs, but I think they're fantastic," Bishop said, and Jennifer nodded in agreement.

"What do you think? Everyone ready?" Cooper asked.

Calling out and mumbling in agreement, they all sat down on their snowmobiles again.

"Same procedure as yesterday," Hemi said. "The GPS on each of your mobiles is programmed with our destination so you can monitor our progress all the time. I'll ride shotgun again, so just follow me. And if you want to talk...."

"Hey Cardo," Jennifer called out.

"Exactly." Hemi sat down and started his snowmobile, slowly set his vehicle in motion, and with a loud growing rumble, a gray stack of smoke rose from his exhaust. When he drove out, the others opened their throttle, and the electric mobiles followed him in silence.

"I really love these electric mobiles," Cooper called out through the com system.

"Okay, okay," Hemi said. "Maybe tomorrow we can change. Let me check out what all the fuss is about."

From Scott Base, they turned north, and soon the buildings behind them were nothing but a small speck in the white and blue plains.

After a few minutes, Cooper sounded through their helmets again. "We're lucky again. The sun's shining bright, and no wind. That's three days in a row, which is quite exceptional."

"And from the looks of it," Hemi added, "the weather will hold for the coming days. When were you planning on returning to the mainland?"

Monroe was the first to speak. "After we found what we're looking for."

"Or get stuck permanently," Bishop added.

***

The Bell 212 Twin Huey helicopter's rotors slowly started to spin on one of the six helicopter pads at McMurdo Station. Scott Base paled in comparison to the American station. Amongst others, there was a firehouse, power plant, water distillation site, a wharf, harbor, several stores, clubs, and warehouses. Miroslav Yakovlev flipped some switches on the cockpit's ceiling when Melnyk, Pavlov, and Nadya arrived at the choppers sliding door.

"Here, let me," Pavlov said, moving in front of Nadya before grabbing the handle and sliding the door open.

Nadya simply nodded and got in.

Melnyk followed quickly, and Pavlov swiftly closed the door after he joined them. Melnyk moved to the front, sat down next to Yakovlev, and strapped in.

"Everybody ready back there?" Yakovlev asked, looking back.

"We're good," Pavlov said.

Nadya, opposite of him, nodded while putting on a headset.

The rotors now started to spin rapidly, and after a short, sudden shake, the chopper took off.

"I understand you had contact with the Americans this morning?" Nadya said into the headset.

"No real contact," Pavlov said. "Early this morning, I stood guard near their base in a four-wheel-drive, and I saw them leave on snowmobiles."

"How do we know where they're going?"

Melnyk took over. "They drove north, and this helicopter is specially equipped for search and rescue missions, so it has ground radar that can locate people, vehicles, and everything else that moves or arrays heat, in almost any weather conditions."

"Cute," Nadya said. "And what do you suggest we do once we find them? It's not as if we're able to swing by unnoticed."

Melnyk cocked his head. "We'll see. We can always 'accidentally' drop in and say hello. Who knows what we might learn once we're down there?"

Pavlov took out his pistol magazine and check it for ammunition.

Nadya took a deep breath. *Great.*

***

After thirty minutes of relatively flat snow and ice, the terrain slowly inclined, and Hemi slowed down a bit. "Mount Erebus," he said, and waved everyone beside him. "Or rather the southwest rim, called Seismic Bluff. You see that cabin over there in the distance? That's the seismic station this slope is named after." A tiny plume of light gray smoke emitted from the top of the twelve-thousand-foot tall mountain.

"And the New Zealand flight that crashed?" Bishop asked. "You said that the wreckage was never retrieved."

"That was on the other side," Cooper answered. "But you won't find anything there without digging. Everything is molted into the ice and covered with a thick layer of snow."

"All right, here we go again. Ready?" Without waiting for an answer, Hemi opened the throttle, and they all followed suit and picked up speed again.

"What are those?" Monroe asked, pointing at a series of tall towers of ice with thin plumes of smoke emitting from the top.

"They look like little volcanoes," Jennifer said.

"In a way, they are," Cooper replied. "They're called ice fumaroles. They're ice towers formed by freezing gasses emitted from extremely humid caves beneath the ice, where starved organisms form carbon dioxide, carbon monoxide, and hydrogen. They can grow up to two hundred feet before collapsing again. Often a new one will then form nearby."

"Never heard of it," Monroe said.

They all seemed to check their GPS screen at the same time; they had about eighteen miles to go.

They left the ice fumaroles behind them, and minutes later, the terrain leveled again. Hemi and Cooper switched positions, and the new lead went full throttle, bringing them to their destination in less than twenty minutes. In front of them, from left to right and as far as they could see, a massive wall of ice shapes appeared. They looked like they were shot out of the ice below, forming enormous towers of blue, glass-looking ice that occasionally reflected all colors of the rainbow.

"The pressure ridges," Cooper said through the system.

"Wow," Jennifer said. "They look incredible."

"*Hey Cardo...* How tall did you say those ridges are?" Bishop asked.

"The sails can be up to forty feet tall," Cooper answered.

"And we should climb over?" Monroe asked.

"We're here." Cooper stopped his snowmobile, and seconds later, everyone parked next to him. "And I don't think we need to climb them. There are often passages through them that should be relatively easy to climb."

"*Relatively* being the operative word," Monroe mumbled.

Hemi worked his GPS while everyone got off their mobiles, took off their helmets, and put their Cossack hats back on.

"What do we do now?" Bishop asked. "Use the GPR again?"

"The radar is of no use to us here," Hemi responded. "I checked the exact coordinates from the rubbing with our position. If they determined the coordinates correctly seventy years ago, what we are looking for should be straight over... there." He pointed to the center of a massive piece of ice sail some thirty feet away.

"You mean..." Bishop said.

Hemi nodded. "Straight in the middle of that sail somewhere."

They walked up to the edge of the ridge.

"And behind the ridge?" Bishop asked.

"Is the Ross Sea," Cooper answered. "Or rather, a vast collection of ice floes in a thin layer of ice. I checked yesterday's satellite images this morning."

"How deep does this ridge run?" Bishop asked.

"It varies," Hemi answered. "It could be anywhere from thirty feet up to a few hundred."

"Wow," Bishop replied.

"What now?" Monroe asked.

"Now we take a look," Cooper said.

Hemi opened the toboggan behind his snowmobile. "I suggest we all take some gear. Take two ice axes, put your cardo on your head, and put on these spiked hiking crampons. You simply fold them around your shoes." He held up what looked like a black rubber sandal with stainless steel jaws attached to it. "One size fits all."

Bishop, Monroe, and Jennifer clumsily tried to attach the rubber soles to their feet.

"Simply put them on your shoes, the man said," Monroe mumbled. Then he watched Cooper and Hemi put them onto each other's feet. "You could have said so." Monroe shook his head and grinned.

"And miss you fumbling around?" Hemi laughed.

After helping each other, soon everyone had their spikes on and were armed with two ice axes.

Hemi said, "I suggest we split up, with about fifty feet between each of us, and follow the ridge from left to right."

"Towards the sun," Cooper added.

"What are we looking for?" Jennifer asked.

"A way into the ridge," Cooper suggested. "Any reasonably way into the ice. If there's anything to be found in there, it'll probably be reachable by what looks a little like an access path, a place where the ridges in the past drifted apart. Such access could be frozen closed again, so use your axes freely, and mind where you put your feet."

"Is there a risk of falling through the ice?" Monroe asked.

"It's not that. The ice everywhere is at least several hundred feet thick. But the floor can be very slippery and slanted, so chop your spikes firmly, and with force, into the ice every step you take. All right, everyone ready?" Cooper, without waiting for a reaction, stepped up to the ridge straight in front of him and watched left and right as everyone took their place a bit farther on. "Everyone ready?"

"Ready."

"All right."

"Yes."

"Let's go."

"All right, let's go," Cooper said. "Please be careful, and whenever in doubt, call out, and I'll get to you immediately."

They slowly walked the edge of the ridge and inspected every foot of the wall.

Bishop was the first to slash an ax into the ridge, chopping a chunk of ice with a loud crackle. *Nothing*, he thought, looking at the closed ice formation a few feet inside the ridge.

A few seconds later, Hemi started chopping off ice, followed by Cooper. Again they found nothing.

Then Bishop found a way into the blue ice.

Monroe, walking somewhere behind him, said, "You got something, Matthew?"

"I'm not sure," Bishop said, and followed a narrow path into the ice, placing his feet cautiously on the treacherous ice shelves on the floor. Then he walked up to a large sail of ice that blocked the rest of the way. He hammered the ice with his ax a few times, but it wouldn't budge. "It's a dead end. I'm coming back."

After finding his way back, he continued along the wall, and the rest of them followed again. Then he noticed Jennifer in front of him disappearing into the ridge. "You found something, Jennifer?"

"There's definitely some kind of a path leading in," she responded.

"Please be careful," Monroe said.

"You didn't say that to Matthew when he walked in!" Jennifer complained.

"Sorry," Monroe replied. "I care too much for you, I guess."

"Thank you," Bishop replied, grinning. "I knew you were my best friend."

"Nothing personal," Monroe said.

"With you, it's never personal," Bishop joked. "So how is it going with you, Jennifer? ...Jennifer?"

There was no response.

"Jennifer!" Cooper now called out. "Are you there?"

Seconds passed without a sound.

"Everyone gather at Jennifer's location. Now!" Cooper shouted out. They all ran as fast as they could on their spikes, and within a minute, they stood at the gap where Jennifer walked into the ice.

"I'll go in first," Monroe said, and set one foot into the ridge.

"Let me go," Hemi said. "You don't have the experience."

"But I got us here," Monroe replied.

"And Hemi can get you out safely," Cooper said. "Let him go in first, and we all can follow."

Monroe took a deep breath and then stepped aside.

Without hesitation, Hemi walked into the narrow path, pulling himself forward by chopping his axes on either side into the ice and dragging himself along.

Monroe and Bishop followed his example, trailed by Cooper, who planted a small flag at the entrance as they worked their way through the riff.

"Stop," Hemi said, and went down on his knees.

"What is it?" Monroe asked.

"Jennifer," Hemi called out. "There's a fresh hole in the ice. I think she fell through it."

"I thought you said you couldn't fall through the ice," Bishop whimpered.

"Sorry, she didn't fall *through* the ice," Hemi clarified. "She fell *into* the ice." He stuck his head deep below the ice. "There's some kind of an open space or tunnel down there."

"Hello." Jennifer's voice suddenly sounded again, crackling through the com system.

"Jennifer," Bishop said. "Are you okay?"

"I'm fine. I just fell through a thin layer of ice and lost my headset on the slide down. I just found it back."

"Thank God," Monroe said. "Can you get back up?"

"I can, but I don't think I should."

"What do you mean?" Bishop asked.

"I think you should come down here and see for yourselves."

Bishop and Monroe turned to Cooper.

"What do you think?" Cooper asked Hemi.

Hemi took a deep breath and nodded. "All right, let's go see what's down there."

He sat down on the side of the hole with both legs over the edge, and let himself slide down until his shoes touched the floor below. Then he let himself go and, standing straight, his head stuck out just above the hole.

"I guess it's not too deep," Monroe said.

"Easy peasy," Hemi replied. "Stay here until you hear from me." He sat down on his butt and let himself slide away. "Here we goooo...." His voice rapidly faded away.

"Are you there?" Cooper asked through Cardo.

Monroe already prepared himself to get down there.

For several seconds, the line stayed silent.

"I'm here," Hemi said. "Sorry, I got distracted. Yes, get down here. You should."

"All right then," Monroe said. He lowered himself into the hole and let himself slide.

Bishop and Cooper followed his example.

"That was fun," Bishop said as he stepped out of the way to let Cooper slide in.

"Wow," Cooper said, balancing himself as he slid in so he could easily get back on his feet.

Bishop took it all in. "Wow, indeed. What is this place?"

The five of them looked around the square-looking ice-room.

"It looks almost man-made," Cooper stated. "The walls are almost flat, like they've been carved out."

"And where does the light come from?" Monroe asked.

"Good question." Bishop watched the blue ice walls, lit up and glowing like the light of a flame lightbulb.

"Thin ice," Hemi offered.

"Could it be the ice somehow is so thin and transparent the sunlight gets through?" Bishop asked.

"This deep?" Hemi shook his head. "We must be twenty feet or more below the surface."

"And how about... umm...?" Monroe pointed at the floor, which also lit up light blue.

"Good question," Cooper said. "Light-emitting algae, perhaps."

"Bioluminescence, in sub-zero temperatures?" Hemi frowned.

"It isn't unheard of," Cooper answered. "Was that why we had to come down here?"

"Jennifer?" Hemi pointed at her. "It's your finding."

"Yes, well, my eyes were immediately drawn to a darker space in the ice-wall in the back. With my gloves, I could easily wipe off a thin layer of ice when this emerged." She took a step aside.

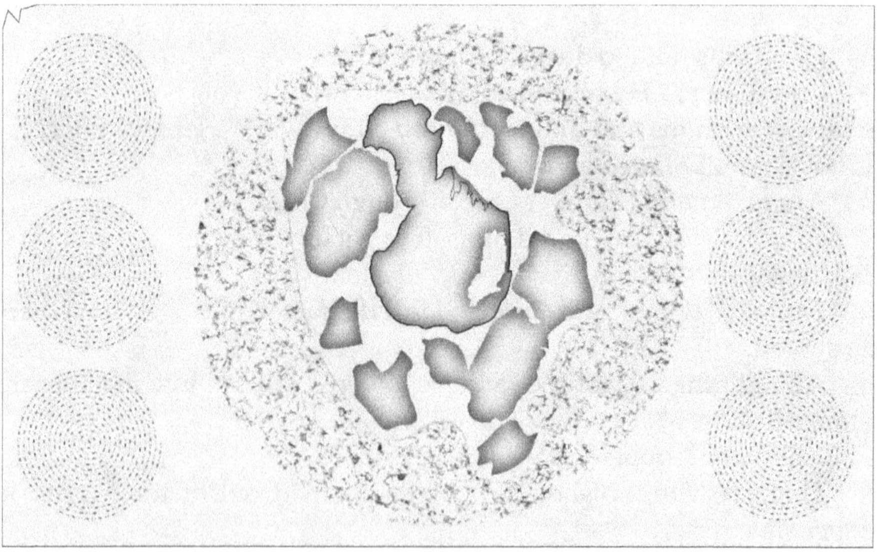

A copper or gold-looking plate in the wall materialized.

"That's it," Monroe said. "The rubbing."

Bishop stepped up to the wall and took a closer look. "I believe you're right. Look at those spirals. I think we've seen spirals just like that before."

In the center, a large circle with what looked like darker spots in it was drawn on the plate, while on each of the sides, three spirals were etched.

"What could they say?" Jennifer asked.

Bishop shook his head. "I have no idea."

"The big circle," Monroe said. "I'm sure I've seen that image somewhere before."

"Where?" Jennifer asked.

Monroe shrugged. "I don't know. Can we take it off?"

"I tried for a second, but it seems to be embedded in the wall somehow," Hemi answered.

"Here, let me try." Monroe wriggled his fingers around the plate and pulled. "Wow, that's tight."

"Wait a second," Hemi said, and put his fingers on the other side. "Now pull again."

Both men grunted as they pulled as hard as they could, but the plate wouldn't budge.

"Take pictures," Bishop said. "As many as we can, and also take details of the spirals."

They all took out their phones and cameras and started taking pictures.

Jennifer said, "And what do you think about this?" She pointed at an arched shape in the ice about two feet wide and four feet tall.

"A doorway for little people?" Monroe suggested, grinning.

Bishop snickered. "Funny, but you're right about one thing. It looks like an opening that froze shut again." He punched it with his hand.

Hemi offered him his ax. "Here, try this."

"I've got one." Bishop took the ax dangling from his belt and smacked it into the wall. Pieces of ice broke off and scattered around the room. He hit the same spot again and again, until he broke through the ice.

"What's that?" Monroe asked as everything around them began to shake. "Did you do that?"

Bishop looked around. "I don't think so."

The five of them looked around the trembling room as small pieces of ice from the wall and ceiling broke off and fell onto the ground with the sound of broken glass.

After a minute, the shaking slowed down until it came to a complete stop.

"Earthquake?" Bishop asked.

"Or eruption," Hemi suggested.

"In any case, I suggest we don't stay too long," Cooper said.

"I'll chop faster," Bishop said, and plunged the ax into the wall again.

***

On the surface, the Bell helicopter's rotors had come to a full stop.

"Let her run," Melnyk ordered the pilot.

He got out of the chopper with Pavlov and Nadya, and the three walked up to the five snowmobiles parked some fifty feet away.

"Where could they be?" Nadya asked.

"Radar didn't show any movement or other heat signatures besides those from the snowmobiles," Melnyk replied.

"That means they have to be in the ice shelves somewhere, where radar can't find them," Pavlov said.

"Or somewhere below," Melnyk suggested.

"There." Pavlov pointed to a small red flag with a black 'x' on the edge of the rift.

"X marks the spot." Melnyk smiled.

"You want to go and say hello?" Nadya asked.

"I think it's time," Melnyk said. "Will you take point?" he asked Pavlov.

"Of course, sir." Pavlov pulled himself onto the riff.

A few minutes later, they all leaned over the hole in the ground.

"Hello," Melnyk called down. "Hello."

Nothing came back.

"Strange," Nadya said.

"We don't know how far that tunnel goes," Pavlov said. "They must be out of reach. You want to get down there, sir?"

"We've come this far, so...." The heavyset man lowered himself into the hole and let go of himself.

A couple minutes later, Nadya landed on the floor in the room, where Melnyk and Pavlov already waited.

"Woah," she said. "Nice crib."

"And they left the lights on for us," Melnick said. "What's that?" He pointed at the plaque on the wall.

"No idea," Nadya said, and they walked up to it. "Looks like an etching of something."

Melnyk grabbed it and tried to pull it off. "Thought so."

"What do you mean?" Pavlov asked.

"If it were easy to take it off, they probably would have done so before us. Take pictures," he ordered Pavlov.

"Here," Nadya said, standing at an arched hole in the ice wall.

"This must be where they went through," Pavlov said.

"Hello," Melnyk shouted into the hole.

The ice began to shake, and grew in intensity. Large chunks of ice broke off from everywhere, and the ceiling started to break down.

"We need to get back, sir," Nadya called out as she grabbed Melnick at the shoulder.

Melnyk hesitated for a moment. "Damn, I think you're right. Let's get back. What's happening?"

On their hands and knees, they crawled back into the tunnel, and within two minutes, they ran outside, where the helicopter's rotors were winding up.

"What are you doing?" Melnyk cried out when he opened the helicopter door.

"What do you mean?" Yakovlev asked.

"What's with the ruckus?" Melnyk pointed at the rotors.

"The temperature, sir. Because of the freezing cold, I speeded up the rotors. That way, in case we needed a speedy withdrawal, we wouldn't need to let the engine run warm first."

Melnyk shook his head. "Get us out of here. Now!"

"Yes sir." Yakovlev took the controls and lifted the chopper into the air. 'What's up?"

***

"I think we'd better not stay down here too long," Cooper said.

"I think you're right. Did you feel that tremble again?" Monroe said. "The whole place could come down on us."

"What distance did we cover down here since we went through the archway?" Cooper asked Hemi, who looked at his smartwatch.

"About three hundred meters," Hemi answered.

"Do you feel that?" Bishop asked.

Jennifer nodded. "There's a draft."

"Smells like the sea," Hemi added.

"Before we head back, let's see what's out there beyond that corner." Bishop pointed some hundred feet ahead. "If there's nothing there, we'll go back. I promise."

"All right, let's go," Cooper agreed, waving a hand forward.

Bishop took the lead, and a minute later, he turned the corner and yelled out, "Wow!" He grabbed on to the walls and let himself fall back onto the floor.

"What is it?" Monroe quickly stepped up and took a look around the corner.

Some hundred feet above the ice floes, a hole in the immense ice shelf ended their journey.

"What is it?' Cooper asked.

"See for yourself," Monroe suggested as he helped Bishop back on his feet.

"Damn," Hemi said. "That's been a long walk for nothing."

"This path must have led somewhere," Bishop said, stroking the wall with his glove. "It's too meticulously carved out."

"It probably did," Hemi agreed.

"Then where is the rest of it?" Bishop asked.

"That seems to be the question at hand," Cooper said.

"What now?" Monroe asked.

"Now we get the hell out of here," Hemi said. "Before the whole damn place comes down on us."

"Agreed," Cooper said. "Let's go. I'll lead."

For another ten minutes, they snaked back through the tunnels, until Cooper suddenly stopped after taking a turn.

"What now?" Monroe asked.

Cooper took a step back and let Monroe pass.

"What?" Monroe called out.

Cooper took deep breaths as they all inspected what was beyond the corner.

"What does that mean?" Jennifer asked.

Cooper sighed. "That means the cave we took in here has collapsed, and we have no way out of here."

CHAPTER 27

Back at the Site

The Ross Ice Shelf, Antarctica, January 27, 1940

The Antarctic Snow Cruiser slowly drove the final mile to the place where they made the rubbing. Jay Simons was glad to head back to the site—'his spot,' as he had called it—and was eager to find out more about the mysterious tunnel and golden plaque on the wall.

For the past week, Simons had driven the Cruiser around with a small group of scientists led by Jack E. Perkins, the key botanical researcher on the Little America Three expedition. For days, he'd heard the proud Perkins talk about his search for new plant life and lichens. Apparently, a combination of fungi and algae was found growing in the sunless, damp environment in the cracks of rocks along the Antarctic coast.

He could still hear Perkins in the back of his mind. '*We've already collected twenty-four new plants, fifteen bryophytes and lichens, and nine brand new species of algae.*'

During his last week of driving, the rubbing had been on constant display in front of Simons on his dashboard. Intrigued, he watched and scrutinized the six spirals and large circle with seemingly random spots in the center.

What was it, and why was it there? Who could have put it there? Especially when you consider the fact that we were the first to visit the place... ever?

Every time he looked at it, he came up with more questions than answers. At one point, while focused on the rubbing, he would have driven off an ice-cliff if one of the scientists, by accident, hadn't bumped into him just in time.

In the evening, after dinner, he'd located Kippler and discussed their finding, up to the point that Kippler had, in a friendly manner, urged him to '*Find a new friend!*'

Somehow, he couldn't let it go. For days, he'd kept bugging Poulter for another trip to the site, but Poulter had made a promise to the botanical team that they would be driven around in the Cruiser for a week.

Yesterday, that week was over.

He was glad that he, Kippler, McConnel, and Poulter would be back at the pressure ridge in little over an hour.

"What do you think?" McConnel climbed over Simons' shoulder to the front. As he sat down next to him, he held up a picture he'd drawn of the Eagle and the Turtle.

"What do you think?" McConnel repeated as he signed it.

"I think you missed your calling." Simons smiled.

"You're joking."

"No, I'm serious. You might just be a better artist than you are a pilot."

McConnel chuckled.

"But seriously, Dougal, why did you become a pilot?"

McConnel lit a cigarette. "My father was an airplane designer early this century, a real pioneer, so to say. He worked with the Wright brothers at the time they made their first controlled, sustained flight with a powered, heavier-than-air aircraft. I often picture myself there when the Wright Flyer flew for the first time, on December 17, 1903. You see, it was contagious. Only I wanted to fly myself."

"Content?"

"With my profession?"

Simons nodded.

"Absolutely. Especially when it leads to places like this that no one has seen before, especially from the sky. You never know the circumstances you'll be confronted with, in the air."

"Unfortunately, we didn't get to fly much yet. Only a few supply-runs between Admiral Byrd's camp and ours."

"That's okay. I also like our little trips. They've been adventurous so far."

"Let's see if I can keep it interesting for you." Simons grinned.

Kippler stuck his head around the corner behind them and said, "Are we there yet?"

"It should be just around the next snowfield," Simons said, laughing.

"You better wake the captain," McConnel said.

"I don't think he likes it when you call him Captain," Kippler said, and disappeared into the back again.

Kippler was right. Ever since Poulter started working for the military, they had tried to push him to accept a military rank. That way, if things went wrong and they had some kind of fallout, they could always try him in a military court. Of course, Poulter knew that, and insisted that he was duty- and contract-bound to the Armour Institute of Technology.

"That's it." Simons pointed at a wooden crate sticking out of the snow. "There's our marker."

"I see it," McConnel confirmed. "Amazing. You found it."

Simons tapped on the oil-filled compass on the dash. "Never go driving the Antarctic without it. Did you know that the compass was invented by the Chinese almost two thousand years ago?"

"Good morning, everyone." Poulter moved into the front and sat behind the two. "We're here?"

"Morning, Captain," McConnel replied.

"Chief," Simons said to McConnel, and then turned to Poulter. "Yes, over there's the crate we left behind last time."

Poulter stretched his arms as they neared the crate, and within a minute, Simons brought the Cruiser to a metal-screeching halt.

"The weather could have been better." Poulter pointed at the dark sky.

"True, sir," Simons said. "But if we're lucky, we'll be inside the whole time."

"That's true. Okay...." He looked at his watch. "I suggest we have an early lunch here before we head out."

"Sounds good to me," Kippler responded from the back.

"I bet it does," McConnel said softly as they all started to climb back.

An hour later, Simons and McConnel cleared the table of army biscuits, the left-over sardines, mixed berry jam, and York ham, while Kippler did the dishes, wiping them clean with a wet cloth.

"Ready?" Poulter called out, fully dressed in his sheep wool jacket and seal fur Cossack hat and mittens. He waved a flashlight in one hand and a pickax in the other.

"Almost," Simons replied.

The rest finished dressing up, and were ready a minute later.

When Poulter opened the door, a cold wind laced with flakes of ice and snow blew into the vehicle. The flying bits diminished the sight, making it impossible to see the crate that should be some twenty feet straight ahead.

"Our sight is diminishing rapidly now," Poulter shouted over the sound of the gushing wind. "I suggest we move inside as quickly as we can." He put on his snow goggles and stepped out fast, followed by the others.

Simons closed the door behind them, and the four of them, holding each other at the shoulders, slowly moved up to the ridge.

Poulter nearly stumbled over the crate before he noticed it and stopped. He turned to McConnel behind him. "Mind your step. We're getting in here."

They cautiously found their way into the riff again.

"I suggest we skip the sliding part this time," Poulter said. He pointed his flashlight ahead to the path, as they remembered it from a week before.

Ten minutes later, Poulter said, "I think I see it. There's the entrance."

"Great, Captain," McConnel shouted, shaking his shoulders. "Not a moment too soon."

With their hands still on each other's shoulders, they walked into the tunnels again a minute later.

"Good God," Simons said, shaking the ice and snow from his body. "It's getting pretty nasty out there."

"You can say that again," Kippler said. "I suggest we stay inside until the storm subsides."

"Flashlights, everybody, before we run out of light," Poulter said. He took out his own and shone it into the darkening tunnel. "Shall we?"

"After you, Captain," McConnel said.

"For once and for all, stop calling me Captain." Poulter started walking, closely followed by the others.

"Aye, sir."

"I know your enthusiastic, Jay," Poulter said. "But I'm still wondering what we expect to find here this time?"

"I'm not sure myself, sir," Simons replied. "But yesterday evening, Dougal and I flew over the region one more time, and the shadow was still there."

Kippler laughed. "What did you expect? It would have flown away, like a flying saucer?"

"Ha, ha, ha," Simons mocked. "Like you have any answer as to what's down there."

"But I'm pretty sure it isn't an extraterrestrial airplane," Kippler replied.

"There's the cave again," Poulter said. At the end of the tunnel, the large square room appeared in their flashlights' crossed beams.

Kippler sighed and said, "It's still amazing how nature can create such a thing."

They walked in and put their gear in a corner.

"Are you sure it's natural?" McConnel asked.

"Are you starting now, too?" Kippler shook his head.

Simons walked up to the plaque again and wiped off a thin layer of ice, revealing the shiny golden plate. "Who could have done this? Who could have created something like this with those flawless carvings?"

"I don't know yet," Kippler replied. "But this time, I came prepared." He took a small hammer and chisel from his pocket and started working on a corner of the plaque. "That's sturdy stuff." He tapped the hammer a bit harder, but the plaque didn't give way.

"Here, let me." McConnel took the hammer out of Kippler's hand, and with a massive swing, he hit the top left corner of the plaque. A small piece broke off and flew away, nicking Poulter's cheek before lodging itself in the ice wall behind them.

"Ouch!" Poulter stroked his cheek. "That's nice." He looked at his bloody hand.

"Oh, I'm so sorry, Captain." McConnel walked up to him and offered him a handkerchief.

"No, thank you," Poulter replied. "I've got my own." He took a piece of cloth from his jacket and wiped his face. "It's just a nick."

"There's your piece." Simons walked up to the small piece of plaque in the wall and took it out. "Can you work with that?"

"I think I can," Kippler said. "Thanks."

Simons tilted his head a little, looking at the ice wall where he'd just plucked out the fragment. While he kept his focus on the wall, he took a few steps back and cocked his face the other way. "That's strange," he mumbled. He walked up to it again, and with his mitten on, he caressed the ice, seemingly following a pattern or line in the ice.

"What are you doing?" McConnel said.

Simons took a few steps back again. "Take a good look at that wall, focus, and tell me what you see."

Kippler and Poulter joined them, and for a minute, the four men gazed at the wall in silence.

"I give up," McConnel said loudly, breaking the silence.

The others ignored him.

"I think you're right," Kippler said after a few seconds.

"What?" McConnel asked.

Kippler walked up to the wall and, using his chisel, drew a line in the ice. "Something like this?"

"I think I see it too," Poulter said.

Simons walked up, nodding. "I think there's something behind this."

"Neh," McConnel said. "I'm not so sure."

"What?" Simons asked.

"There's only one way to be sure." Kippler walked into the corner where they'd stowed their gear, and came back with a pickax. With a big swing, he hit the ice in the center of the line he'd drawn. He hit it again, and the chops of ice flew around, making everyone turn away from him. He hit the ice again and again and again, and....

Silence ensued as everyone stared at a hole in the wall leading to a new open space.

"I told you there was something back there," Simons said.

"There's nothing back there." Kippler laughed.

"All right, wisecrack," Simons replied. "Have it your way."

"Let's chop out the rest of the ice and see what it is," Poulter ordered.

"Let me," McConnel said.

He picked up another ax and, together with Kippler, they carved out the entire opening in just over a minute.

"There you have it," McConnel said.

"Another tunnel," Simons said, taking a peek inside. "What do you say, shall we have a look?" He already set one foot into the tunnel.

"Not without our gear," Poulter said, pointing at the corner. Everyone quickly gathered their gear and came back, and Poulter said, "Who wants to lead this time?"

Without answering, Simons set foot into the tunnel and started on his way.

"Just be careful," Poulter said. "I'll take the back." As they walked in, the ceiling was just high enough for the tall Poulter to walk straight up. "Let's spare our flashlights. Only the front and back men use theirs."

"More tunnels," McConnel complained.

"You'd rather be up there?" Kippler asked.

"I'd rather be at home with a beautiful girl under a warm set of blankets next to a fireplace."

Poulter chuckled. "Who wouldn't?"

"Thank you, Captain," McConnel said dryly.

Simons kept the group moving at a high pace for the next twenty minutes.

"You know we've been walking down for quite a while now?" McConnel said.

"We must be way below the water level," Poulter added.

"Can't we take a break?" Kippler breathed heavily.

"I think we're nearly there," Simons said.

"Where?" Kippler asked.

Simons didn't react; he just kept walking.

After another five minutes of icy walls and beams of flashlights, he turned a corner and suddenly stopped.

"What is it?" Poulter asked from the back.

"Come up, all of you. I think this is the end of it."

"And it ends in what?" Kippler said.

"What the hell is that?" McConnel said as he turned the corner.

Some ten feet ahead, the tunnel ended in a pitch-black wall with a perfectly smooth surface. The edges—left, right, and on top—seemed to run deep into the ice.

"Do you hear that?" McConnel said.

"What?" Kippler said.

"Shhh!," McConnel held up a hand.

In complete silence, they all raised their heads to the sky and listened.

"There's a hum," Simons said.

"Yes, I hear it now too," Poulter said. "A soft hum."

Simons walked up to the wall and cautiously placed his mitted hand flat against it. "I can feel the hum." He put his other hand next to it.

"What is it, some kind of door?" Kippler asked. "Can you open it?"

Simons pushed against the black wall, and nothing happened. "It feels like metal, I think."

"Push harder," McConnel suggested.

Simons followed the suggestion, but nothing happened.

"Here, let me," McConnel said as he tried to push past Simons.

"Let him try first," Poulter ordered from the back.

"Aye, Captain."

Simons traced the edges with his hand, cautiously pushing every now and then, but still, nothing happened.

"You need tools?" Kippler asked.

Simons ignored him, took off his mittens, and handed them to McConnel. Then he slowly he placed both hands toward the wall. Even before touching it, he could already feel the vibrations coming from the black metal. Then he carefully placed both hands against it and held them firmly in place. A soft rumble suddenly sounded, building in rhythm and pace.

"What's happening?" Kippler sounded scared.

"It's okay," Simons answered.

When the rumbling suddenly stopped, the lights from the flashlights went out, and for a second, they stood in complete darkness. Then the black wall abruptly vanished, making Simons fall over.

CHAPTER 28

The Schiehallion Experiment

Antarctica, The Present

Cooper and Bishop tried to remove the large chunks of ice that blocked their way back, but the blocks were too heavy and somehow locked into each other.

"It's no use," Bishop said after a few minutes.

"We're stuck in this tunnel!" Monroe paced back and forth.

"For now," Cooper confirmed, and looked at Hemi.

Hemi checked his satellite phone. "Nothing. I'll walk back into the tunnel and try it at the end. It should work over there when I hold it outside. It'll be able to create a line of sight with the satellite."

Cooper nodded. "Please do so. Who wants to go—"

"I do," Jennifer interrupted him. "I'll walk with him."

"Be careful, you two," Monroe said.

Jennifer grinned. "We'll be all right."

Seconds later, the two turned a corner and disappeared from sight.

"What happens if they can't get a connection?" Bishop asked.

"We'll be stuck a little longer. Nothing else," Cooper assured them. "When we left, we logged a so-called 'at the latest' time of 6 p.m." He glanced at his watch. "That's about four hours from now."

"What happens then?" Monroe asked.

"They'll try to contact us, and when that doesn't work, they'll come for us. They'll take the helicopter and send a rescue mission. I left the precise coordinates in the log, so they shouldn't have much trouble finding us."

"Why didn't we take the helicopter here?" Monroe asked.

"Do you know how to fly?" Cooper smiled.

"Jay-Jay," Bishop said. "What do you think happened? I mean, at the end of the tunnel."

"As I said, that is the big question. Usually, I would say this whole system of tunnels and caves was a naturally occurring phenomenon, and maybe it is, but...."

"What about the plaque?" Monroe finished.

"It's a good thing we already took pictures of it on our way in," Cooper said.

"But," Bishop said, "if it's not a natural phenomenon, it's likely that the tunnels once led somewhere."

Cooper's eyebrows shot up. "I tend to agree."

Bishop pulled his phone from this pocket, pressed a few buttons, and showed the screen to Monroe and Cooper. "Could this be it? It's the picture I took back at your place of the hundred-fifty-foot-tall floating iceberg, with the remains of Little America Three exposed from the side."

Cooper answered. "We *are* near the place where Little America Three was back then, so I guess it could be. The iceberg was a few miles wide and over five miles in diameter, so...."

Bishop took a deep breath, and his expiration condensed in the air.

"Looks like it's getting colder," Monroe said.

Bishop nodded. "It is." Ho thought for a moment. You know, even if the other part of the tunnel continued on the broken-off iceberg, the question remains the same. What was at the end of it?"

"That's the big one," Cooper agreed.

"Don't take this the wrong way," Monroe said, "but your father shared with us theories about Nazi Germans living in the Hollow Earth, and there was supposedly an entrance to it right here in Antarctica."

"Mind you," Bishop added, "he didn't say he believed the stories, but he did say that on his crusade to find out the truth about your grandfather, he spoke to a lot of people who suggested such theories."

Cooper smiled. "I know, and there's a lot of speculation going around on the subject of *Hollow Earth*." He made air quotes with his mittens.

"Especially when it's described as a place for our subterranean afterlife," Monroe said. "There's the Christian Hell, the Greek Underworld, and the Jewish Sheol that's described in detail in Kabbalistic literature like the Zohar." As he spoke the words, Monroe tucked the red string around his wrist away behind his sleeve. "When I did my research on the Little America expeditions, I came across a diary claimed to be Admiral Byrd's, which told of an entrance to a *Hollow Earth* and to a being called *The Master*."

"A hoax?" Bishop suggested.

"Probably," Cooper confirmed.

"Let's just say I don't have a copy of it in my library," Monroe added. "There are, however, plenty of theories about the Hollow Earth." He looked at Bishop. "I already told you about Helene

Walburga Ehrengarde and her theory on the subject, but there are many more out there. Also, the theory about Atlantis is still out there." He eyed Bishop and grinned. "Plato's fan."

"There is, of course, the Schiehallion experiment," Cooper said, making the other two men tilt their heads. "An eighteenth-century French scientist named Pierre Bouguer performed an experiment that allegorically disproves the Hollow Earth theory. Now, I don't understand its science, but he climbed a volcano in Ecuador and conducted a 'vertical deflection' experiment. He lowered himself into the volcano to two different depths, and determined how local mass anomalies affected the Earth's gravitational pull."

Bishop and Monroe both frowned in response.

"Wrong science," Monroe said.

Cooper shrugged. "As I said, I don't understand it myself, but it seems to have disproven the theory so—"

"What's that?" Bishop interrupted.

"What's what?" Monroe asked.

"Shhh." He put a finger to his mouth. "It sounds like someone wearing headphones."

"Wait a minute." Cooper searched his pockets and came back with a Cardo headset with hissing sounds emerging from it, and quickly put it on his head. "*Hey Cardo,* is that you, Hemi?" For a moment, he waited in silence. "That's great. On your end, you say?" Another pause. "All right... I understand... yes... I'm not sure our guests will like it, but I'll tell them, and we'll get going. See you soon." He took off the headset.

"What's that?" Bishop asked.

Monroe sighed. "I don't like the sound of that last bit."

"Well," Cooper said, "the good news is that a rescue party is already on their way."

"But?" Monroe asked impatiently.

Cooper grinned and shook his head. "They've decided not to dig because of the time it will take, and they would first need to determine our exact position underneath the ice. And all of that with the risk of new cave-ins. So...." He waited for a long moment.

"So?" Monroe reacted even more impatiently now.

"So, the helicopter will rendezvous with us at the cliffside and hoist us out one by one. Then they'll drop us off on the shelf again, where we can unstrap. When we're all up again, we can take the snowmobiles back to the base."

"Hoist us!" Monroe exclaimed.

"Don't worry, it's perfectly safe," Cooper explained. "They'll lower a harness that we'll tie you into, and off you go. Within a minute, you'll be safe back at the shelf. If it's any consolation, Hemi told me that Jennifer was actually looking forward to it."

"I bet she does," Bishop said.

"That woman," Monroe said.

"Shall we?" Cooper suggested.

The three started their walk through the tunnels. Bishop took out his phone again, worked the screen, and gazed at an image while walking.

"What are you looking at?" Monroe asked.

"A picture we took of the plaque, or rather, the center part of it." He turned the screen to Monroe. "You said you'd seen that image somewhere before?"

Monroe took the phone from Bishop's hand. "I'm sure of it, but where?"

For the next twenty minutes, they snaked the ice tunnels and talked about the various theories on the image. Bishop kept calling names of random books to try and prompt Monroe's memory.

"*Twenty Thousand Leagues under the Sea* by Jules Verne. *The Lost Continent of Mu* by James Churchward."

"I told you I don't know where!" Monroe uttered when they heard Hemi's and Jennifer's voices.

"I'm so glad you're here," Jennifer said as the three turned the corner.

"Me too," Bishop said.

Monroe just grunted.

"What's with him?" Jennifer smiled and pointed at Monroe, grimacing.

"Oh nothing," Bishop answered. "He's just anxious to be strapped under a helicopter."

"You're just in time," Hemi said. "Listen."

The sound of rotors became clearer, and a minute later, the white Eurocopter AS350 B2, with bright orange stripes on the side, made a wide turn and stopped mid-air, right above of them.

Hemi's satellite phone rang. "Tipene here," he said while waving his other arm at the helicopter.

"You're kind of anxious to get strapped in and dangle under a helicopter?" Monroe asked Jennifer.

She smiled back. "I wasn't at first, but when Tipene explained this was also standard procedure, how they lowered and raised researchers into caverns, I was okay with it. Look at it this way: the weather is great, and try to consider it a great, free carnival attraction."

Monroe shook his head. "I'm sorry, dear, but I get the same feeling I have with bungee jumping."

"You ever do it?" she asked.

"Only watched it." Monroe shivered his shoulders.

"All right," Hemi said. "We're ready—a piece of cake. Jay-Jay, you wanna go first and show them how it works? I'll go last."

"No problem," Cooper said.

Hemi waved up, and the chopper opened its sliding door and slowly lowered a cable. The helicopter moved closer, while gaining altitude to fly over the edge and land the line against the cliff.

Hemi took his pickax as the cable neared and swung it, trying to hook it behind the steel wire. "Miss," he said, and swung again. "Gotcha!"

He pulled the cable into the tunnel and wound it in. Attached to the end of the cable was a bright orange belt, with two V-shaped openings beneath it. Cooper stepped forward and into the V-shaped openings one leg at a time, then hoisted the belt around his waist. Hemi helped him tighten the belt as Cooper put his hands through two loops attached at chest height.

"There you go," Hemi said, tapping him on the shoulder.

"Thanks." Cooper took a step closer to the edge, looked up, and waved.

Then Hemi spoke something into the satphone, and the sound of the chopper grew louder. As it slowly flew away from the cliff, the cable tightened until it dragged Cooper from the tunnel into the air.

"See you soooon," Cooper dragged his words as, spinning, he rapidly flew away from the cliff. The chopper quickly gained altitude, and Cooper disappeared overhead.

"That's one," Hemi said.

"You see," Jennifer addressed Monroe. "Nothing to it."

"Hm," Monroe uttered. "I'm next."

"Courageous," Jennifer replied.

"When you dread something, you'd best get it over with as soon as possible. My life's motto."

"Hemi," Bishop said, "why do you think the cave collapsed? The weather is great, there's hardly any wind, and there's no other movement or work in the area."

Hemi shook his head. "To be honest, I've been asking myself that same question. I don't know. There's no identifiable reason I can think of. Out here, it's usually the weather or a human-made reason that causes something like this."

"Meaning?" Monroe said.

Hemi shrugged. The helicopter came back, made its wide turn, and slowly moved up to the ridge again.

"The harness is empty," Hemi remarked. "So, either they lost Jay-Jay on the way, or he's safely returned to the shelf and is checking out the snowmobiles."

Monroe made a goofy face and said, "Funny man."

"All right." Hemi swung the pickax again when the cable came close, and this time got it the first time.

"Yes." Monroe stepped forward as, on the floor, Hemi opened the belts 'trousers.' Monroe stepped through them, and Hemi quickly hoisted the harness up and tightened the belt.

"Put your hands through." Hemi handed Monroe the loops. "Ready?"

Monroe nodded, tightening his lips.

Hemi talked into the phone again, then put his head outside the tunnel and waved. Immediately the helicopter came in sight again and the line tightened.

"Don't let go," Jennifer said.

The fear in Monroe's eyes grew as the cable suddenly tightened and dragged him out of the tunnel.

"There you go!" Bishop called out after him.

"Enjoy the ride," Jennifer added as Monroe swung in the air.

"He's braver than he looks," Bishop said.

***

Monroe kept his eyes closed tight while, with knuckles straining, he held on to the cable. The sharp, cold wind of the helicopter blew all over his body. When he felt that the chopper was no longer ascending, he cautiously opened his eyes a bit, looked down at the ice floes sticking out of the water, and he imagined how the cold water would feel should he fall. *Don't do it,* he thought. Seconds later, he flew high over the pressure ridge and, sure enough, started to admire the view of the white and blue ice sails that rose high above the ice.

Like the Earth itself had broken open from the inside out.

Another few seconds later, at the end of the ridge, the snowmobiles materialized, and Cooper waved two arms high above his head. Now that he was here, he kind of regretted the fact that it was almost over. The helicopter lowered him carefully, and when his feet hit the ground a few feet away, Cooper walked up and rapidly unstrapped him.

Monroe looked up and waved at the man sticking out of the sliding door. Immediately, the chopper gained altitude, and the harness at the end of the cable drifted off in the air and flew back over the ridge.

"How was your flight?" Cooper asked.

"It was fantastic! Really fantastic. At first, I thought I would shit my pants in fear, but once I opened my eyes and gazed at the amazing scenery.... Wow."

Cooper smiled. "Glad you liked it."

"Everything okay here?"

"Sure, why do you ask?" They walked towards the snowmobiles.

"Well, Hemi suggested that the cave-in would have been either caused by a weather-driven, natural disaster, or else by something created by humans."

"I tend to agree with him, but as far as I can see, there's nothing...." Cooper stopped mid-sentence.

"What is it?"

Cooper wiped a thin layer of snow and ice from his snowmobile's saddle. "I didn't notice it before."

"What?" Monroe insisted.

Cooper took a deep breath. "No wind or snow, so how did our things get under a layer of ice and snow?"

They both looked around but saw nothing but the bare ice fields on one side and the pressure ridge on the other.

"That's really strange," Cooper said.

***

Fifteen minutes later, everyone was back on the ice shelf, swaggering about their airlift and wondering what could have happened out there in the first place.

"All right," Cooper said. "It's getting late, and we have a bit of a trip ahead, so I suggest we get back to Scott Base and have dinner first. Afterward we'll discuss everything that happened in front of a nice fire with a scotch in hand."

"Sounds like a plan," Bishop said. "Are the coordinates in the GPS?"

"No problem," Monroe said. He started his snowmobile. "Who needs GPS? Follow me. I know the way." He kicked into gear and drove off.

Bishop laughed. "Like I said... he's braver than he looks."

CHAPTER 29

Scatterometers

Monroe took the two steps down from the hall into the Scott Base lounge, where they agreed to meet before dinner, and everyone was waiting for him. He walked straight up to the fireplace, sat down on the sill, and stuck both hands almost into the open fire.

"Where have you been?" Jennifer asked.

"In the shower most of the time, trying to get warm."

"You weren't successful?" Bishop asked.

"Not really." Monroe rubbed his hands. "What have you been up to?"

"Nothing much, really," Jennifer said. "We only just got here ourselves. We've been looking at the pictures we took of the plaque, and we ran the center image through some picture recognition sites, but nothing substantial came up. You?"

"I've no idea yet where I saw that image before." Monroe took out his phone and opened the image of the rubbing. After a few seconds, he shook his head. "Nope, but it'll come back to me. Now, what about the theory of the broken-off iceberg?" He eyed Cooper and Hemi.

Cooper let go a big sneeze, took out a handkerchief from his pants pocket, and blew his nose.

"That's old school," Monroe said.

"Yeah, I must have caught a cold somewhere."

"I mean the handkerchief," Monroe replied. "You don't often see cotton handkerchiefs anymore. It's all paper nowadays."

"True, but out here, every piece of garbage counts. It needs to be removed from the continent and taken back to the home country."

"Sounds like a good initiative," Jennifer replied. "We should make that a rule back home."

"Anyway...." Cooper stroked his chin. "We've confirmed now that there was actually a large piece of ice that broke off at that place. We called a friend and colleague of ours at the university, and sent him some pictures that the helicopter made of the ice cliff. He confirmed that the patterns in the side of the riff suggest that over a six-mile-wide area, a large chunk of ice broke off and went on its merry way. He also suggested that from the wear and tear of the grooves in the side of the cliff, it probably happened more than fifty years ago."

"Of course," Hemi took over. "There's still no way of telling where the rest of the tunnel led without actually finding the broken-off piece."

"Where does that leave us?" Bishop asked.

"How do you find this exact iceberg?" Monroe sighed. "You told us that in 1963, the... umm.... What was the name of the icebreaker?"

"Edisto?" Jennifer offered.

Hemi smiled. "Good memory."

"That one," Monroe continued. "The one your father was on. It sighted the iceberg somewhere near the Bay of Whales, three hundred miles west of its original location, and that was the last time anyone ever saw it. It could be just about anywhere out there at this time. In an area twice the size of North America, we'll never find it."

Cooper smiled and cocked his head.

"Or?" Bishop asked.

"Did you ever hear of the SCP, the NASA Scatterometer Climate Record Pathfinder?" Cooper asked.

"The what?" Jennifer uttered.

"Our colleague from the university suggested something," Hemi replied.

"I like the sound of that." Bishop shifted in his seat.

"All right." Cooper also shifted to the edge of his seat.

Monroe stepped up from the fireplace, joined them, and put his phone—with the picture of the rubbing still on screen—in the center of the table. "You never know."

Cooper continued. "The SCP was a NASA project originally designed to measure winds over the oceans from space, using scatterometers."

Monroe said, "What's a—"

"It's a device that measures the return of a beam of radar," Cooper said. "Or light that measures its diffusion when it returns. But that's not important right now. What is important is that nowadays, the project broadened its focus to support climate studies of the Earth's cryosphere and biosphere. Scatterometer data has been proven extremely valuable to the study of polar ice. Two researchers from Brigham Young University in Utah used all the data from those scatterometers from 1987 until now, and developed the Antarctic Iceberg Tracking Database."

"We know where the iceberg is?" Jennifer asked.

"The data only goes back to 1987," Bishop said.

"No, we don't know where the iceberg is, and you're right." Cooper pointed at Bishop. "But we do know where the iceberg was in 1963 and where it was in 1940."

"In 1940, it was here," Monroe said. "Still attached to the ice."

Cooper nodded. "Indeed it was, and in '63, we know where the Edisto saw it. The database NASA's ACP created tracks over five hundred icebergs. Our iceberg may be amongst them or not. The software they created to follow them also uses data from seven different space-born scatterometers, and can interpolate gaps caused by missing data. This way, they can extrapolate and interpolate any place the iceberg was or will be at any time."

"So, it can calculate where an iceberg, which would have been at a certain place in 1963, would be now?" Bishop asked.

Cooper and Hemi responded with broad smiles.

"This could actually work?" Monroe asked.

Bishop rubbed his chin. "That's assuming that the same iceberg that broke off sometime between 1940 and 1963 is the same piece that broke our tunnel in two."

"Could it be that the iceberg broke off while Little America Three was still occupied?" Monroe asked.

"There's no record of it," Cooper said. "The official reason they came back early is that World War II broke out, and the US wanted all their men and material back in the home country. They also thought the risk of being out here was too big with the Germans so close by."

"Still, it doesn't sound illogical," Bishop said. "I figure that if a large part of the expedition washed away, the government would have considered it very bad publicity at the time."

"So it could be the same iceberg," Jennifer suggested.

"It could be, but we can't be sure," Monroe concluded.

"Agreed, we don't know for sure," Hemi replied. "The only way to be sure is when we find that iceberg. Anyway, our colleague was willing to contact NASA's SCP and see if they would help us. So, we gave him the known coordinates of where the iceberg was in 1940 and 1963, and now we'll wait."

"Any idea when he'll get back to us?" Jennifer asked.

Cooper looked at his watch. "There's a nineteen-hour time difference between here and Utah. That makes it around midnight over there."

"Yesterday," Hemi added. "It's like looking into the past."

"We don't have to expect anything before tomorrow," Cooper said. "Maybe by the time we wake up."

"So, how about dinner?" Bishop suggested, rising from his seat.

"Sounds like a plan." Monroe took his phone from the table, and the image lit up bright and showed an incoming call. The screen read 'USGS.' He held up a hand. "Wait a minute."

As he spoke, everyone sat down again.

"Walker Monroe.... Yes, of course, how are you? Isn't it terribly late for you to call?" He paused a moment. "No, it's fine. I'm in New Zealand, so we're about to go to dinner.... Okay, wait a minute. I'm here with my colleagues, so let me put you on speaker."

He put the phone on speaker and placed it in the middle of the table. "Everyone, this is Don Fellows calling from the USGS with, according to him, important news about.... Well, tell them yourself, Don."

"All right. Good evening, everyone. My colleague William Hootkins promised to call you as soon as we had the results back from the uranium-thorium-lead test on the pieces of metal from the sheet. William is out of town, for business, I think, so I thought I'd bring you the news myself."

"And?" Monroe reacted impatiently.

"The results still have to be verified, but the oldest rock ever found was a zircon crystal, found in Australia. It was dated with this method and revealed to be four-point-four-billion-year-old. Your piece of metal came back a few billion years short of that. As it's now dated, the piece appears to be about one-point-one billion years old."

Monroe rubbed his hands over his face. "So, you're saying the piece of metal with the engravings is... over a billion years old?"

"That's what the figures are saying at this moment," Fellows said.

"Could it be that the metal is that old, but that the engravings were made later?" Bishop asked.

"That's highly unlikely," Fellows answered.

Everyone fell silent for a while, eyeing each other and taking deep breaths.

"Are you still there?" Fellows sounded after half a minute.

"Sorry," Monroe said. "Yes, we're here. I guess we're just trying to wrap our minds around what you just said."

"I can imagine," Fellows replied.

"Mr. Fellows, this is Jennifer Porter, a colleague of Walker. What are the chances that the test results are wrong?"

"As I understand it, they already ran the test two times and got the same results. As we speak, they're running the test a third and fourth time, and then we'll be absolutely sure. I felt I needed to tell you as soon as I heard. I have to say that I'd love to chat about the implications of this when you get back to America, but this is all the news I have at this time. Now, if you don't mind?"

"Sure, thank you for taking the time this late at night."

"No problem. I'll keep you informed. We'll talk again soon."

"Have a good night." Monroe pushed the red phone on the screen. "Do you know what that means?"

"I've got to say...." Bishop shook his head. "The logical conclusions my mind is drawing don't process rationally."

"What do you mean?" Jennifer asked.

"I mean, a piece of metal with an inscription on it, billions of years old.... Humankind is only two hundred thousand years old. That's only a fraction relative to what we're talking about here. Billions of years... amazing."

"What did you say?" Monroe asked Bishop.

"Humankind is only a fraction of—"

"No, no, no, the other thing." Monroe took his phone back out.

"Billions of years?" Bishop asked.

Monroe nervously worked his phone. "Anyone have his phone on him?"

"You need another phone?" Cooper asked.

"Yes, please."

"All right." Cooper took his phone out of his pocket and put it in front of Monroe on the table.

"Thanks." Monroe laid his phone next to it, and worked them both.

"What's he doing?" Cooper asked.

Bishop shrugged. "I guess we'll know in a moment."

With the two phones next to each other, Monroe turned Cooper's phone on the table. As he almost turned it 270 degrees, he stopped, took a little distance, and gazed at both screens.

Everyone now did the same.

"What is it?" Hemi asked.

"What am I looking at?" Jennifer added.

"It has to be," Monroe mumbled under his breath. "All right," he suddenly said louder, pointing at the phone on the left. "You see here... this one, on the left? This is the picture of the plaque we took in the cave, only zoomed in on the center circle. Here, on Jay-Jay's phone—" He pointed at the phone on the right. "—is a zoomed-in picture on a Wikipedia page. I know, it's Wikipedia, but this is somewhat of a generally accepted image. This is where I saw the image before. Do you see it now?"

"They're not the same," Jennifer said.

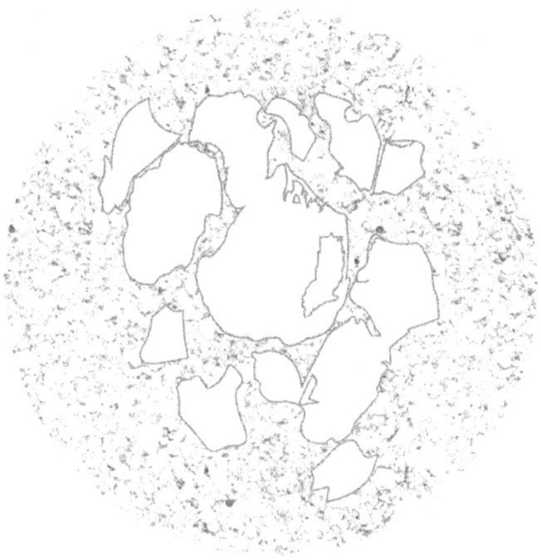

"Of course, they're not the *exact* same," Monroe said. "How could they be? But don't you see the similarities? Those two shapes, like islands on the top right, the two in the center-right, and the large one in the middle.... And what about the small one, all the way on the bottom? Those are almost identical."

"Okay," Jennifer agreed. "I admit, there are similarities. But what am I looking at?"

"Rodinia," Hemi answered.

"Rodinia?" Jennifer asked.

"Isn't that something like Atlantis?" Bishop asked.

"No, it isn't," Monroe said. "Rodinia isn't anything mythical. Rodinia is science." He turned to Cooper, looking for support.

Cooper nodded. "Rodinia comes from the Russian word 'rodina,' meaning 'birthplace or motherland.'"

"It's the continental drift," Hemi added. "There's all kinds of proof that the continents as we know them, over periods of billions of years, drift apart and then drift together again to form one big supercontinent. We are now in a period when everything is drifting slowly together again."

"Correct," Cooper said. "There are already computer models on what the next supercontinent will look like."

"I guess we'll not be there to witness that." Bishop said.

"Depends on how old you're planning to get." Cooper smiled. "If you have another three hundred million years, you could be there."

Bishop shook his head.

"But anyway, our best guess is that Rodinia was formed between one-point-one and zero-point-nine billion years ago, and broke up again four hundred million years later."

"Give or take a few," Hemi added.

"One-point-one billion," Monroe said slowly.

"Like the age of the piece of metal with the inscription that brought us here in the first place," Jennifer concluded.

Tight-lipped, Monroe nodded slowly.

"This is nuts," Bishop said. "There must be something wrong here. The mummy wasn't that old, and how can a Russian woman write in a language that was first, and maybe last, written over a billion years ago."

"I agree," Monroe said. "It isn't getting any clearer yet."

"Clearer?" Bishop almost yelled. "This thing is getting murkier every step we take and with every continent we visit."

Except for the burning wood crackling in the fireplace, the lounge fell completely silent for a few minutes.

Hemi finally broke the silence again. "I don't know about you, but I tend to think a lot better on a full stomach. And after dinner, we can have a nice drink by the fire, and talk some more before getting a good night's rest. What do you say? Shall we?" He rose from his chair.

"Great idea," Jennifer said.

"Best one yet," Cooper agreed.

"I could eat," Monroe confessed.

"Nuts," Bishop added.

CHAPTER 30

Four Icebergs

About fifty people were already having their breakfast at the stretched tables of the Scott Base mess hall. At the buffet, Bishop put some extra bacon on his plate next to the scrambled eggs, and moved on to add some cooked tomatoes, mushrooms, hash browns, and baked beans.

Next to Bishop, Monroe put a small spoon of eggs on his plate with two bacon strips. "How can you eat that stuff?"

"He's not normal," Jennifer said, laughing at the end of the row, carrying a plate with only a glass of orange juice and a small bowl of milk and cereal on it.

"You wait and see," Bishop said. "When we skip lunch again because we're out there somewhere, you won't hear me complaining."

"Sure," Monroe said.

"We'll see," Bishop replied. "I'll join Jay-Jay and Tipene over there." He nodded his head in the direction of one of the tables as he walked off.

"Good morning." He sat down next to Cooper.

"Morning, Matthew," both Cooper and Hemi replied in chorus.

"I thought you didn't eat breakfast," Bishop said to Hemi.

"Somehow I got up hungry this morning," Hemi answered.

"Did you get a good night's sleep?" Cooper asked.

Bishop shrugged. "Not really. I must confess that yesterday's events kept haunting me in my sleep."

"The cave-in and rescue?" Hemi asked.

"No, not that, but our billion-year-old finding."

"Morning."

"Morning."

Jennifer and Monroe joined them, and as three greeted back, Jennifer yawned.

"You also didn't sleep too well?" Hemi asked.

"I slept like a baby," Jennifer answered. "It's just that I can always sleep a little longer in the morning, something that will probably correct itself after breakfast. That's what the coffee is for." She raised her cup.

"I see you two also took a firm breakfast." Monroe nodded at Cooper's and Hemi's plates.

"Of course," Cooper answered. "You see, out here, you never know if you'll be able to enjoy a decent lunch, so...."

"Hmm." Bishop eyed Monroe and Jennifer as he took a bite from his eggs, together with a shiny strip of bacon.

"Any new thoughts on yesterday's findings?" Hemi asked.

Monroe took his phone from his pocket pants and put it next to his tray. "In bed, I did some research on Rodinia." He worked the screen and read from it. "At the time of supercontinent Rodinia, the east coast of North America, as we know it now, was adjacent to the west of South America. And the south and west coasts of North America were connected to today's Australia and Antarctica. It's believed that Texas and Antarctica were attached, and Antarctica on the map would have been just above the equator."

"It must have been warm out here," Jennifer stated.

"It must have been," Monroe replied. "But we know little to nothing about that time."

"That's all buried beneath the ice," Cooper said.

"And when did life on Earth start?" Jenifer asked, and sipped her coffee.

"That one I know," Hemi said. "They assume that the first Eukaryotes formed about two billion years ago, resulting in the first fungi around one-point-five billion years ago. At about the same time, the first multicellular life developed, and species were formed that procreate by sexual reproduction."

Cooper jumped in. "You know the story about Captain Robert Scott, the name giver to just about everything out there?"

Everyone but Hemi shook their heads.

"Although everything around here's named after the man, his expedition to Antarctica in 1912 was a complete failure. After a first, somewhat successful, mission, he came back here a second time just five weeks after the world-famous Amundsen's South Pole expedition. Scott wanted to prove Darwin's theory of evolution. Back then, they thought that an embryo passed through all stages of evolution as it developed."

"Ernst Haeckel," both Jennifer and Bishop said at the same time.

"What? Who?" Cooper asked.

Bishop said, "A German biologist who worked at the same theory. Something we came across a few years ago. Please go on."

"All right. Anyway," Cooper continued. "Scott's team wanted to harvest the eggs of the flightless Emperor penguin. At that time, that bird was seen as the most primitive alive. By researching the embryos, Scott wanted to prove that there was a link between birds and dinosaurs."

"Didn't they know penguins before?" Monroe asked.

"They did see penguins before, but never with their eggs," Cooper replied. "Of course, all their theories turned out to be a failure."

"Again, like Ernst Haeckel," Bishop said.

Cooper grinned. "Scott and a small team left their base camp for a mission. When days later he failed to check in with his supporting dog teams, they went searching for him. Eight months later, 162 miles from base camp, Scott and his team members' bodies were found. They were frozen to death in their tents, probably caught by several blizzards. He left behind several letters saying goodbye to his mother, his former commander, and his wife. He also kept a diary with his last entry, saying, '*For God's sake, look after our people.*'"

"Yikes." Jennifer shook her shoulders.

"Sure," Cooper replied. "But here comes the exciting part. Next to the bodies, they found thirty-five pounds of what were later determined to be Glossopteris fossils, a tree that became extinct about three hundred million years ago and grew only in subtropical environments. Those same fossils were found in parts of Australia, South America, and Africa. Captain Scott unknowingly proved that Antarctica had once been a warm place, connected to other continents."

"Rodinia," Monroe stated.

Cooper tilted his head.

"But where does that bring us?" Jennifer asked. "It proves Antarctica was once warm, and probably all kinds of other species lived here, but—"

"Probably not the kind of species that engraved plaques in strange languages," Bishop said.

"True," Cooper said.

"Then what?" Jennifer asked. "Aliens?"

They all grinned but soon fell silent.

Cooper broke the silence. "Finished?"

They all nodded, mumbling.

"Then may I suggest we go to the Maintenance hall, where we can check on my computer to see if there are any messages from the university."

The five of them cleared their trays and left the mess hall. Seconds later, they were snaking their way through the buildings' connecting corridors.

Hemi walked shotgun. "Our base may not be as big and luxurious as the Americans' McMurdo, but they have to go outside every time they change buildings."

"That seems very ineffective," Jennifer replied.

"It is," Cooper said. "I once stayed there for a short time, but on a bad day, you keep changing clothes. There are plans to completely rebuild Scott Base a bit further down the road and create everything in only three huge, connected buildings." He stopped at a large green door. "Here we are."

They walked into the hall, and Hemi strolled to a table in the far corner, where he started to work on what looked like old engine parts. The rest walked up to a small desk on the right, where Cooper sat down.

"Sit, relax." He pointed at the square conference table a few feet to the left. "This could take a while." He powered up his computer and worked the mouse. "Ah, here we have something." Mumbling, he started to read. "Hi, Jay-Jay, I contacted the SCP and attached...." His mumbling became undistinguishable but kept going on for several seconds.

"By the way," Monroe said, filling the mumbling silence. "Did you know the word iceberg comes from the Dutch word 'ijsberg'?"

Cooper turned back to the conference table and took a deep breath.

"And?" Monroe couldn't contain himself as Hemi walked up to them.

"I have some good news and some bad news. What do you want first?"

"The bad news," Jennifer answered quickly.

"There are four," Cooper replied.

"That's the bad news?" Bishop asked.

"Four what?" Monroe sighed.

"Four icebergs."

Monroe cocked his head and Jennifer moaned.

Bishop frowned and said, "The good news?"

Cooper brightened. "Ah, the good news is that my friend worked the information in the SCP database and extrapolated that to a number of possibilities."

"I guess that number is four," Bishop said.

"Indeed it is," Cooper said. "He found the location of four icebergs. The one we're looking for is possibly amongst them."

"Possibly?" Jennifer asked.

"Well, although it looks like an exact science," Cooper replied. "It isn't. There are too many factors to account for, and the program has to make a best guess now and then. Then there's also the fact that our iceberg may have melted in part, and that the part we're looking for sunk to the bottom of the ocean."

"Or," Hemi took part. "The part of Little America that stuck out in 1963 can be snowed in again, and is now buried under a thick layer of snow and ice, and we won't be able to see it."

"We can use the Ground Penetrating Radar, can't we?" Jennifer asked.

Hemi laughed. "Of course we can, if we had the manpower and time to search four huge icebergs."

Jennifer frowned.

Cooper took over. "Some of these icebergs are the size of Manhattan. You want to take the snowmobile and the GPR and go searching?"

"What are you saying?" Monroe asked. "If we don't find anything sticking out of an iceberg, we won't be able to find anything?"

Cooper cocked his head and sighed. "I guess there's another way. It involves a GPR that you strap under a helicopter, and search that way. But we don't have that kind of equipment."

"I think McMurdo does," Hemi said.

"Ah," Bishop said, and smiled.

"Okay, maybe." Hemi shrugged. "But before we get ahead of things, here, take a look." He pointed at the left part of the screen with a map on it.

"What am I looking at?" Bishop asked.

"We are here," Cooper pointed out. "And these four dots represent the icebergs we're looking for."

"What's the distance?" Monroe asked.

"More important," Jennifer added. "How do we get there?"

"Both valid questions," Cooper replied. "The closest one is about a hundred-thirty kilometers."

"Eighty miles," Hemi converted for them.

"Thanks," Monroe said.

"Anyway...." Cooper pointed at the right part. "This is the helicopter roster for later today. Fortunately, the university has leased more than enough miles for this year. I just made a reservation for twelve o'clock. I hope you had a decent breakfast. Otherwise, you can always take something from the vending machine."

"Hmm," Jennifer grunted. "Anyway, we're going?"

"Only if you want to," Cooper said.

"What do you think?" Monroe asked. "I have a good feeling about this."

"What do you want to do in the meantime?" Jennifer asked.

Bishop looked through the window. "The sun is shining, so who's up for a walk?"

Jennifer and Monroe agreed immediately.

"Hemi and I have some other work to do. So, have fun and stay out of trouble. We'll meet you back here at noon."

"See you later," Bishop said, and took the lead out of the Maintenance hall.

***

Yuri Pavlov leaned back in a Range Rover parked on top of the ridge, with a good view over Scott Base. With his feet on the dash, he unwrapped the cold burger he took from McMurdo's cafeteria, along with a large can of coke and a small box of chicken nuggets.

It might be even better cold.

He worked through the thing in three big bites.

In the distance, the large doors of the Scott Base hangar rolled open. He put his feet down and took a pair of binoculars from the dash, and zoomed in.

Bishop and his company, dressed in thick clothing, stepped outside, and the door behind them rolled back again.

Pavlov held on to the binoculars with one hand, while with the other, he picked up a walkie-talkie and pushed a button. "Are you there, boss?"

The crackling line stayed silent for a few seconds.

"Melnyk here."

"Boss, there's movement at our friends' place."

"What kind of movement?"

"Not sure yet, sir, but I'm looking at them now, and they have just left a building and are walking around it."

"To the parking place?"

"Not sure yet. No, wait.... They turned right, and the parking space is left." Through the binoculars, he followed the path ahead of where they were walking. "I think they're walking to the helicopter platform. At the end of the path, there's a helicopter with the engine running." Pavlov sounded excited.

"Okay, easy. Wait until they get on," Melnyk ordered.

"All right, they're almost there now. One of them is walking up to the pilot. What do you want me to do when they take off, sir? We can't follow them."

"Of course we can." Melnyk sounded calm. "If they take off, you drive back, and I'll take it from here. No problem."

"If you say so, sir. They are now opening the back door, and the first one's in and helping the others."

"All right, that's clear," Melnyk replied. "Now drive home carefully, and we'll meet you here."

"Yes, sir, I'm on my way." He put down the goggles and radio, and quickly took a big sip of his coke, followed by two pieces of chicken nuggets. He then started the car and drove off.

***

Melnyk took his satellite phone from his jacket pocket and started to punch in numbers. "*Stántsiya Vostók* (Station Vostok), do you read me?" he said into the phone. "Good to talk to you... yes, it's time. We could use a ride. Can you pick us up at McMurdo?"

CHAPTER 31

Black Velvet

The Ross Ice Shelf, Antarctica, January 27, 1940

When their flashlights came on again, they shone their light on Simons, who'd fallen on his knees when the black wall suddenly disappeared. Simons crawled forward a bit before he rose from the ground, and his colleagues helped him up. They all shone their flashlights around, but the beams of light seemed to vanish completely a few feet ahead and above them. The only reflected light came when they shone their flashlights onto each other.

"What happened?" Simons asked.

"We're in a new room," McConnel said. "A door opened somehow." He checked out the entrance but couldn't find any openings where a door could have closed into.

"It's like an invisible space," Kippler said.

"Are those walls?" McConnel asked. "I mean, where do our beams disappear?"

"I have no idea." Simons looked around, and kept his light shining ahead as he walked up to the disappearing point. There he gazed at the deep blackness for a second before he slowly put his flat hand against it. A soft humming sounded like before, only this time, it came in a single continuous tone. As he took his hand off the wall again, the sound stopped, and he looked at his hand.

McConnel stepped up next to him. "Everything okay? Did you feel anything?"

"I'm okay. The wall feels a bit like velvet, and somehow, the hum that you heard, I could also feel it in my fingertips."

McConnel put down his pickax, took off his glove, and raised a hand to the end of his beam of light. He stopped a few inches in front of the wall and looked at Simons.

Simons nodded. "It's okay."

McConnel slowly moved his hand forward until his fingertips

touched it. Nothing happened. He looked at Simons again, who shrugged. Then he placed his full hand against it—still nothing.

"Maybe it recognizes Jay." Poulter, who had walked up to them, suggested. "You know, from the door behind us."

"How could that be?" Simons asked.

Poulter shrugged as he also walked up to the end, put his fingers, and then his hand, onto it. Again nothing happened.

"You try it again," McConnel suggested.

Simons cautiously touched it again. As soon as his fingertips lightly touched the black velvet, the humming started again.

"This place gives me the creeps," Kippler said, still standing in the door opening. "Have you ever seen this kind of deep black? Do you realize we can only see each other and nothing else, only feel it? Have you ever heard of something like that before?"

They shone their flashlights around, but only some dust particles, as well as themselves, reflected the light.

"He's right," McConnel said as he walked around and followed the end of his beam of light across the mysterious room. "It feels like it's a room, some ten feet deep and wide, and a little less high. I can feel something of a ceiling."

"A room we can't see, even in the light," Kippler said.

"Burt, get up here," Poulter ordered Kippler. "Feel this end and tell me what kind of material you think it is."

Reluctantly, taking small steps, Kippler moved up to him.

"Touch it," Poulter said.

"Must I?" Kippler slowly moved forward and stopped next to Poulter.

Poulter took the big man's hand and put it against the velvet. Again nothing happened. "You see," Poulter said. "Now, what kind of material do you think it is?"

Kippler stroked the wall, then knocked it a few times, and touched it again. "It's soft, indeed velvety, or like felt. I truly have no idea." He took off his glove for a second and tried to scratch it with his nails, but nothing happened.

"You want me to...?" McConnel took his pickax from the floor and raised it into the air.

"No." Simons grabbed him by the arm and lowered it. "I have the distinct feeling that trying to destroy it is not the way."

"Then what?" McConnel asked. "There's nothing here, just straight ends, black velvet, and nothing else."

"There has to be," Simons said.

"How do you know?" Poulter asked.

"I don't know, sir. It was like I felt it through my fingers as soon as I touched the end."

"Then touch it again," Kippler said. "I won't touch it again, but you, touch it again and describe what you feel."

Simons cautiously placed his hand again on the wall, and the low hum sounded again. "It's just a slight tingling sensation." As he moved his hand over the velvet wall, the sound's pitch slightly changed.

"You hear that?" McConnel asked. "Move your hand."

Simons waved his hand in what looked like thin air, as if he was washing windows. The sound changed as he moved from left to right.

"It seems to intensify when you move right," Poulter suggested.

"It's showing you the way," Kippler said.

"What way?" McConnel asked.

"How do I know?" Kippler replied. "Just try to follow the sound."

"That's actually not a bad idea," Poulter said. "You remember how the sound changed when you touched the entrance to this room? Try to mimic that same pitch."

"But that was a completely different sound," Simons said.

"Just try it, Jay," Poulter urged.

"Yeah," McConnel added. "Just try it."

"Will you all shut up," Simons almost shouted.

When the room was silent again, he put his hands back on the velvet and slowly rubbed it in every direction, listening to the way the sound altered with every change of directions. After trying all possible directions, he walked to the right as if his hand was guiding him. The sound changed from a high pitch to a lower, almost rumbling sound.

"That's it," Poulter said. "Go on, that must be it."

Simons now stretched out his arm to the top right end and then turned the corner. When he moved it farther away from the bend, the sound changed back to a higher pitch.

"Go back," McConnel said.

Simons moved his hand back to the corner and held it there for a second, then moved it down. Again the sound changed the wrong way. He moved up again and beyond the point where he started, in the corner. The rumbling sound came back again and now slowly increased.

"That's it," Poulter said.

The tall Simons stretched himself to the top of his toes, and stopped. "I feel something."

"What is it?" Kippler asked.

"It feels like a hole or something." Simons grunted and stood on his toes.

"How can that be?" Kippler asked. "We don't see a hole."

"We see nothing," McConnel added, as they all pointed their flashlights at his hands.

"And yet there is." Simons put a finger inside. "You see?" Even with the light shining on Simons' hand, the finger completely vanished from sight.

"How can that be?" McConnel asked.

"Must have something to do with the reflection of the light," Kippler suggested.

"How big is it?" Poulter asked. "What do you feel?"

"I feel nothing. Let me see." Simons took out his finger and cautiously moved his hand around the edges. "It's shaped like a vertical mail slot. Let me try something."

"Be careful," Poulter said.

Simons slowly slid in his full hand, and as it disappeared into nothingness, the rumbling increased even further, until the ground beneath their feet began to shake.

"Take it out," Kippler shouted.

"No, wait," McConnel said.

At the top of the edges of the black room, a streak of light appeared, as if the ceiling was raised or the walls slowly lowered.

"It's okay," Simons said. As he took his hand back, the rumbling stopped, and the streak of light disappeared.

"I'm afraid you need to keep your hand in," Poulter said.

Simons took a deep breath and rose onto his toes again. When he put his hand back in, the light appeared again, and a brighter streak of light gave away that the walls were lowering under a constant deep rumble.

"What's behind there?" McConnel asked. The little man jumped up and down but couldn't look over the edge yet.

"Take it easy," Poulter ordered McConnel. "Give it a minute."

The light became brighter, and they all squeezed to keep their eyes adjusted.

"It's as bright as the sunrise," Kippler said. "I can barely look at it."

"It looks like...." McConnel uttered as the black velvet now lowered enough for them to look over it. "I don't know what it looks like."

"It's beautiful," Simons said, still hanging on.

"It's huge," Kippler added as he walked up next to Simons.

"Careful," Poulter said.

"It's okay," Simons replied.

The velvet walls had dropped almost halfway down.

"It must be as big as a football field," McConnel said.

Simons still held his hand in the opening, which was now in a black pillar that stood free in the center of the light.

With a loud bang that made the ground tremble heavily beneath their feet, the black walls disappeared into the ground. Then, for a short moment, complete silence fell, except for their breathing.

Kippler broke the silence. "It's...."

"Shh." Poulter interrupted him. "What's that? That sound?"

They all tilted their heads in the air.

"I don't hear anything, Captain," McConnel said.

"I hear it too," Simons said, still keeping his hand in the slot. "Listen."

"It sounds like a roar or thunder that's coming from there." Kippler pointed at the doorway to the tunnel behind them.

"And it's getting closer fast," Poulter said, and the sound grew louder as he walked towards the entrance.

McConnel and Kippler joined him, and the ground beneath their feet started to shake even more, causing small pieces of ice to break off from the ceiling.

"What's going on?" McConnel shouted over the ever-growing noise.

"The tunnel is collapsing," Poulter yelled.

"The whole place is coming down," McConnel yelled.

"It's not that," Kippler said. "Look!" He pointed at the ceiling some ten feet ahead into the tunnel they'd come from, where under a devastating growl, a large crack formed in the ice.

"Down here too," McConnel added.

"The ice shelf is breaking in two!" Kippler shouted.

"What?" McConnel grabbed Kippler at the shoulders.

Kippler's eyes widened in fear. "The whole place is coming down because the ice shelf where we're standing is breaking in two. Any moment now, it will break off completely and drift into the ocean. We need to go. Now!"

Poulter turned to Simons, who was still holding his hand in the slot and gazing into the room. "Simons... Jay," Poulter yelled. "Come, we need to go."

Simons didn't react.

Poulter walked up to him, grabbed him at the shoulder, and turned him. "What's happening to you, man? Come on. This whole place is breaking off. We need to go."

Simons calmly took Poulter's hand from his shoulder and squeezed it tight. "It's okay, sir. You'd better go. I'll be okay here. Trust me." He shook Poulter's hand a few times before letting go. "Really, it's okay."

"I'm not leaving here without you," Poulter said.

"Captain," McConnel shouted from the door opening.

Poulter looked back at the floor's crack, already a few feet wide, with Kippler standing on the other end of it.

McConnel stretched out an arm in Poulter's direction. "We need to go. *Now!*"

"Come." Poulter grabbed Simons' hand and tried to pull it.

Simons gazed into Poulter's eyes and, without speaking, shook his head and loosened Poulter's grip. Then he nodded, raised an arm, and held his hand up as if starting to wave. But he didn't.

Poulter took a step back and turned towards the entrance, where McConnel now jumped to the other side.

"Damn," Poulter cried out while he stepped back towards the entrance. "Why?"

"Tell my wife I love her," Simons said as a tiny, closed smile appeared on his face.

Poulter nodded before turning, then he took a few big steps and jumped over the now four-foot-wide crack in the ice.

"What are you doing?" McConnel yelled at Poulter. "Why's Jay still there?"

Poulter shook his head. "He isn't coming."

"What? Why? What do you mean?" McConnel cried out, flailing his arms about. "What did he say?"

"He said he was going to be okay, and asked me to tell his wife that he loves her."

"What?"

"We need to go," Poulter urged. He pushed Kippler into the tunnel, and turned to McConnel. "You too."

Simons still had his hand up at the other end of the widening gap.

McConnel now also raised his hand. "Goodbye, my friend," he whispered, and turned to Poulter.

Poulter pushed him after Kippler, and took one more look at Simons on the shelf that now quickly drifted away.

"Run," Poulter shouted into the tunnel, and quickly ran up to the others.

Minutes later, when the rumbling had stopped, they resurfaced.

"What do we do now?" Kippler asked.

"What *can* we do?" McConnel replied.

"I'm afraid we have another problem," Poulter said, looking around.

Kippler's eyes popped wide open. "Where's the Cruiser?"

"My God." McConnel pointed some forty feet in the distance, where his airplane just rose above the snow.

They ran up to the edge of what looked like a big pit in the ice, and there it was, the Cruiser, encased in a hole over thirty feet deep.

"How are we going to get it out?" Kippler asked.

"What about Simons?" McConnel asked.

"What can we do?" Poulter answered.

"What are you saying?" McConnel replied, waving both arms in the air. "We can't just leave him there."

"There's no way to get back there." Poulter pointed at the large wall of ice sails rising from the pressure ridge behind them. "And even if we could get back, there's no way to get back onto the broken-off ice shelf. I'm sorry."

McConnel fell on his knees and put his head in his hands.

"Now," Kippler asked a few seconds later. "How do we get the Cruiser out of the ice?"

"I don't see how," Poulter said. "We can't dig it out. We would need to dig out a ramp, over thirty feet deep and three hundred feet long, without any tools."

"So what do we do?" Kippler asked again.

Poulter took a deep breath.

"I have an idea." McConnel rose on his feet again.

"What is it?" Poulter asked.

"We fill up the hole instead of digging it out."

"What?" Kippler asked.

"You see...." Poulter drew a line in the air at snow level. "The plane is level with the ground we're standing on. If we fill up the hole with snow, I'll drive it off and fly both of you back to the base one by one. And maybe I can even go look for Jay after that."

"And the Cruiser?" Kippler asked.

"It'll have to stay here," McConnel answered. "Maybe someone can come back for it later."

"Maybe." Poulter pointed at the roof of the Cruiser, barely visible buried in the snow. "I think it's a good plan. Maybe I can get in through the hatch and get us some shovels."

"Let's do that," Kippler agreed.

Poulter climbed onto the Cruiser's roof.

***

"Don't forget the keys to the plane, please, Captain," McConnel said, then turned and gazed back at the pressure ridge.

"What are you thinking about?" Kippler asked.

"I was wondering what that place was that we found, and what Jay's doing now."

Kippler sighed and put a hand on McConnel's shoulder. "We might never know."

"Maybe," McConnel replied softly. "I'm still planning on going back there."

CHAPTER 32

The Silurian Hypothesis

Antarctica, The Present

The white Eurocopter flying east and low over the Antarctic coastline cast a large shadow on the ice and snow below. Every now and then, the icy landscape with its hundred-foot tall cliffs changed into a bare rockface beachfront.

"That looks more like a Martian landscape than the South Pole," Monroe sounded through the headset.

"I figure Mars is a bit warmer," Cooper suggested.

"But probably just as inhospitable," Hemi added.

"Maybe," Bishop said.

"How long now?" Jennifer asked.

Hemi looked at his watch. "We should be at the first iceberg in about fifteen minutes."

"Professors," Hemi said. "Any thoughts on what this is all about? I mean, we are flying off in search of a tunnel, based on a plaque with a drawing of an ancient supercontinent. Am I the only one who thinks that's a bit odd?"

"You're right," Bishop answered. "Although oddly enough, I must admit that up till now, this isn't even the strangest thing we've come across in a long time now."

"Do tell, Matthew," Hemi urged him.

"Maybe another day," Bishop replied. "Over a fireplace and drinks."

"I've been thinking about this and started reading up last night," Monroe said. "Did anyone of you ever hear of the 'The Silurian Hypothesis'?"

"The what?" Hemi asked.

"The Silurian Hypothesis," Monroe repeated louder.

"Never heard of it."

"Nope."

"What have you found now?"

"Basically, it's a thought experiment in which we, being modern scientists, try to access our ability to prove the possibility of a prior advanced civilization on Earth."

"You lost me, professor," Hemi said.

"Think of it this way. If the Earth is three-point-five billion years old, modern humans have been around for as little as two hundred thousand years. That leaves 3,498,800,000 years that we know nothing about. That's far more than enough time for a lot of empires to rise and fall."

"And aliens to land and take off again," Bishop joked.

"But how?" Jennifer asked. "If something was here before us, some kind of civilization, wouldn't we find evidence of it—fossils, machines?"

"Plaques?" Monroe added.

"Just a plaque?" Cooper asked.

"Of course, I'm a skeptic too," Monroe said. "But what if, for the moment, we stay at the level of a thought experiment? As geologists, you probably know that the oldest place on the Earth's surface we know of is a piece of Israel's Negev Desert. And that part is only a little over a million years old. That timespan, again, is nothing compared to Earth's age. This is not something that I came up with, you know. The Silurian Hypothesis was recently written, in 2018, by a NASA climate modeler named Gavin Schmidt, and Adam Frank, an astrophysicist at the University of Rochester."

"How do you come from Rodinia to this hypothesis?" Jennifer asked. "And why don't we find anything, like fossils?"

"It's been figured that every three million years or so, the Earth gets completely re-shuffled again. The ocean's bottom becomes the land and forms new mountain ranges, and the land becomes the bottom of the ocean. In between those movements, they form the supercontinents."

"Like Rodinia," Jennifer suggested.

"Exactly," Monroe said.

"Rodinia's only one of them," Cooper confirmed. "Pangea and Laurasia are a few of the others that science theorizes about."

"And life?" Bishop asked. "How did they come to the conclusion of advanced civilizations?"

"Schmidt and Frank searched for so-called 'hyperthermals' on distant planets," Monroe explained. "A hyperthermal is a sudden rise of temperature that could indicate the existence of an advanced civilization. Industrialization leads to a release of carbon in the air that we can measure through time."

"When the Earth would get reshuffled every three million years," Hemi said. "And any physical proof of life would disappear completely, the rise in carbon, however, would still be there and measurable. Doesn't seem too farfetched."

Monroe shrugged. "I'm just repeating what I read."

"And what does Silurian stand for?" Cooper asked.

Bishop laughed. "I know that one. The Silurians were an ancient reptilian-looking Earth race in the British TV series Doctor Who."

"Hey," Monroe said. "Don't look at me."

"And the plaque?" Bishop asked. "The piece of metal from the Kola dig I can make sense of... buried somewhere deep in the Earth, shuffled around a couple of times. But how do you account for an engraved plaque perfectly mounted in a tunnel in the Antarctic?"

"I can't," Monroe said.

"We're here at our first subject," the pilot said through the headset.

"Saved by the bell," Monroe said.

"What do you want me to do?" the pilot asked.

They all looked through the chopper's windows. On the right side, a pointy iceberg emerged in the dark blue waters.

Cooper responded. "Just take us low enough and slowly circle it, so that we can take a good look at the sides of the thing."

"There are binoculars beneath each of your seats," Hemi said.

"You thought of everything," Bishop said.

"Courtesy of Scott Base," Hemi answered as the helicopter lowered to about half the iceberg's height.

"How tall do you think this thing is?" Monroe asked.

"About seventy-five feet," Cooper answered. "But I don't think this is the one. My father described a large flat-topped chunk of ice looking much like a floating island. And this one seems too small in overall size."

"Could it have been melted into a pointy version of an iceberg?" Jennifer suggested.

"I don't think so," Cooper said. "If it was melted, the surface would have more rounded upsides. These sides have sharp edges suggesting it was formed or broke off that way."

Everyone took their binoculars from beneath their seats and started examining the iceberg's surface.

"What are we looking for?" Jennifer asked.

"Somehow, I have the feeling we'll know it when we see it," Monroe answered.

"You're probably right," Cooper said. "The iceberg is all blueish white, and everything else... umm... human-made should stick out."

"And if aliens made it?" Bishop asked.

"Ha, ha, ha," Monroe grunted.

"I see our shadow double," Jennifer remarked. "One vague and a sharper image."

"I think you're right," Bishop confirmed. "That's weird."

"It's not that weird," the pilot said. "It's because there's a second chopper in the air that's straight above us."

"A second chopper?" Monroe asked.

"That's nothing to worry about," Cooper said. "It happens all the time. If it isn't the Russians or the Chinese, it's probably your countrymen from McMurdo. They usually have a healthy interest in what we're doing out here."

"The Chinese also have a base on Antarctica?" Jennifer asked.

"They have four," Hemi answered.

"Wow," Jennifer said. "Didn't know that."

For the next three minutes, the helicopter flew along the ice wall before the pilot came back in the headset. "We've completed our pass. Anything?"

Everyone lowered their binoculars.

"Anything?" Cooper asked.

They all shook their heads.

"You need another pass?" the pilot asked.

"No, we don't," Cooper answered. "Please take us to the next."

"Your call," the pilot said, and took the helicopter higher up and over the iceberg. "We'll be at the next one in a few minutes."

"What a magnificent sight," Bishop said as he looked back and watched the iceberg rapidly shrink.

Cooper nodded. "Never gets boring."

Monroe searched for the coastline, gazing through the windows.

"What are you looking for?" Hemi asked.

Monroe bent over to look outside, and said, "Where are we now? I don't see the coast anymore."

"That's correct," Hemi answered. "The coast is a few miles that way." He pointed out the window. "We're flying off the coast in a north-northeast direction. Theoretically, if we were to fly on, we would end up somewhere in Chile."

"In that case, we can visit the Atacama Desert," Bishop replied.

"Let's not," Monroe said. "Do we even have enough fuel to visit all four icebergs?"

The pilot answered. "Visit, yes. Get back, no. If they all are where they should be, we'll probably make it to three of them."

"And it's always the last one," Jennifer said, and smiled.

Hemi chuckled. "It usually is."

"Here's our next one already coming up on the east side," the pilot called out. "And it's a big one."

They all leaned right to catch the first glimpse.

"Wow, that is a big one indeed," Monroe said. "And this one's flat-topped, like an island."

"Indeed it is." Cooper nodded. "It looks almost like a perfect rectangle."

"The same routine?" the pilot asked.

"Yes, please," Cooper ordered.

The pilot immediately steered the helicopter down until it was about halfway up the hundred-foot tall frozen island. Then the pilot slowly picked up his routine while everyone picked up their binoculars again.

"This one's huge," Bishop said.

"Miles wide," Hemi confirmed.

"I have a good feeling about this," Cooper said as he swiped the binoculars from left to right, as if watching a tennis game.

"That's one side. On to the next, shorter side," the pilot said as he turned a corner.

"One down, three to go," Cooper said.

Halfway through the short side, Hemi lowered his binoculars. "Nothing."

"Were only halfway," Monroe said optimistically. "Trust me."

A minute later, the pilot turned a corner again, and everyone again was tied to their binoculars.

"And the third chance, only one to go after—"

"There it is!" Monroe called out almost hysterically while repeatedly pushing a finger against the window.

At about a third from the corner, half a mile in the distance, a dark black streak, some ten feet below the surface, stuck out of the otherwise white and blue face.

"I must admit that looks a lot like the picture you showed us in your office," Bishop agreed.

"Can you take us as close as possible?" Cooper asked the pilot.

"No problem." Less than a minute later, the helicopter neared the dark part, pulling to within thirty feet. "That's as close as I can get." The pilot hovered the aircraft in front of the dark streak.

"It looks like an empty space," Monroe said, looking through his binoculars. "The darkness appears to be formed by the shadow of the ice above."

"But not completely empty," Cooper said. "Look at the left side, some ten feet in. It looks like metal stakes. Zinc probably."

"I see a bucket," Monroe added. "A little to the right of it and farther into the niche."

"There are all kinds of materials farther in," Hemi said once his eyes were adjusted to the dark.

"I see it too," Bishop said. "Could this belong to Little America Three?"

"It has to be," Cooper confirmed. "This cannot be a coincidence."

"This is our iceberg?" Monroe asked.

Cooper shrugged. "Not to be a party pooper, but it's only our iceberg if we find a tunnel somewhere, and that could still be a needle in a hay—"

"Gentleman, oi!" Jennifer called out. "I appreciate your enthusiasm, but if you look ahead about a quarter mile or so, at about the same depth from the surface...."

They all quickly turned their binoculars to the front of the iceberg and searched the cliff.

"Where? I don't see anything," Monroe said.

Jennifer snuck up behind him, aligned her body with his, and took his head in her hands. Then she turned it towards the front of the iceberg and pushed it down a little. "About there.... You see it now?"

Monroe exhaled deeply. "Oh my God, you're right. There's something there. Can we fly up? Just straight ahead?"

"No problem," the pilot said. "Straight ahead."

"I see it now," Hemi said as the helicopter neared the second half of the cliff. "Five hundred feet ahead."

"Yes," Bishop exclaimed. "There's something there. What is that?"

"I see it too," Cooper said. "Looks like a hole or something."

The pilot flew up to the spot and hovered again midair.

"It is a hole," Bishop confirmed. "Can anyone see how deep it goes?"

"It's too dark," Hemi said. "But it must be ten feet tall and five feet wide or so. That fits our description."

"Shit," Monroe called out. "What now? What do we do? We can't just fly into it."

Cooper chuckled. "What did you think we would do if we found a tunnel sticking out of the side of an iceberg?"

"To be honest, I didn't think that far ahead," Monroe confessed.

"We did," Hemi said.

"Can you put us down straight on top of that hole?" Cooper asked the pilot.

"No problem." He skillfully maneuvered the helicopter onto the top of the iceberg, where he cautiously landed.

"All right, how do you want to do this?" Bishop asked.

Cooper opened a chest behind his seat and took out a rolled-up cable with a climbing harness at the end of it. Smiling, he threw it in Bishop's lap. "What do you think?"

CHAPTER 33

Melnyk

Cooper and Hemi secured an anchor in the ice and tightened the harness onto the snap hook on the cable's end.

"Getting down looks easy, but how do we get back up again?" Monroe asked.

"Look." Hemi took the other end of the rope, where another snap hook was attached. He ran it through a metal eye attached to the anchor and walked up to the helicopter's front. There he attached it to a winch attached beneath the cockpit, waved a finger in the air, and circled it around. The pilot in the cockpit flipped a switch, and the winch started to reel the rope in. "Okay." Hemi raised a full hand, and the winch stopped again. "We simply reel you in."

"Why didn't we use that earlier on?" Jennifer asked. "When we were trapped beneath the ice?"

Cooper walked up to them. "Because there wasn't a place to land on top of the spikey pressure ridge," he answered. "Everything secure?" he asked Hemi.

Hemi nodded. "All set up."

Cooper pulled the rope as hard as he could, until all the slack was out of it. "All right, I'll go down first, Hemi last, and the pilot will stay here to reel us back up later." He took the harness from the floor and held it up. "This harness works exactly the same as we used before, and with this descending device." He held high a metal circular gadget that looked like it had a motorcycle handbrake extending from it. He ran the rope through the gizmo. "Push this handle to control your downwards speed. The harder you push, the slower you go. Let me show you."

He stepped into the harness, secured it, and walked to the edge of the riff. With one end of the rope attached to the helicopter's winch, he threw the other end over the edge, then took a pickax and raised it. "I'll use this to pull myself into the hole. You won't need it because I'll pull each of you in. Hemi will carry a backpack with some other gear we might need. Here we go." He raised a hand. "One second." He contorted his nose, reached into his pocket, and blew a loud sneeze into his handkerchief.

"That's a big one. Bless you," Monroe said.

"Thank you. See you down there." Cooper put the cloth away and stepped backward over the edge. He held himself there for a second and demonstrated how the descending device worked, and slowly lowered himself.

They all leaned over the edge, trying to follow Cooper as he went down, but the cliff was too steep to follow him.

"We'd better back up before one of us tips over," Hemi said.

The rope untightened in less than a minute, and a minute after that, it swung wildly on the edge.

"That's it," Hemi said. "Let's get it up again."

Bishop picked up the rope and reeled it in.

"Who's next?" Hemi asked when the harness came back over the edge.

Monroe stepped forward.

"All right," Hemi said. "You got the hang of it."

"No pun intended," Bishop said, smiling.

Monroe stepped into the harness, grabbed onto the descending device, and quickly walked up to the edge. There he turned. "See you down there." He sounded confident as he stepped over the side.

"I gotta hand it to him," Bishop said. "The British are quick studies."

A few minutes later, the harness came back up again, and one by one, the others lowered themselves into the tunnel. Finally, Hemi appeared before the hole where everyone was waiting for him. Cooper stretched out an arm, grabbed him at the harness, and pulled him in.

"There we are," Cooper said.

Hemi stepped out of the harness and attached it to a snap hook that Cooper had fastened into the ice wall. "Did you already take a look?"

"Up to the first corner down there." Bishop pointed down into the corridor some twenty feet away. "I took a peek around the corner, and it appears to be a real tunnel."

"So, this could be the place?" Hemi opened his backpack and handed everyone a flashlight.

Bishop cocked his head. "We'll see."

"Everyone ready?" Cooper asked.

They all confirmed.

"Do you mind?" Monroe asked as he stepped up to take the lead.

"Be my guest," Cooper said. "Just be careful at each corner."

"No problem." Monroe walked ahead slowly.

"These tunnels sure look a lot like the ones we walked before at the pressure riff," Jennifer said.

"They sure do," Monroe agreed, making the first corner.

"And there's that light again." Cooper turned off his flashlight behind Monroe, and they all followed him.

The farther they went into the tunnel, the brighter the walls seemed to glow. "Still convinced of bioluminescent algae?" Monroe asked.

"What else?" Cooper answered.

Bishop broke off a small ice piece from the wall, and it glowed in his hand like a lightbulb. "It is fascinating."

"Can I see?" Hemi asked, and Bishop gave him the piece. "I once read an article describing an experiment where they tried to grow microalgae in a closed saltwater container to use it as a biological lamp."

"That would be something," Jennifer said. "Lamps without electricity. Did it work?"

"Watch out," Monroe said as he turned another corner and pointed at a large hole in the ground. "Don't trip."

Everyone cautiously stepped over the hole.

"What's that?" Jennifer asked when a soft rumble made the ground shake.

"Probably nothing," Hemi answered. "These icebergs are always on the move, and the ice keeps growing and shrinking. Nothing to worry about."

"Thanks," Jennifer said. "Anyone have any thoughts on what we'll find at the end of this tunnel? I think there's a...." She thought for a short moment. "I think there's an entrance to the Hollow Earth," she said, smiling brightly.

"A pot of gold?" Bishop joked.

"Probably the fountain of youth," Hemi added.

"Ah, let me see," Cooper said. "A perfectly conserved million-year-old alien spaceship that froze into the ice?"

They all laughed.

"What do you think, Walker?" Bishop asked.

"A black panel," Monroe said as he turned another corner.

"A what?" Bishop asked, frowning.

Monroe waved everyone around the corner and pointed some twenty feet ahead.

"Okay, now I understand," Bishop said. "What's that?"

"Be careful," Cooper called out as Monroe started to walk up to it.

They all followed him slowly.

"Is it a door?" Jennifer asked as Monroe stopped at the end.

"There's no door handle." Monroe moved his gloved hand towards the blackness, and cautiously put his fingertips against it.

"What is it?" Hemi asked.

"I don't know." Monroe took off his glove.

"Careful," Bishop urged.

Monroe put his bare fingertips up against the black divide. "It's hard." He stretched his fingers and placed them flat against it. "Kind of warm." He took back his hand and then knocked it with his knuckles a few times.

"Sounds massive," Bishop noted.

Monroe nodded. "It does, doesn't it? Some kind of metal, I guess. Here, see for yourselves." He stepped aside and, one by one, the others moved forward and touched the black wall, rubbed it, knocked on it, and Hemi even banged his torch against it. Nothing happened.

Then Cooper stepped up and stopped one foot away from the black face, and gazed into it.

"What is it?" Hemi asked.

Cooper didn't answer and didn't move an inch.

"Jay-Jay," Hemi now said louder.

Still no response.

Hemi put a hand on Cooper's shoulder and called out again, "Jay-Jay, are you okay?"

Cooper snapped out of his trance and turned towards Hemi. "There's something back there."

"What do you mean there's something back there?" Hemi asked.

Cooper shrugged and shook his head, then took off his gloves and slowly moved his hands towards the black ending. "I feel a vibration in my fingers, and it gets stronger when I approach it." His hands started to tremble just before he placed his fingertips against the blackness. A rumbling sound resonated through the tunnel.

"What the hell is that?" Monroe asked.

No one answered as Cooper placed both hands flat against the black wall.

The rumbling sound increased, and changed into a slow rhythmic hum that rapidly picked up the pace.

"I don't like the sound of that," Bishop said.

"Jay-Jay," Hemi shouted out, but before Cooper could react, the tremble transformed into one continuous tone, and the black wall disappeared, making Cooper take a few uncontrolled steps forward. Hemi stepped up and swiftly grabbed him at his jacket just before he could tip over completely.

"Here's something you don't see every day," Bishop said as they looked at the dark space.

"I don't see anything." Jennifer turned on her flashlight and shone it around, but her light beam seemed to end into nothingness within ten feet or so. "Jeez!" she suddenly yelled out, dropping her flashlight and slapping a hand against her mouth.

"What the hell was that?" Hemi called out.

Everyone moved their beams to the same place, where they saw the frozen, clothed body of what looked like a tall and slender man, sitting on the floor with one arm raised into the air.

"Who's that?" Jennifer asked, still gasping for air.

Bishop walked up to the frozen corpse, which wore an almost pristine Cossack hat, sunken over his shrunken face. The skin on the visible bare hands and neck had lost all its color and looked like leather folded around a skeleton, like a taxidermist had forgotten to stuff an animal.

"What happened here?" Monroe asked.

No one answered.

Bishop kneeled at the body and gingerly raised the hat, and a skimmed, leathery, male face emerged, with a perfect head of dark curly hair.

Cooper took a deep, loud breath.

Hemi whispered, "You think it's...?"

"I think it is," Cooper replied, sighing. "I think this is my grandfather, Jay Clemency Simons—tall, skinny, with dark, curly hair, and gone missing in the Antarctic. What are the odds this is someone else?"

Hemi put a hand on Cooper's shoulder. "I'm sorry, man."

"No need to be," Cooper said. "He's long gone. It's just that a mystery comes to an end, a mystery that obsessed my father during my childhood and ruined our relation till today."

"Perhaps you can give your father some closure now. Patch up things between you two," Jennifer suggested.

"Who knows," Cooper said.

"Are you sure you're okay?" Hemi asked.

Cooper nodded. "Don't worry. I'm fine."

"The question is: why is he here?" Bishop said.

"Indeed," Monroe agreed. "What is this place? What are those walls?" He waved his flashlight through the space, seeing the light end not far from him. He stepped up to where the light ended, stretched out an arm, and suddenly stopped. "It's a wall. A black wall."

They checked out the sides of the space.

"It's a small room," Hemi concluded.

"But what's that material?" Monroe, being the only one who touched the wall without gloves, asked. "It feels soft but sturdy."

Hemi also took off his gloves and touched it. "It feels like a layer of velvet on metal. What do you think, Jay-Jay?"

Cooper stood there frozen, close to where they'd come in.

"Jay-Jay," Hemi called out.

"I'm here," Cooper said. "Sorry, there's just something about this room."

"What is it?" Monroe asked.

"I don't know," Cooper replied. "A feeling. I'm not sure yet."

"What's going on with the light?" Jennifer waved the flashlight onto a wall, and the light mysteriously vanished. "Looks like magic."

"There's nothing magic to it," Bishop explained. "It's just the blackness of the wall. In theory, pure 100% black doesn't reflect light but simply absorbs it all. I've heard that at MIT, they created a new material made of carbon nanotubes that absorbs about 99.995% of the light that shines on it."

"So, these walls are the blackest of blacks?" Monroe asked.

"I think so," Bishop replied. "There's nothing mystical about it. Because of the blackest black, we can only see everything that's directly in the path of our light beams and nothing else."

"But why?" Hemi asked.

Bishop shook his head as Cooper took a few small steps and stopped at the wall in front of him. In one swift move, he put his bare flat hand up against it, and a monotonous vibration sounded through the room.

"Wow," Monroe said.

The sound dissipated when Cooper took his hand from the wall.

"Do that again," Hemi said.

Cooper, now slowly, moved his hand against it, and immediately the sound returned. Then, when he stroked the wall, the pitch of the sound changed. He moved his hand back and the sound also changed back.

"It's like a weird musical instrument," Hemi said.

"I don't think it is," Bishop said. "Please, move it again in any direction."

Cooper now waved his hand over the wall, and the sound changed with every change in its path.

"It's giving you directions," Bishop explained. "Follow the pitch."

Cautiously, Cooper let his hand slide against the wall, stepped over the body in the corner, and continued on the other side. Each of them, with their flashlights, followed Cooper's hand, which seemed to move midair against the blackness.

Monroe shook his head. "It's a bizarre phenomenon that, even with the light pointed at it, you can't see anything."

"It's crazy," Jennifer said.

"Go back, go back," Hemi called out as the sound's pitch lowered again.

Cooper waved his hand back and forward again until he stopped in the corner.

"You need to go up," Monroe said, pointing his flashlight at the body's pointing arm.

"Your grandfather's showing you the way," Jennifer said.

Cooper took a deep breath as he moved his hand up. "I feel something," he grunted, now fully stretched on his toes.

"What is it?" Hemi asked.

"I'm not sure. It feels like an opening, a slot, or something. Let me see."

As he reached in, the walls started to lower with a soft *clunk*, and a bright streak of light appeared between the ceiling and the walls. Immediately, everybody took a step back to the center of the room, including Cooper. When he let go of the slot, the walls went up again.

"What was that?" Monroe asked.

"There's something very bright behind those walls," Hemi said.

"Do it again," Jennifer said.

"Let me," Monroe said. "I'm taller." He stepped up to the corner, reached out, found the niche with his hand, and reached in. They all watched his fingers disappear into thin air, but nothing happened. "That's strange. Did you do something, push a button, or pull a lever or anything?"

"Nothing," Cooper said.

Monroe waved his hand up and down inside the wall, but nothing happened.

"Let me try," Hemi said, and stepped up and changed places with Monroe. Again nothing happened.

"That's weird," Jennifer said. "Could it have been a one-time thing?"

"I don't think so," Bishop said. "Jay-Jay, please...." Bishop pointed at the corner.

Cooper walked up, stretched out again, reached inside, and the walls started down again.

"That's really strange," Monroe said.

"Perhaps not," Bishop replied while the walls kept coming down. "I think it has something to do with the grandfather. I think the grandfather somehow got trapped in here when the ice broke off, found the keyhole in the wall, and learned that his hand worked as a key. And when he died, he made sure he'd literally point us in the right direction."

"Two questions," Monroe said. "If he found the keyhole, why didn't he open the wall himself, and is still here instead?"

"Oumph," Cooper uttered as he let his hand go from the keyhole. He grunted and fell back on his flat feet again, and the walls instantly went back up again.

"There's your answer," Bishop said. "He simply couldn't keep the key in the keyhole long enough for the walls to lower completely. As for your second question...."

"I didn't even ask my second question," Monroe said.

"Let me guess," Bishop replied. "Why does the keyhole only work with Jay-Jay?"

Monroe gave a bright smile.

"Jay-Jay, how's your cold?" Bishop asked.

"Uh, what?" Cooper asked.

"Your handkerchief... do you mind if I borrow it for a second?" Bishop smiled.

Cooper frowned. "What? Why? It's used, you know?"

"Please indulge me." Bishop stretched out his hand.

"All right." Cooper sighed, took the handkerchief from his pants pocket, and put it in Bishop's gloved hand.

"Thank you." Bishop walked back to the corner with the pointing body. He reached out and shoved the handkerchief into the slot. Straightaway, the walls started to lower again. "That's better," he said.

"What? How?" Monroe asked.

"Your second question," Bishop said. "You know that this whole... umm... experience we've had lately revolves around DNA. I guessed that the keyhole responded to Jay-Jay's grandfather first, eighty years ago, and somehow connected itself to his DNA. When Jay-Jay's hand worked as a key and ours didn't, I figured it had to be a DNA lock. The keyhole works only with family members."

"And the hanky contains enough of Jay-Jay's snot to keep the door from closing again," Hemi said.

"As you put it so eloquently," Bishop confirmed. "The big question is: what's behind there?" He jumped to his toes, but the walls were still too high to look over the edge.

"It is exciting, isn't it?" A strange voice sounded from the entrance to the room.

Startled, they all turned back to see three men and a woman blocking the doorway. "I can't wait to see what's behind those walls."

"Hootkins?" Monroe asked.

"Hootkins!" Bishop yelled. "The USGS Hootkins?

CHAPTER 34

The Library

As if nailed to the ground, Bishop, Jennifer, Cooper, and Hemi stood frozen as they exchanged looks between Monroe and the man from the USGS he called Hootkins.

"Hootkins?" the woman next to the fat man asked.

"William Hootkins." He cocked his head and smiled. "Or Andre Melnyk to some. Or, in your case...." His voice turned throaty as he turned to the woman next to him. "You can call me Chief."

The woman's face contorted in surprise. "Chief? I don't understand."

"Neither do I," Bishop added. "What's going on here?"

"So the rumbling we heard before must have been your helicopter," Monroe said.

"Nothing to worry about?" Jennifer said, eying Cooper.

"I'm lost." Monroe stepped forward, and the two men flanking Melnyk and the woman put their hands on the holsters they wore on their belts.

"It's all right," Melnyk said.

Monroe raised both hands for a second and stepped back. "But, if you're not with the USGS, who are you working for?"

"Oh no, I do," Melnyk addressed Monroe. "I do consulting work for the USGS, but I'm also—"

In the corner of the room, Simons' body keeled over backward when the wall was low enough to tip him over. Everyone hushed at the sound of the falling body and looked around. While they'd been focused on Melnyk's arrival, a vast, open, square space—some three hundred feet wide and deep—had materialized.

"Is that gold?" Jennifer asked, looking at the walls and floor as they took a few steps into the great hall.

Monroe shook his head. "I don't think so."

"Why would you say that?" Jennifer asked.

"It's probably made from the same unknown metal the Kola piece is made of."

Everything surrounding them shone like the purest of polished gold. The brightness of the walls and floor was only interrupted by the same kind of etchings they recognized from the piece of metal from Kola, the writings by the crazy woman, and the plaque from the rubbing.

They all walked up to the nearest wall, and Cooper touched it. "It feels kind of warm."

They all took off their gloves and touched and rubbed the shiny, smooth walls, on which spirals were stacked in series of four, from floor to ceiling.

"There must be hundreds of spirals," Hemi said. "They look like the ones we saw on the plaque."

"Thousands, I'd think," Jennifer said. "And much larger in size than we found in Russia."

"Larger means more scripture," Monroe added.

"And the individual characters are so small. Barely recognizable," Bishop added. "There must be thousands of large texts on these walls."

"And look at that floor." Hemi opened his arms and spread them around. The spirals filling the floor were each two feet in diameter and separated by only a few inches.

For a long moment, they moved around the great hall in silence.

Cooper broke the silence. "What do you think this place is?"

Bishop grinned. "I might have an idea." He paused for a moment. "I think this space is right up Walker's alley." They all eyed Monroe, who walked up to Bishop from the other end of the room, where he was trying to count the spirals.

Monroe nodded. "I think you're right." He took a deep breath. "It's a library."

"A library...." Cooper sighed and cocked his head. "Okay, maybe, but made by who?"

"I have no idea," Monroe said. "But I would guess that, whoever they were, they must have introduced themselves in one of these spirals."

"But where?" Bishop spun around on his axis.

Hemi tapped Cooper on the shoulder. When he got his attention, he pointed to the ceiling with his other hand.

"Wow," Cooper uttered as both men gazed up.

"What is it?" Bishop followed their gaze and, as he looked up, gasped. "Oh my God."

A second later, everyone was staring upwards and uttering sounds of amazement.

"Is that what I think it is?" Jennifer asked.

"Earth," Monroe answered.

The black ceiling didn't reflect any light, which made it look like a pitch-dark sky over a brightly lit golden room. Drawn in the roof, white lines lit up in that pitch-black night. Together the lines formed the highly detailed shapes of continents, mountain ridges, and oceans.

"Wow," Jennifer said softly.

"Earth, billions of years ago?" Bishop suggested.

"And the stars...." Monroe pointed at another part of the ceiling. "That looks an awful lot like the Milky Way."

"But not exactly," Cooper said. "It looks different somehow."

"Maybe a billion years ago, it looked like that," Monroe stated.

"Who made this place?" Hemi asked. "Aliens?"

"I don't think so," Bishop said as he pointed at the other end of the ceiling.

"That looks an awful lot like...." Jennifer took a deep breath.

"Ata," Monroe said as he looked at a front and side drawing that perfectly resembled the tiny mummy they saw in Spain.

"But how?" Jennifer asked. "Remember what Elise told us, that Stanford researchers determined Ata was only a few decades old?"

Monroe shrugged. "I remember, but what does it mean?"

"No aliens?" Hemi asked.

Bishop shook his head. "I don't think so. Remember the Silurian hypothesis Walker talked about? Ancient life... a primeval civilization right here on Earth. To me, all this text and imagery suggests a civilization that had its genesis right here, billions of years ago."

"And its demise," Jennifer added.

"One-point-one billion years old," Monroe said. "Like Fellows from the USGS dated the Kola piece."

"I heard about that from my colleague," Melnyk said.

Monroe turned to the fat man. "The U... S... G... S...." He emphasized each letter. "Who are you, exactly?"

"Just someone eager to see to it that all Earth's treasures are equally divided between Earth's dominating nations."

"You're not Russian Foreign Intelligence?" the woman asked. "You're just a hired gun?"

"I'm afraid you don't understand, Nadya," Melnyk replied. "Of course I'm Russian intelligence. I work for everyone and no one. Let me explain. For far too long, the top 5% of leading countries in this world have dictated to the other 95%. My organization believes that by equally dividing the world's resources, we can eradicate poverty in the next twenty years."

"Your organization?" Bishop asked.

Melnyk nodded. "An abbreviation you never heard of. Yet."

"And you're here to do just what, exactly?" Cooper asked.

"That's simple," Melnyk said. "I'm here to ensure transparency."

"Transparency?" Bishop asked, raising a brow.

"Now I remember," Jennifer called out, pointing at Nadya. "You were in the hotel in Spain. Your hair looked different, but it was you. And you were also back at Matthew's office at the university, on that bench. I only got a glimpse of you, but now I'm sure. You've been spying on us the entire time."

Before Nadya could answer, Melnyk stepped forward. "Nadya's been working for me all the way."

"Are you the one that tortured that poor old man in Murmansk?" Jennifer asked Nadya.

"Yes, transparency," Melnyk interrupted. "Tell me, if you would have found this place all by yourselves, would you have told your newly found New Zealand friends? Or your Russian adversaries? Or the Chinese? Or any other country, for that matter?"

For a moment, all stood silent.

"I don't think so," Melnyk continued. "I think you would have kept it for yourselves. You would probably research it first, and then, whatever riches would come from it would probably flow to your country's government or, as usual, to the top two richest industries. And maybe, just maybe after that, you would tell the rest of the world about it."

"We would never do that," Jennifer said.

"Maybe you wouldn't want to," Melnyk replied. "But the real question is: could you prevent it?"

"And your colleague, Fellows?" Monroe asked. "Who is he in all this?"

Melnyk smiled. "Don is an outright loyal and trustworthy government worker."

"Hmm." Monroe shook his head. "Unbelievable."

"What now?" Bishop asked. 'What do you suppose we do now?"

"Nothing," Melnyk replied. "Like I said: transparency. I have a small group of friends on standby. They will arrive here shortly, take inventory, put everything on photo and film, and put it online to share it with the rest of the world. They will also take care of the iceberg for the coming months and see to it that everyone, from everywhere, gets access to this place, and all the information it provides."

"But we have no idea what we've found ourselves yet," Monroe said.

"An ancient library?" Melnyk answered. "You said it yourself. And what is the purpose of a library?" Melnyk paused for a moment. "To share knowledge. How fitting, I would say."

"Knowledge no one will be able to read," Bishop remarked.

Melnyk nodded once. "For now, but that's where people like you come in, professor. I'm sure you or people just like you will succeed in translating everything, given time."

"And you will be there again to share that knowledge?" Jennifer asked.

Melnyk smiled and cocked his head.

"And what do we do now?" Cooper asked Melnyk.

"I suggest you do what you came here to do," Melnyk replied.

Cooper looked the man straight in the eyes and frowned.

"I'm serious." Melnyk invitingly spread both arms. "Look around, discover, take your pictures. Whatever. Don't mind us."

"This is crazy," Monroe said.

"Guys." Bishop gestured to his friends, and they all walked to a far corner in the room.

"Again, what do we do now?" Cooper asked.

"What *can* we do?" Monroe asked.

"Listen," Jennifer said. "Maybe this doesn't have to be a bad thing."

"How do you figure?" Hemi asked.

Jennifer cocked her head. "Are we the ones who would want to keep such a finding to ourselves? I mean, doesn't everyone have the right to know?"

"I doubt that if the Russians or Chinese made this kind of discovery, they would share it with us," Monroe argued.

"Exactly my point," Jennifer replied. "I think you're right, and isn't it time something changed in that regard?"

Bishop sighed. "Maybe you're right. Maybe Melnyk's right, and it is time to start cooperating."

"But that doesn't mean I have to like that fat man's methods," Monroe added.

"Ignore him," Bishop said.

"Look around you," Monroe replied. "How the hell are we going to document all of this? Let alone translate it without a working algorithm?"

"I'm confident we'll solve that problem soon," Bishop said. "I suggest we take as many detailed pictures as we can and get the hell out of here."

"But that will take hours," Monroe replied.

"Unless you have a better idea?" Bishop took a camera from his jacket pocket.

The others followed his example.

EPILOGUE

A Few Weeks Later, Yale, New Haven, CT

The day's last rays of sunshine beamed through the translucent marble panels of Beinecke's six-story–tall, glass-enclosed tower, lighting up the thousands of gold embossed ancient books. Jennifer's heels echoed through the building as she walked up to Monroe, who, back in his dark suit and red tie, was concentrating on his laptop at the desk next to the Guttenberg Bible showcase. She smiled to herself, thinking of the many times she dropped by in the early evening and found the librarian zoned out and focused on some ancient manuscript, only to get startled when she would call out his name.

"Walker!" she called out.

"Damn." He shot up straight. "Woman... when will you stop doing that?"

"Not as long as it's funny."

He caught his breath again and shook his head. "You're going to give me a heart attack someday."

"I'm sorry. Or not. I'm late, and Matthew's even later?"

"As always," Monroe confirmed, still regaining his breath. "How have you been the past weeks? I haven't heard from you since we got back."

"I'm okay, I guess. I've been trying to pick up where I left off when we went on our journey."

"And how's that working out?"

She bobbed her head. "I still can't wrap my head around it. All my adult life, as a linguistic anthropologist, I've lived under the assumption that someday I would be able to know just about everything there is to know about how language influences social life."

"Doubts?"

"I mean, when someone succeeds in translating the millions of pages of text we took from the spirals, it will probably shake the foundation of just about any scholar."

"I think it already does. Until recently, the assumption that a civilization lived on Earth over a billion years ago was considered sheer science fiction."

"And yet we found them," a familiar voice sounded from the entrance.

"Ah, I'm so glad you could make it," Monroe said sarcastically.

"Where have you been?" Jennifer asked.

"Have you been fishing again?" Monroe added, smiling brightly.

"As a matter of fact," Bishop answered. "In a way, I did. Here, let me make it up to you." He handed Monroe a large flat package wrapped in brown paper.

"You shouldn't have," Monroe joked.

"Wait until you unwrap it," Bishop said, smiling.

"Heavy," Monroe suggested, lifting the package and moving it up and down a few times.

"Just unwrap it," Jennifer said, impatient.

Monroe ripped off the paper with one big move and fell silent. For a long moment, he held the large frame in front of him. "Wow, where did you get that?"

"I'm glad you like it. I found it folded between the papers we took from the Cruiser and had it restored and framed."

Monroe handed the frame to Jennifer. "That's very thoughtful," he said to Bishop with watery eyes.

"It's signed." Jennifer noticed.

"That's Dougal MC, it says," Bishop replied. "I checked. Dougal McConnel was the pilot of the Beechcraft 17 Staggerwing biplane they carried on the Cruiser's back. They called it The Eagle. The Cruiser was called The Turtle."

"Apparently, he was also a gifted artist," Monroe said.

"The Eagle and The Turtle. How fitting," Jennifer said. "Isn't there any family left who would want the drawing?"

Bishop shook his head. "McConnel died in '43, flying fighter planes for the British Royal Air Force. He left no family, so...."

"Incredible," Monroe said. "I still can't believe it when I think of what they must have gone through there in the cold, back in those days. But thanks again. It's really a great gift, and I will cherish it and give it a very special place. I forgive you for being late." He put the frame next to him against the table.

"No problem," Bishop smiled. "Did you succeed in connecting with the men at Scott Base?"

"Yes, they should be waiting by now." Monroe opened his laptop, punched a few keys, and turned it around so they all could see the screen. On the screen, Jay-Jay Cooper sat at a desk next to Tipene Hemi. They recognized the maintenance room from the snow scooters in the background.

"Hi, how are you doing back home?" Cooper asked while Hemi waved at the camera.

"Adjusting slowly," Monroe answered, smiling with Jennifer and Bishop waving in the back.

"I miss our snow scooter rides," Bishop said.

"I can imagine," Cooper answered. "I see you're all there."

"It's good to see you both," Jennifer said. "How are things over there? Is that Melnyk still there and giving you a hard time?"

"We haven't seen him in a while now," Cooper answered. "The last time we heard from him was when he came to tell us they were planning on towing the iceberg to the Ross Ice Shelf. That way it could be visited without having to fly there every time."

"That doesn't sound like a bad idea," Monroe suggested.

"Well...." Cooper hesitated. "It does if you count in the fact that the Antarctic has become a pretty crowded place since you left. Every respected scientist in fields of Geology, Paleontology, History, and God-knows-what wants to take a look at the room before the winter sets in and it becomes dark again."

"We've become somewhat of a tourist attraction," Hemi added.

"I guess that's the price you pay for transparency," Bishop said, adding, "I tried to find out more about that organization Melnyk was talking about."

"And?" Cooper asked.

"Nothing but rumors," Bishop answered. "As if they don't exist, or no one wants, or dares, to talk about it."

"I gotta say, however," Hemi said. "I don't think their ideology is all bad."

"Maybe it's their methods I have doubts about," Jennifer said.

"Peaceful protest will only get you so far," Hemi replied.

"Jay-Jay," Bishop said. "Did you contact your father?"

"We spoke a few times over the phone," Cooper answered. "I'm not sure if we're ever going to be all okay, but we had a somewhat normal conversation. I think he felt relieved to learn about what happened to his father."

"What did happen to your grandfather?" Jennifer asked. "The last thing we heard was that there was going to be an autopsy back in New Zealand."

"Yes, indeed. They finished it already," Cooper answered. "There's something strange going on with that. The autopsy concluded that the body was indeed my grandfather's, but also determined that he probably died of old age."

They all fell silent for a moment.

"But how can that be?" Monroe asked. "You told us your grandfather was a young man when he went on that expedition?"

"Twenty-seven," Cooper said.

"How could he have survived?" Jennifer asked. "You cannot live on snow and ice alone, can you?"

"I don't think you can," Bishop said.

"Could it be someone or something kept him alive all that time?" Monroe asked.

"But how? And who?" Jennifer asked.

"Them!" Monroe stated.

"Them as in the Ata people?" Jennifer mocked, and everyone mumbled and shrugged.

"Maybe he gained all the knowledge from the Ata people's library somehow?" Hemi suggested. "Though I'm not sure you could survive on that."

Bishop cocked his head. "Hadeans, we call them now, the Ata people. For lack of a better option, they're named after Hadean, the geologic eon of the Earth four-point-six billion years ago. I recently learned that they found traces of carbon minerals, biological materials from living organisms in four-point-one-billion-year-old rocks in Western Australia."

"So life on Earth started way before we always thought it did," Cooper said.

"And that means," Hemi concluded, "that it's not such a crazy thought that there was a technologically advanced civilization here before us."

"Who's to say there was only one?" Monroe smiled. "Considering the duration of our human development here on Earth, there's plenty of time in history for there to have been a few civilizations more."

They all chuckled.

"Why not," Bishop said. "I'm now ready to believe just about anything. You know, perhaps the translations of the spirals will shed some light on things, maybe even on how Simons could survive for that long."

"Matthew, how are those translations coming?" Cooper asked.

"We don't have anything concrete yet," Bishop answered. "I'm working with several US and foreign universities, and of course, the government is helping, so to say. It's going slow, but I feel we're closing in. Yesterday we had a breakthrough, and we think we now have a way to separate what we think are proper nouns from the texts."

"That sounds like a step in the right direction," Hemi said. "You know what I still don't understand? How do your mummy, Ata, and the other one... what was his name?"

"Alyoshenka," Jennifer answered quickly.

"That one," Hemi replied. "I still don't understand how they fit in. They were both only decades old when they found them. As I understand it, Alyoshenka was even alive when they found him."

"That one had me puzzled too," Bishop said. "And to be honest, it still does, but together with a few other scientists, we developed a working theory. You remember the star map on the ceiling of the room?"

They all nodded.

"Well, we learned a few things from that. For instance, from the pictures of their bodies and the knowledge of translated DNA, we learned that Ata wasn't as young as we thought her to be. She was probably a young adult. The Hadeans were short people. Alyoshenka, we now believe, was a fully grown adult."

Monroe nodded and grunted. "Hmm, okay, that could explain the state of Ata's skeleton, which looked like a full-grown adult, only several times smaller."

"Much, much smaller," Bishop agreed. "And you remember the star charts on the ceiling? Well, it appears that they had locations marked on them. We don't know the exact place of those locations because we haven't been able to correspond them with our star maps, but...." He took a deep breath. "We think it's possible the Hadeans left Earth for that location or locations."

"They left Earth?" Cooper asked. "Why?"

"And how?" Hemi said.

"Maybe Earth couldn't sustain them anymore," Jennifer answered. "I mean, if you look at us, we're kind of on our way to overexploit Earth. So who knows... in a few decades, our Earth might also not be able to sustain us any longer."

"As for the how," Bishop answered. "We know they were, or are, a highly advanced civilization, so—"

"So the idea of colonizing Mars might not be such a bad one after all." Jennifer gave a tiny smile.

"But still," Hemi said. "Are you saying they came back from the stars, Ata and Alyoshinko?"

"Alyoshenka," Jennifer corrected him.

"Who knows," Monroe said. "Maybe we'll know for sure when we translate the spirals."

"I don't think so," Jennifer replied. "Those spirals date back over a billion years ago, so how could they?"

"I don't mean those spirals," Monroe said. "I mean the spirals that made the Russian woman crazy."

Jennifer nodded. "That's a good one. Come to think of it, how do you think she learned how to write those spirals? Did that Alyoshenka figure possess her?"

"Who knows," Bishop replied. "Anyway, that's our working theory for now. Maybe you remember that strange interstellar object in 2018 that entered our solar system?"

"Oumuamua?" Cooper suggested.

"That one," Bishop said. "The Messenger."

Everyone frowned.

"That was a cigar-shaped object, discovered through a telescope in Hawaii, which they found to be the first interstellar object in our solar system. Somehow it never got much attention, but a well-respected and published scientist named Abraham Loeb, professor and chair of astronomy at the Harvard Smithsonian Center for Astrophysics, wrote a paper on it."

"What did it say?" Monroe asked impatiently.

"I was coming to that. He argued that our civilization, including the IKAROS project and the Starshot Initiative, created 'light sails' with similar dimensions as Oumuamua. A technology that one day might be used for transportation of cargos between planets or even systems. He theorized that this would account for Oumuamua's unusual cigar shape, geometry, low thermal emission, and strange trajectory. One thing is for sure: it also wasn't a regular comet because it didn't have a tail of melted glass behind it."

"Are you suggesting Ata and Alyoshenka traveled to our world on that cigar?" Hemi grinned.

Bishop shrugged. "I'm just saying...."

"Well, let's say they came back from the stars," Monroe said. "Why?"

"Maybe they wanted to point us in a certain direction," Bishop answered.

"What direction?" Monroe asked.

"The direction we've been taking the past weeks," Bishop said.

"Again, why?" Jennifer asked.

"I don't know," Bishop answered. "I don't have all the answers. Maybe they came to help us. You said it yourself: we're making a kind of a mess of our planet these days, and maybe they have knowledge of how we can change that."

"Wouldn't that be nice," Hemi said.

"There's only one way to find out," Bishop said.

Cooper nodded. "I understand you need to get back to work."

"No problem," Hemi added. "Take care, and let's talk again soon."

"In a few weeks, we'll be back in New Zealand, and let's talk again before then," Cooper said.

"Sound like a plan," Monroe agreed, and while the others waved, he closed the laptop.

"What now?' Jennifer asked.

"You heard them," Bishop said, smiling. "I need to get back to work and try to piece together some way of translating those spirals."

"Do you think we'll ever know?" Monroe asked.

"I'm sure we will," Jennifer replied. "I'm more afraid of what we'll do with the knowledge once we've obtained it."

Bishop gave a tiny smile. "I think you're right. I believe a wise man once said: 'Knowledge is knowing that a tomato is a fruit. Wisdom is knowing not to put it in a fruit salad.'"

WE HOPE YOU ENJOYED... OH WAIT....

INTERLUDE

Two Years Later, Yale, New Haven, CT

"Walker, it's me, Matthew. You must come to the dungeon. Now! And bring Jennifer. We did it. I did it."

***

For just over two years, Matthew Bishop lived his life somewhat a recluse, withdrawn to the office that his friends and colleagues named the dungeon, where he worked and slept, seven days a week. The university had let him be on the premise that he was on the brink of an earth-shattering discovery, should he ever be able to translate the 1,023 spirals—or the Hadean Volumes, as they called them now. Al the volumes were copied from the walls of the Hadean Vault, the name they gave the iceberg holding the ancient texts. All the volumes were made public by a mysterious organization, starting a global race where governments, academics, and amateur enthusiasts began working on the translations.

In his first year of reclusiveness, Yale had forced Bishop to appear in public and share his results. His appearances had been erratic. He looked confounded, messy, and his work seemed logical but was inimitable. His reputation had preserved his status as a professor, though he hadn't spoken in public for students in over twenty months.

Where most of his friends and colleagues had lost faith in his ability ever to translate the spirals, and had looked upon him as lost, Walker Monroe and Jennifer Porter had never stopped believing in him. His best friends and colleagues had coordinated their visits to him and visited him at least four times a week. At their visits, they kept him in the loop on current events, and he would explain his progress. Not that they understood his work, but they admired his always present enthusiasm and optimism. Every visit, he somehow succeeded in convincing them he made a new, small, but significant step. In the beginning, researchers from all over the world had visited him live at the campus. Still, after a year and the absence of results, contact had diminished to an occasional video conference. He was mostly contacted by students who thought they made a groundbreaking discovery. It seldom played out, and when it did, those were minor discoveries he'd already made himself. Disappointed, Bishop always kept encouraging students to keep up the work and never give up.

In the second year, the world lost some of the interest. The news coverage on the Hadean Vault and the Volumes diminished. The belief that he would one day be able to translate the volumes faded away. Only the biggest governments, with time and money to waste, a handful of enthusiast amateurs, and Matthew Bishop were relentlessly working on the Volumes in their basements and attics.

September 7, 2:00 PM

Standing between the wall and his desk, with a marker clenched between his teeth, Bishop gazed at his smartboard for a long moment before turning to his laptop. His desk was filled with stacks of printed paper that had all kinds of colored markings on it. Even the floor was littered with piles of paper and books on mathematics, ciphers, and ancient languages.

He bent over, took the marker from between his teeth, and started scribbling signs and English text on his glossy desktop next to the computer. He put the marker back in his mouth, turned around to the smartboard, back to the computer, and to the smartboard again. Then he took a deep breath, took two steps back, bumped into his desk, and looked over the board again. When he turned his head from left to right, his mouth opened slowly, dropping the marker on the floor.

A big sigh broke the silence.

Then he held his breath while, moving backward, he walked around his desk until he bumped against the back wall. After one more big exhale, he closed his eyes and slapped his hands against his face. Then he lowered his hands and slowly opened his eyes again. A deep inhale, and with two big steps, he rushed to his desk and started throwing off papers, searching.

Shit, where is it?

When he finally removed a small stack next to his laptop, he found his cell phone. With shaking hands, he took it and noticed that it wasn't on. He impatiently pressed the button on the side and held it.

Come on, come on, come on. As the splash screen appeared, Bishop wiggled on his feet before he started pacing the room. "Yes!" he called out at the sight of the opening screen. Still trembling, he opened the phone app and started punching numbers. The dial tone sounded for at least a minute. *Where are you? Come on.*

Suddenly a man's voice sounded, clearing his throat. "Monroe here. This better be good."

"Walker, it's me, Matthew. You must come to the dungeon. Now! And bring Jennifer. We did it. I did it."

"Who? What? What are you talking about? You did what?"

"I know the system. I can read it. I mean, not all of it—that will take some work—but I know how to do it. You must come. I'll show you. Now, please."

"Calm down," Monroe said, still waking up. "Are you saying you actually—"

"Yes, please, now. I can explain. It's a form of symmetric-key algorithms, but then again, it's not. It does use the same cryptographic keys for the encryption of the text and the decryption of the ciphertext, but only with another level of—"

"Stop!" Monroe called out. "I have no idea what you're babbling about, and I don't want to know at two o'clock in the damn morning."

"But you have to come so I can show you," Bishop urged.

"Yeah, yeah, sure. It's okay," Monroe replied. "I'm going to hang up now. You try to calm down, and I'll be there in half an hour or so."

"Hurry, and bring Jennifer."

***

Monroe looked at the phone's screen, hung up, and dialed. After three dial tones, the line silenced. Monroe waited for a second. "Jennifer, are you there?"

"Do you know what time it is?"

"The madman did it," Monroe replied. "The madman says he did it and wants us to come over to the dungeon."

"Now?" Jennifer's sleepy voice said. "Are you sure? What did he say?"

"He started rambling about cryptographic encryption of the ciphertext. What do I know? He sounded convinced. He wants us to come, and now."

"Do you think this is real?" she asked, now alert.

"Somehow, I think this could be it. I'm going anyway. I said I'd be there in thirty minutes."

"Give me thirty minutes, and I'll pick you up," Jennifer said.

***

Fifty minutes later, Jennifer and Monroe walked up the steps of 451 College Street. The door to the dark building was ajar, and as they entered, they noticed light coming through a crack at the end of the hallway.

"Do you think he really did it?" Jennifer asked as they walked the hallway.

"I guess we'll find out soon enough." Monroe stopped at the door in the back and carefully placed his flat hand against it. He glanced inside through the crack, and when he couldn't see anything, he turned his head slowly and listened.

"What are you doing?" Jennifer asked, and she put her hand above Monroe's, and with one big push, the door swung open. "There we go. We were invited, weren't we?" She pushed Monroe inside and walked in after him.

They looked at the mess and stepped over dozens of documents lying around on the floor. Jennifer swiped them aside with her feet as she walked up to the desk where Bishop sat, concentrating on the screen and mumbling. His traditional three-day beard had grown into an inch-long, salt-and-pepper beard since she last saw him a week ago. His hair, frequently trimmed by Jennifer herself, was tied together with a band in the back, giving him a short reddish ponytail with curls.

"How are you, Matthew?" she asked.

He kept mumbling and reading on the laptop.

Monroe looked around the office and shook his head. "How are you doing, my friend?"

He joined Jennifer, and they both stared at the professor bent over his laptop screen.

"You're late," Bishop mumbled. "Come." He circled an arm, pointing them to flank him. "Here, look at this." He pointed at the screen.

"Are you okay?" Monroe asked.

"Stop asking if I'm okay. I'm fine. Look at the screen." With his mouse, he continuously shaded and unshaded a row of signs. "Do you see that?"

"Okay, sure," Jennifer said.

"Those are similar to the signs we found in the spirals," Monroe said.

"They are from the spirals," Bishop replied. "Now watch this."

On the right side of the screen, he clicked on a green button. Over the signs, regular Roman alphabet letters started flipping as if they were slowly forming words. When the flipping stopped, a sentence with what looked like words had formed.

"You see?" He pointed at the screen again.

"Gnorf alag mefferique attancsa wormana lodat ik?" Monroe tried to pronounce.

"That's just the first layer," Bishop said, as if explaining something.

"You're not making sense, man," Monroe said. "Maybe start from the beginning."

"All right, all right." Bishop sounded excited. "From the beginning. I mean, we all tried to translate the text by using cryptographic primitives, based on symmetric ciphers in a single layer. But that way always needed a symmetric key block cipher that I didn't know and couldn't recreate. By adding multilayers, I skipped the need for a single cipher and employed a maximum distance separable matrix. That way—"

"Okay," Jennifer interrupted him. "Maybe not all the way back to the beginning. Skip to the part where you said you did it, and from there, treat us like any of your first-year students."

"Okay, sorry. Listen. Try to look at it like this. A translation of an unknown language is like writing something in a secret code. Umm... like this." He started typing on his laptop. "'*Now Walker can read this okay,*' becomes, '*yako siht dear nac reklaw won*'."

"You typed it backward," Jennifer noticed.

"You wanted it simple," Bishop replied, raising two hands.

"Keep going," Monroe urged.

"All right." Bishop typed again. "Now, '*siht dear nac reklaw won yako.*' "You see what I did there?"

"You moved the first word of the sentence to the end," Jennifer said.

"I did. Now, what if this was the first sentence, and what if for the second sentence, I would move not only the first but also the second word to the end, and so on, and so on."

"It's that simple?" Monroe asked.

"No, it isn't." Bishop shook his head. "But you wanted it explained in a simple way. What I'm trying to say is that there is more than one layer of translation necessary to make sense of it."

"Then why didn't you just say that?" Monroe asked.

"I did, but you—"

"All right, okay," Jennifer came in between. "Play nice. Are you saying that you can translate all the volumes with this multilayer approach?"

"I already did." Bishop leaned back in his chair.

"What?" Monroe grabbed Bishop at the shoulder and turned his chair towards him. "You translated all the volumes already? Can you please repeat that?"

"I translated all the volumes already," Bishop said. "They're right here on my laptop. That was what I was reading when you came in. It took me some time to sort them in the right sequence, but once I knew where to look.... Well, it was a push of a button and ten minutes later." He worked the keyboard again. "Here."

On the screen, a numbered table appeared. Monroe took the mouse and scrolled the pages down.

"There are 6,068 books translated from the 1,023 volumes," Bishop said. "Judging from the titles, they can be categorized much the same way as we do our books, with genres like history, fiction, poetry, folktale, and even cookbooks. Every book translated from a volume has an index."

"So the Vault is a library in every sense of the word," Jennifer said.

"It is," Bishop confirmed.

"Six thousand and sixty-eight books." Monroe spelled out the numbers before he let go of the mouse. Then he leaned over Bishop, wrapped his arms around him, tightened them, and started shaking him around in his chair. "You did it, you crazy bastard. You did it."

"Amazing." Jennifer took the mouse and scrolled through the list. "One question," she said, reluctant. "Where do we go from here?"

Monroe let Bishop go. "That's a good question. What do you think, Matthew?"

"I think I need a bath and a shave, and then I suggest we take some time to read before we make a public announcement."

Monroe and Jennifer nodded in silence.

"But where to start?" Jennifer said.

"We first start cataloging the books by their names and indexes," Monroe suggested.

"A lot of that work is already done," Bishop said. "Like I said, all the books are already in genres."

Jennifer took a deep breath. "I say we start by trying to get the answers to our most wanted questions, like: who were they, where did they come from, did they leave Earth, why, and where did they go?"

"Sounds like a plan to me," Monroe said. "Now we only have to find the right history book."

***

"Again, one step ahead of you," Bishop said.

"Incredible." Monroe shook his head. "How do you do that?"

"Hey, it took you an hour to get here, so...." Bishop smiled. He hadn't felt this excited since his father took him on his first fishing trip, and he caught that ten-pound largemouth bass at Lake Montgomery, off the Ocmulgee River in southern Georgia. "I found what looks like a kind of 'General history of the world in a nutshell,' series of books. Though it's still three volumes of 300,000 words each, I think it's a good place to start."

"Show us," Monroe said, pointing vigorously at the screen.

"Yeah, show us," Jennifer agreed.

"All right, okay. Take it easy." Bishop worked the screen. "Here, you see." He rose from his chair. "I already read the first pages, so sit down and have a look while I freshen up. If you want, I believe there's still some coffee in the thermos. However, that might be from this morning or yesterday. I'm not sure."

Jennifer and Monroe appeared not to have even heard him, as they read the first lines on the screen and were immediately drawn into the text.

I know the feeling, Bishop thought as they read.

'We count the year of Alpha-46/72, and war has finally come to an end. Who knew that after all these ranges of time and death, the walls would finally come down, we would overcome our differences, unite the families, and leave this world together....'

AND SO IT BEGINS....

ACKNOWLEDGEMENTS

Special thanks and love to my wife Nathalie for her support and rereading the *Atacama* manuscript.

Thank you, Rose, for keeping me—and the story—consistent.

Thank you, Erica, for reading and re-re-reading the manuscript and finding the finer points (and commas).

Special thanks to all those others involved who contributed so much. You know who you are.

ABOUT THE AUTHOR

Dutch renowned author, Clinchandhill, had long-discovered his passion for writing at a young age. Despite past career detours, his love for worldbuilding and the written word were rekindled into a furious blaze. He has since penned his acclaimed political thriller, *Kursk*, and its equally compelling sequel, *47 Hours*, and will be releasing *The Mogadishu Encounter* in late 2020.

His irrefutable fascination for credible stories and true events is evident throughout all his fictional works, including this latest novel, *Aldaraia* [Evolved Publishing], and its upcoming sequel, *Lemuria*.

Clinchandhill now writes full-time in the Netherlands, with his beautiful wife of 20 years. In his spare time, he enjoys sipping tea with a good book and delving into his own adventures out on open waters.

For more, please visit Burt Clinchandhill online at:
Website: www.clinchandhill.com
Facebook: @Clinchandhill
Instagram: @Clinchandhill
Twitter: @Clinchandhill
LinkedIn: Burt Clinchandhill

MORE FROM EVOLVED PUBLISHING

We offer great books across multiple genres, featuring high-quality editing (which we believe is second-to-none) and fantastic covers.

As a hybrid small press, your support as loyal readers is so important to us, and we have strived, with tireless dedication and sheer determination, to deliver on the promise of our motto:

QUALITY IS PRIORITY #1!

Please check out all of our great books,
which you can find at this link:

www.EvolvedPub.com/Catalog/

Thank you!

CPSIA information can be obtained
at www.ICGtesting.com
Printed in the USA
LVHW111744260422
717291LV00006B/338

9 781622 536122